THE REWARD OF WIZARDRY

◇◇◇◇◇◇◇◇◇◇◇◇◇◇◇◇◇◇◇◇◇◇◇◇◇◇◇◇◇◇◇◇◇◇◇◇◇

A rickety cart pulled by ancient horses was making its way through the muddy ruts. It stopped, and Magni beckoned Starkad and Svanlaug to approach the tailboard.

"We found two bodies in the burned inn," he said. "We believe they might be the wizard Thurid and the Norskar that traveled with him. You must look at them and tell us if what we suspect is true."

Starkad's heart stood still as he looked at the burden the cart carried. There was no mistaking Thurid, his marble features washed clean by the soft rainfall. Nor was there any doubt that Raudbjorn had perished with him, still gripping his halberd. No flame had touched them, yet they had lost their lives in the fiery conflagration.

By Elizabeth H. Boyer
Published by Ballantine Books:

THE SWORD AND THE SATCHEL

THE ELVES AND THE OTTERSKIN

THE THRALL AND THE DRAGON'S HEART

THE WIZARD AND THE WARLORD

The Wizard's War

THE TROLL'S GRINDSTONE

THE CURSE OF SLAGFID

THE DRAGON'S CARBUNCLE

LORD OF CHAOS

LORD OF CHAOS

Elizabeth H. Boyer

A Del Rey Book

BALLANTINE BOOKS · NEW YORK

A Del Rey Book
Published by Ballantine Books

Copyright © 1991 by Elizabeth H. Boyer

Library of Congress Catalog Card Number: 91-91980

ISBN 0-345-36302-7

Printed in Canada

First Edition: October 1991

Cover Art by Greg Hildebrandt

Some Hints on Pronunciation

◇◇◇

Scipling and Alfar words sometimes look forbidding, but most are easy to pronounce, if a few simple rules are observed.

The consonants are mostly like those in English. G is always hard, as in Get or Go. The biggest difference is that J is always pronounced like English Y, as in Yes or midYear. Final -R (as in FridmundR or JolfR) is equivalent to -ER in undER or offER. HL and HR are sounds not found in English. Try sounding H while saying L or R; if you find that difficult, simply skip the H—Sciplings would understand.

Vowels are like those in Italian or Latin generally. A as in bAth or fAther; E as in wEt or wEigh; I as in sIt or machIne; O as in Obey or nOte; U like OO in bOOk or dOOm. AI as in AIsle; EI as in nEIghbor or wEIght; AU like OU in OUt or hOUse. Y is always a vowel and should be pronounced like I above. (The sound in Old Norse was slightly different, but the I sound is close enough.)

Longer words are usually combinations of shorter ones; thus "Thorljotsson" is simply "Thorljot's son" run together without the apostrophe.

Of course, none of this is mandatory in reading the story; any pronunciation that works for the reader is the right one!

Chapter 1

◊◊◊◊◊◊◊◊◊◊◊◊◊◊◊◊◊◊◊◊◊◊◊◊◊◊◊◊◊◊◊◊◊◊◊◊◊◊

The great river known as Svart-strom divided the black-hearted fells and carved its way across the emerald valleys in a mighty seam from north to south. From their high vantage point in the fells, Leifr and his companions saw it curling through the broad valley below, filling the air with a dull roaring. Its powerful churning against the rocks in its course filled the air with mist, almost obscuring the wet black cliffs and skarps on the far side, where a riot of vegetation clung in the perennial bath of moisture. With gloomy misgivings, Leifr gazed at the expanse of foaming water, plunging waterfalls, and deep swirling pools.

"We don't have to cross it, do we?" he asked Svanlaug, noting with disapproval that Gedvondur was riding on her shoulder, all atwinkle with anticipation.

"Only if we want to get to Hringurhol," Svanlaug snapped testily.

"So how are we going to get across that?" Starkad demanded, waving a hand at the river in a hopeless gesture. "Since it's spring, it's in spate, too."

"We'll get across farther down at Ferja," Svanlaug retorted, twisting up a handful of her hair and scowling in thought. "It's a nasty little settlement, where they'd rather stab you and murder you for a gold tooth than take you across to the Hringurhol settlements, but if we're careful we can manage it. Two more days will put us at Ferja. That will give us some time before Brjaladur."

"Brjaladur! Madness?" Thurid queried sharply.

Svanlaug nodded. "In ten days the stars will line up for the first day of summer. During the final three nights of their rule, the Ulf-hedin go mad. They fight and destroy everything they can lay their hands on. Shifts in seasons often invite chaos."

Thurid plucked at his nether lip worriedly. "I'll need some

1

time inside their fortress if I'm to find this Pentacle they're building, much less destroy it before Brjaladur. Is Ferja the only crossing?"

"The safest, but not the only," Svanlaug said. "The Council has their own ferry boat, to which I was once entitled, when my father Afgang was alive. It's a great dragon ship that comes across to fetch guests of the Council, and it crosses without oarsmen or sail or rudder. It would be a quiet way to arrive at Hringurhol, without all the riffraff at Ferja knowing about us and spreading the word on both sides of the river."

Thurid snorted. "It sounds like a way to arrive as prisoners. I'll have nothing to do with any enchanted dragon ships of the Council's conjuring. Tomorrow we'll make our way to Ferja."

"And waste another two days?" Gedvondur demanded, his carbuncle stone sparkling in the firelight like blood. "Don't be such an old woman, Thurid. I crossed the river once in the Council's dragon ship."

"And look how you came out," Thurid said. "Slaughterhouse leavings are in bigger pieces than you. I don't wish to argue about it; I've made up my mind for Ferja."

"Well, I haven't," Gedvondur retorted, thus commencing a furious argument that lasted until sundown.

The river mist seemed to thicken with the onset of twilight. The travelers made a camp in the rocks above the shore of the river, overlooking the crumbling ruins of a boat stand, half covered by the high water of the river. Across the roiling expanse of the river was Hringurhol, crouching on the brink of a green hill above the jetty, a crumbling, black old encrustation of ruins and walls and towers and blocked-up gates, sparkling with watch fires. The twinkling lights of small settlements crowded around its lower walls, strewn in decreasing frequency across the plain and fell behind its bulk. The faint sounds of voices carried across the water, swift and flat. Above its towers, the lowering cloud hovered, flickering with suppressed lightnings and muted thunderings. All their eyes were drawn to the fortress and the cloud bank in silent fascination, no matter how many times they resolutely looked away.

"It seems a bad place for a settlement, right under the noses of the Council," Starkad said.

"Their merchants are like the fleas living on a bear's hide," Svanlaug said. "They are vermin, but the presence of the Council and the Ulf-hedin and the Dokkur Lavardur make them arrogant and bold. It's impervious to attack from land or water, as if anyone would dare attack the Dokkur Lavardur. The river traders take full advantage of that protection. Ferja is a thriving little pesthole, and so is Throngur on the Hringurhol side.''

"And the Pentacle?" Thurid questioned. "Did you see it when you were there with your father?"

"Certainly not," Svanlaug answered. "It's far too potent a device for casual visitors to view. But I can tell you this much— I know which building it's in. Heidur's well, on the top of a hill. No one is allowed near it, so I believe there's something hidden inside it that is very important to the Council. The Ulf-hedin hold their assemblies in there. It's open to the sky and that thing they call the Dokkur Lavardur.''

Curious, Leifr followed her glance upward toward the sky, seeing nothing but the bellies of low-hanging clouds that always seemed to threaten, without breaking loose in a storm. The clouds moiled and shifted, reminding him of the shapes he saw in Thurid's blue orb. The mist rising from the river and the low clouds filled him with an ominous feeling of brooding doom. He hadn't seen or felt the sun since Skaela-fell, and the lack of it was beginning to build into a desperate longing to return to places that didn't drip and ooze with the clammy coldness of the Dokkalfar realm. It put him in mind of a slow and reluctant spring, or a particularly dark and miserable late autumn.

Raudbjorn hooted a soft warning, beckoning to Leifr from his watching place on a rock overlooking the boat stand. Then he descended toward the river. Leifr left the camp and made his way down to the riverbank, moving cautiously over the wet, slimy rocks. Pointing silently across the water, Raudbjorn cupped one hand behind his ear to listen. In a moment Leifr heard the steady hiss and slap of a boat's hull coming through the water. In a few moments the shadowy shape of a high-prowed ship came gliding steadily through the mists roiling over the water. It was a dragon ship, and Leifr gasped a little at the length of it. He had seen plenty of ships of war in his short and brilliant career as a coastal marauder, but none as long from lofty nose to trailing tail.

Leifr's admiration faded almost instantly as the strangeness of the dragon ship suddenly struck him. No one manned the oars, and no mast and sail stood erect to catch the wind, which was considerable over the face of the river. As if it were alive, the ship crept toward the boat stand and glided to a halt, tossing lightly in the eddying current in ghostly silence. No one was aboard.

Leifr backed away and nearly collided with Thurid who had approached to peer over his shoulder at the ship. Svanlaug and Starkad stood behind him, barred from closer approach by the way Thurid held his staff to block them, like a shepherd with a couple of sheep.

"They must know we're here," Thurid whispered, his eye flickering with a gleam of challenge. "They sent their boat for us."

Svanlaug shifted her hood restlessly to free her black hair, gazing at the boat with keen interest. "Well? Are we going to cross?"

"What, and find a dozen or more wizards waiting for us?" Thurid retorted. "It's exactly what they want. We've got to be extremely cautious now. We'd lose these weapons, and the world would lose the battle with the Dokkur Lavardur. Besides, they sent the boat across, so they'll be expecting us. They'll have every advantage."

"Who says the wizards would come out best?" Leifr asked grimly. "I'd take plenty of them with me before I died."

"And maybe miss the chance to dismember Sorkvir yourself?" Thurid queried incredulously. "Not likely. We'll wait for a safer way across the river, thank you."

Svanlaug clenched her fists in disgust. "They have a ferryman on the other side who watches and sends the boat back and forth. They don't always know when someone is coming across or who it is."

Thurid glared at her. "I think you're rather too anxious for us to get into this boat and be ferried across like a load of dumb sheep. Doubts have been called forth, Svanlaug, and once they're freed, they're hard to recapture, even for those of us who have no cause to fear."

"Doubts!" Svanlaug spat. "How could you seriously doubt, after all I've done for you? Maybe I've done too much. Maybe I've told too many secrets of the Dokkalfar realm for you to trust me. If I wasn't a Dokkalfar, you wouldn't dream of making your jaundiced accusations!"

She whirled and stalked away in a rage.

"Come away from here," Thurid commanded. "I don't like the looks of this ship at all. Don't loiter about staring at it like a yokel, Leifr, it's not a natural sort of ship."

"It's a beautiful ship, Thurid," Leifr said.

"Beautiful and undoubtedly haunted," Thurid said with a nervous shudder of his shoulders. "You'll never catch me setting one foot in that thing, and if you want to live, you won't either. Are you coming along?"

"Yes, but don't natter about it," Leifr growled. "I shall have a good look at this ship first."

Thurid stalked away, prodding a reluctant Starkad ahead of him like a prisoner. Leifr gazed a moment at the prow piece of the boat, thinking it was one of the better representations of a dragon that he had ever seen. Even in the dim twilight night he could see its scales, eyes, nostrils, and teeth, which were bared in a frozen grimace of rage. There was even a gaping socket where the carbuncle stone would have resided in a real dragon. Wondering what sort of wood had been used, Leifr paced along the length of the boat stand, inspecting the rest of the boat, noting how great wings had been incorporated into the design of the ship, folded back to form the gunwales. It gave the boat a deeper draft than the typical viking ship, which could be brought aground on almost any shoreline in water shallow enough for the raiders to wade through.

Thurid stood on the cliff's edge and watched the ship awhile longer, until he tired of the damp rocks and mist and returned to the camp in quest of a semblance of dryness. Raudbjorn returned to his watch post, making his way along the riverbank. Leifr paced along the boat stand, still watching the boat and the other side from whence it had come until it was time for him to relieve Raudbjorn on guard. The troll-hounds padded at his heels, silent as usual until he returned for a closer look at the boat. They whined uneasily as he stepped onto the boat stand, but Kraftig loyally clung to his heels, pawing his leg in silent appeal whenever he stopped to stand and gaze.

Kraftig pawed at him again, growling softly, so Leifr acquiesced to his wishes and turned to retreat, wondering how long the wizards would leave their boat on the opposite side of the river before they called it back.

A soft hissing suddenly drew his attention to the shadows near the boat stand, and Kraftig growled, his back fur standing up in a ridge. Leifr drew the sword, circling around to get off the boat stand before his enemy attacked.

"Leifr!" came a whisper, and he recognized Svanlaug's voice. "Put away that sword! They'll sense it, over there. Or do you still think I'm an Ulf-hedin?"

Leifr put the sword back into its sheath, not without reluctance, but she had shamed him into it.

"I never did believe that you're an Ulf-hedin," he said in a careless, half-impatient tone, which concealed his doubts rather nicely, he thought. "If you are, you've missed plenty of chances to kill us all. I suppose you could be just a cowardly and stupid Ulf-hedin—"

"Have I ever been cowardly and stupid?" Svanlaug interrupted fiercely. "Haven't I repeatedly risked my life for the lot of you? And with precious little thanks, I might add, and only because you didn't like my methods."

"Did you come down here just to have another argument?" Leifr asked wearily. "If you did, I can do without it."

"Yes, I have, as a matter of fact," Svanlaug replied. "That old goose Thurid has lost his nerve. We've got to get across this river tonight, Leifr, while we're here at the crossing and not two days south at Ferja. It's going to be Brjaladur in only ten days. I have a feeling that the Pentacle is going to be either completed or destroyed on one of those nights. Ten days is not much time to find the other four stones that go with the one Thurid's got."

"You'll have to argue it with Thurid," Leifr said. "My duty is protecting him and that orb."

"Duty? Don't be pious," Svanlaug snorted. "Revenge for Ljosa is what you want. When you kill Sorkvir this time, he won't be coming back from Hela's cold embrace. If you wait, you might not have the satisfaction of seeing him die on your sword's end, spewing his stinking guts and melting away like rendering lard. Your honor is at stake, Leifr. You know what lies he must be spreading, how he must be boasting about beating you at every turn. If you could slip into Hringurhol and pluck Sorkvir right out of their midst, think what a shock it would be to the Council. It would rock them back on their heels. It would show them that you are a force to be feared."

Leifr stifled an impatient sigh. "Svanlaug, I've come to know you well. You've got some axe of your own to grind or you wouldn't want me to go over there without Thurid. What is it you really want? You couldn't give two hoots about what I might consider my honor."

"Well put, and to the point," she replied. "I must admit, you're seeing better and better. You're not the fool you once were, even for a Scipling."

"Get to it, or I'm leaving," Leifr said.

"It's Ulfrin," Svanlaug said in a low voice. "She's over there. I know she is, I can feel it. She's my sister, and much as I hate her, we are as near as two sisters can be. She's in danger, Leifr, and I must rescue her."

Leifr scowled at her incredulously. "Rescue her? If she's in danger, you should be rejoicing. If she dies, you ought to dance."

"She's my sister. I can't allow such a fate to befall her as she might encounter in Hringurhol. She's a fool, she's arrogant, she's mean, but she can also be used by the Council to drastic effect, Leifr. She's a Sverting, a young and haughty one, true, but possessed of dazzling powers. They've got her and they'll use her against us."

"What about Thurid and the orb and the Pentacle?" Leifr asked warily. "How can I leave him here unprotected?"

"With Heldur's orb, he's in no need of sword protection," Svanlaug said. "Thurid will have Raudbjorn and Gedvondur to protect him. You can go places where Thurid cannot, Leifr. The Council has four other stones, each as precious and powerful as the one Thurid's got. They know exactly where the fifth one is and how close it's getting. Only you can slip into Hringurhol and find my sister. You're a Scipling, one of the new race, and they can't see you as well. Will you do it, Leifr? It's not just for my good, or Ulfrin's. With her out of the way, the road will be cleared for Thurid to wreak whatever havoc he chooses upon the Council."

"You really do care about your sister, don't you?" Leifr asked. "Worthless and spoiled as she is, you're worried about her safety."

"Of course," Svanlaug said. "She's my sister-kin. She may have banished me from my clan, but I have not banished the clan from me."

"You're certain she's in there?" Leifr nodded toward the sheaf of sparks glowing in the night that was Hringurhol, spread across the opposite side of the river.

"Positive," Svanlaug said. "Will you do it, Leifr? It won't take long, and while you're gone, Thurid will have Gedvondur to protect him."

As she spoke, Gedvondur came floundering indignantly out of her pocket and gripped her wrist, and she spoke aloud the words he wanted to say.

"No, he won't have Gedvondur to protect him," Gedvondur's voice declared. "I'm going with Leifr. The pigeons are coming home to roost at last, and I want the Council to know it. They thought they were rid of me. I have dreams of revenge of my own, Leifr, and you're going to fulfill them for me."

"No, I'm not," Leifr protested as Gedvondur clambered off Svanlaug's arm and clamped onto his shoulder. He heard himself add in Gedvondur's voice, "Yes, you are. You can use my help."

"I don't need it," Leifr answered angrily, trying to shake Gedvondur off again, not quite daring to do him any violence and thus give Gedvondur another reason for hating him, besides that early attempt at Fangelsi to throw Gedvondur in the fire. "You take away my strength. Your help is no help at all."

"I won't harm you or interfere unduly," Gedvondur replied. "I'll be the carbuncle you don't have. Believe me, you're going to need a third eye after you cross this river. It won't be as easy to get Ulfrin out of there as Svanlaug would like you to believe."

Leifr hated the feeling that he was talking to himself. As nearly as he could tell, however, Gedvondur wasn't attempting to control him in any other way, except to use his voice to communicate.

"You won't try to take me over, as you did Thurid?" Leifr asked suspiciously.

Gedvondur sighed, and Leifr felt a wave of impatience and frustration. Suddenly he understood Gedvondur's situation. Powerful, intelligent, but he was hopelessly inadequate without a body to channel his brilliant strength, either for good or for ill.

"Never mind, forget that I asked," Leifr hastened to answer his own foolish question. "If you'd wanted to do that, you would have done so long ago."

"And maybe I should have," Gedvondur's voice rasped in his throat. "We would've had much less trouble."

Kraftig's ears lifted suddenly and he growled a warning, raising his long nose into the air to sniff.

"Horses," Svanlaug said quickly, pointing back the way they had come. "Take cover!"

"Your ears aren't as good as Svanlaug's," Gedvondur said to Leifr, without speaking aloud. "You should have heard them yourself."

They dived into the cover of a jumble of river rock as a dark knot of horsemen came plunging down the cliffs at a heedless gallop. Red eyes flashed, and the cold night light gleamed on weapons and the wolf faces of the Ulf-hedin. The dark forms of the lesser fylgjur-wolves surged around the horses' legs as the riders clattered onto the boat stand. Their leader threw back his wolf cape, a white-maned one, revealing a familiar shock of white hair, last seen by Leifr in a low, smoky room in Haetafell, thick with the cloying scent of eitur.

"Hvitur-Fax!" The name came to him with a soft nudge from Gedvondur's presence. "Wolf master of the Ulf-hedin. I knew we'd meet again."

Hvitur-Fax lingered while the others were urging their horses to step into the boat, with rattling snorts and much spirited prancing. He gazed around warily, and Leifr crouched ready with his hand on his sword hilt. When the last flygja-wolf had leaped over the gunwale, Hvitur-Fax followed the rest into the boat, still suspiciously scanning the cliffs surrounding the boat stand, as if some instinct had warned him of Leifr's presence. The ship eased away from the stand and turned slowly into the rippling current of the river, taking a downstream gliding path until it disappeared in the mist. Leifr expelled a pent-up sigh, half relieved, half disappointed.

"We won't be crossing with that boat tonight," he said.

"And why not?" Gedvondur answered him, giving him a great start. "When Fridmarr and I were here, all we had to do was stand on the boat stand and the boat would be sent. Those wizards aren't much concerned with who comes over, but they are highly particular about who leaves."

Leifr found himself rubbing Fridmarr's carbuncle with his thumb. It had indeed recognized the place, filling him with the reassurance that Gedvondur had spoken the truth. The rivalry he had sensed between the two was now replaced with a trembling anticipation.

"All you must do is stand upon the boat stand and wait," Svanlaug said. "It will come back for you."

"Then we'll wait," Leifr said. "But one final thing—I want it understood that I'm going alone. You're to stay behind and do your best to protect Thurid and the orb."

"The orb doesn't need such as she to protect it," Gedvondur said, strutting and preening on Leifr's shoulder.

"You'd do better to take me with you than that thing," Svanlaug said. "At least I've been into Hringurhol and gotten out again, many times, without being dismembered."

"I, at least, am a Ljosalfar," Gedvondur retorted.

"You were, you mean," Svanlaug said. "You're nothing now but a piece of carrion and a carbuncle. Was a hand all that you could save of yourself when the Council got you? A really decent carbuncle could have done better."

"Silence, both of you," Leifr said. "I don't appreciate being in the middle of your quarrel. Gedvondur is enough of a headache when he's not drawing his power out of your very vitals."

"He's nothing but a leech," Svanlaug said. "You'd better be careful of any errand he wants you to do."

"And rescuing your nasty-tempered sister is a worthwhile endeavor?" Gedvondur snapped in return. "I think she should be left there to perish with the rest of the Council. She's rotten with their evil influence. But enough talk; this is costing you. I'll speak when you need to hear it."

"When I speak, you'd better answer," Leifr said, feeling rather better when Gedvondur released his hold upon him and dropped into his pocket.

Inscrutable as a cat, Svanlaug perched on a rock and sat motionless for an interminable wait, while the faint sounds of the Hringurhol settlement came to them across the water.

Raudbjorn whistled softly from his watch point, beckoning Leifr to come back to the camp. Leifr whistled to Starkad, perched on the other side, and Starkad waved back.

"What is it?" Leifr asked Raudbjorn, who was sniffing the air and testing the sharpness of his halbred with one thumb. "More wizards going to Hringurhol?"

Raudbjorn shook his head, baring his teeth in an unpleasant

grin of pleasure. The troll-hounds wagged and pawed around him, growling in anticipation and showing their teeth in similar anticipation.

"Not wizards," said Raudbjorn. "Naglissons."

Chapter 2

He found Thurid pacing about in a foment, with the blue orb glowing and smoking.

"What is it?" he demanded. "Sorkvir?"

Leifr shook his head quickly. "It looks more like the Naglissons and their repulsive parent. What ill-assorted marriage of misfortune and stupidity has given them this ridiculous determination to pursue us?"

"Naglissons!" Thurid snorted. "I thought that sizzling I gave them in Skaela-fell would have discouraged them. But it seems that the reward on our heads is large enough to make thief-takers lose all reason." He grunted, throwing his tea on the ground and reaching for the satchel to haul out a handful of rune sticks. "Let them come. I'll make fritters out of them. Blast these wands! I need more power than a lot of mumbling and grumbling!" He threw the sticks back into his satchel and scowled into the smoky depths of the sphere a moment. "Yes, there they are, Nagli and his sons, like a recurring case of mange."

"Blast them with that orb, then," Svanlaug advised. "We don't need them holding us up, now we're this close."

"And waste the strength of this precious orb on Naglisson slime?" Thurid snorted. "What do you think I've brought Leifr and Raudbjorn along for? I'm hoarding every bit of my strength, and we'll be lucky if it's enough when the fat is finally cast into the fire, which is going to be very soon."

"Brjaladur," Svanlaug said, nodding in agreement. "Old spells must be renewed, and new ones cast."

"A most inauspicious night," Thurid said. "The calamitous night of disarray on the border of spring and summer. If my calculations are correct, that will be the time of the challenge between the Council of Threttan, the Dokkur Lavardur, and the

12

wise ones who have brought us so far. We can brook no interference by Naglissons.''

Thurid held up the glowing orb, as clear and bright as a
bubble, and the tiny slinking figures of the Naglissons were
revealed, crouching behind a jagged rib of stone above the place
Thurid had chosen to stop for the night.

Raudbjorn squinted into the orb and chuckled with anticipation, baring his teeth in a fierce grin.

''Death finds Naglissons at last,'' he rumbled, giving himself
a thump on the chest as if the epithet were his own.

''Wait until they're closer,'' Leifr advised. ''I think they'll
come right into our hands. They don't know we can see them.''

''Don't kill them now.'' Gedvondur scuttled up Thurid's cloak
to his shoulder to deliver the message. ''We can't predict what
would happen if life forces were released with that orb so close
to the other four. Nor do we know who can see us. This place
is crawling with influences. The Council must be holding their
breath and rubbing their hands with glee, the nearer we get.''

Leifr nodded, aware of the restless atmosphere surrounding
them. He glanced up frequently, sensing the storm lurking overhead, filled with the crackling energy of an incipient cloudburst
and lightning show.

''We shall spare the Naglissons, Raudbjorn,'' Leifr replied.
''But this will be the last time.''

Raudbjorn's crestfallen expression brightened. ''Last time,
Leifr. Then Naglissons belong to Raudbjorn.''

The Naglissons separated and spread out to encircle the camp.
With the aid of the all-seeing dragon's orb, Leifr watched in
grim anticipation, with Gedvondur perched on Thurid's shoulder. He waggled one finger warningly in response to Raudbjorn's restless snorts and grumblings.

''Halloa!'' came the triumphant shout from the scarp above
their camp. ''We meet again! It's time to talk, old friends. We're
willing to let bygones be bygones and forget what happened at
Skaela-fell!''

''Let that be your mistake, not ours,'' Thurid returned, striding forward with the staff and orb spewing blue smoke. ''Skaela-
fell should have been your warning, Nagli.''

''It was all just a misunderstanding,'' Nagli answered in a
whining tone. ''We've given up on Djofull's blood price.''

''Then why are you still following us?'' demanded Leifr.

"We wish to become your allies," Nagli replied. "See, we come in peace. Allow us to come nearer, so we won't have to shout into all the hostile ears that might be listening. Believe me, what I've got to say is worth hearing. There's enough gold forthcoming to line all our pockets." He stepped out from behind his hiding place, holding his hands wide apart to show that they were empty of weapons.

Thurid cast one startled glance at Leifr. "A likely tale!" he muttered. "Allies! I'd sooner be snake-bitten."

"Get him down here and Raudbjorn will welcome our new friend," Leifr said grimly.

"He mentioned something about gold," Svanlaug said. "Perhaps it will be worthwhile to hear him out."

"It won't hurt to listen," Thurid replied. "For a while, at least. Halloa, Nagli! We are eager to listen to you. We, too, will lay down our weapons."

Leifr shot him a scandalized glare.

"Do it," Thurid ordered. "And tell Raudbjorn to stop scowling."

Reluctantly Leifr placed his sword and weapons upon the ground and stepped back a pace. Raudbjorn followed suit, but not without audible inner turmoil of a highly rebellious nature.

Nagli crept from rock to rock, as if direct, upright procedure of any sort was unfamiliar to him. Grinning and rubbing his hands, he edged nearer until he stood at the edge of the firelight.

"That's near enough," Leifr said. "We know your sons are still out there, still armed and waiting for your signal to attack us."

"Don't be so hasty in your judgment, my young Scipling friend," Nagli said. "They will not attack. Perhaps I am only guilty of a father's pride, but they are a fine lot, don't you agree?"

"I couldn't agree more," Thurid said. "Now speak your piece, thief-taker."

"You understand I carry no grudge against you," Nagli said, grinning and licking his lips in a craven, cunning manner. "In my line of work, I find it safer not to become any more involved than a butcher who slays an ox. If the ox kicks, I'm not surprised."

"You're not killing anything here except time," Leifr said. "Get on with it, we're getting impatient."

"To put a cap on it," Nagli went on swiftly, "we've received a better offer for you than Djofull's kinfolk. An offer that we'd be fools to pass by, just as we'd be fools to take it up.''

"What's stopping you then?" Leifr inquired. "It sounds like something you'd jump on, being the greatest fools I've encountered. You'd like nothing more than a chance to kill us all for the blood price.''

Nagli shook his head vigorously. "No, no, you'll come to no harm. You'll see, all will be well, once we join forces against Sorkvir.''

Thurid hoisted one eyebrow attentively. "Sorkvir is it now? You've taken on a powerful opponent this time, Nagli. Someone has put out a blood price on Sorkvir, and you want us to join with you and split the reward?''

"Exactly," Nagli said. "But I freely admit, I've not got what it takes to kill a wizard, especially a draug wizard, especially one such as Sorkvir. I know the lot of us could do it together, though, with the aid of that sword.'' His eyes made a nervous and greedy dart toward *Endalaus Daudi*, shining at Leifr's feet.

"Who has offered this blood price?" Starkad asked from behind the safety of Raudbjorn's massive backside.

Nagli tapped his nose slyly and his voice dropped to a smooth and conspiratorial murmur. "Sorkvir is getting to be a nuisance and an embarrassment to the Council, they say. He might even be coveting Alfrekar's seat, they say. Djofull and his experiments with Hela were made an end of, without any regret from the Council. You didn't see Alfrekar offering any gold for the capture of Djofull's killers, did you? A word here, a word there, that's all it takes to let the world know who can be profitably killed for pay. We came upriver to Ferja by barge and found the word awaiting us. It helps to know where to look, and there's a cozy private place that belongs to old Varudur, who looks out for those of us that like to do a bit of killing now and then, in an honest fashion, to earn their pay in this wretched world—''

"The Council wishes to be rid of Sorkvir!" Thurid cast Leifr a speculative stare. "And you think that we can be of help to you in getting him.''

"How much are they offering?" Svanlaug demanded.

Nagli folded his arms, bared his teeth in a snaggly grin, and shut his eyes briefly, as if to savor the ecstasy.

"One thousand marks in gold," he said in a voice that quivered slightly. "And a thousand marks in silver. Did you ever hear of such a price? And I heard it myself from a member of the Council of Threttan. He was hooded and cloaked to conceal himself, but I knew what he was. You can feel it in the air around them that has to do with the Dokkur Lavardur.'' He whispered the last bit, almost hoarse with reverence, and cast his hands about in the air as if feeling for influences.

''That's all well and good,'' Leifr grunted. ''I wouldn't mind being paid for my trouble, since I intend to kill Sorkvir anyway. But you and the Naglissons are among the last men in the world I'd want at my back for such an enterprise, profitable though it may be.''

Nagli shook his head regretfully, his expression genuinely pained. ''Profitable indeed, if we could only come to trust one another. My friends, it's not my fault that I can't trust you entirely. It's simply my nature to distrust everyone; but rest assured, there's no one I would rather trust or distrust more than you, and I mean that in the most complimentary of terms. I keep a knife in my hand when I sleep, even with my own sons around me, but that's not to say I think the less of them for merely distrusting them. I admire those who give me reason to distrust them. I know I'm in the presense of greatness when I feel my life endangered. So what I propose is this—an exchange of hostages, as an inducement to keep our friendship warm and cordial. One of my sons for one of your friends. It is my hope that you value the life of your friend enough to refrain from attempting to cheat me out of my fair share of the blood money, if I keep him in my possession for a while. When you yoke yourself with a bull you must keep your hand upon a club to keep him civil.''

''I'm yet to be convinced that you and the Naglissons will be of any use to us at all in killing Sorkvir,'' Leifr replied dubiously.

''Sorkvir came to us,'' Nagli said. ''He offered us a fine price for killing you and bringing him that sword. Sorkvir himself sent us after you at Djofullhol. Promised us a fine reward if we caught the lot of you and turned you over to him, and it wasn't all just gold and goods. Promised us powers, like real wizards. We'll be his liege men and share all his spoils after the Great Dark One rules the Alfar realm. But it wasn't as much as the Council offered us for killing him. He believes we are earnestly pursuing you for his reward. It would be very easy for you to get close enough to kill him, with him thinking you were perhaps one of the Naglissons, or somesuch treachery. He doesn't fear us, thinking quite rightly that ordinary thief-takers are no danger to him, even if by chance we did overwhelm him—a thing that we wouldn't do, since we've sworn never to attempt destroying draugar. You see, it's a perfect situation for the two of us. You to kill him, once we have drawn him into our net and brought him to you, unsuspecting. One can't work without the other, you know.''

Thurid clasped his hands behind his back and took a few paces one way, then back. Leifr watched him narrowly, keeping one eye upon Nagli, who was trying to conceal a triumphant grin behind one grimy hand. Raudbjorn squinted at him and sniffed his pervasive atmosphere as suspiciously as the growling troll-hounds crouching around his knees.

''What you propose is not without merit,'' Thurid said at last, pondering. ''Our task would be simplified without our personal quarrel with Sorkvir to complicate the situation.''

''Who's going to be the hostage?'' Starkad inquired warily.

''You, of course,'' Thurid said. ''Neither Leifr nor I could do it, and Svanlaug—well, not Svanlaug. Raudbjorn is too valuable for our defense, so you're all that's left.''

''Why not draw lots?'' Nagli suggested. ''Let fate decide who is to be the hostage, and no one will be angry or have cause to blame you for choosing. I have a bag of rune stones that I consult for guidance whenever I am in doubt. We'll say that whoever draws the stone of the most powerful sign shall be the hostage.'' He drew a small greasy pouch from inside his jerkin and shook it with the inviting slithering sound of smooth stones sliding over one another.

''Rune stones,'' Thurid mused. ''Yes, that would be a fair method to arrive at a decision.''

''I don't think these rune stones have done such a good job of guiding Nagli and his sons thus far,'' Svanlaug said. ''I don't know if I want to submit myself to their influence or not.''

Thurid's eyes gleamed with the reflection of the blue orb. ''It will work out splendidly,'' he said. ''It is only fitting that fate should have a hand in our endeavor, since fate is what has brought us this far. Choose a stone and keep it in your hand until we've all chosen.''

Beginning with Svanlaug, who delved around among the

stones before selecting one, they all chose a stone and held it hidden. Raudbjorn fumbled with the bag, unable to insert more than two fingers into its small maw, and ultimately gave it up and shook one out on his hand.

"Now then, reveal what you have drawn," Thurid said, holding his up. "I have drawn Perth the Unknowable. I doubt if any of you will draw higher than that."

Starkad held up his. "Ehwaz the Horse."

"Good, good," said Thurid. "It is what I would have expected. You are making gradual progress toward your goals, as would a man on a horse. Good but not strong enough to beat Perth. So far I am their man. Svanlaug?" Thurid turned to her. She stood gazing at her stone a moment, then clenched her fist around it.

"Isa the One Who Impedes," she said. "I believe this is a trick, and one that I don't find amusing. I've done nothing deliberately to impede your journey, yet I'm continually blamed for everything that goes wrong."

"At least you are spared from being the hostage of the Naglissons," Thurid said. His gaze slid uneasily over Leifr and came to rest upon Raudbjorn, who was squinting with his one good eye at the stone he had drawn, turning it this way and that with a lip curled in disdain. Then he held it up for all to see.

"The Thorn," Thurid said. "A rune of nonaction. You are not the one, Raudbjorn."

All eyes turned to Leifr. He extended his hand with the unmarked side of the stone upward. Thurid reached out and turned it over, revealing that the other side was also blank. The breath went out of him in a long hiss.

"The rune of destiny," he said, turning it over again as if to make certain. "The Alfather's rune. He has chosen you."

"It is the right choice and I welcome the opportunity," Leifr said. "I have the greater cause to kill Sorkvir. When I have finished with my private quarrels, I can turn all of my energy toward the Council of Threttan and their Pentacle."

"You're putting your neck upon the block with these Naglissons," Svanlaug said. "If Thurid should happen to fail to fulfill his end of the bargain, they have the right to kill you."

"The right, maybe," Leifr said, "but do they have the talent? I think not, as long as I have *Endalaus Daudi*."

Nagli shook his head vigorously. "You must relinquish your

weapons to us. That sword must be put into something so we can handle it. When the times comes for you to kill Sorkvir, I shall put it into your hands, but not until then. You are, after all, a hostage, and you can't go about fully armed and capable of leaving whenever you feel like it. That's not the nature of a hostage, you know.''

''I can't allow it,'' Thurid said. ''Take me as your hostage.''

''The runes have spoken,'' Nagli said. ''We wouldn't dare oppose them now. Much as I would like to get my hands upon that blue abomination on the end of your staff, even I know when my greed overreaches itself. There are great deeds afoot here, my friends, with the forging of this alliance. The wizards of the Council will quake in their boots because of this conjoining of forces.''

''I doubt if they will do much quaking,'' Thurid said with a snort of disdain. ''But I can see where it might startle them somewhat. Where do you propose to meet with Sorkvir next to work this treachery?''

''Ferja,'' Nagli said. ''At the house of old Varudur three nights hence. But we must not be seen traveling together. It would not look right at all. I must appear to have captured the Scipling for Sorkvir's blood price. I and the hostage will go in advance, while you come slyly behind. Sorkvir will arrive at midnight, and you must be there waiting for him. He will think that I have captured the Scipling for him, and he'll be lured into our trap like a goose-stealing fox.''

''How do you propose to divide the blood price, once we've got it?'' Svanlaug inquired shrewdly.

''I'm a fair man,'' Nagli said. ''We'll split it right down the middle.''

''It seems to me that the one who kills Sorkvir ought to have the greater share,'' Svanlaug said. ''You're doing nothing, actually, except meeting with Sorkvir at Ferja, while Leifr and Thurid are the ones who will do the actual fighting and the killing. It's not going to be easy, even with weapons such as they've got. He's enormously powerful—a draug who has tasted death seven times.''

''Then you may take six hundred of the thousand marks,'' Nagli said, licking his lips.

''We must have eight,'' Svanlaug said.

''That makes it hardly worth the danger,'' Nagli said, a

stricken expression drawing his wizened face into sorrowful lines. "Dealing with draugar and wizards is always dangerous, and when the wizard is a draug, the danger is tenfold. Each time we deal with a draug, we swear we'll never do it again."

"Seven hundred, then," Thurid said.

"Done," Nagli said, and they shook hands upon their bargain. "Now then, nothing remains except to exchange hostages and be on our different ways to Ferja. Remember, three nights from now at Varudur's inn, at midnight."

"We'll travel at dawn," Leifr said. "My horse is tired after traveling all day. We'll still have plenty of time to meet Sorkvir."

At dawn the Naglissons approached the camp warily, muffled to the eyes in protective black wrappings or masks. They kept at a wary distance, letting their father and the hostage come closer. Raudbjorn gripped his halberd, rumbling and glaring as Nagli and his son rode their horses into the camp.

"This is my firstborn son, Modga," Nagli said, pointing out the designated hostage, who crouched on his horse in a resentful slump, darting seething glances toward his father.

Raudbjorn stepped forward to take command of the hostage, depriving him at once of a considerable heap of knives and daggers extracted from the most cunning of hiding places.

"Modga is heir to all I possess and as dear to my heart as blood itself," Nagli said with a mocking half bow. "I give him to you as a sign of my great trust in our partnership."

"Spare us your blather, Nagli," Leifr said. "We know you're not capable of trusting anything except yourself."

"No harm had better come of this exchange," Thurid warned, with the blue orb perfuming the air with its smoky stench. "If you attempt the slightest deceit, Nagli, you'll have this blue abomination to contend with."

"Never once has the thought of treachery crossed my mind," Nagli said with an oily smile. "Are you having second thoughts, Thurid? Remember, the rune stones themselves chose the Scipling as the hostage."

"That's what concerns me," Thurid said. "This is a hostile realm for Sciplings as a species. It's cost me a great deal of effort to train him properly for his role."

"I'm capable of taking care of myself in this realm, Thurid," Leifr snapped, bristling at the implied affront. "Remember,

Endalaus Daudi is right here within my reach, while your blue abomination will be miles behind. Let these carrion-hunters do what they will; there's only three of them now, and they're still no match for me, once I get my hands on my sword.''

"There will be no need of that, I assure you," Nagli said. "I wouldn't give up this chance for such a blood price for that small a treachery. The Scipling is worth only three hundred marks in gold to Sorkvir, and Sorkvir dead is worth a thousand in gold and a thousand in silver. Anyone can see which side of the bread the butter is on. The Scipling will be my honored guest as long as we share one another's company.

"And you," Nagli added to his son, giving him a great dusty cuff on the ear, "mind yourself now, and do what you're told. I'll not have you causing others to form an ill opinion of your father and his example by your misbehavior. We are a proud breed, and you're lucky to have me for a father, so remember who you are." He gave Modga another clout on the ear to remind him.

Endalaus Daudi was wrapped in a sheepskin and tied behind Nagli's saddle, where it smoked menacingly. The Naglissons sniffed worriedly at the smell of burning wool and made surreptitious signs to ward off evil and kept their distance from it. Leifr mounted his horse.

To Raudbjorn he lifted one hand in silent salute, and Raudbjorn replied with a slight nod, grimly baring one yellowed tooth in a semblance of a smile. Modga would have scant chance of escaping with such a captor hovering over him and, judging from his sullen expression, he considered his prospects bleak indeed.

"What an honor to travel with such exalted company," Nagli crooned, guiding his horse alongside Leifr's to goggle up at him with a sneering grin bedizening his scrofulous countenance. "The ones that I travel with usually aren't up to much conversation, if you take my meaning, and I've traveled with plenty of fine fellows in my time, I can tell you. There was Bardi Bog-Foot and Red Hundsfotr and Killer Hjalgrimr, but all were strangely silent about their midsdeeds that earned them their outlawry. I suppose having their heads in one place and their carcasses rotting in another had something to do with their silence."

"I suppose it did," Leifr said curtly, "and I wish the same could be said for you."

Nagli cackled nastily. "You outlaws all talk the same, big and bold until the blade is at your throats for the last time, and then the whimpering begins. I've seen it a thousand times, outlaws you wouldn't suspect of a grain of pity, begging for it with all their might as if they had any right to expect it. The promises I've been offered would have made me the richest man in Skarpsey, had they been worth anything at the time, but I always chose to whack off the head and take it to whoever wanted it, even if the reward was somewhat small. Who would want to be always looking around for some blood-crazed outlaw you'd allowed to buy himself off? You wouldn't survive a year, men's memories of gratitude being as thin as they are."

Leifr did his best to crowd Nagli's horse off the path at every chance he got, but Nagli cheerfully caught up with him again as soon as the way widened again, oblivious of the affront. By the end of the first day, Leifr was well acquainted with many of the noteworthies Nagli had slain for gold, and had decided that only a very fine line separated a thief-taker from his quarry.

"We haven't got the fine victuals I daresay you're accustomed to," Nagli said with an apologetic leer as his two sons silently set up the camp and scratched together something to eat. "But I've had worse and less in my days. Six winters ago we had to eat Grenjadr Hook-nose. All of him, and he wasn't a small man. Winter had set in early, and my sons and I were in a cave with him, and outside were about eight of his friends and kinfolk trying to starve us out before they ran out of supplies. Their horses froze to death, and after eating most of their horses, they still hadn't starved us out, because, you see, we had Grenjadr to work on, and the weather was keeping him fresh, so they had to give it up, and we survived and got a nice blood price for Grenjadr's head. I always felt grateful to him for that, and I don't know why, because he certainly wouldn't have helped us out of that predicament in any other way, if he hadn't been dead and past caring."

All the while he was talking, Nagli chewed at a strip of blackened dried meat, having courteously offered Leifr several. After a cautious nibble, and after Nagli's story about eating Grenjadr got well underway, Leifr found he had no appetite for the suspicious black meat.

"Not hungry, are you?" Nagli chirped, whose darting eyes didn't miss anything. "Have some bread and cheese then, or try the ale, it's a real ripper."

So saying, he hoisted aloft a leather bottle and guzzled down a great draft until his face turned a deathly dark purple and his eyes started to protrude. Snorting and sputtering like a man who has nearly drowned, he came up for air at last, reeling slightly already. In a very short while he succumbed to the effects of the sour-smelling ale. His head fell back against a rock with a solid thunk, and the bottle slipped from his nerveless fingers. His hairy lips parted in an idiot smile, and from his throat issued the first of several thousand of the grating snores Leifr heard that night.

Leifr eyed the two Naglissons watchfully. They sat on either side of the small fire and eyed him just as warily. They kept their weapons close at hand and jumped twitchily whenever Leifr made a slight move to make himself more comfortable. Their eyes were narrow and close-set, and their relentless staring was almost as irritating as Nagli's snoring.

"Ovild and Lygari, is it?" he asked conversationally.

They exchanged a suspicious glance and just barely nodded in response.

"If I had a father like yours," Leifr continued in a friendly tone, "and if I thought that I'd one day be anything like him, I'd do the world a favor and cut my own throat."

There was no more response than if Leifr were speaking a foreign language. The two of them sat and stared at him expressionlessly through curtains of lank greasy hair.

"Your eyes are too close together," Leifr added. "Scarcely room enough for an axe blade, I'd say. Now it's your turn to say something insulting to me, if you've got any manners at all."

One of them blinked and shifted uneasily, and his brother gave him a sharp jab in the ribs with his elbow. The jabbed one, evidently the younger, moved away from his brother with a sudden flicker of rebellion smoldering in his narrow eyes.

"Is it true," he asked intently, "that them you kill with that sword shrivel up like a pork crackling and their souls run out of their mouths like melted black tar?"

"Something like that," Leifr replied. "If you want a demonstration, all you've got to do is lay your hand on the blade of *Endalaus Daudi*."

The Naglissons' eyes shifted to the bundle that covered the sword, smoking and steaming on the far side of Nagli, just within reach.

"I'd like to see it, just once," the younger Naglisson said in a reverent tone.

"Ovild! Hush!" the other commanded in a strained whisper. "It's cursed. Pabbi said we wasn't to talk to him. As if he was more clever than us." He darted Leifr a triumphant leer at his feeble attempt at an insult.

"Now that's better," Leifr said. "That was said almost the way a true warrior would say it, but you ought to be more rude. I would have said something like this—if your brains were spilled, it would make only a very tiny spot on the ground. One that you could cover up with a leaf."

Ovild shook his head. "Pabbi doesn't hold with a lot of fancy talk. He just offs the head and goes on his way, without any challenges or honors or anything."

"A knife in the back is the quicker way," Leifr said contemptuously. "And the safest, when you're not much of a fighter, such as your father. Thief-takers generally don't care much about fame and honor—just the gold."

"Aye, the gold," the elder brother spoke up in a sudden fever of greed. "Council gold as well as Sorkvir's gold. We'll be rich as jarls when we're done here. There's nothing we won't be able to buy—even a chieftancy and rich brides for us all."

"You'll be able to buy anything you want, except honor," said Leifr. "But I suppose even that can be bought somehow by such as your father."

Nagli gave a particularly boistrous snore and turned over in his sleep, cradling the leather ale bottle as if it were a cherished infant. A familiar little pouch dropped out of one sleeve pocket, and Leifr reached out and picked it up with a soothing chatter of polished stones.

"Let's consult the runes," he said. "Ask the stones if you're going to be rich and powerful one day."

He loosed the mouth of the bag and held it out invitingly. Ovild raised one hand to reach for it, but his brother slapped it down again.

"What harm will it do, Lygari?" Ovild sniveled, leaping back like a kicked hound.

"Them's Pabbi's stones, and no one should mess with them,"

Lygari said with a scowl. "Now put an end to this chatter. He's an outworlder, a Scipling, and there's no telling what powers he's got or what plans he's making. We're to watch him, not to talk to him."

They went back to their silent and dreary scrutiny. Leifr made himself comfortable, still holding the bag of rune stones. For amusement, he drew out a spread of stones as he had seen his father do to determine his course of action. He placed the stones facedown on a section of his cloak, shielded from the flat stare of the Naglissons. The first stone he turned over was the Alfather's rune, the blank stone that had got him into this situation. With a resentful glare at it, Leifr turned over the next stone. It, too, was blank. Astonished, Leifr slowly turned over the rest of the stones. They were all blank, as were the handful he pulled out of the bag. He was certain it was the same bag Nagli had used to choose his hostage, yet somehow, by some sleight of hand, Nagli had tricked him into drawing from the bag of blank stones.

Leifr returned the stones to their bag and replaced it beside Nagli where he would be certain to see it when he awakened from his stupor. So fate had had nothing to do with his selection as the hostage after all. Leifr smiled coldly to himself, taking scant comfort in that thought. At least he would be prepared when Nagli sprung whatever trap his devious mind had formulated.

Sorkvir's gold, his memory whispered. He glanced narrowly at Lygari, who had mentioned it. The Council's gold for Sorkvir, and Sorkvir's gold for Leifr. It seemed a breathtakingly audacious plan, even for one as greedy as Nagli.

Chapter 3

◇◇◇◇◇◇◇◇◇◇◇◇◇◇◇◇◇◇◇◇◇◇◇◇◇◇◇◇◇◇◇◇◇◇◇◇◇◇

Varudur's inn crouched under the onslaught of rain, its turf roofs blackened with age and sagging under the weight of decrepitude. Grimy urchin faces peered at the travelers as they made their way past the barns and paddocks into the dooryard. The dooryard was a sea of mud, slop, and refuse from the kitchen. A door stood open, leading into the kitchen, which blazed like a forge in the general gloom of the wretched settlement and the weather. A huge black hog lay in the doorway, with half a dozen bedraggled chickens pecking around in the dirt for crumbs fallen from tables or platters.

"We're in time for supper," Nagli said cheerily, wiping his nose on his sleeve. "Didn't I tell you it wasn't worthwhile to let a bit of wet weather stop us?"

"Yes, you did, and now we're here a day and a half early," Leifr said in cold fury. "We could have waited a few hours and arrived tomorrow without having soaked ourselves to the skin. You seem to be in a great hurry to get here for no reason."

He eyed Nagli as he said it and saw the fellow's fleeting glance into the horse byre, searching, perhaps, to see if someone had arrived ahead of him.

"It might have been worse tomorrow," Nagli returned. "No sense in waiting for it to clear, when waiting gets you just as wet as riding."

Leifr shivered as he dismounted, glad of arriving at last where a roof would keep the weather off and he would be able to get some sleep. For two nights Nagli had snored until midnight; then he awakened and announced that they had rested enough and they must be off again. At dawn he called a stop and rested until noon for another stint of riding until sundown. On the second day the rain had started shortly before dawn; instead of finding shelter among the skarps, Nagli had decreed that they would ride until they reached Ferja. The horses were staggering with exhaustion by the time they got there, shivering and steaming in the downpour. The hostlers led them away, and Nagli led the way into the inn, carrying the sword bundled up under his arm and obscured by his cloak.

Inside the inn, old Varudur was cheating at quoits when the travelers came dripping in. Other than him and the two Dokkalfar he was cheating, the inn was empty. Strongly perfumed by the odor of boiled cabbage and onions, the room was dark and smelled of moldy wood and peat.

"I bid you greetings," Varudur said, a dry little Dokkalfar with a rusty red beard wired with silver. "Make yourselves welcome. It's a night not fit for man nor beast to be out." He pressed his withered hands together, darting a nod at the other two Dokkalfar, who immediately thought of business pressing enough to take them back out into the rainstorm. His deep-set eyes inspected his guests, lingering curiously over Leifr and the bundle that Nagli stowed under a table before doffing his wet cloak.

"Not fit indeed," Nagli said. "Unless he knows there's a place such as yours waiting ahead of him. This is truly an island of hospitality in a sea of danger and despair."

Leifr draped his wet cloak over a rack for that purpose and sat down before the fire to let himself dry, after rousting another pig off the hearthstones. Grunting, it went around to the other side and flopped down again with a piggy glare of reproach at him. Varudur's inn was indeed an island of some sort, but Leifr could see few signs of hospitality. The fire was low and smoky; chickens and pigeons roosted in the rafters overhead and accordingly peppered the ground below with their droppings. Guests were evidently expected to fend for themselves when it came to competing with the pigs and dogs for space by the fire. Leifr didn't relish the thoughts of sharing the warmth with pigs. Sheep and goats were one thing to share a house with, but his own personal fastidiousness drew the line at pigs.

Old Varudur sat down at the table nearby and talked with Nagli while they ate the food brought from the kitchen annex. From his glimpses of that haven of culinary skill, Leifr was glad he wasn't privileged to have a complete look, or he might have lost his appetite for the food that came from there. The cook was a powerful-looking woman with red arms and a red face

like a hard winter apple. She commanded a fleet of kitchen
maids and lads who were evidently unable to function without
being first slapped or bellowed at. Interspersing the whacks were
curses at the livestock, which had moved in to get out of the
rain. At least twenty cats paraded haughtily in and out while the
food was being fixed, begging for scraps in cajoling feline fal-
settos liberally sprinkled with hissing and growling. Once a
great fight broke out with a pack of dogs, which frightened all
the pigs and goats out of the kitchen and into the hall. Disgrun-
tled, the beasts sidled up to the hall fire and cannily waited for
the food to be brought from the kitchen.

By the time it arrived, Leifr was too tired to care. He was
nearly dry and could think of nothing better than sleep, even if
dogs and pigs shared the hearthstones with him.

Nagli grew merrier, with a fresh flagon of ale helping to improve his attitude.

"You must have some of this," he urged Leifr, delving around
in his pack and coming up with a horn cup. "It's a marvelous
ale Varudur brews himself from mangels and hedge apples, not
at all like the usual slop you get at inns, made of any sort of
garbage that will ferment. It's as sweet and soft as a young girl's
cheek, it is, truly." He peered into the cup and gave it a swipe
with the tail of his sleeve to remove whatever objectionable particles he saw remaining inside. Unsteadily he poured a dose of
the dark ale into the cup and handed it to Leifr. "It will warm
up your insides after riding all day in the rain. Tell me now,
wouldn't you rather be here now instead of out there in the scarps
with night coming on? We'll be as snug as bedbugs in a feather
tick tonight and tomorrow, while Thurid is still out there slog-
ging along."

Nagli laughed inordinately at the idea. Lygari and Ovild sat
like two sticks, staring at Leifr or their father like apprehensive
young hounds let into the house for the first time. Varudur also
stared at Leifr with his hard, bright, half-hidden eyes, but he
turned away quickly to pretend to study something else whenever Leifr looked back at him. It was not a group he felt inclined
to get jolly with, but the sooner Nagli drank himself uncon-
scious, the sooner he could attempt to get some sleep. Not even
Nagli's snoring was going to keep him awake tonight.

"If ever my vitals were in need of warming," he said, taking an experimental swallow of the ale, "it must be tonight. You ought to be hanged for dragging us along in that rain today."

Nagli cackled with mirth. His eyes were glinting points of light. "Go on and drink," he urged. "Is that the way you Sciplings swallow an ale? Tiny little sips, like a minnow?"

"We can't all be whales like you, Nagli," Varudur said in his dry old voice.

Leifr found the taste of the ale not as unpleasant as he expected, although it had the usual bitter edge preferred by Dokkalfar. As he emptied the cup, the ale warmed the inside of him with a cozy glow. In its warmth, the wretched inn suddenly took on a friendly, comfortable aspect, as if he had swallowed a great deal more ale than just a single cupful.

"Hah," Varudur said, peering into his face. "Perhaps another draft?"

"Are you feeling better now?" Nagli inquired, his narrow face swimming in and out of sharp focus.

Leifr found he was unable to form an answer. His mouth seemed paralyzed, and he was losing contact with his fingers and toes. The warmth spread through him like a blanket of feathers, and his head began to feel too heavy to hold up. The cup rolled away across the table with a clatter, which he heard as he slowly slumped forward onto the planks.

"It worked," Nagli said to Varudur. "I told you it would. It just takes longer for these big hulking fellows. My cup hasn't failed me yet." He retrieved it and let one drop roll out onto his tongue with a grateful sigh. Then he gave Leifr's inert body a shove, helping him to fall limply onto the floor. "Now then, do your sleeping on the floor. The table is for doing business, and our business partner is soon to arrive."

Leifr could hear perfectly; only his body refused to respond.

The door opened with a blast of cold air.

"Here he is now, and earlier than I expected," Nagli said.

"Draugar," Varudur muttered, making covert signs to ward off evil. "I shouldn't have ever agreed to this scheme, except for your wheedling—and except for your payment." To the recent arrival he added in a slightly more hospitable tone, "Come in. I bid you welcome to my humble home" revered Meistari. Sit down and take a cup or two with us to fend off the damp."

Sorkvir ignored him, striding across the room to survey Leifr's limp carcass sprawled on the floor and the sword in its bundle under the table.

"So you've got the Scipling and the sword," he said. "That's better work than I expected from you, Nagli. Put the sword on the table and unwrap it so I can see if I've been deceived or not."

Nagli licked his lips and grinned nervously. He carefully hoisted the bundle out from under the table. "Of course, of course. And you haven't been deceived by me. That's the Scipling, and here's the sword. Carrying it has been a nuisance, I can tell you, what with the way it keeps burning whenever it's away from its master."

"Unwrap it," Sorkvir said. "I know there's at least one copy of it in existence."

Reluctantly Nagli pulled away the scorched sheepskin. "It's a vile thing," he muttered plaintively, turning his face away. "I can feel the evil coming off it. Ugh, what a creation! It gives my heart palpitations."

"That's enough," Sorkvir said harshly. "That's the cursed sword, the only one that can stand in the way of the Council's Pentacle. Now wrap it up again. You've done better than I had expected. Fetch a cart to the door and dump the Scipling into it."

Varudur beckoned, and a small boy entered reluctantly from the kitchen.

"A cart, and be quick about it," he said.

"And then," Nagli said, swallowing with a throat that sounded rather dry, "we can talk about my payment for getting the Scipling to you."

"We shall talk later, after I've also got the wizard," Sorkvir returned harshly. "He's been traveling fast, and he'll be here before long, with that blue dragon's carbuncle, and he's already suspicious."

"I told him exactly what you told me to tell him, no more and no less," Nagli said plaintively. "It worked exactly as you said it would."

"Never mind, we'll deal with the wizard when he arrives," Sorkvir said. He gave Leifr a prod with his toe. "Now carry him to the cart and get well away from here before Thurid arrives, if you value your lives. Make certain this sword remains safe. I shall meet you at the agreed-upon place to discuss your reward.''

Sorkvir turned away with a swirl of his cloak and stalked from the hall into the rainy dark.

"Lygari. Ovild." Nagli motioned toward Leifr. "Carry him out to the cart. I fear," he added with genuine regret, "that it's back to the rain for us for a little while."

"Curse that miserable wretch," Thurid growled, peering into the depths of the blue orb. "He's plotting something. I should never have allowed Leifr and that sword out of my sight. It seemed such a good scheme at the time, though."

"Nagli will be sorry if he crosses Leifr," Starkad said stoutly. "I thought it seemed like a good scheme for ridding us of Nagli and a couple of Naglissons." He bestowed an arrogant glower upon Modga, who glowered sullenly back and smirked in his infuriating way.

"I won't tell you anything," Modga said. "If you think Pabbi is cheating you, that's your lookout."

"I think Pabbi is doing more than cheating us," Thurid groused. "When we get to Varudur's inn, he'd better be there, and Leifr had better be there, or I'll fry his heart in his own belly-fat and feed it to you if I have to force it down your throat."

"We'll be there by midnight," Svanlaug said, "and you can stop your fretting. Or you can kill Modga, depending upon how reliable Nagli has been."

"Or depending upon how much he values Modga's life," Starkad said. "He's got two other sons. Perhaps he doesn't mind losing this one."

"Pabbi will be there," Modga said, baring his teeth in a wolfish grin of malevolence. "I'll be after him myself if he's not, and he knows it."

When they arrived at Varudur's inn, they found the yard empty and quiet, except for the rain pattering down steadily in the mud.

"I don't like the look of this," Thurid muttered, hesitating at the gate despite the barely concealed impatience of Svanlaug and Starkad to get inside where it was dry. "An inn yard ought to be full of carts and the byre full of horses. The place ought to be crowded with drovers and carters and wanderers. It's far too quiet for my taste."

"It's only the second night," Svanlaug protested wearily.

"We're an entire day ahead. Nagli can't have suspected you'd get here this soon and laid a trap. We're freezing, Thurid."

"You wait here and I shall go for a look," Thurid said. "Keep a close eye upon our Naglisson. He might be privy to all that's happening here."

Raudbjorn growled, "Let Raudbjorn find out, wizard. Raudbjorn pull the truth out of him, along with guts."

"That won't be necessary, Raudbjorn," Thurid said. "If I don't like the look of this place, I'll be back and I shall do it myself."

Starkad groaned softly, earning a reprimanding glare from Thurid before he dismounted and went stalking off through the slop toward the inn. The weary horses sidled around restlessly, edging into the shelter of a hay barn where they eagerly attacked the hay stacked inside. The respite from the rain was welcome for their riders. They dismounted and stretched their saddle-weary legs.

"Thurid's being an old woman," Svanlaug grumbled. "I can't believe Nagli would double-cross us now. Not if he cares a whit about Modga."

Starkad did not take his eyes off Thurid. "I should have gone with him," he muttered uneasily, watching as the dim figure of Thurid skirted the muckiest parts of the inn yard, taking advantage of the slight shelter of the walls of barns and pigpens.

"And what use would you be with all your skill?" Svanlaug demanded. "Thurid's had to nurse you along the entire way just like an infant."

"I may be incompetent," Starkad said, "but at least Thurid knows he can trust me."

Svanlaug answered with a disdainful snort and set about wringing some of the water out of her cloak. Starkad shivered, but at least they were out of the wind now. Even Raudbjorn uttered a satisfied chuckle, the sound coming eerily from his huge black shadowy bulk as he squatted on his heels and leaned against the haystack.

At that instant, a great silent flash illuminated the mucky inn yard with its surrounding squalid huts and barns and paddocks. All their faces were blanched white in the momentary glare, including the fleeing shape of Modga, caught in the act of climbing over a fence. Then a mighty explosion knocked Modga off his precarious perch and blasted soot and rain and bits of turf in all directions as a large portion of the inn's roof disintegrated.

"Thurid! Thurid!" Starkad gasped in horror, staggering into the rain on legs numbed by shock. Another furious explosion blew out one wall of the inn, the fury of its impact driving Starkad backward, blinded and deafened.

Reeling under the onslaught on his senses, Starkad was next knocked breathless against a post by something large charging past him in the sudden darkness after the flash, bawling like a maddened animal. He thought it was one of the terrified horses, but another smaller flare from the inn revealed Raudbjorn plowing through the mire straight toward the front door, which had been blown completely off its hinges. With a berserk bellow of challenge, Raudbjorn plunged into the flaming interior.

"Raudbjorn! No!" Starkad yelled, and started after him, but Svanlaug arrested him by grabbing the tail of his hood, jerking him to a choking halt.

"Don't be a fool! You'll die!" she shouted into his face as he struggled to get out of her grip. "You can't do them any good! After Modga!" she hissed, "He knows something about this! Get him, Starkad!"

Starkad collected his stunned wits, suddenly infused with a blazing thirst for vengeance. Lowering his head, panting for breath, he charged after Modga, who was getting up on the fence again. With a mighty plunge, Starkad grabbed his foot as it was going over and held on with all his might while Modga dangled from the other side a moment, yelping and snarling. Starkad lost his hold, letting Modga drop into whatever was on the other side. Vaulting over the fence, Starkad fell almost on top of Modga, who was sputtering under a faceful of pigsty, with what sounded like a dozen young piglets squealing around them both. The sow gave a savage bark of rage and came plowing through the mud, champing her jaws murderously. Another screaming flare from the inn illuminated her deathly visage to excellent advantage, and also revealed her attackers. She took them around the pen twice, barking and grunting, scattering squalling piglets in all directions, before Modga found a handhold and vaulted over the fence, closely followed by Starkad. They dropped in a tangle in the wet grass, where the pursuing troll-hounds surged around them, trying for a mouthful that was not Starkad. All around in the surrounding huts and hovels, the alarm was going up and people were running through the rain toward the inn. They all stared at one another for a second, gasping for breath, and then, leaping up, Modga wheeled and ran, with Starkad at his heels, huffing and snarling at least as savagely as the old sow. They raced a good long time, hurdling ditches, rocks, and clumps of furze and gorse. The troll-hounds were closing the gap when they missed a leap over a ditch. Hunting by sight, they had their eyes upon their quarry, and Starkad had his eyes upon the hounds. With a jarring crash he plunged into the ditch also, landing against the opposite bank full force. By the time he struggled to his feet, aching in every bone, there was no sign of Modga or the troll-hounds haring over the moors. Limping painfully and gulping huge wracking breaths, he hobbled back to the inn yard, where the inn was in full conflagration now, with a host of thralls and frightened livestock and other interested observers standing about with a few small piles of salvaged possessions.

The sooty form of Svanlaug rose suddenly from the shadows of the hay barn and snatched Starkad out of the light.

"This isn't a healthy spot for strangers just now," she said. "Not after what Thurid's done to Varudur's inn."

"Where's Thurid? Where's Leifr?" Starkad asked between painful gasps. "And Raudbjorn?"

"I don't know," Svanlaug replied rapidly, shoving him toward his horse. "We've got to get out of here before we're connected with this and hanged from the nearest roof-tree."

"But what about Leifr?" Starkad demanded. "He's in danger! We've lost our hostage!"

"That's unfortunate," Svanlaug said grimly. "I'd give much to get my hands on a Naglisson now. I think it was all a hoax to lead us into Sorkvir's clutches. There was no thousand marks in gold blood price from the Council, I'll warrant. I fear Leifr's Scipling fascination for gold has led him into a very bad situation."

"You were just as charmed," Starkad said.

"We were all deceived," Svanlaug retorted. "Even those rune stones were a deception, I'll warrant. Well, there's nothing for it now but to find a safe place to hide until the furor blows over. Then we'll start to search for Leifr."

"If he's still alive," Starkad said drearily. "He might have gone up with the inn and everyone else in it."

"We don't know that he was there," Svanlaug said. "We must assume there is still hope. Otherwise, the Council and their Pentacle are now completely unopposed."

"Where are we going?" Starkad demanded as Svanlaug turned her horse onto a well-traveled road and urged it into a smart trot. In silent shame, the troll-hounds slunk out of the shadows, their entire aspect reflecting defeat in their enterprise. Determined resistance was the only thing that could have turned them back from their prey.

"To a safe place," Svanlaug said impatiently, her head turning from one side to the other. "My instincts inherited from my sorcerer father Afgang will guide us. Now be silent; there are settlements on both sides of this road."

Starkad found himself gazing longingly at the lights as they passed each settlement. His ribs still ached from the tumble into the ditch, and his entire being ached at the realization that they might have lost Leifr and Thurid in one fell swoop. The troll-hounds trotted behind him in a similar state of embarrassment, heads drooping and bedraggled tails curling low at their heels.

They rode a long time, passing house after house. A steady roaring sound increased gradually in volume as they went along, until the road suddenly dipped down between two shoulders of rock and they found themselves standing on the bank of the Svart-strom once again. Ahead lay a crumbing boat stand.

"What are we doing here?" Starkad demanded. "Is this the best your sorcerous instincts can do?"

"Be silent," Svanlaug said. "Everything that happens has its reasons."

"Svanlaug! Look!" Starkad gasped and pointed across the dark, turgid waters. A vast dark shape was coming toward them out of the mist, with head and tail held arrogantly high. "It's that haunted ship again!"

Svanlaug gaped at it a moment, and the troll-hounds whined and growled uneasily.

"Back! Get away from this place!" She turned her horse and plunged away from the boat stand. "It followed us! The Council will have a perfect idea of where we are, thanks to this cursed ship!"

"How could they know we'd gone upstream to Ferja?" Starkad sputtered, taking on a mouthful of rain in his gaping at the dragon ship over one shoulder.

"That cursed orb of Thurid's!" Svanlaug said, tossing her wet hair out of her eyes. "It's like a beacon light, pointing out right where our location is."

"Where are your fine inherited instincts now?" Starkad demanded. "I think they're leading us right into the Council's lair for destruction!"

"Perhaps we must cross to the Hringurhol side now," Svanlaug said, slowing her horse to a walk, then stopping to turn and look back. "We must cross sometime. Sorkvir could have easily taken Leifr across, before the fire. He could be alive, Starkad. We might have lost Thurid, but I'm not ready to give up yet."

Starkad swung around to glare from her to the ship waiting at the boat stand. "You may be right," he growled, "but I'm not setting foot in any haunted ship just yet."

Starkad led a fast retreat from the riverbank. They urged their cold and weary horses along by main force, with Starkad finally resorting to leading his exhausted mount despite his aching bruises. Halting suddenly, Svanlaug turned half around to gaze down a faint track leading toward a single light burning about a mile from the road.

"There's our refuge," she said wearily.

At the end of the track, winding between stone walls that encouraged the road to become a ditch in rainy weather, stood a crumbling turf house with adjoining barns and paddocks, all in a state of decay and disrepair and overgrown with nettles. The light came from a single unshuttered window in what had been the main hall. Svanlaug rode up to the window and knocked, taking advantage of the opportunity to peer within.

"I don't think anyone is home," she said. "More's the pity, there's a nice fire and a big haunch of meat on the chain over the coals. It looks as if everyone left in rather a hurry."

Starkad stifled a moan. "Well, that's no help for us. They probably went to look at Varudur's inn burning. Maybe we could shelter in one of the barns. No one would object to that, I don't think, especially on such a night."

Svanlaug didn't appear to be listening. She dismounted and led her horse over to the door and knocked more loudly. The sound echoed in the house beyond, faintly answered by a barking dog somewhere, but it didn't come any nearer. After a moment of considering, Svanlaug gave the door a shove, and it opened quite willingly.

"No one would mind us sheltering by their fire," she said. "Even the Dokkalfar have a few rules of hospitality. Let's take the horses to the stable. Someone might be here by the time we get back."

"This isn't a good idea," Starkad said, following her to a nearby barn, where a few horses stood in large clean stalls, along with ten empty stalls that had been recently occupied.

Starkad's arguments became more feeble after they returned to the hall and spread out their wet cloaks by the fire. His protests died altogether when Svanlaug carved off a juicy slab of the succulent meat. They ate it with their fingers in silent, half-starved haste, and washed it down with ale from a jug on a nearby table.

"Pass the bread," Starkad said. "Might as well make ourselves as comfortable as possible, thanks to our kind hosts, unseen though they may be."

The moment the feast was finished, Starkad forgot everything except the pressing prerogative of sleep. Leaving Svanlaug drying and brushing her hair by the warmth of the fire, he garnered a couple of sheep fleeces and instantly fell asleep. It was a deep sleep, punctuated only by short intervals of cold when the fire burned low. Scarcely awakening, he pushed more fuel onto it and fell asleep in the restored warmth.

The next thing he knew, a gust of cold fresh air fanned his face, powdering him slightly with a cloud of ash. A low rumble of voices and the tramping of feet suddenly filled the silence of the hall. Opening his eyes slightly, Starkad was treated to the sight of ten Ulf-hedin trooping into the hall with their wolf capes dangling over their shoulders as they came and stood staring at him and Svanlaug in mute amazement.

Chapter 4

◇◇◇

Svanlaug sat up and stared back at them without losing a trace of her haughty composure. "It was raining and we were wet and cold," she said. "I hope that even Ulf-hedin have the kindness to share a fire and a roof for one evening. No one was at home, after all, so we troubled no one, except your joint of meat."

"Did you ever see such audacity?" one Ulf-hedin demanded with an unpleasant laugh.

"Leave them alone, Birtingr," said one who had entered the hall last, standing slightly apart to survey the situation. "They mean no harm. Just a couple of ragged wanderers who wanted a dry place to stay."

"We'll be glad to leave at once and cease troubling you," Starkad offered a trifle too eagerly.

"What, day-farers are you?" inquired the leader, coming forward with a faintly curious frown. "There was a great to-do last night, caused by day-farers at Varudur's inn."

Starkad and Svanlaug made no answer. Starkad kept his eyes upon the Ulf-hedin, scarcely daring to twitch a muscle lest he betray himself in a thousand different ways.

"I think you can see, Magni, they're not the sort to have caused such a conflagration," another Ulf-hedin drawled, turning away in disinterest. "That was direct sorcery, mark my words, or I'll eat them."

"Eat who?" Starkad inquired uneasily.

Magni chuckled coldly, his eyes not softened by the warmth of mirth. "You're not what he was talking about, little nithling. What has brought you to Ferja? I don't recall seeing either of you two around before, begging at kitchen doors and tent flaps."

Svanlaug shrugged and replied, "What brings any beggar to Ferja? The hope of a comfortable place to stay awhile, with no one to cause trouble, until it's time to go on again, usually through no fault of our own.''

"But beggars usually don't have horses," Magni said. "We found yours in the barn."

"I never said we were beggars," Svanlaug said. "We have every intention of paying for what we used last night. A piece of mutton, several cups of ale, a loaf of bread, and whatever hay the horses ate—''

"There is no need," Magni said. "But you will have to bide with us a short while until our chieftain Hvitur-Fax takes a look at you. These are unsteady days, these last days before Brjaladur.''

Birtingr sidled a few steps nearer with a fawning grin for his superior and a contemptuous smirk for the uninvited guests. "I shall guard them until Fax returns, Magni. Are you certain he's going to be sufficiently interested in these two nithlings to warrant bothering him? If I were the ranking Ulf, I'd deal with them without annoying Fax. Kill them and throw them in the river.''

A grizzled Ulf-hedin looked up from taking his boots off nearby and said, "Is that your solution for every problem, Birtingr?''

Birtingr whirled on him furiously. "You're not the leader of this pack any longer, Ongull, so why do you talk? No one is going to listen, least of all me! Why don't you hold your tongue before someone cuts it off?''

"Still envious, Birtingr?" Ongull drawled, undiscomfited as he shook a pebble out of his boot. "You might be leader of a pack someday, but I hope I don't live to see it.''

"Take yourself away, Birtingr," Magni snapped. "Fax must be consulted. Halmur, come forward. You shall be the one to guard our guests. Keep your eyes upon them and see to it they come to no harm.''

He cast Birtingr a malevolent leer and strode away to a sleeping platform where he threw himself down with a grunt. No longer amused by the novelty of the situation, the other Ulf-hedin wandered away to eat and drink or sleep.

Starkad turned slowly to look at Halmur, advancing from the back of the pack. He was one of the youngest of the group of Ulf-hedin and moved among them deferentially, with lowered eyes and nervous care not to draw attention to himself. Starkad's blood chilled and his heart came to a brief and painful standstill before commencing a leaden pounding that churned out a pint of cold sweat over his body. It was the same young Halmur he and Leifr had seen unwillingly invested with the Ulf-hedin cape and belt in Skaela-fell, a Halmur now as lean and stealthy as a yearling wolf.

Neither betrayed the slightest recognition, had anyone been paying much attention.

"You must follow me," Halmur said in a low voice. "The higher elders will take affront if less worthy ones crowd the fire."

He led the way to the sleeping platforms along the side of the room and squatted down watchfully on his heels.

"You're in grave danger here," he whispered. "I know who you are. I can't keep the secret much longer, for fear of them." He nodded his head slightly toward the others.

"I'm nothing to Fax," Starkad answered.

"You're something if you're involved with the Scipling and the wizard Thurid," Halmur said. "They'll expect you to tell them where he is."

"I don't know where he is," Starkad said. "They'll have to ask the Naglissons that question."

"The Naglissons and their father are in Ferja," Halmur said. "The Ulf-hedin will find them."

"How do you like being an Ulf-hedin?" Starkad asked. "Is it as great as you'd thought?"

Halmur looked away a moment. "Every day I think of home and my father. I shall never return and I may not live very long. But I made my choice and I must live with it as long as I can. We must stop talking before someone gets suspicious."

Starkad glanced over the other Ulf-hedin. Some were already asleep, others sat apart by themselves in sullen silence, glowering in red-eyed offense at anyone who happened to come near. After a long night, it was Halmur's misfortune as the youngest to draw the duty of guarding prisoners, instead of making himself comfortable as the others did. He sat on a narrow stool with his arms folded over his chest, struggling manfully to stay awake.

Svanlaug passed the time by sitting up stiffly, eyes shut, consulting some inscrutable oracle somewhere within the recesses of her own mind. Starkad leaned his head against the wall and alternately thought of home and Ermingerd, or dozed uncomfortably.

Near midday the grizzled Ulf-hedin Ongull rose from his bench and prodded Halmur.

"I shall take your place," he said. "Go and sleep."

Halmur nodded gratefully and left his place to Ongull, who sat down on the stool and gazed at the captives, his one faded eye perusing them from its leathery recess. The creases on his face were interspersed with several ancient white scars and one fairly recent one still glowing a livid red. It made a gruesome journey from one blinded eye socket downward almost to the hollow of his jaw where a wound could end a man's life in moments. His own hair was white and wiry, and the decrepit wolf cape hanging over one shoulder was worn almost hairless in spots and matted and scruffy throughout.

Starkad took in all the details of him with interest, particularly the fearsome battle wound.

"You're old," he blurted out.

"And content," Ongull replied, lighting his pipe and blowing out fragrant clouds. "I've led this pack for a good many years, and now it's Magni's chore. He'll be a good leader. He's the one that gave me this scar that you're staring so hard at. Lovely, isn't it?"

"It's one of the best I've seen," Starkad stammered, looking away in embarrassment. "Another jot to the left and he would have had your throat out along with the eye."

"The fool took pity on me at the last instant, though I told him not to," Ongull said serenely. "I trained the pup myself from his early days, like that young Halmur. He's the one I would pick to take my place."

"You don't seem like an Ulf-hedin," Starkad noted. "You seem like anyone else—right now, at least. I never imagined an Ulf-hedin getting old."

"It does happen, if they don't manage to get themselves killed," Ongull said with a weary sigh.

Birtingr looked around his shoulder and said, "You should have managed it long ago, you old crowbait."

"You did your best to take over," Ongull said, "and it wasn't good enough. Nor will it ever be. With one eye gone, yet I could still beat you senseless."

"You yielded to Magni," Birtingr snarled. "You allowed him to win the pack from you."

"And Magni will keep it from you just as well," Ongull said. "I can trust him to do that."

"Stop your quarreling or take it outside and finish it for once and for all," someone nearby growled. "Can't you see we're trying to sleep?"

Near twilight, the Ulf-hedin began to awaken and make preparations for their nightly departure.

"Where's Fax with the eitur?" Birtingr growled, pacing up and down the hall in a growing frenzy. His eyes glared as he cast about for a suitable scapegoat, settling upon the luckless Halmur, who was minding his own business in a far corner.

"So," he began jeeringly, "the infant from Skaela-fell is riding with us still. I wonder how much longer he's going to last. He looks to me as if he misses his old home and his family and would like to go back. Wouldn't they be glad to see him on a full moon night, when he changes to wolf-phase and comes at them to rip out their throats?"

Halmur turned away, pale with anger, but Magni overheard and ended the situation summarily by shoving Birtingr against the wall with a crash.

"It's your throat that will get ripped," he said with a lowering glare. "It would sound much better than what we have to hear coming out of it, day in, day out. I'm not amused by you, Birtingr. If you wish to challenge me for this pack, I'm willing to fight you anytime."

"Not I," Birtingr said, shrinking back in a craven manner that was not entirely sincere. "I'm not destined to lead—only to follow."

"Then do as you're told," Magni snapped. "Be silent and trouble no one any further."

"It's the fault of Fax," Birtingr said in a nasty whine as he slunk away, casting an avaricious eye around the room for signs of sympathy. "He's never been so late with the eitur."

When Starkad looked at Ongull, he thought the old Ulf-hedin winked at him in wry amusement, but with only one eye, Ongull was always winking.

Hvitur-Fax arrived considerably later, well past their usual hour for departure. He strode into the hall on a surge of cold outside air.

"Come forward according to rank," he ordered brusquely, positioning himself behind a table and removing a familiar flask from an interior pocket. Each Ulf-hedin possessed a small cup scarcely bigger than a thimble, which was filled with ruby drops of eitur and either swallowed in one greedy gulp and a fiery gasp, or savored in the mouth before swallowing. Last of all to come forward was Ongull, the former pack's leader. He was a savorer of the eitur, gazing at it and smelling its sweet fragrance in great appreciation before tipping it onto his tongue. Birtingr, who was one of the avid gulpers, watched his performance in exquisite envy.

"Now for the business at hand," Fax commenced, his eyes sliding over the ranks of Ulf-hedin. "We know the hiding place of the outlaw Leifr Thorljotsson. An incompetent idiot, Nagli, is holding him for ransom from the Council of Threttan. It's a ticklish situation. A forceful attack is not the answer this time. The Most Exalted Meistari Alfrekar is dealing with a traitor on the Council."

A low mutter ran through the Ulf-hedin, and Ongull winked at Starkad and Svanlaug. "They're all traitors," he whispered slyly, rather louder than a whisper ought to be. Several nearby Ulf-hedin turned and looked at him uneasily, and others pretended to have heard nothing.

Fax paused a moment at the slight disturbance before going on. "Until information about the traitor is extracted, we must wait for instructions from Alfrekar and keep our eyes upon Nagli. The sword that menaces the plans of the Council is still unfound, as yet."

"The Dokkur Lavardur knows all things," Magni said. "Why doesn't he reveal us the location of the sword?"

"The affairs of such paltry creatures as mortalkind are of little importance to such a great and ancient being," Fax replied. "The Lord of Chaos will be consulted by the wise ones who have the skill and powers to do so. Continue as usual until you are told otherwise. Those who burned Varudur's inn are still prowling about somewhere. Out of five marauders, we can account only for the Scipling. We cannot rest until all of these outlaws are captured or killed."

"We have two captives," Magni said. "One a day-farer and one a Dokkalfar woman, strangers to this region. No one else who knows this place would have pushed open our door while we were gone and sheltered in our hall."

Fax turned and a pathway opened before him, leaving Starkad

and Svanlaug facing him unobstructed. Fax approached slowly, his boots making scarcely a sound, as the other Ulf-hedin stood motionless, watching. After a long moment of silently surveying the prisoners, he permitted himself a grim parody of a smile.

"This is the sort of unexpected luck one never dares hope for," he said, his eyes boring into Starkad. "Perhaps you've repented of your decision on Skaela-fell not to make the conversion to the clan of the Ulf-hedin. You saw how easy and relatively painless it was. Perhaps now you've come to join our ranks in Ferja."

Starkad shook his head as much to break the effect of Hvitur-Fax's hypnotic stare as to signify his answer.

"No," he said, "I don't wish to become an Ulf-hedin. I didn't then and I don't now."

"Nor do I," Svanlaug said with a challenging tilt to her chin. "You already have one female Ulf-hedin in your ranks, and that is enough."

Fax's eyes widened a split second, then narrowed. "We have no female Ulf-hedin in our numbers," he said coldly. "Common men are easier to control than women with their dark and mysterious powers."

"Then what's to be done with us?" Svanlaug demanded.

"That depends. Were you the ones responsible for burning Varudur's inn?" Fax demanded, and Starkad nodded slightly. "I thought it seemed the sort of thing a wizard might do. Where is Thurid hiding now?"

"If he's alive, we have no idea," Svanlaug answered. "As nearly as we can tell, Thurid went into the inn and it burned before he could get out. There was only one door. The Norskur also was lost at that time. Why else do you suppose the two of us are left on our own, blundering into Ulf-hedin fortresses and stealing their food?"

"I was just marveling at such audacity," Hvitur-Fax said. "It seemed so clever, until you fell asleep and allowed yourselves to be captured. Perhaps you had thought it was a good way to get inside Hringurhol and nearer to the unfinished Pentacle."

"Scant good it would do," Svanlaug said. "We don't have the sword nor the dragon's carbuncle from Thurid's staff. We are exactly what you behold before you, a youth who is a common Ljosalfar and a Dokkalfar healing physician from the clan Bergmal. Afgang the Martyr was my father, however."

"Martyr!" Fax grunted. "It should be Afgang the Traitor."

"Plenty of Dokkalfar don't want to return underground to the dark days, any more than he did," Svanlaug retorted with a spirited toss of her head.

"Ferja is not the place for those who wish to argue on that point," Hvitur-Fax said, starting to turn away. "And I have no time for it besides. Magni, you've done well. Your good luck must have drawn these captives here. Only the wizard and the Norskur must be accounted for, and perhaps they are dead. It was a fortuitous night, Magni."

They walked away a few paces, but Starkad could still hear their low voices. He slumped on the sleeping platform in a dejected pose with his head buried in his arms, but he still listened.

"Tonight we will search the ashes of the inn for the bones of Thurid," Magni said. "The rain should have cooled them by now. Perhaps we will soon have the blue orb of Galdur in our hands at last. This is where it belongs."

"Carry on, Magni," Fax replied. "But don't go near the north end of the settlement tonight. Some very nervous thief-takers are holed up in the mill tower. They have sent a message to Alfrekar that they have something he wants."

"The Scipling!" Magni said. "And the sword!"

"We don't know for certain if it's anything but a hoax," Hvitur-Fax replied with a shrug. "These seem to be a shabby lot, even for thief-takers. Regardless, I don't want them taking flight before Alfrekar meets with them, in case they have got the Scipling."

"I'd wager that the Scipling died in the fire," Magni said. "It was clearly a clever trap."

"Clever indeed, and I wonder who set it," Fax mused. "Certainly not those thief-takers at the mill. Nevertheless, we must be certain. Carry out your search of the burned inn and keep well away from the north end. I've got Tostig's pack watching the mill from a distance. I'll leave these two prisoners to you awhile, as well as the finding of Thurid and the crystal."

"Ingolfr's got the best nose, but there won't be many traces in all this rain," Magni said. "We'll search each house individually from cellar to attic. The wizard won't go far without his swordsman. If either of them are still alive, we shall find them."

The Ulf-hedin pack had donned their wolf capes by now,

milling around restlessly and snapping at one another as they waited for their leader.

"Away then," Magni commanded. "Saddle the horses and proceed to Varudur's inn. All except you, Halmur. It will be your duty to guard the prisoners tonight. The rest of us will sift the ashes of Varudur's inn, if necessary, to find the blue crystal."

Halmur removed his wolf skin and resumed his watchful position on the stool. When the rest of the pack had trooped outdoors and shut the door after them, the hall was suddenly very silent.

Svanlaug drew a deep breath and exhaled an impatient sigh. "Once again, Halmur, you are given the least desired duty. It must be a burden being the youngest and least experienced among Ulf-hedin. Have you been allowed to kill anyone yet, or is that a sport reserved for the leaders?"

Halmur raised his sullen stare from the floor to glare at her malevolently. "I have the same powers as any of them," he said. "If I were not thought capable of guarding two prisoners, I would not have been left here, so your taunting is in vain if you think to trick me somehow."

Svanlaug strode up and down a few quick paces, plucking at the heavy locks of her hair, matted from the rain.

"While you were in the Hringurhol," she said, "did you see the Sverting sorceress? I have heard about her."

"I saw her from a distance," Halmur said. "A lowly one such as I would not dare come near to the exalted ones."

"Such as Alfrekar and the Council and the Sverting?" Svanlaug questioned.

Halmur nodded. "We are there for nothing but the work of keeping peace in the realm so the Dokkur Lavardur can overspread it all."

"Is the Sverting an Ulf-hedin?" Svanlaug asked.

"I know not," Halmur said, "but it would upset a great many Ulf-hedin if she were. They would not take kindly to females in their ranks."

"But this Sverting runs with the Ulf-hedin," Svanlaug persisted. "She uses a wolf cape and shifts shapes and uses Ulf-hedin powers. Therefore, she is an Ulf-hedin, and she must then take the eitur, the same as you, wouldn't you agree?"

"She only pretends to be an Ulf-hedin, I think," Halmur

said. "She struts around with a cape, but she does not partake of the eitur as we do. None of the exalted ones do. They wouldn't dream of submitting themselves to its slavery."

"If any of them once was lowly and rose to power," Svanlaug said, "would he still be addicted to eitur?"

"Naturally not," Halmur said. "There is an antidote, and the lucky ones would take it and be cured. Any of us might one day be so lucky, if we prove ourselves consistently over the years."

"Does Hvitur-Fax take eitur?" Svanlaug asked. "Is that the only way Alfrekar keeps him in submission to the Council of Threttan? The Ulf-hedin are so many, and the Council is only Thirteen—less than thirteen now."

"The Ulf-hedin are ever loyal to Alfrekar," Halmur snapped.

"You are very young to be an Ulf-hedin," Svanlaug said. "Don't you miss your family and friends back at Skaela-fell?"

"I am dead to them, and they are dead to me," Halmur said in a wooden tone, his eyes dull from the effects of the eitur. "I am an Ulf-hedin, and always was, and always will be. Now you must be silent. I have no further interest in talking to you or answering your questions. You are prisoners and I am here to guard you, nothing more."

Starkad sat and watched as the last sparks of Halmur's own identity were smothered in the darkening effect of the eitur. An entity not Halmur looked out from his eyes, cold and ancient and evilly wise. His natural youthful grace slouched into something stooped and distorted. A crooked half-smiling sneer curled his lips, and his breathing rattled in a peculiar manner. Repelled, Starkad turned away, feeling a strong sense of revulsion and fear rising in his throat.

"Who are you?" Svanlaug demanded after watching in silent horror at the transformation. "Where is Halmur?"

"Halmur is young and foolish," a hoarse voice coming between Halmur's stiffened lips croaked, which slurred the words and didn't form them properly. "And you are young and foolish, also. Everyone around me is infantile and stupid. I am the greatest of the last and most wise. I was here before anything was, and I shall be here when everything is gone. I am Nameless, Nafnlaus, Enginn, Nobody. Sooner or later everything comes back to me, the Lord of Chaos."

Svanlaug gripped Starkad's arm painfully and drew him away with her until they stood beside the hearth. The cold eyes of the entity in Halmur followed them, relentless and unalarmed as Svanlaug busied herself and Starkad in building up the fire.

"What is the matter with you?" Starkad grumbled.

"It's him," she said, her voice almost trembling with fear. Her eyes were wide with a sort of reckless excitement. "Or some of him. Can't you see it? Feel it? It's like a hammer pressing down on your heart."

"I feel it," Starkad said, "but who is it?"

"The Dokkur Lavardur," Svanlaug said in a low voice. "By the eitur, they are enslaved. They are him."

It was shortly after daybreak when the Ulf-hedin returned, standing around outside the door with a lot of restless muttering and growling. Starkad awakened from an uneasy doze, instantly suspicious, wondering why they did not come trooping in for their supper and beds. He darted a quick look at Halmur, who was standing up and stretching, quite himself again, as Starkad could tell at a glance by his silent, dolorous demeanor.

Magni opened the door and entered the hall, tearing off his wolf cape as he did so, with much the same startling effect as if he were skinning himself.

"Bring the prisoners outside, Halmur," he commanded. "We've found something in the ashes. Perhaps it can be identified by these two."

Halmur silently pointed, indicating they were to follow Magni outside. Squinting slightly in the low-angle rays of the early sun, Starkad edged warily out the door. The Ulf-hedin cleared away for him and Svanlaug; some stood staring at the prisoners in surly distaste, and some gazed away down the road behind the house.

A rickety cart pulled by an ancient horse was making its way through the muddy ruts. One ragged figure walked alongside encouraging the horse, and three others huddled on the seat like a knot of shabby crows. As it came into the dooryard, approaching the hall, several of the Ulf-hedin made covert signs behind their backs and sidled away from the cart and its three occupants.

The cart stopped and Magni beckoned Starkad and Svanlaug to approach the tailboard.

"We found two bodies in the burned inn," he said. "We believe they might be the wizard Thurid and the Norskur that traveled with him. You must look at them and tell us if what we suspect is true."

Starkad's heart stood still as he looked at the burden the cart carried. There was no mistaking Thurid, his marble features washed clean by the soft rainfall. Nor was there any doubt that Raudbjorn had perished with him, still gripping his halberd. No flame had touched them, yet they had lost their lives in the fiery conflagration.

"You're mistaken," Svanlaug said, after too long a pause. "We have no idea whom you've found here, but it's not Thurid and Raudbjorn."

"She lies, as I knew she would," Magni said triumphantly and pointed to Starkad. "You see it there? The lad's face tells it all without speaking a word, while the Dokkalfar woman fills our ears with lies."

"So you may think," Svanlaug said. "If this is Thurid, where is the blue orb on the end of his staff? Staff and crystal seem to be missing entirely, as well as his satchel. Are you certain this is not merely a leikfang, an image left behind by the wizard to deceive you? He's very clever at the old spells of the Rhbus. If you found no satchel and staff," she continued over the rising uneasy murmuring of the Ulf-hedin, "I'll warrant Thurid is hiding somewhere nearby, waiting for his chance at you."

"We have it from Varudur that it was an ambush," Magni said, silencing the murmuring with a sharp scowl. "A wizard of considerable reputation was waiting for him. I believe the satchel and staff were carried off by this wizard before the inn was set ablaze. Notice how these corpses did not seem to perish by fire. Rather, it seems more like ice, does it not? I have it on authority from Hvitur-Fax himself that a rogue wizard, possibly even a member of the Council of Threttan, is conspiring against the Council and the Dokkur Lavardur himself."

"At least we can thank this rogue for dispatching Thurid," one of the Ulf-hedin muttered, and the others nodded in agreement.

"We can thank no one until the crystal is found," Magni said sharply. "In the wrong hands, it will do as much damage as these ill-starred day-farers thought to do."

"They will fail," someone grunted. "All the others have."

Magni snorted and shook his head. "Such thinking will one day lead you face to face with one who may not fail, and he'll use your severed head as a stepping-stone into Hringurhol and its secrets. Now then, away with you all. There's no reason for you to stand around staring.''

"Wait," Svanlaug said in a rather hurried tone, catching at Magni's sleeve as he brushed by. "Perhaps I was a little over-hasty. It's true, I attempted to lie about the identity of the bodies. It is Thurid and the Norskur. I now think the time for pretense is past. There is much I can tell you about the Scipling and the sword and the wizard who is conspiring against Alfrekar.''

"I shall listen with great interest," Magni said.

"Svanlaug!" Starkad cried. "You can't tell them anything! They're Ulf-hedin!''

"It's over, Starkad," Svanlaug said with a sad smile. "Thurid is dead and Leifr is, too, or captured. There is nothing more to do than barter for our lives with what information we have." She turned and started to return to the hall, leaving Starkad standing rooted to the spot, seething in an intolerable stew of grief, rage, and betrayal.

"Come on, then, back inside," Halmur urged.

Starkad hesitated a moment for one last uncomprehending look into the cart at Thurid and Raudbjorn. Never in all his days of relatively sheltered living at Fangelsi had he felt such a wild and bereft condition descending upon him. From the stables came the voices of the troll-hounds raised in desolate wailing howls from whatever prison that held them, as if they, too, were sharing in his rending grief.

Halmur broke into his trance by giving him a poke in the back to urge him to return to the hall. A great wave of desperate fury broke over Starkad. With a bellow of rage, he swung around and charged at Halmur, taking him right off his feet in the suddenness of his attack. Plowing Halmur's head into the ground, Starkad leaped to his feet and was well on his way down the lane with the full Ulf-hedin pack charging at his heels when one of them finally tackled him around the knees, bringing him down under a heap of snarling and cursing Ulf-hedin, determined that he would go no farther. To do him credit, it was Halmur who had tackled him, a feat that garnered him some congratulatory back-slapping and growls of approval.

Starkad's rage was quite over when they brought him back, puffing and bruised and ashamed. Svanlaug turned away from her silent scrutiny of the bodies in the cart and dealt him a withering scowl.

"Truly, Starkad, I don't believe my eyes," she said contemptuously. "Did you believe you could get away, bolting off like a runaway horse?"

She turned a slanting glance toward Magni, and Starkad knew with a flash of inspiration that she had been talking to him while he was pelting away down the lane like a fool. She must have seen the sudden suspicion in his eyes. She smiled at him coldly and tossed her head.

"Oh, no. Svanlaug, you wouldn't turn on us again!" he gasped. "Not after all we've done for you!" He lunged at her with a second surge of enraged fury, but a couple of Ulf-hedin had a good grip on his arms. "I've put my neck on the block the last time for you!" he raged. "Thurid would have left you a dozen times, but I was always the one who took pity on you! Now I see what an idiot I was!"

Magni nodded toward the other side of the hall. "Put him in the cooling house," he said. "He won't get out of there. What a rage he's in! An Ulf-hedin at full moonrise could scarcely do better."

"Traitor! Liar!" Starkad spewed as they hauled him away.

Svanlaug shrugged her shoulders. "I must be true to myself and my own kind," she said. "Especially now that I can see these day-farers can take me no farther."

"We have much to discuss," Magni said, turning toward the doorway to the hall. "There's no more to be seen here, now we're certain the great Thurid is thoroughly dead. I fear you haven't been very comfortable here since your arrival."

As he turned to go, a ragged brown figure scuttled a few steps after him. Svanlaug whirled around with a startled gasp, exclaiming, "Who touched me?"

Just as quickly, the brown figure scuttled back into the shelter of the cart.

"What is it you want?" Magni demanded.

The little brown figure edged forward, bright eyes peering at him from a withered nutlike face. Nervous fingers scuttled up to grip the ragged fabric of the threadbare cloak more firmly around the throat.

"If you're finished with the carrion," a harsh female voice cawed, "we'll take it off the premises for you and dispose of it in a fitting fashion. If you wish to give us a small bit of something for our trouble, we'd be so grateful, being such as we are."

"Ketilridir, isn't it?" Magni asked as he dug into his belt pouch for a coin.

"I'm Beitski," the little scavenger said with a nearly toothless grin. "My sister Ketilridir is on the cart, with Jarngerdr and Grimssyna. She's afraid of Ulf-hedin."

"Who are these women?" Svanlaug asked with a tremor in her voice.

"The knacker-women. Rag- and bone-pickers," Magni said with a shrug. "They carry away dead bodies no one wants and get rid of them."

"She touched me," Svanlaug said with a shudder. "I felt as if something evil was there."

Magni glared at the four old women. "Clear out of here at once. And don't come back unless you're sent for. And don't hunt around at the inn any longer. You've got what you came there for."

"Very good, very good," Beitski chirped, rubbing her dry hands together like a disreputable cricket. "And so we have, so we have."

Chapter 5

◇◇

Leifr awakened with a pounding headache and a mouth as dry as wool. His ears were filled with a terrific buzzing that soon resolved into the murmur of voices and the crackling of a fire.

"Hah, he's waking up," boomed a voice that made his head throb.

Leifr opened his eyes a crack to admit a searing beam of light into his fevered skull. A monstrous distorted face floated before his eyes, breathing its foul breath into his face. Automatically his hand reached for his sword, but his fingers still felt numb and clumsy and seemed to have lost their memory for finding the sword. His entire body felt as heavy as lead, particularly the back of his skull. In a moment he recognized the face, not as some dread monster or troll, but as Nagli the thief-taker, grinning at him in complacent glee.

"I'm afraid there's no gold in this bargain for you after all," Nagli said with a regretful clucking of his tongue and a shake of his head. "It's a pity and all that, but clever men such as I will always reap the harvest of blood money placed upon the heads of honest but unlucky men such as you. I think there's a great truth there somewhere. It doesn't always pay to be on the right side, does it? If there are enough people who decide to get rid of you, all they have to do is announce a blood price, and fellows such as I will do the job for them."

"Get out of here, Nagli," Leifr growled, giving his head a shake to clear it for a better look around him.

Behind Nagli was a fire and the three Naglissons sitting around it leaning against a blackened stone wall behind them. He realized he was lying on a heap of old straw with some smelly horse cloths thrown over him. Slowly he gathered his wits, and the memory of Nagli's treachery with the poisoned cup returned to him. He turned over a fleeting memory of a jouncing ride in a cart, concluding that he had been taken away from Varudur's inn to this place, wherever it was. It had the smell of a disused barn; judging from the nearby sounds of horses eating and snorting and pawing, it was now being used as one again.

"Whatever you wish," Nagli said, moving back. "I've always allowed condemned men one last wish, providing it was reasonable."

"I'd like a sword and a chance to kill all of you," Leifr replied.

"I'm afraid that's not a reasonable request," Nagli said with a cheery grin, rubbing his hands together.

A light tapping sounded at the door, and one of the Naglissons by the fire got up to open it. The dark hooded form of Sorkvir stepped into the room, drawing back from the fire quickly.

"Close that door, you fool," he commanded in a hoarse snarl, "and stamp out some of that fire. There's too much light and heat in here. Alfrekar and Hvitur-Fax received the message only moments ago and they are on their way here now. Is the Scipling awake yet, or have you killed him with your poison cup?"

Not waiting for Nagli's answer, Sorkvir strode across the room to verify the condition of the prisoner for himself. With his staff he whisked away the horse cloths and prodded at Leifr for signs of life. Leifr's eyes snapped open and he seized the end of the staff with both hands and gave a great thrust, impelling Sorkvir toward the fire behind him. A jolt of icy cold seared his hands. With surprising agility, Sorkvir leaped aside, avoiding the licking flames reaching out greedily after him. He raised the staff, words of a spell forming on his wizened lips.

Leifr found his feet in an unsteady lurch and braced himself against the wall behind him. A chain fastened around his leg hampered his movements, but at least he was on his feet as a warrior ought to be for his last moments.

"Come now, this won't do!" Nagli said sharply, waggling his hands deprecatingly. "You mustn't kill him, Meistari Sorkvir. Not until we're done with our scheme. We can't do much without the sword and the Scipling, you recall."

Sorkvir abruptly abandoned his hostile stance and turned his back to show his scorn.

"As I said, Alfrekar and Hvitur-Fax are on their way," he

continued. "You must pretend to cooperate with them, but insist upon the price we have set. Even if they pretend to get angry and walk away, stay firm. They will respect you for that."

"But what if Fax sends his Ulf-hedin sniffing around?" Nagli questioned, his grinning confidence suddenly knotted up with apprehension. "They can do whatever they wish with us, and that door won't stand against an Ulf-hedin."

"After they see this place tonight, we shall have to hide the Scipling and the sword elsewhere," Sorkvir said. "Otherwise you'll be overrun, killed, and the sword taken. Leave the Ulf-hedin to me. I shall see it to Hvitur-Fax doesn't get in."

"You're doomed, Nagli," Leifr said. "You're in the palm of Sorkvir's hand, as helpless as a quail. You've got no defense against the Ulf-hedin, and you'll find that out very soon when Sorkvir decides he doesn't need you for his bargaining with the Council. He's turned on Alfrekar; do you believe he'll show you the slightest mercy?"

Sorkvir turned and pointed one finger toward Leifr. "Thagga nidur, Scipling," he pronounced, and Leifr found himself silenced. No amount of effort would summon the words from his thoughts to his tongue.

"Now then," Sorkvir continued contemptuously with a gripping gesture with one fist, "I could have just as easily crushed his heart or stopped his wind. But you see I am a patient man and accustomed to dealing with small and easily frightened creatures such as yourself. Don't worry about Alfrekar and Fax. They are mine, and I shall deal with them when the time comes. You are less than an insect to me, and it will amuse me to make use of you, then set you free as a gesture of my great power. When I take Alfrekar's high seat and chieftancy of the Council from him, I will need clever fellows such as you, Nagli, to ferret out nests of resistance and rebellion."

"Ferreting is what I am best at," Nagli said with a weasely grin. "Particularly if the pay is good."

"Bah!" Leifr said, suddenly shaking himself free of the silence spell, to his own amazement. "He'll crush you like a bug, Nagli."

Sorkvir glared at him furiously and took a step forward.

"Halloa!" Nagli exclaimed suddenly. "Meistari, you're burning! You're too close to the fire!"

A tiny tongue of flame danced upon the withered flesh of

Sorkvir's forearm. He appeared not to feel it, gazing at it a moment with an inscrutable expression before calmly crushing it out with his other hand. The Naglissons fell back against the wall, staring and making signs and rubbing amulets in a fever of terror.

"It's nothing," Sorkvir said. "Just a warning that time is running out for this wretched carcass. Handling that Rhbu sword has hastened the process. Preparations must be made for taking another one that will serve me better." He darted Leifr a venomous glare. "And by the way, bring me a handful of the Scipling's hair. A hairlock spell will make him far easier to control."

"He's already on a good stout chain," Nagli said uneasily. "You're certain that isn't enough?"

"More control is needed," Sorkvir said, stalking toward the door. "A Scipling is an unruly influence. Remember, Nagli, to insist upon your price."

When he was gone, Leifr flung himself down on the straw in supreme disgust. "Nagli, you're a worse fool than I ever suspected," he snorted. "Your greed for gold and power is going to get us all killed—or worse, enslaved to Sorkvir, if he succeeds in his mad scheme to take over the Council."

Nagli rubbed his hands together nervously and licked his lips. "Yes, well, it's a bit of a gamble, but it's a good plan. For me, at least. I'd hate to be in your shoes, though. He's looking for another body, and I think you're it. Then he'd have that sword of Endless Death."

"Sorkvir in any form could not touch that sword," Leifr said with sudden fiery inspiration. "No unclean thing can touch it, and Sorkvir will always be unclean, as will anything he touches." Silently he thanked Fridmarr for his encouragement. "That includes you, Nagli. You think you're a clever fellow for capturing me. This I promise you—you're going to come to a bad end because of it."

"Tush!" Nagli said. "I've heard worse threats than that from doomed outlaws. You're a fierce bunch, breathing threats you'll never fulfill and swearing vengeance you'll never take. I'm not the least bit frightened."

A heavy knock thundered at the door, and Nagli jumped like a startled horse. "It's them!" he gasped, all color draining from his face. "Merciful gods of all thief-takers everywhere, defend us now! Ovild, open the door!"

"Me? Why me?" Ovild whimpered, edging away from the door and eyeing it as if it were a dragon. "Because I'm the youngest and you think you can spare me? Pabbi, you've gone one too far this time. They're going to kill us."

"And what a good riddance it will be," Leifr said, bracing his back against the wall once more.

"Open it!" Nagli commanded, assuming a false posture of confidence and command.

Ovild unbarred the door and scampered back out of the way as it swung open a few inches.

"Halloa! Come in!" Nagli croaked, adding a violent "Hem!" to clear his constricted throat.

The heavy door was thrust aside by a hairy paw and Hvitur-Fax stepped into the room in full wolf regalia. Wolf eyes scoured the room and came to rest upon Leifr with a fiery glow of recognition. Yellow fangs gleamed in a throaty snarl and the white mane of fur that gave Hvitur-Fax his name bristled on in anticipation. Then, with one hand, Hvitur peeled back the wolf skin and turned to the heavily cloaked figure standing behind him.

"Most Exalted One, it's the same Scipling I saw in Skaelafell," he said. "He had the cursed Rhbu sword with him then, but there's no sign of it here."

Alfrekar stepped forward, a wizened stick of a man of tall and angular proportions. He looked draug-thin to Leifr, yellowed and withered from serving as a vessel for unclean powers. Clutching an elaborate staff taller than himself, Alfrekar surveyed Leifr in silence a moment, his cold flickering gaze as paralyzing as that of a snake.

"Are you indeed the bearer of the Rhbu sword known as *Endalaus Daudi*?" Alfrekar rasped.

"I am," Leifr said. "It has brought me here to destroy you and your Pentacle and the Dokkur Lavardur." An unknown deep well of inner calm cleared his senses, and it was as if he heard Fridmarr's voice speaking in his ear. "*Endalaus Daudi* is coming home to finish the work for which it was forged long ago by the hand of the Rhbu called Malasteinn. He is the grindstone and I am the sword sharpened for your doom. I am only the tool of the will of the all-powerful Three who still rule the

Rhbu tribe. Kill me and another will come in my place, until this blot you have created is erased from the earth.''

"I have heard those words before," Alfrekar said with a jittery twitching in one jaw. "You have spoken with the ill-fated Fridmarr, or his associate Gedvondur. And still you didn't take warning from what befell them. Dreams of power and glory have taken away your common sense. You must know that you will die here. A Scipling has no hope of surmounting the challenges of Hringurhol. You have no powers, no carbuncle, no guidance. The New People have no power against the Old People.''

"I was chosen by Fridmarr," Leifr said. "He would not have brought me this far only to fail and die. He was wise. The eitur made him wise before he died.''

Alfrekar's eyes narrowed and he pursed up his lips, like the mouth of an old leathery bag, as if he had suddenly gotten a very bad taste. With a dusty snort, he turned his attention to Nagli, who was grinning and writhing in an ecstasy of dread.

"Well?" he barked harshly, causing Nagli to jump. "You have captured the Scipling, but where is the sword? One's no good without the other.''

Nagli made a stiff half bow. "Most Exalted Meistari, the sword is in a more secure place for safekeeping. I did not deem it wise to keep the sword within reach of the Scipling, in case he somehow managed to free himself and get to it. In that case, our lives would not be worth the nether parts of a gnat, I fear.''

Hvitur-Fax never removed his eyes from Leifr. "He knows enough to keep his bargaining chips well apart, Meistari," he grunted. "So he can demand of you twice what they are worth and thrice what you are willing to pay. I could crush him for this audacity.''

"No, no, Fax, he's entitled to attempt to use his wits and audacity against us," Alfrekar said. "I would not expect less from one such as this.''

"I had the chance to catch both prizes in Skaela-fell," Fax rumbled, his eyes catching the firelight in a red glow, like a wolf's eyes. "Right in my hands, they were.''

"You presume to question, Fax?" Alfrekar demanded.

"No, not I," Hvitur-Fax said in a chastened mumble. "I lack your patience, Exalted One.''

"You see, Fax, the pieces are all coming into my hands without any effort on our part," Alfrekar said with a contemptuous snap of his fingers. "It is the working of destiny. We have the Scipling now, and the sword is soon to follow." He turned to Nagli with a negligent shrug of his thin shoulders. "I shall pay you five hundred gold marks."

Nagli allowed a sickly shadow of his avaricious grin to twitch at his greedy features. "I will take two thousand marks in gold," he said in a hoarse croak.

"Two thousand marks!" Alfrekar stood staring at Nagli, seething a moment in silent outrage. Then he glared at Hvitur-Fax, as if he were responsible for such madness.

"A worthy bargain," Leifr said. "It may be the last you ever make, one that men will remember."

"And then you will want another two thousand to reveal the hiding place of the sword?" Alfrekar gripped his staff as if he would end Nagli's presumption then and there. Hvitur-Fax strode forward and caught Nagli by the collar, baring his teeth in a hungry snarl.

"Is that your final offer?" Fax growled into his face.

Nagli cowered back in his grip, the sweat bursting from his brow in yellowish beads of unclean ichor. His eyes rolled in desperate evasion.

"As far as I know," he sputtered. "You mustn't kill me, you know, or you'll never find that sword. In fact, I don't know where it is now. I'm only an agent in this matter, a rather minor agent at that."

"Just as I suspected. He's not working alone in this matter," Hvitur-Fax said. "I smell a conspiracy, Exalted Master."

"And so do I," Alfrekar replied with a sharp, impatient sigh. He tapped his staff upon the ground. "The Council is rotten with sedition. I wonder which one of them it is. Askell, perhaps. Or Styrla. He's been restless lately. I'd swear it was Afgang, but he's already dead. When I find who it is, I'll have him purged until he's as witless as a newborn babe, and then I'll have him set out on the Troll-heath to wander and starve. Come along, Fax."

Hvitur-Fax cast a reluctant glance toward Leifr. "You're going to leave them here?" he asked.

"For now," Alfrekar said. "Let this greedy maggot think about his asking price while I find who it is standing behind him to give him all this courage. He'll go nowhere, with the promise of such a pot to be made.''

Hvitur-Fax released his hold upon Nagli's throat with reluctance. ''We could kill them,'' he suggested softly.

Alfrekar considered a moment. ''No, I want to find out who's betraying me behind my back almost as much as I want that sword. That name,'' he added, turning a grisly semblance of a smile toward Nagli, ''is what will make you a wealthy man, my friend.''

''I have the name and I will have the sword,'' Nagli gasped. ''Spare us and they are both yours, if the price is right.''

''I like a bargaining man,'' Alfrekar said with a seamy grin shriveling his features. ''He's audacious, greedy, and won't hesitate to cheat if he can. It will be a pleasure to match wits with him. Come, Fax. We must consider this noble thief-taker's offer.''

When they were gone, Nagli flung himself into a chair, still gasping for breath. The Naglissons still huddled in a craven heap, only their eyes showing signs of life.

Leifr shook his head slowly as the chill of Alfrekar's presence dissipated.

''What a man knows,'' he said, ''is often more important to saving his life than what a man does. Right now there's very little between you and death, Nagli. I could have told Alfrekar it was Sorkvir, but we've got to buy all the time we can. You were a fool to have cast your lot with Sorkvir. He's going to see to it that you don't get out of this alive. Unless Alfrekar tortures you to death first.''

Nagli gripped a double handful of his hair, as if he could pull some inspiration out by its roots. ''I hate getting involved in wizards' spats,'' he moaned with a twisted grimace. ''Every time I swear it's the last I'll have to do with them. Give me a good honest murderer any day or a thief or a house burner. No more wizards!''

''All you have to do,'' Leifr said, rattling the chain manacled to his leg, ''is take this off and tell me where to find the sword. I'll see to it Alfrekar and his Council of Threttan never bother anyone else again.''

For a moment Nagli weakened. He looked yearningly toward the door, and the Naglissons gazed at him with the mute appeal of three worried hounds. Then he shook his head resolutely.

"No, no, I've started it, and I'll finish it," he declared with a fanatic gleam in his eyes. "I could still make a pile from this deal, if I work it carefully."

Leifr threw himself down on the straw in disgust. "You're doomed, Nagli. You can't play both ends against the middle much longer."

"Long enough to get some gold out of them is all I need," Nagli said feverishly. "Then I'm going to marry a fat and comfortable rich widow and give up thief-taking and live a very quiet life. I'll find rich wives for my sons and we'll never have anything to do with wizards or Ulf-hedin again."

"All that won't help you now," Leifr said. "I could get you out of this alive, if you'd have the sense to help me get my sword back."

Nagli wavered a moment, his eyes darting around the tower like trapped rats. His sons gazed at him with mournful hope. "No, no, not at this point," he said finally. "We shall ride it out and see what happens."

On the following day, Sorkvir appeared at the mill, wrapped securely to the eyes, which burned like two coals through the wrapping rags. A smoky pall followed him into the room, reeking like a smoldering fire of old bones and hides. Quickly he threw off his cloak and searched for the source of the smoke, discovering a small glowing spot eating a hole through his clothing in the region of his heart. In great irritation he slapped at the fire and doused it with a dipper of water from a bucket.

"We haven't much time," he growled to Nagli and the Naglissons, who gaped at the proceedings in open-mouthed fascination. "The Ulf-hedin have discovered this place, thanks to Alfrekar's visit last night. We shall have to move our captive now, while it is daylight and no Ulf-hedin are about. We shall wait a few days and then send another message."

Nagli nodded faintly. "I do hope we conclude our business before Brjaladur. I'd like to put some distance between myself and here by then. I hear the festival is going to be a tremendous one this year, celebrating the ascendancy of the Lord of Chaos at last—that is, if the blue carbuncle stone is found in time. But I fear I shall have to miss it. I have pressing matters to attend to at quite some distance. I plan to get married soon, you see."

Sorkvir's reply was a contemptuous snort. 'Your personal

concerns are of no interest to me. If our business is not finished, you'll go nowhere.''

He swung around to face Leifr, who rose to his feet in readiness for any attack.

''I have some news for you,'' Sorkvir said. ''Something that you'll be greatly interested to hear.''

''Everything else falls short of the news of your destruction,'' Leifr said, ''but tell on, if you wish, and I shall attempt to be amused.''

''It is I who am amused,'' Sorkvir said. ''The Ulf-hedin have pulled two corpses from the ashes of Varudur's inn. Your esteemed traveling companion Svanlaug unhesitatingly identified them as the noble Thurid, late of Dallir, and a great clot of a Norskur, known to have also been a companion of yours.''

''Svanlaug is a liar,'' Leifr said. ''She's as crooked and devious as a twisted root. I would no sooner believe anything she says than I would believe you for telling it.''

''Believe,'' Sorkvir said. ''I saw them myself before the old knacker-women carried them off. Was I not the one who trapped him so thoroughly at Varudur's inn? You were there, although you rather carelessly allowed Nagli to poison you with that sleeping drug. It was clever and worked exactly as I planned. I reversed the fire-spell Thurid attempted to use on me through that crystal, and the exploding forces ignited everything that was burnable in one splendid bonfire. I hadn't counted upon the Norskur blundering into the fire in an absurd attempt to rescue Thurid, but we're well rid of him, don't you think? Soon it will be just you and me, Scipling, and that blue carbuncle stone.''

''Then you don't have it yet?'' Leifr queried. ''After all your trouble, you neglected to get it from Thurid?''

Sorkvir glowered at him in silence, and a wisp of yellow flame suddenly burst out of his heart region again. Furiously he slapped it out again. Drawing a small sharp knife from his belt, he probed around in the charred area until a bright yellow stone about the size of a bird's egg popped out and landed on the ground at his feet. He snatched it up quickly in one claw and stuffed it into a pouch, darting Leifr sinister glances all the while.

''Then who's got the carbuncle stone?'' Leifr persisted. ''You haven't, and Alfrekar hasn't or we'd have heard about it by now, and I certainly haven't. All this trouble is hardly worth it without that crystal, is it?''

"Spare me your Scipling reasoning," Sorkvir snarled. "There are higher principles involved here than such a maggot as you could ever comprehend. With Thurid and the Norskur dead, how do you think you're going to get out of this situation you're in? Had you thought of that yet?"

"I shall escape," Leifr said. "Sooner or later, one way or another. Fridmarr and Gedvondur have not brought me so far only to fail now."

Sorkvir answered with a harsh coughing sound that might have been a laugh. "Failures! Both of them. And you shall be the third. Perhaps that will put an end to the fascination that Rhbu sword holds over weak minds. I shall find the last jewel in the Pentacle, and that will be the end of all resistance. Nagli!" he added suddenly, bringing Nagli up to attention with a nervous jerk. "Are you ready to depart? Fetch the cart around to the side. No one must see the Scipling. Cover him up with straw, so you'll look like an ordinary ne'er-do-well about your useless business."

The move was effected without incident. Leifr was bound and loaded into the cart with an old hide thrown over him. From the fleeting glimpses Leifr was able to snatch of his surroundings, he was unable to form much of a conclusion about even the direction he was being taken. Nagli sat hunched on the seat with his cloak pulled up to his eyes, and two of his sons rode behind with the horses. Modga sat in the cart with his drawn sword hidden under the straw, doing his best to discourage any escape attempts.

After a lengthy period of time, wherein Nagli drove back and forth across the same bridge and passed houses that were the same or similar, the cart came to a halt in the yard of a disused house. Its owners were either away on an extended stay at some other house or they were dead. The present tenants were rats, birds, and feral cats, with traces of wild goats and pigs. All appeared to be longtime residents and hostile to the rude invasion of the Naglissons. On the first night rats chewed up a saddle, savoring the salty horse sweat on the leather, and the fighting of the stray cats kept the dark hours lively at frequent intervals.

The trespassers took up residence in the kitchen and waited glumly for Sorkvir's next visit. At dusk one of the Naglissons slunk away with a basket and returned with provisions from the market stalls of Ferja—black bread that was stale, cheese that defied all knives and teeth to cut it, and a scrawny joint of meat that seemed to have come off some half-starved creature not normally considered edible by human beings. Privately Leifr decided it was a large dog, which put him into a gloomy mood as he thought about his loyal troll-hounds. Fortunately, the rats carried off the leftovers from their dubious feast, and Nagli vowed never again to send an infant such as Ovild to dicker with the hardened old hags of Ferja's market stalls.

They remained at the old house for three days. By day Leifr tracked the faintly warm pool of light that fell through the high narrow windows, as best he could with one leg manacled to a post. The mill had been far colder and damp from the water that still poured over the unused mill-race. By night they all listened for signs of the Ulf-hedin. Distant howls were plentiful, but it was not until the third night that they knew they had been found. Stealthy footsteps ran across the roof, and the hosts of crickets that chirped outdoors were completely silent. The horses sharing the other end of the kitchen were restless, holding their heads high to listen, their eyes glowing like coals in the low firelight.

"Maybe Sorkvir's got the carbuncle," Lygari whispered, his narrow face pinched with dread. "Maybe he's just going to leave us here for the Ulf-hedin to find."

In the morning a bloody spiral adorned the door, and each of the Naglissons and their father discovered a thumbprint in blood on their foreheads, placed there sometime during the night, although they had taken shifts of watching, so someone was awake at all times.

"We've been marked!" Ovild squeaked in a paroxysm of terror, staggering about as if blinded. "We're their next prey, Pabbi! We'll be taken and drawn and quartered and fed to them like raw meat!"

"Hush! Hush!" Nagli commanded, hastily scrubbing the dried blood off his head, leaving a rubbed place that was the only color on his pasty countenance. "I can't think with all that moaning and whimpering. You'd think you were whipped pups instead of Naglissons. If the Ulf-hedin had wanted to kill us, what was to stop them? They know we're the only link they've got to the Rhbu sword."

"They also want you to know they've got you in the palm of their hand," Leifr said.

No bloody mark had touched him, but a faint ring scratched

in the dust encircled his pallet. When he arose and stretched and ventured to step across it, he felt a slight tingle as if some power lingered there, and the mark had vanished when he returned to look at it again. Whoever had made it had not made the bloody marks upon Nagli and his sons. Privately he marveled, greatly encouraged by this sign that he had not been forgotten.

"We must move," Nagli said. "I shall tell Sorkvir the moment he arrives."

Sorkvir arrived at dusk, bringing with him the usual cloud of acrid smoke.

"Tonight," he announced in grim triumph, "an exchange is to be made. Alfrekar is coming, lured by the promise of the sword and its handler. But he is suspicious, so great care must be taken not to alert him. Saddle your horses and follow me. Ask no questions and do exactly as you are told, and this night will see you become as wealthy as earls."

"Or as dead as salted mackerel," Leifr added to encourage the Naglissons, who were sweating and trembling as if they had just sprinted for a mile or more.

Leifr's arms were bound behind him and he was tossed onto a horse, with his feet also secured, and a long cloak thrown over him, covering even his face so he had soant idea of where he was being taken. They rode out of the settlements, away from the distant noise of the market square and the endless rumble of the river. Not another soul passed them on the road they took. When the horses slowed and halted at Sorkvir's command, he heard the Naglissons murmuring in a steady undercurrent of whining protest, quicky silenced by their father.

Leifr was hauled off his horse and half dragged, stumbling, down a rocky path and finally down a rocky incline that felt something like steps. A thick door grated stolidly aside to admit them. Even smothered under the cloak, Leifr knew where he was being taken. The cellary smell mingled with the unmistakable smells of ancient decay and death. A faint bit of light penetrated the fibers of the cloak and he got dim glimpses of earthy walls and stone slabs. He attempted to jam his feet against any further progress, but Nagli and the Naglissons shoved him along bodily. With two on a side, they were practically carrying him by the time Sorkvir called a halt.

"Tie him there," Sorkvir's voice said. "Securely. He mustn't escape before I am finished."

They shoved him against a pillar and lashed the ropes around him. With enough struggling, he managed to toss the cloak aside to see where he was. By the smell alone he recognized the place as a barrow, though he could see little beyond where he stood. A single lamp rested upon a stone slab, cluttered with bits of rags and bones. With his staff, Sorkvir impatiently swept the clutter off the slab with a scattering of dust and fragments that included bits of hair, teeth, and the brief glimmering of a few bits of gold and jewels. The Naglissons and Nagli shrank back from such wanton desecration of the dead, fluttering with hopeful gestures and frantically pawing for protective amulets.

Sorkvir next lit five small braziers positioned around the slab, which cast the rest of the barrow into sullen red illumination. On ledges around the sides, like sleeping platforms in an ordinary hall, lay the dusty little heaps that had once been fighting men, their wives, and descendants. Banners hung on the walls, surprisingly bright yet, although the faint breath of fresh air that had come into the barrow with the intruders was gently unraveling the tapestries nearest the door and turning them to dust.

Sorkvir next shoved at the stone slab in the center of the barrow, revealing a stone box underneath. He reached into it and pulled out a long bundle bound in scorched sheepskin, which he placed upon the slab. Then he removed a sack, which suddenly lurched and rolled about when he set it down. Leifr's heart lurched, also. It was the right size to be a cat, but he immediately steadied himself with the thought that it could be any cat captured at any kitchen door, and not Ljosa.

"You don't believe it is truly her?" Sorkvir asked in a dry whisper. "Listen to this, Scipling!"

A faint voice penetrated the heavy air of the barrow. "Leifr! Where are you? Help me, Leifr! I can't get out! Come and help me!"

"It could be a trick," Leifr said, his heart pounding thickly. "I saw her killed."

"You saw what the Ulf-hedin wanted you to see at that time," Sorkvir said. "It was only an illusion and it served its purpose. A force was released then, which has preserved me from our lady Hela's clutches until now."

"You're nothing but a leech, preying upon living people to keep that dead carcass alive!"

"I wouldn't say a leech is nothing," Sorkvir said. "If they

take enough blood from you, you will die." He broke off his triumphant leering suddenly when a small fire broke out on his shoulder. He pummeled it out with one hand, grimacing in helpless fury.

"Enough idle chatter!" he barked, looking himself over suspiciously for more traces of spontaneous combustion. "We must be ready when Alfrekar comes to make his bargain. Nagli, you and your offspring will stand on either side of the door. Only Alfrekar must be allowed into this chamber, no Ulf-hedin. Alfrekar must be subdued and placed upon the table. Silence!" he snapped, when Nagli opened his mouth to protest. "Stay out of my way and I shall do it."

"You intend to take Alfrekar's body!" Leifr gasped.

"It's a small thing," Sorkvir said. "Hela will have Alfrekar, and the Council and the Pentacle and the Ulf-hedin will be mine. I doubt if anyone will be the wiser."

"You talk as if the blue orb were yours already," Leifr said, "when it's not and never will be as long as Thurid lives to protect it."

"Thurid is dead," Sorkvir said. "So is the Norskur, and the other two are in the hands of the Ulf-hedin. Your journey is almost finished, Scipling." With a sound like a chuckle, he commenced wrapping his face in black strips to conceal his identity from Alfrekar.

Chapter 6

◇◇◇◇◇◇◇◇◇◇◇◇◇◇◇◇◇◇◇◇◇◇◇◇◇◇◇◇◇◇◇◇◇◇◇◇◇

"I won't be fooled by anything you say," Leifr answered. "If Thurid was dead, you'd have the blue orb, and if you did, you wouldn't be in this barrow now preparing one of your sordid body-snatching incantations."

"Perhaps not," Sorkvir said. "I wasn't able to steal the orb before the fire became too hot for this carcass to endure and not catch fire. Thurid knew he was trapped. He did everything he could to destroy me along with him. For that reason—" He paused and held up his hand, showing a small bluish nimbus of flame dancing over the withered flesh of his knuckles. He smothered it quickly and continued, "I am now plagued by unwanted combustion. Thurid plunged into the deepest, hottest part of the fire to thwart me. By the time the embers of the inn cooled, the Ulf-hedin were there looking for the carbuncle stone. They did not find it. At any rate, if they did, they didn't turn it over to the Council. One thing I am certain of, Thurid is dead. One other thing I know, you shall help me to trap Alfrekar."

"I won't," Leifr said. "I refuse to assist you with your unclean spells and would even if I was able. I'm only a Scipling, with none of the powers of Ljosalfar or Dokkalfar."

"You are able enough," Sorkvir said. "A crude source of life powers, but one with no natural defenses or training. A curious lot, you Sciplings. If you only dreamed of the strengths you possess, you could be more powerful than all the Alfar people, but you ignorantly shut your eyes and keep killing one another with axes and swords, like the senseless barbarians you are. There are many wonders you haven't dreamed of, Scipling. A pity you don't wish to remain and see what I intend to do, once I possess the Council and the completed Pentacle. Now that I have this, your wishes shall cease to exist. I expect resistance from the Ulf-hedin. With that sword—" He made a faint nod toward the table and the sheepskin bundle. "—and the hand that wields it, I shall control the Ulf-hedin, also."

"I can't believe everything is as perfect as you seem to think," Leifr said. "You're gloating and you haven't got the orb, Alfrekar, or even a decent corpse to house your ugly and perverted spirit. I think you're acting out of desperation, Sorkvir. Time is running out for you."

"Silence!" Sorkvir snarled. "It is all in the palm of my hand now." Turning his back, he strode to the center of the braziers, arranged at the points of a pentacle scratched in the earth. He opened up the mouth of the sack and withdrew the cat, scratching and biting to no effect. It was a gray cat with long soft fur like smoke, and Leifr's heart gave a jolting leap, despite his efforts not to deceive himself. Sorkvir held the cat with both hands, and gradually she stopped struggling. He held it up so Leifr could see her, lolling in his draug hands as if half asleep. Her amber eyes gleamed in the light of the braziers, and she lashed her tail in angry disapproval that was slowing to feeble twitches.

"Don't harm her," Leifr burst out.

Sorkvir shot him a malevolent glower. His dry lips were pursed, as if blowing out a candle flame, except that he was drawing in his wind and drawing the spirit out of the cat. Her form diminished in substance, like mist, before Leifr's horrified gaze. Sorkvir turned his back when the form of the cat was nearly gone. When he turned around again to face Leifr, it was the image of Ljosa that suffused his form and figure. She gazed around, her eyes wide in fear, and her pale hair flared untidily around her head. Slowly she turned, taking in the rows of crumbling corpses with a startled gasp. She looked almost as solid as real human flesh.

"Ljosa!" Leifr breathed, scarcely daring to believe she was more than merely a conjured image to trick him.

"Leifr!" She turned and saw him at once, and came a few steps forward, but when she attempted to cross the boundary of the pentacle, a sputter of icy green flame halted her.

"Leifr, help me!" she gasped, reaching out with her hands, but more sparks of green flame repelled her.

"Ljosa, where are you?" Leifr asked.

"I don't know," she answered. "In a place of death, and I can't escape. You're my only hope, Leifr. He keeps me here and drains my strength until I can't fight any more. I can't escape. You must help me regain my power, Leifr."

"I thought you were dead," Leifr said. "If that was a trick then, how do I know you're not a trick now? Or if it wasn't a trick then, you're just an illusion of Sorkvir's."

"I'm no illusion," she replied in a desolate tone. "He has kept me captive and uses my strength. He has no life, only a terrible sort of hateful energy that preys upon living things. You must do as he wishes and help him conjure Hela. She'll take Alfrekar as her offering."

"Who is speaking? Ljosa or Sorkvir?" Leifr demanded sharply. "Is he forcing you to speak for him, Ljosa?"

"Yes!" she cried in anguish. "But don't listen to what I say! He lies, he—" She broke off with a shriek, shaking her head and flinging out her arms like a drowning swimmer.

"Ljosa! Don't! He's hurting you!" Leifr lunged against the ropes. Her image was beginning to fade.

"It's five days until Brjaladur, Leifr!" she panted, her voice growing faint and rapid. "You can save me then, when their forces will be in disarray. Come to the Council Hall. I am at the Council Hall. It's a threshold spell—"

Sorkvir made a banishing gesture, and she vanished with a wailing cry, leaving the skeleton figure of Sorkvir behind, snatching and pounding furiously at several small combustions that had burst out on his back, chest, and arms.

"Die, you monster!" Leifr spat in a fury, jerking at his bonds until the timber quaked and a handful of earth was dislodged from the low ceiling. "I hope to see you burn and melt away like candle wax!"

"She is here, inside this cadaver!" Sorkvir snarled, slapping at the sullen red flakes of fire burning in his chest. "If I die, she goes to Hela with me, and once Hela's got a morsel, she won't let it go, unless you can bargain as I have done. Give me your strength, if you want to spare the girl. There's scarcely anything left of her. I require a living force!"

"Then take me and let her go!" Leifr demanded, giving the post another heave. The Naglissons cringed and whimpered as more clots of turf powdered down on them. He strained, intent on bursting free. No sizzling green fire would stop him from hurling himself into that unclean pentacle, getting his hands around Sorkvir's throat and tearing his head off, strewing his dusty blood and shriveled entrails across the floor. Somehow he would free Ljosa by gratifying his furious impulse, he was certain.

The flames in the braziers leaped to four times their former size, searing the ancient timbers that supported the barrow. One nearby tapestry disappeared in a sudden puff of flame, a priceless treasure reduced to ash in an instant.

Sorkvir spread wide his arms and commenced his chanting. In strange waves, Ljosa's image battled with his, her voice mingling with his, calling out to Leifr in a garbled manner he could not understand, but it seemed to him she was fighting and suffering. Leifr felt an irresistible rage flowing within him, thinking of her trapped within the same body as his hated enemy Sorkvir, struggling against him to voice her warnings. A cloud of faint light surrounded him, causing his ears to buzz and his hair to stand slightly on end with its invisible energy. His next mighty heave dislodged the post a notch from its moorings.

Sorkvir's chanting poured forth in a torrent. He looked around, gnashing his teeth in a rage.

"It's not enough! It's not enough!" he roared. "Hela, goddess of the dead! I summon you, I command you to appear! I have a bargain to make with you, old woman! Where are you?"

The mist thickened, but no form appeared. Leifr felt a presence drawing near, draining his will to resist. He stopped his struggles and hung gasping like a salmon on a gaff. A dim voice called out, echoing down many long cold corridors, "You have made enough bargains. You have not kept your word. Now your soul belongs to me!"

"One more trade!" Sorkvir croaked hoarsely. "This will be the best one yet, Sovereign Lady! I shall bring you Alfrekar, chieftain of the Council!"

"Alfrekar's time is already short," Hela's voice replied, implacably grim. "Send me someone of value and greatness!"

"I already sent you Thurid!" Sorkvir returned. "Was that not enough to satisfy you?"

"I received not Thurid," Hela replied. "You seek to cheat me, as usual. I granted you life until Brjaladur and no more. Yet here you are begging again."

"If you have not received Thurid yet, then you soon will," Sorkvir said through his clenched teeth. "I had him in my grasp, and he escaped! But he shall be ours, my Queen. Before Brjaladur, I swear it, or you may take me. I shall give you Alfekar for nothing.''

. "I shall take him then. And if you get me Thurid before Brjaladur, then I shall grant you life until Samhain."

"Samhain! Half a year!" Sorkvir muttered with a vile grimace. "You are most generous, my Sovereign."

"You would live forever?" the goddess sneered. Her face came faintly into view, gaunt and implacable. "Then bring me Elbegast, or any one of the Three Rhbus! Then I would grant you immortality!"

With a windy gust, the mist vanished and the soaring flames of the braziers died away to sputtering coals.

"Samhain!" Sorkvir snorted. "Half a year!"

Then he lifted his head and listened. "Alfrekar comes! To your positions! Remember, no Ulf-hedin must set foot in this barrow. And you—'' He turned and regarded Leifr a moment. "Listen very closely. Against both Alfrekar and myself, you have no hope. You must dismiss any idea of attacking and escaping. Reveal my name to him and you and Hroaldsdottir perish instantly. But if Alfrekar becomes unruly, it is in your best interest to go for him rather than me. He seeks you only for the purpose of destruction.''

"By force is the only way I would ever be of use to you,'' Leifr said with an involuntary shudder at the memory of the last hairlock spell Sorkvir had forged. His strength was slowly returning, and he tested it against his bonds again, resulting in a sinister creak from above. "Now that I know Thurid is alive and still in possession of the carbuncle, I'll fight you to the death, you stinking pile of bones and offal."

"Well and good," Sorkvir said, baring his yellowed teeth in a snarling sneer. "But remember, when I perish, I take the soul of Hroaldsdottir with me to Hela. Now be silent until my trap for Alfrekar is sprung. And afterward, I hope you'll have the sense to remember not to betray me when I am Alfrekar, or you shall never see the girl again.''

Leifr clenched his jaws and fumed inwardly. Sorkvir retreated behind the braziers, safe within the perimeters of the pentacle. He debated sounding a warning to Alfrekar, but in the end he kept his silence when the Naglissons brought Alfrekar into the barrow.

Alfrekar snorted and coughed in the close air, fanning away

the smoke and dust with a blast of cold mist from the end of his staff. Suspiciously he gazed toward the dark and inscrutable figure awaiting him beside the stone table.

"Who are you, traitor?" he demanded.

"Did you bring the gold?" Sorkvir's voice rasped, unrecognizable in its harshness.

"I did," Alfrekar replied with a wizened scowl and a wary glance behind him at the Naglissons. "It's far too high a price to demand, even for the sword of Endless Death. Nevertheless, I have brought it and it waits outside on the back of a horse. Now show me what you have to offer in return. I have waited a long time to get control of that cursed sword. Or must you examine the gold first?"

"I have no need for gold," Sorkvir said in his dry voice, sounding drier than ever. "Except to use it to manipulate others who are weak and stupid enough to like it. Rest assured, all your gold will be going right back to the Guild coffer. It was nothing but a ruse to command your attention."

"You are one of my own," Alfrekar said. "Could we not have spoken face to face like trusted comrades? What did you think to achieve by robbing the coffers of the Council? And for these?" He made an incredulous gesture to include the Naglissons and Nagli, all cringing and listening with their jaws agape. "You could have done much better, almost any time. As one of the Council, you could have commanded some Ulf-hedin to do your work."

"That would hardly have been appropriate, considering my plans," Sorkvir said.

Alfrekar warily turned and bestowed a dubious glance upon Nagli and the Naglissons. "I do not understand your choice of tools," he said. "But you have brought us the Scipling, at least. Now where is the sword?"

"In good time," Sorkvir said in a choked tone, tapping the stone table with the point of his dagger. "We have more matters to discuss than the sword and the Scipling. I believe I am more fit to sit in your seat at the head of the Council of Threttan. Surrender it to me, and the sword of Endless Death is yours."

"Jealous of my position, are you?" Alfrekar said softly, his fingers tightening upon his staff. "Then you are rebelling against me, aren't you? We have all thirteen worked together to control the Dokkur Lavardur. It is neither seemly nor necessary that you should covet the high seat. We are all equals in power, equals in freedom, and equals in the victory over the Ljosalfar that will come when the Dokkur Lavardur restores the Fimbul Winter.''

"We are not equals," Sorkvir rasped. "You are mortal and one day you will die. I have been promised immortality by the goddess Hela. She said that your time was short.. The guardian and guide of the Lord of Chaos should not be a fragile stalk that will quickly perish. It should be one who will live forever. Seven times I have died and gone to Hela's realm, where all wisdom resides with those who have already died.''

"Are you challenging me here, now?" Alfrekar asked.

"Yes. I must act before Brjaladur. The contest will be with swords.''

"Swords, and not magical powers? If you wish, it will be done." Alfrekar removed his cloak and loosened his sword in its sheath. "When you are ready, comrade.''

"Done," Sorkvir said. "Nagli, step forward. I command you to cut the ropes that bind the Thorljotsson.''

"What are you plotting now?" Alfrekar demanded.

"The Scipling is my factor in this duel," Sorkvir said. "The sword is _Endalaus Daudi_, the sword of Endless Death.''

"You tricked me," Alfrekar growled, darting glances at Nagli sawing Leifr's ropes off and at the long bundle upon the stone table.

"It's a legal device," Sorkvir said. He crooked one long yellow finger at Leifr. "Come forward and take your cursed sword. Remember all that I have told you.''

Leifr rubbed his raw wrists, sizing up Alfrekar as an opponent. He was small and wiry and no doubt very quick, judging from the way he was loosening up his muscles by swinging his sword in experimental cuts and thrusts.

Sorkvir reached out with his dagger and cut one of the cords binding _Endalaus Daudi_ with extreme caution. He sniffed loudly and prodded at the bundle a moment before cutting another cord. When the cords were out of the way, he gingerly unrolled the sheep fleece to reveal a long, dark, sword-shaped image burned into the fleece, but there was no sword.

"This is interesting," Alfrekar said in a voice of deadly calm, "but there is no _Endalaus Daudi_ here.''

The Naglissons inhaled a horrified gasp, exchanging a lightning glance between themselves. In a concerted rush, they charged at the door, jamming into each other in their haste as they all pawed for the latch.

"Stop!" Sorkvir commanded, flinging aside his muffling cloak and halting the Naglissons with a single warning ice-bolt shattering against the door above their heads. They slunk backward, muttering self-righteously. Sorkvir strode forward until they were cornered and could go no farther.

"What have you done with it, you bog-slime?" Sorkvir demanded in a voice of deadly calm, reaching out one claw and fastening a hold on Nagli's collar.

"I did nothing with it!" Nagli sputtered, his eyes rolling back in his head as if he were already dead. "You took it at the inn, remember, and took it right away with you, after you looked at it and said it was the right sword, and I never would have dared try anything so outrageous as stealing it from you, since I value my life, such as it is, and things like swords like that are best left to others such as you and such as him who—"

"Silence!" Sorkvir roared, adding a dusty cough that rattled inside him like dry seeds in a gourd. His eyes blazed through the bandages with a crazed fever and his wretched body gave a strange series of twitches and shudders, as if trying to be free of his consuming grasp on it. With a visible effort he regained control. "Someone has come in here and stolen the sword despite the wards I placed upon the doors," he continued in a menacing growl.

"Your trap is sprung, comrade," Alfrekar said, sheathing his own sword and putting on his cloak, "but your prey has escaped. We still have a challenge that must be taken up before Brjaladur. Whether or not you have the Scipling and his sword to champion you, I shall find out who you are and destroy you—comrade!"

Alfrekar added an injudicious cackle before he opened the door with no resistance from the Naglissons and whisked outside. The imposing form of Hvitur-Fax stood silhouetted against the silver shield of the twilight sky, wolf ears alert and listening for his footstep returning from the lintels of the barrow.

"You are safe, my lord," Fax said. "Is the traitor still within? Should we ferret him out and disembowel him?"

"No, Fax. We must remove ourselves as quickly as possible. I do not wish his name to be generally known just yet, to anyone except me."

"And the gold? What of the sword and the Scipling?"

"The Scipling is there, but by some strange mischance, the sword was stolen from our traitor. There will be no exchange of gold for the sword."

"More treachery, Master. He never intended to give it to you. Perhaps it was a trap."

"An unsprung trap, as yet, Fax. A challenge has been issued for a duel."

"We can find and kill this traitor. The Ulf-hedin will defend the Council from all threats."

"Great care must be taken not to frighten this traitor away, or into injudicious and harmful action. He is a crazed creature, now driven to the very edges of his reason, but he will reveal himself soon. This is a far more dangerous opponent than I had originally feared."

"Nagli and his sons?" Fax inquired dubiously. "They are nothing to us, Great One."

"Very true, but they guard the Scipling while our traitor is presenting an innocent face to the rest of the Council. I want them closely watched, in case they lose their courage and decide to bolt, taking their prisoner with them. Worse yet, they might free him. I have no doubt, if freed, he would very soon find that sword, and trouble would begin. These are perilous times, Fax. The Fimbul Winter is hanging in the balance, and perhaps all our lives, until that sword and Galdur's carbuncle are found. I want three of your best men, Fax. They must follow the traitor and the thief-takers to their next hiding place without being seen. They must keep their eyes upon that place, listening and watching, and not betray themselves."

Hvitur-Fax nodded, his silvery mane bristling. "Gris and Galladur," he said, running his eye over the waiting Ulf-hedin. "And young Halmur. The rest of you, away. At dawn replacements will be sent."

The Ulf-hedin departed, leaving the chosen three flattened against the ground, scarcely breathing as the Naglissons came out and looked around warily. Seeing nothing to alarm them, they fetched their horses from an adjoining open barrow. Of the traitor they saw nothing but a dark cloak vanishing into the deep shadows of the barrow field. The thief-takers took their captive southward, toward the settlements, starting at every small sound.

A stray dog barked from the top of a barrow, startling them into a panicky retreat, as if a pack of Ulf-hedin were on their heels.

The three genuine Ulf-hedin hugged the earth, contemptuous and amused at the idea that Ulf-hedin would be so easily detected. When they moved, it was like shadows crossing the ground. Once the thief-takers passed almost within arm's reach of Gris without the slightest clue.

After some deceptive maneuvers that were totally wasted upon the three Ulf-hedin, the thief-takers sought the shelter of an abandoned house in a narrow dark ravine. With no near neighbors and plenty of surrounding thickets and skarps, the house was well hidden from all except the Ulf-hedin. The soft breeze that sighed through the thickets concealed the sound of stealthy feet creeping near enough to look in through the cracks in the shuttered windows. When one of the Naglissons crept outside for a few bits of firewood, he did not notice the soundless shadow that followed his every move. Galladur turned back at the doorstep, but he could have easily followed Modga into the house without being seen.

Halmur kept well back and kept his eyes upon his two companions, aware that this exercise was a reward for his earlier vigilance and capture of Starkad. His fur bristled with the energy of the Ulf-hedin power, making him as strong and quiet as Gris and Galladur. In one easy leap he could cover the distance between the earth and the rooftop. His ears twitched in the faint spring breeze, catching the sounds of mice far below ground, and the faint tattoo of the heart of the quail hiding in the middle of a clump of gorse nearby.

Just before dawn three replacements arrived as silently as owlflight, gliding into position without sound to betray their presence. Halmur trotted home at the heels of Gris and Galladur, keeping well back out of respect. When they arrived at the hall, they removed their wolf pelts.

"That was well done, for a youngling," Gris said, giving Halmur a companionable shove with one shoulder.

"You'll go far, for a Ljosalfar," Galladur added.

Halmur remained outside the hall, lingering a few moments to watch the sunrise tinting the low bellies of the perennial cloud cover. In the quiet of the frosty morning he could relish his satisfaction at being chosen by Hvitur-Fax himself for an important mission. For such a youth as he was, and a Ljosalfar besides, it was a great honor. He caught himself thinking of home at Skaela-fell, and hastily quelled such thoughts. As he aged as an Ulf-hedin, he knew, he would gradually forget his past before his indoctrination, until the Halmur of that old life was altogether dead.

"Halloa, what are you doing here?" a familiar voice demanded roughly, as a great buffet between his shoulder blades caught him by surprise and knocked him off his feet. Birtingr leered down at him a moment, then thrust a basket into his arms. "You can go take this to the prisoner in the cooling house, since you're being chosen for everything honorable these days."

Halmur gathered his legs under him and got to his feet. "It's your task, you do it," he snarled.

Birtingr's response was a rude laugh. He doubled up his fist and knocked Halmur down again.

"And when you're done with the prisoner's breakfast, then you can stand watch for me until Atli shows up at sundown, since you Ljosalfar are so fond of sunlight. Don't let anyone approach the prisoner or you'll lose your ears."

With a nasty laugh, Birtingr turned and swaggered back to the hall. Slowly Halmur got to his feet, glaring furiously after his adversary and tasting blood from his split lip. Gripping the basket, he turned his back upon the sunrise as if it did not exist and stalked toward the cooling house.

The cooling house was a low building made of stone and turf, set into the cool earth in the past when the farmstead had been owned by people who worked with the earth and the animals for a living, for the purpose of cooling milk so the cream would rise. Now the little house was used as a prison for unruly Ulf-hedin during unfavorable moon phases or peculiar reactions to the eitur. Sometimes when the moon was full, a madness would grip an Ulf-hedin in a frenzy of destruction, and the only solution was to confine him until the fit passed or the moon phase changed.

Halmur followed the well-trodden path past the byres and rotting haystacks and sprouting grain ricks. As he rounded the corner of a granary, he stopped in his tracks, watching. Someone else was already at the cooling house, talking through the grate in the door, someone in a long dark cloak. Stealthily he approached, reached out one hand, and seized the intruder by the shoulder.

With a gasp, Svanlaug whirled around and faced him. Instead of the blazing wolf-madness of the Ulf-hedin, she saw the quiet gaze of golden Ljosalfar eyes gazing at her questioningly from a thin young face, framed by matted hair the color of ripe wheat.

"Halmur!" she breathed with a sigh of relief.

"You're not supposed to be here," he said gruffly. "I'll have to tell Magni. You're lucky it wasn't Birtingr who caught you. Why are you here?"

Starkad's face peered out suspiciously through the grate. "I don't want her here," he said. "She's taunting me, after betraying everything I've worked for. If I ever get out of here, her throat will be the first thing I want to get my hands on."

Svanlaug gave her head an arrogant toss, with a small cold laugh. "You'll never get out of there, you savage," she said. "You've no idea how pleased I am to see you finally getting what you deserve."

"You must come away," Halmur said. "Approaching the prisoner is forbidden."

He put down the basket and escorted Svanlaug away from the cooling house, down the path toward the hall.

"Is it true what they say about that sword of the Scipling?" he asked in a low voice. "That it can destroy the Pentacle the wizards are making? And that the wizards are deathly afraid of it?"

"Yes, it's true," Svanlaug said carelessly. "Luckily it's no longer in his possession. Fortunately for the future of the Dokkalfar people, the Scipling is dead."

"No," Halmur said, "he's not dead. I saw the place tonight where he is being held captive by the thief-takers."

"Not dead!" Svanlaug drew in a deep breath and slowly expelled it in a sigh. She darted Halmur a nervous glance to see how closely he was watching her. "Well, then I would say there's going to be more trouble. Although I am a Dokkalfar, I can see he's destined to do what he must with that sword."

"I am—or was—a Ljosalfar," Halmur said, giving his head an angry shake. "Few of the Ulf-hedin are Ljosalfar."

"All are the same, once they are Ulf-hedin," Svanlaug said when he stopped and seemed unable to go any further. "You are all brothers, packmates, loyal and true to each other. All are equal in the pack, are they not?"

"Of course," Halmur said fiercely, looking all around for eyes that might be watching and ears that might be listening. "Nothing is as glorious as the pack."

"They would never torment and take advantage of you because of your youth," Svanlaug said. "And you would never have to stand watch in the daylight because you were a Ljosalfar. Some would call you slaves because your lives depend upon the eitur that your elders give you. Some would think the short and miserable life of the Ulf-hedin is not worth living. And when the Scipling finishes the work he was fated to do, what will be left? I must say, it takes courage to be an Ulf-hedin now, with such a threat right here beneath your noses."

Halmur stopped walking and gazed at Svanlaug mutely.

"I shall go on alone from here," she said. "I'm sorry to have transgressed the rules, and you may be certain I won't do it again."

"Good. See you don't," Halmur said. "I don't think you are trustworthy."

"Indeed," Svanlaug said. "The pot is calling the kettle black, I think." She turned and stalked away with a toss of her head, covering her face with a veil to shield it from the sun's pallid rays.

Halmur returned to his post. He handed Starkad his breakfast through the grate and squatted down with his back against the door. If he dozed, there was still no way anyone could tamper with the door without alerting him. The sun was warm, and a nap was very tempting, while all the other Ulf-hedin slept heavily indoors in the chilly dark hall after a night of their usual revels.

At noonday Halmur knew he was supposed to trudge to the kitchen to fetch the prisoner's dinner, a humiliating task for any Ulf-hedin. A light but soaking rain had begun some hours ago, so the warmth of the squalid kitchen felt good, but his visit was brief. The key to the lock hung from a ring on Magni's belt, and Magni was curled up on the floor asleep with the rest of the pack scattered around him, wrapped in their wolf pelts.

"I thought it was Birtingr who was guarding," Magni growled when Halmur awakened him for the key.

"We decided to trade," Halmur said, not adding that he had

traded a split lip for Birtingr's sleeping all day as the others were. He tried not to shiver conspicuously.

"Well then, if you like daylight so well, you can guard him again tomorrow," Magni said, tossing him the key. "Don't trouble me returning it. Tonight we're hunting for that cursed orb again—except for you. You'll need your sleep if you're guarding tomorrow."

"Good luck in your hunt," Halmur said. "Has the Dokkalfar woman been of any help in finding the orb?"

Magni glanced in the direction of Svanlaug reposing on a sleeping platform, hands clasped, feet neatly crossed at the ankles as tidily as a corpse laid out for cremation. He scowled and lowered his voice. "Yes, she's got a good idea who's got it—the same person who is holding the Scipling for ransom, the one who was at the inn when it was burned."

"Alfrekar's traitor," Halmur said. "If we could but find out his identity—"

"That's not your concern, youngling. Leave these matters to the ones older and wiser than you. We shall turn both the prisoner and Svanlaug over to Alfrekar tonight. Let Alfrekar extract the information he requires. Now take that mess out to the prisoner; the smell of it is disgusting."

Halmur obediently trudged back to the cooling house and unlocked the door. Starkad sat sullenly in a corner, wrapped up in his cloak.

"I thought you were going to starve me," he said. "Go ahead and try it. Torture me if you wish, I won't tell you anything."

"Torture is for Alfrekar," Halmur said. "You're going to be turned over to him tonight, and so is the Dokkalfar woman. Prisoners have a way of never returning from the Ulf-hol, at least, not as they were before."

"Alfrekar will never take me alive," Starkad said fiercely. "While I live, there is yet hope for smashing the Pentacle and the Council. Is this edible?" Starkad sniffed warily at the pot of watery soup, made of bones, meat scraps, a few bits of vegetables and grains, with a thick layer of grease on top. "Leifr and I had a great many adventures together, which have served to train me in the methods of escape, evasion, and battle. I have the additional advantage of being a Ljosalfar, besides. My native powers will serve to guide me."

"How are you going to escape from here?" Halmur asked in

a contemptuous tone. "You are doomed, as well as the Scipling. He's hiding in the house in Svin-gill, but the Ulf-hedin of course know all about it. We're merely waiting for Alfrekar's command to take them all. Tonight, perhaps."

"I knew Leifr was still alive," Starkad said, stuffing his mouth with coarse bread. "Look, there's plenty of this soup for both of us. You might as well sit in here out of the rain and share it."

"Thank you for your kindness. I shall," Halmur said, sitting down cross-legged on the smooth-packed floor.

"I don't mind the company," Starkad said. "I've been terribly lonely in here with no one to talk to. I like company. It was difficult when I lived at Fangelsi-hofn, the house of my aunts and uncles, because none of them were very chatty souls. I expect I'd be all glum and gloom, too, if I had the same curse on me as they did; although, if Leifr hadn't arrived when he did, I suppose I would have come down with it sooner or later."

"Curse?" Halmur repeated. "What sort of curse?"

Starkad launched himself upon the tale, his enthusiasm fueled by the privilege of a fresh audience. Between the two of them, as he talked, they devoured the pot of soup, except for a last bit in the bottom containing well-chewed bones and a tough cabbage stem. It was rather pleasant in the cooling house after that; at least it was dry and out of the wind. Halmur stretched out his legs to get more comfortable, reluctant to return to his post outside. The story was fascinating, but Halmur's head began to nod. Several times he stirred himself to get up, but Starkad's eyes seemed to hold him riveted to the spot, his arms and legs almost nerveless from yearning for sleep.

At last his eyes closed and his head rolled forward. Starkad leaped to his feet, his eyes upon the door. It stood open a few inches, beckoning him to freedom. As he moved toward it, his toe caught one of the legs of the soup pot and sent it clattering across the floor. Halmur's eyes popped open instantly and he gathered himself for a powerful spring. Starkad seized the kettle and hurled it at Halmur's head, clipping him a grazing blow that, nonetheless, served to send Halmur reeling backward. Blood spurted from a small wound in his scalp, and the last of the soup sprayed across the wall. Startled, Halmur staggered back a few paces. Starkad lowered his head and charged like a bull, ramming his head into Halmur's midsection. His impetus thrust Halmur against the wall and finished knocking the wind out of him completely. Leaving him gasping, Starkad flung himself against the door in a headlong rush, flinging it open right in the face of a dark-clad figure standing just outside. He was moving so fast he had no time to stop, and found himself colliding headfirst with the snarling wolf mask of an Ulf-hedin.

Chapter 7

◇◇◇

"They're outside, I know they are," Lygari moaned, crouching beside the tiny fire with his cloak pulled up over his head. "There! Did you hear that?"

A sound like a whine came from the back of the house, and something like a nose sniffing intently in the door crack.

"It's only the wind," Modga snapped, but his teeth were chattering nonetheless.

"Perhaps they are," Nagli said with a sickly grin. "But if they'd wanted us, they would have taken us at the barrow fields."

"They didn't want you just yet is the only reason," Leifr said. "It's like a game of cat and mouse. The cat likes the game better when it lets the mouse think it's got a chance to escape. It's so much more real for the cat."

Nagli hitched up his trousers a notch and paced up and down the room. "We're getting closer now to our gold. I feel it in my bones. As soon as Sorkvir settles his score with Alfrekar, he'll pay us and we'll be on our way. No doubt he'd like us to stay and help him control the Dokkur Lavardur and the Fimbul Winter, but if we've all got to go back underground, I think I'm going to catch a ship off the island and see what it's like someplace else. I expect other lands have their share of wealthy widow women."

Even Leifr was scarcely listening to him. As he was talking, a fine cloud of dust began sifting down from the roof, as if someone were walking across the turves. The wind suddenly puffed under the crack beneath the door, sounding very much like an Ulf-hedin nose sniffing there.

"Tomorrow," Ovild said in a voice with a fine tremor, "I think we should move to another place, whether or not Sorkvir tells us to move. Sorkvir will find us easy enough. This place is too isolated."

"I think we should get out now while we're still alive," Lygari added.

"Just leave the Scipling," Ovild said. "He's what they want anyway, and once they've got him, we're nothing to them."

"Nothing but bugs to smash, you mean," Modga said.

"Don't be fools," Nagli snarled. "I tell you, we're almost done here. What do you think, the Ulf-hedin are going to break down the door to get at us?"

He had scarcely got the words out when the door suddenly burst apart as if it had exploded, and an Ulf-hedin came hurtling into the room, closely followed by two others. Wolfish forms rushed at the Naglissons, snarling and baying. The Naglissons and Nagli flung themselves into a corner that had once been the cow stall and drew their swords.

"Put down your weapons, unless you want to die now," the Ulf-hedin growled. He was rather a small one, but the snarling and snapping jaws of the beasts beside him were enough to make the Naglis throw down their swords and cower back in the stall.

"Take him and go," Nagli said with a nervous grin, nodding his head toward Leifr. "We want nothing out of this but our lives, and that's a small enough boon to ask, isn't it? Although we captured him and brought him here to you, thinking we were deserving of some small reward, we're content to ask for nothing except to—"

"Silence!" the Ulf-hedin snapped, sparing a glance in Leifr's direction. "Where is the key to that manacle?"

Trembling, Nagli withdrew the key from a greasy little pouch around his greasy neck and held it out gingerly. The Ulf-hedin snatched it and strode away, with a warning glance over one shoulder that boded ill for any of them who dared to move.

"I've got the key," he muttered to the other two, and in a moment the manacle fell away.

"Quick now," one of the others said.

"Starkad? Svanlaug?" Leifr looked from one to the other. "In wolf capes? Who's this with you?"

"It's Halmur from Skaela-fell," Starkad said. "Leifr, where's the sword? Get it and let's go."

"Sorkvir had it, and now it's stolen," Leifr said. "Thurid will have to help us find it."

Leifr fastened on his cloak hastily and briskly tightened his bootlaces, fending off the delighted greetings of the troll-hounds.

With a sinister glare toward the stunned Naglis, he said, "There's something else we've got to take care of before we go."

"But there's not much time," Svanlaug said rapidly. "Magni's going to miss us any minute."

"This will only take a moment," Leifr said. "Tie their hands behind their backs and saddle four horses."

Bound hand and foot, the thief-takers were stacked like so much firewood at Leifr's feet.

Leifr gazed at them with contempt, and the scruffy Naglissons rolled their eyes with apprehension under his scrutiny.

"Leifr, we must hurry," one of the Ulf-hedin said, lifting the wolf mask enough to peer out apprehensively, revealing the face of Starkad.

"You! You're not Ulf-hedin, none of you!" Nagli snarled in astonishment and regret, commencing a belated struggle against the ropes that securely bound him.

"I wouldn't say that," Halmur growled throatily, showing his very genuine wolf teeth in a fearsome snarl and reaching out with his great clawed hands for Nagli's throat. "You creatures, if you knew what powers you tampered with so heedlessly, you'd run like whipped dogs."

The Naglissons cringed and whimpered.

"Good, Halmur! Show him who's boss!" Starkad exclaimed, giving the nearest helplessly bound thief-taker a prod with his toe. It happened to be the elder, Nagli himself, his aggrieved and grimy face upturned from the earth with a sneer.

"You won't be laughing long," Nagli cackled, straining at his bonds. "Do with our carcasses what you will, but you were doomed from the moment you laid eyes upon that slinking Fridmarr. Doomed as all day-farers are doomed—to freeze and perish in the dark."

"Put a cork in all that blather, or I'll fashion one not much to your liking, I daresay," Leifr said. "None of this surprises me, except that Sorkvir couldn't find better quality thief-takers. That's power for you, when you don't have to sully your own hands. Plenty of fools are eager to curry a bit of favor. We'll show Sorkvir what we think of his rogues."

"Remember, no bloodshed," Svanlaug's voice said, muffled under a wolf skin. She pointed one finger skyward to the roiling of the sinister clouds. "That would be exactly what that monster craves to nourish it."

"I've got a plan nearly as good," Leifr said. "These dung-worms aren't worthy of being killed by us. I wouldn't sully my hands with entrails such as theirs. Now listen carefully."

They all listened to Leifr's instructions, Starkad especially, with a dawning expression of malicious pleasure. He vanished into the half gloom and returned promptly with the Naglissons' horses. It was an easy job with the four of them hoisting and heaving, and they tied the Naglissons and their father onto their horses facedown over the horse's rumps.

"Let this be a warning and an insult to the Council," Leifr said when the job was finished, and the horses stood dancing restlessly with their ill-sorted riders. "When you meet with your draug-master Sorkvir next, tell them we have no fear of him or his Council nor of anyone they might send after us. Everyone at Ferja will know it and laugh at such an insult."

"We won't forget this shame!" Nagli snarled, his warped features twisted into knots of fury. "You'll live to regret not killing us when you had the chance!"

Starkad and Halmur drove the horses off at a gallop, and the horses headed southward with a barking escort of troll-hounds toward the distant roistering sounds coming from the ferry landing of Ferja.

Leifr grudgingly had to admire the Naglissons' perseverance, but he hated them all the more because of it. It was the only decent quality they possessed, and they did not deserve it.

"Now then!" Svanlaug said in a fever of impatience. "We must get away from here and away from this side of the river! Magni won't take long to discover we've tricked him!"

Halmur stood still as she led the way to the door. Starkad halted in his tracks and returned to grip Halmur's arm. "Come along, you fool, you can't stay here and wait for them. They'll kill you now, after helping us escape."

"Let them," Halmur said. "I don't want to live as an Ulf-hedin. Death would be better."

"Death is a waste of talent," Leifr said. "You know the Ulf-hol, don't you?"

"Somewhat," Halmur said. "All the novices are kept there until their training is complete, if you want to call starving and beating training."

"You still have your own will, despite it," Leifr said. "Come with us, and you'll get your revenge upon the Ulf-hedin in the time you have left. But you've got to take that wolf skin off. All of you, take them off. I hate the sight of them. How do you know you haven't fallen under some sort of spell by using those things?''

Halmur pulled off the wolf skin. ''It's the belt that contains the spell,'' he said. ''Are you certain you want my help? Can I be trusted?''

''I've been wondering about that,'' Leifr said. ''Why did you suddenly change sides? Just what happened?''

Halmur frowned, trying to organize his thoughts. Starkad broke in. ''They had me locked in a little prison beyond the house, and Halmur brought me my dinner. Then he came inside to share it with me. But I managed to overcome him and started to escape—right into the arms of a big Ulf-hedin.''

''It was Magni, our pack leader.'' Starkad took over the story. ''He saw me, just getting up. What he said was ugly. Then he locked us both in, forgetting I had the other key, I guess. That did it for me. Everything had been going badly, and that was too much. So when Svanlaug slipped out again to talk to Starkad, I told her I wanted to help.''

''I didn't believe him, of course,'' Svanlaug explained. ''But he convinced me. He gave me the key, and I let them both out. Halmur had his wolf skin, but we needed two more, so I slipped inside and stole them while everybody was asleep. We couldn't have done it without Halmur.''

Leifr nodded, partly convinced. ''What about the eitur, though? You're going to need it, Halmur. Then what?''

''It's not long since the last ration,'' Halmur said. ''I can get by without for maybe three weeks. Then, if we haven't won, I'll kill myself. I'm not going back to them!''

Leifr nodded again.

When they were well away from Svina-gill, Starkad brought Leifr's retreat to a halt on a brushy hilltop. ''There's something you must know,'' he said. ''Thurid and Raudbjorn are both dead. We saw them in the knacker-women's cart.''

''Dead?'' Leifr repeated. ''Sorkvir doesn't think Thurid is dead. He spoke of him as if he were still alive and still in possession of the carbuncle.''

''We saw him dead,'' Starkad insisted. ''I don't think those knacker-women would have been interested in him otherwise.''

"Where are these knacker-women?" Leifr asked, turning to Halmur.

"Not far from here," Halmur said. "By the river, where there's fewer people to complain about the smells. Plenty of horse and troll barges keep them supplied with dead animals for their business. Besides what they find in Ferja, with the fighting and killing done by the Ulf-hedin."

"Take us there, Halmur," Leifr said, ignoring Svanlaug's muffled and indignant protests. "I want to see for myself if Thurid and Raudbjorn are dead. We've got a bit of time before the Naglissons get to Ferja."

The smell that Halmur mentioned soon became evident, and Leifr thought of old Gotiskolker, before he knew him as Fridmarr, stirring his rendering pots in ill-humored solitude and waiting for him to begin the entire cycle again. Fridmarr had been here, Leifr knew, by the restless sensations coming from the carbuncle stone hanging around his neck. Warnings, fears, and yearnings—it was all mixed together into a heady brew of anticipation that drew him on without resistance.

A greasy pall of smoke hung over a tiny settlement well away from Ferja, downriver and downwind. They hurried through a yard full of stacked bones. The old blackened turf houses beyond were ornamented with skulls, patched with hides, and half sunken into the greensward of their own weight and antiquity. In a neatly swept yard, a vast kettle stood over a bed of coals, boiling vigorously and emitting an unbelievable stench. A wiry little figure in a brown cloak was poking at things with a long pole from the vantage point of a cart loaded with bones and skins.

"That's Beitski," Halmur said in a low voice. "She's the eldest of the four sisters. Everyone fears her, as if she were a living sister of Hela."

"How do you do?" the knacker-woman greeted them cheerily, hopping down from her perch like an inquisitive little sparrow. "What have you got for me today? Ulf-hedin have usually got something or other they no longer want cluttering around."

"We don't have anything of the sort you'd put in your rendering pot," Leifr said. "We're thinking you might have taken something of ours that wasn't exactly in your usual line of work."

Beitski turned her head to one side and looked puzzled. "Eh? That's not too likely. There's only one line of work around here, and that's rendering out dead things for grease and meal. You must be thinking of some other place. Now if you've wasted enough of my time, I'm off to my work again.'' She was already half turned away, but she whirled around again and looked more sharply at Leifr. ''You're not a Scipling, are you? I've heard that one was lost around here someplace and plenty of people are looking for him. You'd better come inside, before some of them see you standing about.''

Leifr darted Halmur a questioning glance, and Halmur nodded slightly. They followed her inside, leaving the troll-hounds to explore a paradise of bones and smelly things dear to the hearts of hounds.

The interior of the house looked as if it were scrubbed with a vengeance every day of the week. Two old women looked up inquiringly from their weaving.

''Fetch Ketilridir,'' Beitski said to one of her sisters and pointed to some severe chairs lined up stiffly against the wall. ''You may sit there and make yourselves comfortable while you wait for Ketilridir.''

Beitski sat down facing them, her alert eyes picking over them sharply. ''What an interesting assortment,'' she observed, lacing her fingers together primly. ''Scipling, Ljosalfar, Dokkalfar, and Ulf-hedin. Where could you possibly be going together?''

''To Hringurhol,'' Leifr said. ''As soon as we've reclaimed certain personages who were brought here by mistake—or by design.''

''You're clever,'' Svanlaug said. ''There's more than one line of work going on here. I know a house of healing when I see one. My mother is a physician and I was raised to be one. Your knackering business keeps most people at a distance, so who is it you practice your arts upon?''

Beitski shook her head and smiled with a prim expression that declared her secrecy to be inviolate by any ordinary means. ''I shall ask the questions here,'' she said. ''I have to look out for my younger sisters.''

Ketilridir came into the room from a low doorway in the back. She wore a white starched apron pinned to her shoulders with broaches, and a white bonnet adorned her head.

''It's all right, sister,'' she said in a voice of comforting calm. Her entire manner was one of stately repose and inviting peace. ''They may come this way and see for themselves.''

She beckoned for them to approach, allowing them to file into the adjoining room one by one. Leifr had to duck his head and stoop to clear the low doorway.

Beyond was a whitewashed room, sparsely furnished with a table and chair and a neatly made bed with a woven coverlet. A little fire burned on the hearth against one wall, sharing its warmth with the room beyond. Fleeces and rushes made the stone floor more comfortable. A single window allowed the daylight to enter the room, and a lone figure was seated in a chair beside the window, looking out and paying them no heed whatsoever. One hand was stretched out across the table, and under it reposed the blue carbuncle stone from Heldur's forge, sparkling from the depths of its cloudy core.

"Thurid!" Leifr said, crossing the room to his side. "I knew you wouldn't be dead! Only you could burn an inn down around your ears and still survive it!"

Thurid made no move, as if he had neither heard nor seen their arrival. He gazed steadily out the window, like a statue, his skin as pale as marble, his hair hanging loose and wispy on his neck. His hair and beard, Leifr noted with alarm, had turned completely white. He looked almost transparent.

"He doesn't hear you, not yet," Ketilridir said in her soothing voice.

"What's wrong with him?" Leifr demanded. "Why can't he hear me?" Reaching out, he ventured to touch Thurid on the shoulder, and leaped back a step as a current of energy repelled him.

"He's not quite ready," Ketilridir said. "He was dead, you realize, and it takes time to call them back when they have gone."

"Dead?" Leifr took another step backward, keeping his eyes upon Thurid's still form. "He's nothing but a draug, you mean? Like Sorkvir? You make bargains with Hela also?" He tore his gaze away from Thurid to stare at Ketilridir.

She smiled gently. "No, of course not. We're not necromancers. We're healers, changers, and shapers. Hela and her realm of tortured souls are only one aspect of death—the only one generally known to living mortals, unfortunately. We brought back the essence that is Thurid to his body which was dead. All of him is not yet quickened. It is much as if you poured water into dry earth. It takes awhile for the new material to be assimilated into the old.''

"What is the new material?'' Leifr demanded. "Will he be the same old Thurid I knew? I don't want him to be different.''

"He will be the same old Thurid,'' Ketilridir promised. "But think of the place where his essence has been. Think of all that he has learned. Think how busily his mind must be storing away all manner of new knowledge.''

"I can't,'' Leifr said in a mixture of fear and puzzlement. "I've never heard of such things before. Who are you women? How can you do these things?''

Ketilridir took up a heavy, long-handled spoon from the table and held it up. "What is it that makes a spoon a spoon?'' she asked.

"Metal or wood,'' Leifr said.

"What makes metal metal?'' she pursued, and Leifr gazed at her in stumped silence. "What makes a substance metal, and not wood or glass or hair or flesh or air or water or fire? Why is anything one substance and not another?''

"Because it always was whatever it is?'' Starkad asked.

"But it wasn't,'' said Ketilridir. "Everything was chaos at the beginning. Everything was nothing. When all things and substances were formed, they were formed of quite similar materials. The most ancient of all peoples still possess the secrets of forming whatever they desire from pure chaos. A spoon, a cup, a mountain, a river, it is all there before your eyes, waiting to be called into form.''

An errant sunbeam pierced the gloom of the sky and briefly illuminated the room, filled with dancing dust motes whirling and spinning when she passed her hand through them several times. "All things are made of tiny motes like this. The trick is to command them to form what one wishes. The ancient ones knew the secrets. When a good and true one such as Thurid dies, he goes to the same place with those shapers and changers and menders of all things. We are only poor creatures compared to them, in search of the light they possess. We do what we can to mend these poor shabby mortal carcasses. Come, let us leave him now. His healing is proceeding well, and he will be himself very soon.''

She replaced the spoon on the table and turned away. Leifr stared at the spoon in astonishment and disbelief. The heavy metal was perfectly spiraled, as if powerful hands had twisted the spoon handle around and around a dozen or more times. He looked at the dust motes still dancing in the bright air, dimming gradually as the clouds swallowed the sunbeam once again. Warily he stretched out one finger and touched the spoon. It was cool to the touch.

"It is time to go," Ketilridir reminded him gently.

"What are we to do?" Leifr asked when she had closed the low door behind them. "We need Thurid and we need that blue carbuncle stone. How do we know Thurid and the stone are safe here? What if the Ulf-hedin follow us to him?"

"They won't find him," Ketilridir said with a note of surprise and reproach in her tone. "They will find nothing but four odd little knacker-women eking out a bare existence from making tallow for lamps and candles."

Leifr saw her make a sweeping gesture with her hand. When he turned to look back, the low doorway into the next room was no longer there. He saw nothing but another stray beam of sunlight, filled with whirling dust motes.

He closed his mouth, which was getting very dry. With no further questions, he allowed the knacker-women politely to escort him and the others outside. For a moment they stood in the smoky courtyard in stunned silence, while Beitski, Jarngerdr, Ketilridir, and Grimssyna beamed at them and shook each one by the hand, chirping words of encouragement.

"Go ahead now and cross the river," Beitski said. "You can't stay here because the Ulf-hedin are looking for you on this side. They won't expect you to cross the river. The sword and the blue stone will be restored to you at the proper times, never fear. You must go ahead sometimes, even when the way seems impossible, never fearing that you may fail. There is deliverance," she said as she shook Halmur's hand and gazed into his face with a fierce intensity, "so do not be discouraged. Away with you, don't delay any longer. The ones who seek you are not far behind."

"Wait," Leifr said suddenly. "What about Raudbjorn, the great Norskur, who was with Thurid?"

"The same, asleep," Grimssyna said shortly, nodding her head for emphasis. "I think you should leave those dogs with him. They'll only get you into trouble on the other side." She glared at them severely, and they left off their happy sniffing and shoulder-rolling in a heap of offal and guiltily crept over and crouched at Leifr's feet, grinning and tail-thumping in apology. "Now go straight to the river. There's a path. If you take it you'll be in the right place."

They went in the direction she pointed, following a crooked path that led them down into the chasm of the river and again into view of Hringurhol perched upon the far side. Wreaths of mist and rain enshrouded it, allowing brief glimpses of spires and rooftops to penetrate before engulfing them again. If the Wizard's Guildhall had been awe-inspiring, Hringurhol was ten times the size and grandeur. Blackened towers of a dozen shapes and sizes rose above the rooftops and walls, raking the belly of the cloud cover, and lofty fronts of halls towered higher than any Leifr had ever seen, roofed with black thatch or green turf. It all stood in a state of perilous, decaying ruin, sagging and broken away, a mocking parody of its past grandeur.

"What do we do now?" Starkad questioned, looking about the ruins of the boat stand. "Getting here is one thing, but getting across is quite another."

"This is the way it is done," Svanlaug said.

Svanlaug strode to the center of the crumbling boat stand. She hoisted one arm into the air and waved vigorously, although the opposite shore was hidden in mist. Then they waited, straining their ears to hear over the grumble of the deep water. Just as Leifr was about to succumb to his suspicions that a boat was not coming, he heard the slap of waves against its planks and the hiss of the bow-wave curling under its prow. He saw its dim form taking shape in the mist and wavered between waiting for it in a bold stance on the boat stand or taking a more sensible position among the rocks where there was cover. Svanlaug stood still, waiting for it as if she had every right to its services, so Leifr stood to one side of her—the side nearest the rocks.

The boat was unoccupied, with no sail or oar to move it, yet it glided up to the boat stand and halted, its proud dragon's head upthrust in frozen defiance.

"Again we meet," Leifr murmured, drawing a deep breath. "Well, I guess it has come for us at a time we can't turn back. It's like destiny—you can't escape it."

While Svanlaug stepped over the gunwales and settled herself on a bench, Leifr looked it over warily from nose to tail. He stepped gingerly into the dragon ship and knelt one knee on a bench, his hand automatically reaching for the hilt of his sword, which wasn't there. The boat eased away from the boat stand, swinging around toward Hringurhol as if an invisible hand were at the rudder. With misgivings, Leifr looked back, watching the shoreline receding behind them.

The boat glided steadily through the rough current at the center of the river and coasted through the mist toward the mooring. Leifr stood ready as it bumped gently. He saw no one waiting; he saw only the ruins of a tower of some kind flanking the stone platform; beyond was an ornate balustrade, mostly crumbled away, leaving only a raddled ghost to remind anyone who cared of its former glory. Stairs rose from the side of the boat stand, broken and clogged with dirt, moss, and a few struggling saplings. As Leifr gazed around, not liking the place, his eyes suddenly fastened upon a living bit of antiquity, in the form of an old brown cloak huddled around a withered old man, who sat on a rock overlooking the river.

"Who's that?" he demanded hoarsely.

"The ferryman," Svanlaug said in a low voice that betrayed a little tremor of fear. "Have you got anything to offer him? A bit of bread, perhaps? He doesn't require much sustenance, but if we give him something now, he may be more inclined to send us across when we return."

She must have known about the hunk of hard bread Leifr had shoved into his hood's tail pocket. He dumped it out and watched as Svanlaug approached the ferryman's rock and held out the bread. A dark claw of a hand snatched it from her instantly, but the creature never turned his head away from the river. The ragged hem of the cloak was dragged aside by the movement, and Leifr saw that a shackle bound the ferryman to the rock with a chain.

"It's our hope you'll remember us when we come back," Svanlaug said, stepping back quickly from the rock.

The ferryman gnawed at the bread with a voracious grinding sound, never sparing them a glance. In a growling voice he replied, "I'll remember, if the need arises. Them that comes seldom goes back. Unless they be Ulf-hedin."

Svanlaug made no answer and gave Leifr a hurried nudge toward the stairs. They climbed up to a rubbly terrace, where some carved pillars stood around in drunken poses, their usefulness long forgotten. The stairway lost itself in fallen scree and dirt, giving way to a well-trodden road winding around the flank of the hill. From time to time a wall or a cornice appeared, half smothered, as if the hill had grown up around larger and more ancient structures, engulfing them over the centuries.

A decayed-looking archway gave access into the present settlement of Hringurhol, dominated by its central tower, which rose in rings and terraces and arches, unlike any construction Leifr had ever seen. Through the crumbling arches he could see the low-hanging clouds, lurid with suppressed lightnings and unnatural glowings.

"That's the Ulf-hol," Halmur said, slowing his pace and casting uneasy glances all around. "I think the Masters and servants are in a ceremony. No one's about the streets."

"If there's a ceremony," Svanlaug said, "Ulfrin's bound to be there."

"Ulfrin!" Leifr groaned. "Are you certain we can't just forget about her?"

"Positive," Svanlaug snapped. "We've got ample time before Brjaladur."

"I wouldn't call four days ample time," Leifr retorted. "How can we even get into that hall for a look? There's guards all around it."

"Follow me," Halmur said. "We'll find a way."

Following Halmur closely, they plunged into the network of alleyways and avenues fanning out from the Ulf-hol. Surrounding the Ulf-hol were perhaps a dozen halls cast up of turf and stone, robbed from older and grander buildings, some of them fantastically spired and ornamented, taking inspiration from the ruins they were built upon. Crowding between the halls were the huts and hovels of the humble serving folk bound to the heirs of the grand halls, and the smoke of their cooking fires filled the air with the stench of burning dung and the seared hair and feathers of the meat that went onto the fine tables in the fine houses. A few dogs barked and came slinking out to sniff at the strangers, but of the servants and thralls Leifr saw nothing except the occasional pale flash of face in the crack of a doorway. He had the feeling that the place was sealed up tight and corked with fear, and his own inclinations were similar.

"Everyone keeps his head out of sight on nights like this," Svanlaug said grimly, and Halmur nodded in agreement.

After threading a circuitous course around the Ulf-hol,

Halmur led them to an area of greater ruin and decay, where they crouched behind a partially fallen wall. Uneasily Leifr peered toward the central hall with its crown of broken arches. From the roofless interior came the sounds of repetitious chanting, interspersed with yells and screams of a savage nature and the muttering of quite a few voices. A low fire burned beside a black doorway, and a lone guard stood against the stones, resting first one foot and then the other and pacing up and down a few steps like a man who is very bored indeed with a useless task.

As they watched, two cloaked and hooded figures came hurrying along the curve of the building and turned into the doorway without a glance at the guard. Not only was he useless, he was ignored. He clasped his arms over his chest and sighed loudly, peering into the doorway and clearly yearning to leave his post and join the others. Another latecomer came striding up to the door and hurried inside.

Svanlaug poked Leifr sharply. "Well? Are you ready?"

"Ready? For what?" He grunted in alarm as she rose to her feet purposefully, pulling her hood down to her eyes.

"Just follow me and look like you're hurrying," she whispered, and strode directly toward the doorway. He and Halmur had no choice but to follow, hurrying along in a convincing style, with Leifr muttering invectives under his breath with such fury that the guard shrank back from him, waving one hand in a hasty gesture to ward off evil powers.

Svanlaug tossed her head and strode confidently ahead, selecting a place on the edge of the ring of observers. Perhaps a hundred dark figures stood around watching in small knots of two or three, not coming close to filling the space available.

The interior of the tower was vast, and lit by a pair of large braziers in the central court, towering with greenish flames. A wall arose behind the braziers, which Leifr at first believed to be intricately carved; but a closer look revealed that the artistic scrolls and crenellations and details were all formed by human bones and human skulls. A gibbet was permanently established as part of the decorations, and three withered corpses dangled over the heads of the Council of Threttan, who were seated upon the dais in thirteen chairs carved from stone. They wore ceremonial headdresses, tall, mitered crowns ornamented with the personal devices of their bearers: wolves, eagles, foxes, dragons, serpents, and other emblems glinted in silver, gold, and precious gems.

Hvitur-Fax and a pair of Ulf-hedin stood within a circle made with a dark substance Leifr suspected was blood, and between them they held a captive, who offered pitiful resistance when he was dragged forward. A trial of some sort seemed to be the nature of the proceedings, with the Ulf-hedin giving evidence on one side and the Council listening on the other.

"That's Alfrekar in the middle," Svanlaug whispered, her eyes like coals, burning with hatred. "My father used to sit on his left, but now Sorkvir's got that spot. Djofull was on his right. The two of them connived against Afgang, the last voice of reason in this entire foul conspiracy. Afgang died, and his bones have been added to that hideous wall of infamy, consisting of those who have dared resist the Council and the Ulf-hedin."

Leifr's hair lifted with horror as he contemplated the incredible number of bones and skulls ornamenting that wall and wondered if one day his own would come to grace it.

"Where's the Dokkur Lavardur?" he asked in an uneasy undertone. "Is that empty seat beside Alfrekar his?"

Svanlaug turned to look at him, still for a long moment, then her eyes turned upward toward the roiling clouds. The clouds glinted like scales, reminding Leifr of the belly of the dragon he had seen flying over his head to its doom.

"That's the Dokkur Lavardur," she whispered. "The Lord of Chaos, Darkness, Ice, and Death. The Fimbul Winter is what falls in his footsteps. The learned wizards call him an elemental. The thralls and simple ones call him the Sky Dragon, or Stormurganger, the Storm Walker."

As Leifr gazed upward incredulously, a spout of cloud spun itself into a long snout that lashed about like a dragon's tail, barbed with lightning.

"What can a sword do against something like that?" Leifr asked, awed into an unpleasant state of humility.

"I don't know if it can do anything," Svanlaug answered, "but it can wreak havoc with creatures such as Sorkvir and Alfrekar. They are the ones who have conjured the Dokkur Lavardur and bound him to do their will—but not completely, just yet. They required Heldur's orb to finish their binding of the Dokkur Lavardur."

The captive of the Ulf-hedin suddenly interrupted Leifr's

questioning with a shrill scream of terror, which was drowned in a gurgle. Leifr supposed they had cut the poor villain's throat, but when he turned to look, it appeared that Alfrekar himself was pouring some sort of fluid down his throat while another Ulf-hedin held his jaws. The familiar sweet fragrance of eitur drifted over the crowd. The watching wizards nearest Leifr and Svanlaug uncorked small bottles and sniffed delicately at the exuding fumes, as did every other within view.

"Eitur!" Leifr muttered, reaching for the carbuncle almost protectively. It seemed to throb with life in his hand, recalling Fridmarr's pain.

For the first time, Leifr noticed a heap of dead bodies cast negligently behind the ranks of waiting Ulf-hedin. Then he saw the huddle of captives waiting to be judged worthy or unworthy of the Ulf-hedin curse. Among them were the luckless Naglissons and their father, all watching with frozen horror on their faces.

The captive dosed with eitur thrashed about for a short time and suddenly went as limp as a sack in the grasp of his captors. Hvitur-Fax then motioned to another Ulf-hedin, who came forward with a freshly skinned wolf cape, which was arranged over the head and shoulders of the initiate and bound in place with a wide belt anchoring the skinned legs and tail of the wolf. He was then dragged to a pillar and lashed into place, with a small brazier burning at his feet, cloaking him in acrid smoke.

"This can't go on," Leifr said, hoarse with fury. "That fellow doesn't want to be an Ulf-hedin."

"No one does, at the last," Halmur said. "They're all taken against their will and poisoned with eitur. If they don't obey, they suffer and die horribly."

A ripple of grim amusement ran through the crowd as a pair of Ulf-hedin dragged forth one of the Naglissons. The ritual was repeated, except that instead of binding the spell with the pelt of a wolf, it was the hide of a yellow-haired mongrel that was tied over the Naglisson's head. Somehow it seemed a fine joke to the ones who watched, but Leifr saw the hapless wretch's struggles with nothing but disgust and mounting anger. When Nagli was hauled forward, kicking and howling, Leifr uttered an involuntary growl of disapproval that made several wizards turn around to look at him querulously.

"Hush," Svanlaug whispered, gripping his arm with sudden

and painful intensity. "You can't do anything, not alone, and not here. Those are your enemies, the Naglissons. Men of that sort ought to be slaves, for the protection of the rest of us. As Hundr-hedin they won't be as dangerous as Ulf-hedin."

"Dogs instead of wolves?" Leifr grunted skeptically.

"Yes. Craven, slinking, flea-biters," Svanlaug said impatiently. "Very much what they deserve. But we have another problem, Leifr, a much worse one, and we've got to deal with it immediately.

Leifr followed her eyes to a knot of wizards. His heart gave a sudden stutter as he discerned a female warrior among them, with her Ulf-hedin cape thrown back over her shoulders. But instead of Ljosa's pale nimbus of hair, it was a cascade of black hair, like Svanlaug's, tossing in accompaniment to a trill of mirth at the antics of the hapless Hundr-hedin.

"It's Ulfrin," Svanlaug muttered with an angry groan. "And I fear she's become Ulf-hedin!"

Chapter 8

◇◇◇◇◇◇◇◇◇◇◇◇◇◇◇◇◇◇◇◇◇◇◇◇◇◇◇◇◇◇◇◇◇◇◇◇◇◇

"That's the Sverting!" Halmur exclaimed, his tone a mixture of awe and contempt. "She's your sister? You came to get her out of here?"

"Yes, she is my sister," Svanlaug said, "and we've got to get her out of Hringurhol before it is destroyed. She's young and foolish, or she wouldn't be here, shaming her heritage and her clan."

"She is also dangerous," Halmur said. "Alfrekar won't part with her easily. How will you convince her to exchange the supposed powers and glories of Hringurhol for your quiet little village of women in the mountains? I remember how it was to covet such things."

"Perhaps she has come to her senses by now," Svanlaug suggested, pulling her wolf skin farther down over her eyes. "Come, let's get a little nearer to her."

They edged warily closer, until they could hear Ulfrin laughing and chatting in high spirits with the wizards surrounding her. They were well dressed and rather gaudily ornamented, and all were considerably younger than any wizard on the Council. Other wizards and Ulf-hedin nearby moved away with disapproving scowls at the irreverent chatter kept up by the group of dandies.

Svanlaug kept her eyes upon Ulfrin, as if burning a message into her shoulder blades. Uneasily Ulfrin turned and looked around several times, before she suddenly met Svanlaug's eyes with a visible start. Detaching herself from her admirers, she approached her sister, her eyes glittering and her countenance ashen.

"What are you doing here?" she demanded. "I thought you were dead!"

"You thought you killed me, you mean!" Svanlaug spat. "No

101

doubt you're disappointed that you failed, but luckily for you, I'm still alive, thanks to Thurid. I've come to take you home, Ulfrin.''

"What? Indeed! This is more my home now than Bergmal ever was,'' Ulfrin said.

"Do you want to be buried in your new home or do you wish to live in Bergmal?'' Svanlaug demanded. "Hringurhol is doomed to destruction.''

"How?'' Ulfrin inquired with an insolent glance in Leifr's direction. "At the hands of this horse-thief? Thurid is missing and probably dead, the carbuncle is gone and in who knows whose hands, and the great sword of Endless Death is missing. Alfrekar has told me all.''

"I'm not a horse-thief,'' Leifr retorted. "And I'd be content to let you perish with all the rest of the unclean hosts living in Hringurhol, if not for Svanlaug's foolish determination to save your life.''

"I could have all of you captured and hanged,'' Ulfrin snarled, her eyes coming to rest upon Svanlaug. "I suppose it's a weakness, but I'm going to let you escape this time, but only because you're my sister, and I know no real harm is going to come of it. Hringurhol will stand forever, and I shall stand with Hringurhol.''

Halmur stepped forward and uncovered part of his face. "Hringurhol will not stand forever,'' he said. "I shall stand with the Scipling. Already the First Seal is breaking. If you want to be spared, you'll go with them, away from Hringurhol.''

Ulfrin gasped. "A traitor! How do you dare show your face here, after the oath of fealty you have taken? Do you know what you are doing?''

"Breaking the Covenant of the First Seal,'' Halmur said, "and I hope more will follow. I hope to see all five of the Great Seals broken and the Dokkur Lavardur driven out of Hringurhol and out of the Dokkalfar realm.''

"It shall never happen,'' Ulfrin said with a toss of her head. "When Hvitur-Fax gets his hands on you, he'll make an example of you that no one will ever forget, and your bones will one day adorn the Traitors' Wall.'' She inclined her head toward the wall of bones and skulls. "All your bones, unless you are wise enough to make your escape now before anyone discovers you are here.''

"Don't try to frighten us," Svanlaug said. "We've come for you, and we won't leave without you. If you live long enough, you might be able to outlive the shame you've brought upon the Bergmal clan with your Ulf-hedin antics."

"You are a fine one to speak of shame," Ulfrin retorted. "Look at what you've done, haring off like a wild thing and taking up with wandering wizards and outlanders on this hopeless mission of revenge and destruction."

"Hopeless!" Svanlaug snapped. "It will succeed!"

"It won't," Ulfrin said. "And I shall prove it to you. As soon as the ceremonies and the drumming-in are over, I dare you to meet me on the top of Heidur's hill, outside the small eastern gate." She twitched one shoulder toward the east, where the black bulk of the mountain rose above the fortress. "If I convince you, you must promise you'll return to the other side of the river and go back to Bergmal and abandon your attempts against the workings of the Council."

"Heidur's hill it is," Svanlaug said defiantly. "If you're trying to frighten me, you're failing miserably, Ulfrin."

"You were always too afraid to go to Heidur's hill when we were children visiting our father," Ulfrin taunted. "Too afraid the Dokkur Lavardur would come out of the sanctuary and get you!"

"I'm afraid no longer," Svanlaug said. "I, at least, inherited the wisdom of Afgang. I know, as he knew, that the Council must be stopped. And if we convince you, you must promise to go back to Bergmal and leave us to our work."

"Agreed," Ulfrin said, slapping her palm against Svanlaug's. "Now be off. It won't do for me to be observed talking to common people. You'd better wear those wolf capes or you'll likely be hauled away and thrown in a pit somewhere."

Turning swiftly, she strode away and vanished into a nearby doorway, covertly glancing back at them over one shoulder as she ran lightly up a winding flight of stairs.

"After her," Svanlaug ordered. "I don't trust her. She's likely going straight to Alfrekar to set up a trap for us. I don't want to let her out of my sight for a moment."

Svanlaug started after Ulfrin, but Halmur put his hand on her shoulder. "Ulf-hedin can't go up there," he said. "That's for Exalted Ones only, and we'd be suspect at once."

"Take this then," Svanlaug snapped, almost throwing the

wolf pelt at Leifr. "I'm not afraid to go after her. Exalted Ones, indeed! Am I not Afgang's daughter, the same as Ulfrin? Did I not spend half my childhood here under the tutelage of the Council? Let them stop me if they dare." Svanlaug elevated her chin haughtily and strode away after Ulfrin.

"She mustn't go up there!" Halmur said. "She'll be captured for helping me escape. I saw Magni and his pack in the crowd. I'm sure he's brought word to Alfrekar and Fax by now of what she did."

"Go after her then," Leifr said. "We'll wait here."

"Put on your wolf cape," Halmur said, "and don't do anything to attract anyone's attention."

"I will. Go," Leifr said.

Leifr pulled the muzzle of the pelt over his face with a shudder of revulsion. He felt it shape itself to his head and neck and shoulders, running down his arms with a rather pleasant tingle of power. It was a shock to see his arms and hands transformed to hairy black paws, but he had never felt such power transforming his travel-weary body. Looking at Starkad, he saw a young Ulf-hedin in a dark-gray pelt, bristling with energy.

"It's splendid, Leifr," he said in a growling voice. "You look terrible."

Their whispered exchange took only a few moments, but it attracted the attention of a silver-tipped Ulf-hedin leaning against a pillar and keeping a negligent eye upon a pack of about twenty Ulf-hedin. He straightened up to look at them more attentively.

"It's Ufsi, the kennel master," Halmur warned. "Keep your heads low and look like humble novices. I'll be back as soon as I can."

Halmur glided away, and Ufsi continued to watch them, eventually interpreting their guilty glances as suspicionable of misconduct. Pulling his wolf cape down over his face, he sauntered toward them. Starkad nudged Leifr and started sidling through the clumps of wizards, onlookers, and Ulf-hedin. Just as they were certain they had evaded him, he suddenly came up alongside and seized Starkad by one of his wolf ears.

"What are you fools doing?" Ufsi snarled, giving Starkad a shake by one ear, eliciting a yelp of pain. Other Ulf-hedin standing about nearby looked around and grinned unpleasantly. "You're both novices, aren't you? Slinking around by yourselves, are you? I saw you talking to the Sverting and annoying her. You must have a strong desire for death to be so audacious. Whom do you belong to? Where did you come from?''

Starkad sputtered and gasped like a fish on a gaff, and Leifr stood frozen to the spot, which seemed to be considered appropriate behavior in such a situation.

''The third standard kennels, I'd say, old Svidi's lot,'' an onlooking Ulf-hedin said, turning away when he realized the situation did not promise much interest. ''I heard he wasn't bringing them up to the initiations, for punishment. Old Svidi must have left the lock off again and these two sneaked out to see the initiations. His eyes aren't what they used to be.''

''Hurry up and get rid of them, Ufsi,'' another silvery old Ulf-hedin snapped. ''You're raising too much racket.''

''In the kennel for other crimes already, and you sneaked out?'' Ufsi repeated in a growl, giving Starkad another shaking. He glared at Leifr and Starkad, who did a convincing job of cringing and slinking, with the hot and fetid breath of the Ulf-hedin in their faces and a hundred other Ulf-hedin within easy calling range.

''We didn't want to miss the ceremony,'' Leifr muttered.

''Plucky lads,'' Ufsi said after a moment of lowering at them, ''but old Svidi is going to flay your hides. Now get along with you back to the kennel. Hah, there he is himself. He must have missed you. Svidi! Come over here, I've got something for you!''

He signaled with one arm as a squat dark shape lumbered out of a shadowy gallery, scratching one frayed ear.

''Two of your pups have strayed,'' Ufsi said. ''See here, I found them for you.''

Svidi swung his heavy scarred head to scrutinize Leifr and Starkad a moment from the one good eye remaining in his wolf mask. In a low and growling voice he uttered something that Ufsi seemed to understand the most part of; but Leifr and Starkad could only stare at him.

He suddenly lashed out with the whip, making a loud crack.

''Yes, a taste of Svipa is what they need,'' Ufsi said. ''Get them out of here, Svidi.''

Svidi's hairy face split with an enormous grin of sheer pleasure, revealing a mouthful of stumpy and yellowed teeth. He lashed his whip around in a frenzy of cracking and hissing, backing his captives toward a dark gate in the wall behind them.

He pointed, gestured, and made more hideous gargling and growling sounds.

"What's he saying?" Starkad whispered, not taking his rounded eyes off Svidi. "what should we do, Leifr?"

"He's had his tongue cut off, I'd say," Leifr replied, "and I think he wants us to go through this door."

The whip sizzled past Leifr's head, near enough to sting his ear without actually touching him. Svidi barked something in his peculiar language that sounded like an order compounded by bad temper, so Leifr plunged through the doorway. At once he was struck by an overwhelming odor—musk mingled faintly with the sweetness of eitur. He pawed at the wolf mask plastered over his face, feeling stifled, but he couldn't pry it up for a good breath of air. It seemed to grip his face with an insidious life of its own.

The few furtive Ulf-hedin or wizards who were traversing the tunnels paid scant heed to Svidi and his unlucky prisoners. The vicious cracking of his whip was enough to send most people scuttling into alleyways and into the shadows of fallen heaps of masonry. Leaving behind the lights and fires and shrieks of the initiation and purging ceremonies, they headed down a ramp to the levels below the surface of the earth, taking turns or not turning when Svidi gave the signal by suddenly going into a frenzy of whipcracking and garbled shouting. He trotted along with surprising agility for such a short and stumpy individual, fueling his energy with the rage generated by the apparent stupidity of his captives. They repeatedly tried to go up the wrong turns, deliberately to enrage him. Such temerity must have astounded him; Leifr and Starkad both felt the sting of the lash more frequently as his temper degenerated.

"Leifr, we can't keep going," Starkad panted. "We've got to jump on him and get out of here."

"You want to jump on an Ulf-hedin?" Leifr asked.

"We're Ulf-hedin, too," Starkad retorted.

"No, we're not! We haven't got eitur in our blood! We haven't got half the strength he's got!"

The walls and pillars were far older the deeper they descended. The unmistakable sounds of misery and captivity echoed desolately from the dripping walls, moans and whimpers and the rattle of chains. At one time the place had been catacombs, with narrow niches carved into the stone for burial vaults, but now the niches were prison cells, each with a wooden door and a small grate. A pair of Ulf-hedin of Svidi's general type waited beside a small watch fire, grinning in ruthless expectation as the prisoners approached. They, too, carried whips coiled at their belts.

"Two strayed sheep, brought back to the fold, eh?" snarled one of them. "They got away and up to the ceremony almost faster than you did, Svidi."

The other grinned maliciously and nudged his companion with an avaricious gleam in his eyes. "They get faster every year," he said. "Soon they'll be too fast for old Svidi to catch, and then what do you suppose will happen to old Svidi?"

Svidi menaced them with his whip, sending them scuttling for cover as he filled the air with vicious cracking and singing leather. Then he pointed down the corridor of cells and gabbled some nonsense. Humbled now, the other two jailers at once seized Leifr and hauled him bodily along the corridor, while Svidi brought Starkad along in the rear, taking advantage of the opportunity to kick and cuff him for his supposed offenses.

They were hauled into a low and fetid chamber, illuminated by a single grass-wick lamp on a spike thrust into a small crevice. After stumbling over and stepping on six or eight other human forms shackled to the wall, which aroused no small amount of ill will, Leifr and Starkad were also staked out by means of chains and thick collars around their necks. Then the jailers clumped away to sit beside the fire with a jug of ale and direful chuckling as they mocked old Svidi in his own peculiar tongueless gobble.

Scarcely daring to move and call attention to himself, Leifr peered around in the gloom, fearing that one of the shadowy forms chained nearby was going to shout out that the two new prisoners were not Ulf-hedin. Counting slowly, he thought he discerned at least twenty pair of eyes glowing softly in the gloom and dark motionless shapes leaning against the wall or curled up on the floor.

Starkad at once commenced lashing around and struggling with his chain and collar as if he intended either to jerk the chain out of the wall or tear his head off. Leifr explored the contraption around his neck with his fingers, and discovered it was simply buckled on, like a dog collar. Yet these captives were so cowed they didn't take them off and revolt.

"Starkad, you fool, it's only a buckle!" he snapped.

"Silence that racket or we'll have some real noise!" one of their captors roared, glaring into the kennel and giving his whip a significant crack.

"This is worse than Hogni and Horgull!" Starkad growled in a low voice, after a bit. "We're not beasts to be tied up this way!"

"We are now," Leifr whispered grimly. "Save your strength, Starkad, you're going to need it. If this was a scheme of Svanlaug's, it certainly worked well."

"I can't believe she could have planned something this clever," Starkad moaned. "From the moment we found ourselves in Magni's hall, she was working her wiles on those Ulfhedin, pretending to betray us. Until she came to help Halmur get me out of there, you would have thought she had gone over completely to their side. Maybe this time she really did it. Maybe this idea of hers to rescue Ulfrin was just a trap. Ulfrin certainly doesn't seem to need or want rescuing."

"Do I hear talking?" the jailer roared, stalking forward to glare around at the cowering prisoners. "There is a way of dealing with Ulf-hedin who keep talking. Old Svidi will show you what talking earned for him—a personal acquaintance with a pair of red-hot tongs!"

A desolate whimpering throughout the kennel answered the threat. They sat in glum silence, listening to the sounds around them, and were not cheered by what they heard. Leifr's blood grew more chilled the longer he had to listen to the misery and degradation of the place, welling up and filling each dark corner like a black and evil spring. He considered Halmur with new compassion, wondering that the youth's will and integrity had survived the calculated onslaught upon his humanity. Survived and triumphed, even, in order to have rebelled and brought them this far.

The two masters sat and argued beside the fire, their quarrel growing more heated.

"I'll prove it to you," one of them finally exclaimed. He arose tipsily and seized a lantern and unsteadily tried to light it. "He's got two of somebody else's recruits. We weren't missing any. You know he can't see any better than the down-side of a flounder."

"We didn't know we were missing any," the other objected. "They can't just disappear."

"Exactly what I've been saying. We should count them. That will prove it."

"Count them then. I'll wager five marks there's twenty-one, just as there should be."

Leifr groaned softly, and someone across the way answered feelingly with another groan. "Maybe we should have jumped on old Svidi after all," he muttered to Starkad.

The two jailers were moving along the row of recruits and counting. They passed by, then returned, still counting.

"Well, you were right, there's two extras. What should we do with them?"

"Does it matter? Who's going to admit they lost two recruits from their pack? They might still be ours, strayed away, and two of the others might be somebody else's from another day. Svidi isn't particular."

"The old blind fool. They could all be a pack of trolls and he'd never know the difference."

"Maybe we ought to try it. Bring in a few trolls, just for a joke."

"It wouldn't work. They'd eat the recruits. You know how poor the food is down here."

"Maybe they're Myrda's. His kennel is so close, two might have strayed from him. He's so drunk he's usually seeing double and wouldn't miss half his pack. Let's go over and count what he's got. Let Svidi watch awhile."

They tramped away, leaving the kennel in its usual dank misery. By the light of a small fire, old Svidi sat blocking the doorway, and they had to step carefully over him. He opened his one eye with a suspicious snort as a foot grazed his ear, and slowly closed it up again as his snoring recommenced.

Starkad sat cross-legged with his chin in his hands, heaving miserable sighs at frequent intervals.

"What are we going to do, Leifr?" he moaned. "We can't stay down here."

Leifr thumbed the carbuncle in search of a small shred of comfort or inspiration.

"Isn't it strange," Leifr said with a wry smile, "how circumstances repeat themselves? Fridmarr was forced to become an Ulf-hedin, and now the same thing has happened to me, except for the eitur. I think we'll have similar luck in getting out of here and away from Hringurhol and back to Dallir one day, as he did.''

Starkad looked up from pressing his skull between his palms, as if it were a nut and he was trying to crack it and get at the contents.

''If I possessed a carbuncle of that size,'' he said, ''it would be power enough to get me out of almost any situation. You Sciplings are a difficult lot to understand sometimes. It's yours for the taking, yet you continue to refuse it. What I wouldn't give for such an opportunity!''

''I wish someone had it who knew how to use it,'' Leifr said. ''If you did have it somewhere in your body, what would you do to make it work for you?''

''Why, you could simply concentrate on the thing you wanted or the objective you desire; with the power to form it in your thoughts, you also have the power to bring about the result you wish.'' Starkad's tone was softened with awe.

''Hst! No talking!'' came from someone nearby. ''We all get punished for your disobedience.''

Leifr pressed the stone between his palms and silently concentrated. What he wished more than anything was that Halmur would come in search of them, but he found his thoughts continually skipping from place to place, dwelling on Thurid and the knacker-women awhile, Ljosa, his father and mother, Ulfrin, Hvitur-Fax, or Svanlaug and the question of her perfidy. With mighty effort he resumed his silent call to Halmur, time after time.

Old Svidi lay in a dozing heap beside the small peat fire, his hands laced over his sagging belly, his thick chin sunken on his chest. His ears were frayed at the ends from many fights, his broad skull was seamed with scars, and his matted pelt was almost completely white, although no honor had come of the passage of years in the service of the Council of Threttan. So much time had passed since he had last removed the Ulf-hedin pelt that there was no longer much man left in him, and he would not have been himself without the wolf cape. The supernatural strength that knotted his muscles would depart and leave him helplessly weak, a small and scuttling Dokkalfar of no importance. His only friend was Svipa, his whip, braided lovingly by his own hands, which was coiled and fastened to his belt. It was always there to command order from the ranks of recruits that passed through his kennel, fear from the rebellious, and courage from the reluctant.

As he dozed there on the floor, his bulk blocking most of the only doorway into the kennel, his ears twitched at the faint and accustomed sounds of his charges. One of them at the far end was coughing. Svidi half wakened as a thought swam briefly into his consciousness. The sound probably indicated an aversion to the damp underground quarters of the recruits that would eventually result in a slow and consumptive death, which would no doubt spread to several others before the disease ran its course. What with bad food, bad air, and the damp, plenty of recruits perished before ever seeing battle with the recalcitrant Ljosalfar settlers on the other side of the river. Training recruits was a nuisance, though he had made the use of Svipa sheer artistry from years of experience.

Making a mental note to find out who was coughing so he could toss the wretch in an isolation pit, Svidi settled himself more comfortably on his back and let his jaws sag in a comfortable snore.

Suddenly the liver and lights were nearly smashed out of him by a staggering blow just below his breastbone and just above his belly where his hands were clasped. All the air went out of him with a great *whoosh*, leaving him croaking faintly. To worsen his predicament, his attacker shoved a dirty wad of sacking into his mouth, rolled him over on his face, and quickly tied his hands behind his back, making good use of Svipa for the deed. By the time he was finished, old Svidi was beginning to kick and growl and thrash around in helpless fury.

"You prisoners! Unfasten those collars and get on your feet like men! You're beasts no longer! You're free to go! Throw off those wolf pelts and stand up! It's better to die as men than to live as brutes!"

The voice rang in the startled ears of the recruits. Their deliverer seized a smothered brand in the fire and whirled it around until it burst into bright flame, revealing Halmur striding through the middle of the kennel, urging them on. After a moment of shock and struggling hope, most of them leaped up and tore off their chains and wolf pelts. The ones who lingered were suddenly galvanized into action by the realization that the others were actually escaping, leaping over Svidi's snarling bulk and dashing out the door.

Leifr and Starkad tore off their own chains and helped the last of the recruits to free themselves, while Halmur urged them to be off and away. Leifr paused to tear at the wolf cape in an effort to discard it, but Halmur stopped him.

"Keep it on, or they'll know you're different," Halmur said. "Keep moving. Ulf-hedin never wander around as if they don't know what they're doing. At least there's not so many Ulf-hedin belowground right now, with the ceremonies going on."

"We're not going back to the Ulf-hol, are we?" Starkad asked. "Did you follow Svanlaug and warn her?"

Halmur shook his head. "She eluded me. She knows the upper regions better than I do. Follow me. We'll have to hope she meets us at Heidur's hill. I know another way out."

He moved with no sign of haste; but, once they were into the hallway beyond, he broke into a purposeful trot as if he were on familiar ground. Leifr and Starkad clung to the heels of his fleeting form, guided by the glare of torches thrust into the rough and broken walls at infrequent intervals. Other tunnels branched off, all packed hard and worn smooth by the passage of many Ulf-hedin for many years. Halmur stopped, looking up and down the branching tunnels.

"Are we lost?" asked Starkad.

"Not quite," said Halmur. "There's a bolt hole here somewhere that leads straight to the surface. A little farther, I think, past the fifth-standard kennels."

A series of doorways opened into an area barely lit by a few small fires, glowing like red eyes in the dark. Still, there was enough light to show banners on the walls, orderly rows of shields and swords and other weapons gleaming dully in the scant light. Leifr halted in his tracks.

"Any sword is better than no sword," he said. "I'm going to go steal one."

"Novices aren't allowed to carry swords," Halmur said. "We'll draw less attention as humble young initiates. We'd be expected to be in the wrong place doing something foolish. But not if we're carrying weapons."

"We aren't going to be novices for long," Leifr said. "Just until we get out of this place."

"Be quick then," Halmur whispered. "Oryggi is likely to be

up above with his students, watching the initiations, but he might have given them a night of liberty to celebrate the coming of Brjaladur. Be careful and don't make a sound.''

The kennel was more like a large warren. The ground around the fire pits was worn as smooth as polished marble. A few personal possessions were carefully stowed in small niches in the rock and on natural ledges. Leifr moved along the wall, considering the weapons, while Halmur remained in the corridor beyond as a watchman.

''There's a good one,'' Starkad whispered, pointing down the row. ''Look at that blade. Too long for the average Dokkalfar unless he's a giant among Alfar.''

''That's Oryggi's,'' Hamur said. ''Don't touch it!''

Starkad advanced as he spoke and reached for the sword. His foot connected solidly with a large lump on the ground. The lump instantly leaped into the air with a savage scream and the rattle of a chain. It was an Ulf-hedin, flying right into their faces with snapping jaws and glaring eyes. Fortunately he hit the end of the chain fastened around his neck and fell back with a strangled grunt before he got his claws on Starkad. Then he was up with a resounding roar that awakened the echoes in miles of tunnels.

''Silence, you swine!'' another voice bellowed from nearby, followed by the savage crack of a whip and a yelp of pain. The Ulf-hedin fell back, and the trespassers scuttled away in the shadows.

''Master Oryggi, someone's here!''

''Friends of yours, no doubt,'' Oryggi snarled, lumbering into the rim of the firelight, pulling the wolf snout over his face. He thrust his nose in the air and sniffed loudly. ''I know you're out there,'' he rumbled, ''and you're none of my crew. I can smell you out there, sweating and trembling. Whoever you are, you're messing with Oryggi, and I'll use your guts for garters if I get my hands on you.''

Halmur poked Leifr and motioned down the corridor, pulling him along to follow.

''I should have known he'd have someone detained from the fun,'' he said when they had retreated to a safe distance.

''Do you think he caught a scent of us?'' Starkad asked worriedly. ''Would we smell different?''

"Oryggi's nose is famous for not smelling," Halmur said. "He couldn't smell a wagonload of spoiled fish."

"He might tell someone else that we were here," Leifr said. "Particularly someone who is looking for us. Ulfrin might have alerted Hvitur-Fax by now. Are we almost out of this yet, Halmur?"

"Someone's coming," Starkad whispered. "Listen!"

It was a clamorous rushing sound of trampling feet, interspersed with sharp eager yelps and whimpers and the infrequent cracking of a whip.

"It's a pack coming!" Halmur hissed. "Follow me!"

He pulled the wolf cape over his head, motioning Leifr and Starkad to do the same. Leifr recoiled in horror as Halmur's face altered to that of a wolf and his eyes turned red and livid.

"It won't harm you," Halmur said through the transformation, his eyes glowing. "You have not the wolf belts, nor the curse of eitur running through your blood. The pelt is enchanted; it will help you run faster and longer, and increase your strength."

"You're quite certain it won't try to seize control over us?" Leifr asked, still tugging at the pelt tentatively to get it off his face.

"The pelt alone is no bondage," Halmur replied. "Quick now, we must hurry."

Leifr still muttered and pawed at the pelt, loath to submit to a spell of any nature.

"They're coming!" Starkad exclaimed. "It's too late to outrun them!"

"Stay with me," Halmur said, diving into the shadows. "Do just as I do."

The pack came charging down the corridor with jubilant howls. When they were almost abreast of the fugitives' hiding place, Halmur leaped out with a wild howl of challenge. Leifr and Starkad followed suit, surprising even themselves with the savage howls they uttered. The power of Leifr's lunge carried him right into the faces of the startled leaders, young Ulf-hedin considerably smaller in size. Unable to stop, two of them bowled into him and bounced away in disarray, tripping several others in their rush.

The pack instantly scattered with terified yells, ignoring the shouts, curses, and whip-cracking of their master coming along in the rear.

"What's the meaning of this!" he roared, catching sight of Leifr's larger bulk racing away in the gloom of the tunnel. "I'll have your hides for this! Wait until your master hears about this!"

Halmur snickered, slowing to a trot once they were beyond the scattered pack of younglings.

"It's quite easy to scare the younger lads," he said. "Flogged continually as they are, they get edgy. Strakur will be busy trying to find them for quite a while. Follow me and be quiet. We'll be cutting through some secret places, where novices shouldn't be."

"What kind of places?" Leifr inquired, glancing uneasily from side to side at larger rooms opening up. Columns of stone and earth had been left supporting the overburden, but the columns showed no sign of any marks of tools. They were smooth, symmetrical, free of any design or ornament, as if the wind had carved them.

"The best ones of us are brought here," Halmur said, gazing around the empty halls. "To the best masters, the ones who are true Ulf-hedin, not merely half-savage warriors under the spell of eitur, the expendable fodder of warfare. This is what I hoped for when I became an Ulf-hedin—to become one of the Masters of Chaos one day. But I see it was a foolish dream. I could never become an Exalted One."

"What is a Master of Chaos?" Starkad asked in a hushed voice as they padded through the silent vaulted chambers.

"It's a power of destruction, a control over everything," Halmur said, his voice soft. "You can touch a thing and change it to dust, or make it disappear. Like these rooms and tunnels— they weren't dug out with tools. The Masters use their Chaotic powers, and the earth comes away like steam or mist. They can do the same to people, I've seen it."

"At Skaela-fell, at the initiation ceremony," Leifr said. "Fax made one of the Ulf-hedin seem to be everywhere at once."

"Chaos," Halmur said. "The most clever ones, like Fax, can restore what they've destroyed, but not many of the Masters care about anything except rendering Chaos."

"How do they learn it?" Starkad asked.

"It's very ancient—like the Dokkur Lavardur. Some say the power comes from him."

"What's that sound?" Starkad whispered suddenly.

A whistling, tearing sound was following them down the long dark corridor, moving so fast that it was upon them scarcely had Starkad spoken. A powerful gust of wind blasted dust into their eyes and burned their faces with searing cold. Then it was past, leaving the tunnel almost airless in its wake.

"Hvitur-Fax!" Halmur gasped, when he was able to draw his breath again.

"Fax? What—how—" Leifr sputtered, then he saw by the guttering light of a torch that both of his companions bore the spiral mark in blood on their foreheads. "Marked!" he gasped, rubbing his own forehead frantically. His hand came away smeared with fresh blood.

Chapter 9

Halmur rubbed the spiral off his forehead with a groan.
"What does it mean?" Starkad gasped.

"It means we haven't much time," Halmur retorted. "Ulfrin must have warned Fax somehow. I wager he'll be waiting for us at the hill."

"Was he here?" Starkad stared at the blood on his hand. "How did he do this without being seen?"

"He's only taunting us," Halmur replied angrily. "To him, when he's using the powers of Chaos, we stand in one place like statues. He wants us to know he could have killed us if he had wished. He wants us to be frightened. Come, we've been warned, we'll have to turn back."

"Turn back?" Leifr repeated. "How long have we been wandering around down here? I have the feeling that dawn is not far off, and we're no nearer Heidur's hill than we were standing in the middle of the Ulf-hol. There's not much time left, Halmur."

"We can't press Fax," Halmur said. "I know another way out of Ulf-hol. Follow me and be as quick as you can. These tunnels go beneath all of Hringurhol. Wherever you want to go, you can go underground. Follow me close now, it wouldn't be a good place to get lost." He turned and sped away, with Leifr and Starkad running easily at his heels.

The tunnel eventually widened into an avenue, worn to glassy slickness by the passage of many feet. Several times they encountered Ulf-hedin sauntering along in twos or threes, and they ducked their heads in a servile posture and hurried past without attracting anything more than a few warning growls.

"Don't worry," Halmur panted, "this is a shortcut. We're almost there."

A breath of fresh cool air fanned Leifr's face and he inhaled deeply, gratefully. A few moments more and he could see a dim doorway opening up to the lesser darkness of the sky. Halmur paused in the doorway, his wolf ears pricking alertly as he glanced from side to side. From the sounds rising from behind the great wall, the ceremonies had degenerated into a wild revel. Then he signaled and dashed outside. Leifr and Starkad followed his dark form darting through the rubble that surrounded the Ulf-hol. With amazing strength and power, they scaled walls and ran across the tops, spanning the gaps with incredible leaps. They trotted along the steep rooftree of a large hall, sure-footed with catlike grace and sublime confidence. Leifr looked at the astonishing feat he was performing and felt no fear, only a heady exhilaration. It was no wonder the Ulf-hedin life appealed to so many. With only a little effort, he was able to leap across a wide span between rooftops that would have thwarted an ordinary mortal.

They stopped on the roof of a barn to look back at the Ulf-hol and catch their breath. Starkad flung himself on his back and rubbed his shoulders on the green turf of the roof, chuckling with sheer enjoyment.

"I could be a wolf," he said. "I'll never want to plod along like I used to again. I never imagined what it could be like, having such power."

Halmur's smile was small and grim. "But the price you must pay is far too high. Now that the sun is rising, you're going to lose all that glorious strength. You have no eitur in your blood. Your pelt is becoming nothing but a limp piece of old hide."

"It is!"

The dawnlight was defintely making an attempt to pierce the gloom of the eastern sky. Starkad's pelt fell away from him and he sat up, suddenly clutching for a handhold on his precarious rooftop perch. Leifr threw off the pelt with a sigh of relief, taking care to balance himself carefully on the rooftree.

Pausing a moment on the roof of the last house to listen, Halmur raised his hand warningly. "Someone is following," he whispered. "Follow me quickly now."

A collapsed section of the roof gave access to the hall below, and a crumbling spiral stair led down to the front doors and the courtyard beyond. Halmur bounded down the stairs, easily gliding over the empty spaces where the stair-stones had broken off from their central column. The doors had been blasted off their hinges at some faraway date in history, and subsequent wood

pickers had taken away everything they could pry or chop free
of the great rusted hinges. A troop of wanderers who had taken
shelter in the ruins with their ragged packs and skinny ponies
leaped up in terror at the sight of them, goggling in amazement
at the sight of three Ulf-hedin racing through their encampment
with scarcely a glance right or left.

They took a deeply trodden path, winding upward until they
reached a crumbling wall near the top. A gateway stood open
to the wind and sky, which was beginning to show more pronounced signs of approaching dawn. Halmur halted within the
shelter of the doorway, motioning them to stay low. The courtyard at one time had been securely walled away from outside
intrusion, but now its rugged walls were mostly heaps of fallen
masonry, chinked with moss and tuffets of emerald green grass.
A few goats were grazing on the tops of the remaining walls,
indifferent to the significance of the silent courtyard below. Two
massive doorposts and a great double door prevented access into
the ruins of a towering old hall, and four Ulf-hedin lounged
watchfully in the shadows.

They saw no sign of Svanlaug or Ulfrin. After crouching and
watching for a while, they saw the great door open to emit a
hooded wizard with a staff, for a moment revealing a dim, roofless interior. Ranks of broken columns reached skyward, holding up nothing. Empty windows offered scant light for row upon
row of elaborately carved tombs crowding together on that hal-
lowed ground. The moment the door opened, Leifr sensed a
brooding presence, and it was a singularly evil one. It made his
hairs stand on end, and all his instincts for self-preservation
clamored alarms in a way more unpleasant than simple physical
danger would have done. This evil endangered something more
important than a mere physical body. It was hungry for life
forces, a veritable soul-eater that took the spirit and left the body
a useless husk.

Leifr clenched his hand on the empty place where the hilt of
Endalaus Daudi was supposed to be and backed away, feeling
terribly the loss of that powerful talisman.

The lone wizard hurried away, his feet making insignificant
pattering sounds against the massive monuments of stone. The
Ulf-hedin guards hunched up their shoulders, peering around
desolately. Leifr shuddered at the cold and clammy feeling that

filled the old courtyard like dark water in a forgotten and poisonous well.

"What is this place?" Leifr whispered, noticing Starkad delving about in his ill-assorted clothing for forgotten amulets and lucky pieces.

"A sanctuary for the one whose name does not bear mentioning," Halmur whispered with a significant glance upward at the heaving skyful of lowering cloud. "Offerings are done here to placate the great one."

"Shouldn't there be more than four guards to protect this place?"

"There is no need," Halmur said. "No one wants to go beyond that door. It is the place where the Dokkur Lavardur was bound by the Council's spell-casting. No one even wants to come here—except Ulfrin."

He pointed toward a small doorway giving access to the moldering courtyard, where more memorials stood crumbling and forgotten. A slender shadow stood against the feeble morning light, with a wolf cape dangling rakishly over one shoulder. They followed the shadow of the wall until they were at the edge of the ring of red firelight that bathed the great door and its seals. Ulfrin's face also was bathed with the ruddy light as she gazed at the seals intently. With a reverent gesture, she reached out and touched the one second from the bottom, her face suffused with a pleased smile. When a bit of dry moss crunched under Starkad's foot, she whirled around and stared into the darkness in their direction.

"Who's there? Show yourself," she challenged them. When they moved into the light, she stared, then chuckled delightedly.

"So my sister was too afraid to come," she said, lifting her chin arrogantly. "I am not surprised."

"Svanlaug will arrive," Leifr said.

"You're nothing if not determined, Leifr Thorljotsson. You ought not to have allowed my sister to talk you into this. You don't know the danger."

"I don't know why she cares," Leifr said. "She ought to let you die with Hringurhol."

"Die!" Ulfrin laughed, the sound echoing unpleasantly in the gloomy courtyard. "No one is going to die, except the lot of you for your ill-advised attack on the Council. You must be mad to come here without your sword and without Thurid and the carbuncle.'' Her voice dropped to a lower pitch. "If you were to reveal to me where that stone is, I could get you a pardon from the Council. I could send you to a faraway safe place, a wealthy man.''

"All I want is the destruction of that Pentacle and the Dokkur Lavardur,'' Leifr said. "The rest will follow: Hringurhol, the Council of Threttan, the Ulf-hedin, and anyone else who is foolish enough to get in the way.''

Ulfrin shook her head incredulously. "It simply does not appear that way from where I stand. I am on the side of power and might, and you are nothing but insolent usurpers. And you, Halmur, are going to come to a very bad end as a traitor, which is not to be tolerated among the Ulf-hedin. Perhaps you can convince your masters that you are very young and foolish and were led astray by these intruders. If you are not killed, you shall never hunt with a pack again. Likely, if you are allowed to live, you'll spend the rest of your days chained to a wall somewhere as an example to the others of what can happen.''

"I believe the Scipling is destined to succeed,'' Halmur said. "So I'm not afraid. Come with us now to safety. Your sister awaits. You see who I am. You must know that the Covenant is going to break soon, and all the others will follow.''

"The First Seal,'' Ulfrin said, pointing to the bottommost band and medallion and smiling arrogantly, "is in no way endangered by your rebellion. It is not breaking, as you said. This Seal will stand forever as a covenant between the Council of Threttan and the Dokkur Lavardur. I know how the Seals were made and I know what it will take to break each one. Believe me, the rebellion and loss of one insignificant Ulf-hedin is not enough to imperil the Covenants seriously. Look at them, all five as strong and solid as the finest metal. The Wolf Seal is for the Ulf-hedin, whose loyalty is unquestionable. Next is the Black Sorceress, which is my own Seal, which shall never be broken as long as I have breath and fealty to offer to the Council of Threttan. The Third Seal is the Dragon, vanquished enemies of the Dokkur Lavardur, hunted now to extinction by carbuncle hunters. Fourth is the Seal of the Five Jewels—four of which we already possess, and when we have the fifth, our control of the Dokkur Lavardur will be complete. The Fifth Seal is unknown as yet, but the wisdom of the Council will prevail and a suitable covenant will be offered to the Lord of Chaos. Perhaps you can imagine the power and wisdom that has gone into the forging of these Seals. Perhaps that will convince you that you are nothing to the Council except small irritations, like buzzing gnats, which can do nothing to halt the advance of the Dokkur Lavardur and the Fimbul Winter. It makes no difference what you do. You could not break these Seals, even if you had that Rhbu sword. Too much power and magic courses through them. You would be destroyed if you touched them. Do you not now see how futile your journey has been, how useless it is to resist what has already been done?''

"Hst! Someone's coming!" Halmur said. "I knew she'd take word to Fax or Alfrekar!"

"They would not bother with you," Ulfrin said in lofty contempt. "It's only Svanlaug, at last."

Svanlaug approached warily, her figure wreathed in the rising mist. For a moment the two sisters faced each other in haughty silence.

"I have come to take you home," Svanlaug said. "What would our mother say if she could see you now, abusing the powers you were born with? Our little clan Bergmal is not a prosperous one, but we have our pride. You've done nothing but bring us all shame."

"Shame! Is that what you call it?" Ulfrin retorted. "I call it a glorious opportunity. How else am I to learn, if I stay at Bergmal with women who work with their hands?"

"Our clan has never produced a Sverting before," Svanlaug said. "It's true, we don't know what to do with you. But I assure you, this is not it. A suitable mentor will be found for you, Ulfrin. But only if you come away before it is too late."

"Mentor!" Ulfrin laughed. "Who could be found more suitable than the Council of Threttan?"

"The Council killed our father Afgang, you seem to forget," Svanlaug said. "They are corrupted by the power of the thing they hold captive here—the Dokkur Lavardur. One day it will rule them and all of the Dokkalfar realm. Is that what you want to see?"

"Svanlaug, you're nothing but an old woman," Ulfrin said. "The Council is in no danger, as long as the Five Seals are intact, and I assure you that not even the Dokkur Lavardur can break free of the spells bound into those Seals."

A startling burst of brilliant orange flame pierced the sullen red glow of the brazier's light and threw the entire door into a new and brighter glow. Leifr crouched, suspecting an attack of some sort, but Svanlaug uttered a triumphant cry and pointed to the Seals. A small curl of metal on the First Seal was separating from the rest of the Seal in a fiery burst of light. Ulfrin fell back a pace, her eyes wide in shock, reflecting the brighter glow. After a moment it ceased, leaving a blackened shard of metal curling on the edge of the Seal.

"There you have it," Halmur said. "It is beginning, and I am the beginning of the destruction of the First Seal. How can you doubt any longer?"

Ulfrin tossed her head, but not as arrogantly as before, and cast a nervous glance around the courtyard. "It was only a very small bit," she said in an altered tone. "Hardly enough to break the whole Seal."

"There will be others," Halmur said. "Come with us. If we fail and Hringurhol triumphs, you can always return."

Ulfrin darted another glance at the damaged Seal. "Perhaps we should talk, Svanlaug," she said. "I might have known your jealousy of me was going to cause me grief one day. We must have a place where we won't be disturbed. The old observatory, where we used to play when we were children—although we did more quarreling than playing. Meet me there tonight."

"We shall talk here now, Ulfrin," Svanlaug said. "Unless you were afraid and told someone to follow you here to protect you from us."

"Of course not. I'm a Sverting, am I not? What have I to fear as future black sorceress of the Bjartur clan? I'm not afraid to talk to you. I've got Alfrekar practically following me around on a string, like a pet sheep. I'm not really a member of their Council, but he allows me to sit in the empty seat at his right, mostly to enrage the rest of the Council into fits of the most amusing envy. He wants me to learn about the control of the Dokkur Lavardur. One day I'll be his most powerful ally, he believes, although he hasn't said it in so many words."

"Ally!" Leifr grunted skeptically. "You should beware of flattering words from a man in such a position of power. First they flatter you, then they put you to work for their own purposes."

"I don't believe it," Ulfrin said. "Nothing you can say will convince me. But I find no harm in listening to your side of the argument, being a fair-minded person. Go ahead, speak. Try to convince me.''

"You're nothing but a slave,'' Svanlaug said. "And you're too blinded by your own pride to see it. They're using you to imprison this elemental. They're going to enslave all the Alfar tribes, and you'll be partly to blame, Ulfrin. Break that Seal and come home, before it's too late and you go down in Dokkalfar history as one of the most evil of sorceresses. Come away while you can, Ulfrin.''

"Nonsense, I can leave at any time I wish,'' Ulfrin said, lifting her chin to an arrogant tilt.

A ringing howl came from outside the gate, a desolate sound full of savage triumph. A burst of icy wind gusted at the brazier, flattening its flames. Within the bound door, a powerful roaring sound commenced, far down in the bowels of the earth, like the voice of a mighty wind. Ulf-hedin appeared on the walls around them, their eyes glowing in the the last of the night shadows. A group of cloaked men strode through the crumbling archway and stood at the wary distance from each other that denoted auras of power. The shaggy white mane of Hvitur-Fax glinted in the light of a flaring torch that revealed the cruel, narrow features of Alfrekar. Behind him, surrounded by a slight miasma of fetid smoke, lurked Sorkvir. His ashen countenance had taken on the phosphorescent sheen of a rotting log in a swamp.

"Ulfrin, come away,'' Alfrekar commanded. "You've done your duty very well once again.''

"You betrayed us!'' Svanlaug hissed furiously to Ulfrin. "And me your sister! How could you be so faithless? This will destroy all ties to the Bergmal clan—as if your filthy Ulf-hedin cape weren't enough! Now you'll have my death and Leifr's to account for!''

"But this isn't what I intended,'' Ulfrin protested, turning to Svanlaug in desperate appeal.

Svanlaug peeled her searing glare off Ulfrin to confront the wizards making their wary way into positions of advantage around their prey. "Stop where you are!'' she commanded in a voice that awakened the echoes. "As one who had broken bread with you and been your guest in this hall, I demand the protection of this roof by the laws of Alfar guest right. Let no harm befall me nor my companions, or may this place be cursed by guests who come to plunder and kill. If our blood is shed in this place by your hands, let it cry out for vengeance until the third generation has passed.''

Sorkvir snorted, but the others stopped in their tracks, making signs to ward off evil influences. ''Bah! She can't curse us. She's got no real power,'' Sorkvir sneered.

Alfrekar replied, ''She's Afgang's daughter, and she's invoked the law of guest right. That's plenty of power—enough for us to be careful. You're not beyond being careful, I should hope, merely because your blood is nothing but dust.''

''There's no one to avenge them,'' Sorkvir protested harshly, gripping his staff. ''The Scipling is an outcast in this realm, and the Bergmal woman has been banished from her clan. Keep them alive, perhaps, until you've got Thurid and the orb in your hand, but none of them can be allowed to live after seeing what they have seen.''

''You forget about Prestur,'' Svanlaug said. ''I've been signed over to my father's clan. They'll still be smarting over my father's death. News will reach them, and they will lead the attack that brings the downfall of your scheme.''

''We paid them well for Afgang,'' one of the wizards at Alfrekar's back muttered.

''But they'd be glad for an excuse to come after us anyway,'' another voice added. ''Give them the protection of guest right, Alfrekar.''

''We can't afford to be arrogant now,'' someone else said. ''It might mean the complete downfall of it all.''

''Guest right is a powerful spell,'' another murmured.

Alfrekar raised his arms to still the growing tide of mutters and complaints. ''Very well, I will grant them the protection of guest right. See to it that none of you cause harm to our guests, lest you bring her curse against us. They will depart from here only with our blessings.''

''Old women,'' Sorkvir growled, smothering a small ember burning in his cheek.

''Your greed has cost us enough, Sorkvir,'' Alfrekar said, barely containing the fury within his raddled carcass. ''I'll brook no more of your interference. Besides the sword, precious time has been lost because of you, as well as two of my most skillful counselors. Djofull's plot against Afgang cost Djofull his life. And how long do you think the fumes of eitur will preserve you, as you are? That leaves only nine of us, when you are gone. I don't have Djofull's knowledge or skill at robbing Hela. A pity Djofull was too jealous to share his knowledge with anyone, except you, and I daresay half what he told you was deception. Nothing has worked out as you planned. If we fail to obtain Galdur's orb now, with it nearly in our grasp, we may never get another chance. We may not last through the summer until Samhain."

He turned to Ulfrin next and continued, "Ulfrin, this is not a good place for you to come alone. I don't know why you agreed to meet these outlaws here, but I am not pleased by it."

"I can go about by myself if I choose," Ulfrin retorted. "I get weary of you or Fax treading at my heels and seeing everything I do."

"These outlaws are dangerous rebels," Alfrekar said. "Luckily I saw them and followed. What if you came to harm at their hands?"

"I am not afraid of them," Ulfrin snapped. "You seriously underestimate my powers to defend myself."

"I think not," Alfrekar said. "I am concerned only for your safety. I demand that you keep yourself apart from them, even though Svanlaug is your sister." He turned to Leifr with a cold stare, including Halmur. "Guest right is declared. You and your company are free to go wherever you choose in Hringurhol, but remember Ulf-hedin are very likely to get carried away after a fresh dose of eitur, and Brjaladur approaches. I wouldn't want our guests to come to any harm at the hands of any rogue Ulf-hedin." He gave Halmur another sinister glower.

"Thank you for your hospitality—and the warning," Leifr said. "We don't intend to stay long."

"And Fax, take the Sverting with you and escort her to her rooms, lest some other whim seize hold of her."

"What about that one?" Fax demanded, darting a lowering glare toward Halmur, who returned it with the bristling defiance bred of fear and desperation. "Shall I take him and make an example of him?"

"Not just yet," Alfrekar said contemptuously. "We shall study him, Fax, when we have the leisure."

He turned and stalked away to contemplete the Five Seals, taking the other wizards of the Council with him, while Leifr's party edged warily toward the gate. Sorkvir stood and glowered back at Leifr, as if he were meditating some way to get around the law and curse of guest right to do some harm to his enemy.

Ulfrin's voice, upraised in protest, followed them, and Svanlaug looked back, her hair seething around her shoulders. "We've lost her!" she muttered.

"Now go away, Fax," Ulfrin was saying, "and quit troubling me. You shouldn't be missing the initiations. I'm going back there myself as soon as you get these outlaws out of my way."

"I am anxious to see to your well being," Fax said. "I shall accompany you back to your rooms at once. It is Alfrekar's orders."

"I do not wish to go to my rooms," Ulfrin said. "And you can tell Alfrekar I said so. I shall watch the rest of the initiations."

"I am sorry," Fax said, "but I must obey Alfrekar first despite your wishes."

"Fax, I thought we were friends," Ulfrin said.

"So we are, lady sorceress, but that is all," Fax replied. "Alfrekar is the master, and all Ulf-hedin must obey him. Now come away."

Warily they descended the path from Heidur's ruins to the settlement below, clustering around the walls of the Council Hall and the Ulf-hol like scrofulous growths. Svanlaug led them to a ruined house to shelter for the night.

"This used to be my father's house," she said bitterly, looking around at the damp and ruin that had intruded. "I've lost him, and now my sister."

"Why do you care about her?" Starkad demanded with a hearty shaking of his shoulders, as if to rid himself of a burden. "She's completely evil, Svanlaug. She can't see what she's got herself into."

"She's my sister," Svanlaug said. "I don't want to put my life on the line for her, but I have to. It's born in the blood that clans protects their own. You'd do the same for Ermingerd, wouldn't you?"

"Yes, I'd gladly die to defend her, but Ermingerd is not at all like Ulfrin," Starkad said virtuously.

With the rising of the sun, Hringurhol and the revels at the Ulf-hol quieted. Leifr dozed intermittently and without much satisfaction; his sleep was plagued by dreams and images that tormented him like half-forgotten answers to riddles dangling

just beyond his conscious grasp. Near sundown he was awakened by the officious departure of Svanlaug for the market stalls
of Hringurhol.

"You're quite certain it's safe enough?" Leifr grumbled.

"Certainly," she retorted. "I'm a Dokkalfar, aren't I? Most
of the people in Hringurhol are Dokkalfar, and more trustworthy
than any Ljosalfar who has deliberately chosen such a life."

"You'll come directly back?" Leifr went on. "You're not
going to search for Ulfrin again, are you?"

Svanlaug tossed her hair. "For the moment, no, I'm not going
to look for Ulfrin. I've got more immediate responsibilities,
such as seeing to it we all don't starve. I'd thought that if I went
to the market, it wouldn't attract as much attention as you would,
lurking around and looking completely like a barbarian Scipling."

"Go then, but not alone," Leifr said. "Take Starkad and
Halmur with you in case you get into a tight situation."

"I don't need an escort," Svanlaug answered haughtily. "I
believe you're not so worried about my safety, Leifr, as you're
worried that I might do something while I'm out of your sight."

"It's enemy territory," Leifr said. "Only a fool would go
into it alone."

With ill grace, Svanlaug conceded and allowed Starkad and
Halmur to accompany her, provided they kept their distance.

While they were gone, Leifr sat with Fridmarr's carbuncle in
the palm of his hand, concentrating as he never had before.

"Tell me what I should do, Fridmarr!" he silently implored.
"I need your help!"

As he was struggling to hear some kind of message, he heard
something scratching at the door. Instantly he leaped up to peer
out through a crack and met the pale stare of an eye trying to
peer within.

"Halloa, Scipling!" a familiar voice called.

"Vidskipti!" Leifr opened the door and Vidskipti hurried inside, pulling it shut after him.

"I brought you something to restore your strength," the trader
said, placing a jug of fresh milk on the table and producing a
loaf of warm bread from under his cloak.

The bread was the best Leifr had ever tasted, and all he could
manage for a reply was a grunt and an appreciative rolling of
his eyes. A long swig of the milk from a cup proffered by Vid-

skipti freed up his throat somewhat so he could speak, so he said, "What's happening out there, Vidskipti? Tell us and be quick about it."

"Clever lad!" Vidskipti said. "You've already determined that I come not with merely gifts for your deglutition, but to inform you of a circumstance that will astonish and alarm you. You've observed the Ulf-hedin donning their disgusting disguises and scurrying about like the rats that they truly are, riding to and fro with ridiculous self-importance. They, too, are astonished and alarmed, I can well assure you, and rightly so, considering their origins in the foulest, most vile dark sorcery ever devised by the most warped and crazed minds seeking to do the rest of the world the most outrageous villainy, having a profound sense of their own unworthiness and no desire to anything but the worst evil—"

"Speak, Vidskipti," Leifr interrupted impatiently, growing more choleric and each tortured phrase formed by Vidskipti's lips. "Your alarming circumstance will be upon us before you get all the words spat out. Now what is it? What's going to happen?"

Vidskipti pursed his lips a moment, as if more eloquence was bursting to get out, but he restrained himself in an admirable fashion. He said portentously, "It's some old acquaintances of yours and Thurid's. They've smelled you out somehow and followed you, but knowing of them, I can't claim an overwhelming amount of astonishment. Their talents at seeking and finding are legendary, their determination to find their quarry equal to that of wolves in midwinter, their knowledge of—" Seeing Leifr's expression slowly darkening, he finished hastily. "It's the Inquisitors, Leifr, and they're coming up this side of the river from Haeta-fell."

Chapter 10

◇◇

Leifr paced to the window and back, scowling in agitation. "The Inquisitors!" he groaned, almost unable to believe his bad luck. "I thought they decided to let Thurid go! I thought they were done with him!"

"As I was going to say," Vidskipti replied, "their determination is unequaled in the two realms, perhaps even in the three realms, and once they've got a prey in mind, they can't be shaken off it any more than your troll-hounds could be shaken off a troll once they've got their teeth all into it. They might have pretended to let him go, but it was probably a mere ruse to see where he would lead them. Which reminds me of something— we all thank you for what you did for poor old Vonbrigdi. He was most pleased to return and die among his own kind, few of them as there are, but it was a great comfort to him nonetheless to be released from the hold of the Fire Wizards' Guild."

"We couldn't have escaped without him," Leifr said. "Since you know what hideous things happen to Rhbus held under the dominion of the Guild, I'm sure you've no intention of allowing Thurid to fall into their hands. We've got to get him out of the knacker-women's house at once, Vidskipti, before the Inquisitors divine his presence. When I saw him last, he was in no condition to defend himself."

"Not to worry," Vidskipti said with an airy and somewhat drunken sketching of one hand. "No one dares to go contrary-wise of the knacker-women. They've got an undeservedly bad reputation in these parts, I fear, and for no good reason I can think of except they like to pick up dead bodies and cook them down into something useful for man or beast, but as I was about to say, you needn't worry about Thurid, either. He's quite all right, skeptic that he is. Besides, he's not there, he's here in Hringurhol. Answered the third summons from the Council—"

"Thurid's here?" Leifr interrupted. "Why didn't you say so before? What summons did he answer?"

"Yes, yes, I was getting to it, what with the Inquisitors and all." Vidskipti mopped his face with an oily rag, looking very anxious. "He's here, summoned to the Council Hall to answer the accusations of the Council of Threttan. He came across with the knacker-women. They came over with their cart to fetch the carcasses the Ulf-hedin heaped up during their initiation ceremonies—a disgusting ritual if ever I've seen one, but I assure you Brjaladur is far worse, and you don't want to see it for yourself, and you won't either if you are—"

"In the Council Hall?" Leifr repeated, aghast. "Why did he go there? Is he a prisoner? Have they got the orb from him? Is he all right?"

"I fear I can't answer any of that," Vidskipti said, blinking his eyes in an injured expression. The old trader pursed up his lips and his eyes slid away obliquely to peruse the ceiling, and Leifr realized his direct questioning was an affront and a danger to the old wanderer. "I really must be going before I'm seen here. It wouldn't go well for any of us wanderers, I'm afraid, if I were."

Leifr groaned. "I thought the knacker-women told me he'd be smarter when he got back from wherever they thought he'd gone to!"

"I don't know where that might be, except behind their barn in the icehouse, where they keep fresh carcasses from time to time," Vidskipti said, his eyes wide and innocent.

"I could go and speak for him," Leifr said, harrowing up his hair with his hands. "In my own realm, friends of the guilty are allowed that much. How can I get into the Council Hall, Vidskipti?"

Vidskipti paused, his eyes darting around warily. For a moment he shook off his oblique, sliding, slinking trader manner and he looked at Leifr directly. "Don't worry yourself about getting into the Council Hall to speak for Thurid," he whispered rapidly. "You'll get your chance. You're going to be summoned to the Council Hall yourself at sundown. Someone is on the way to fetch you."

Leifr strode up and down the length of the room, rapidly deciding whether or not to make his escape before the summons arrived. Vidskipti divided his attention between Leifr and the door, sidling toward one then the other. In a burst of confidence he said, "Don't worry, Leifr. I have a feeling you're going to make it. Of course I felt that way about Fridmarr and Gedvondur, too, but I greatly fear that both of them have come to rather undesirable circumstances. I hope your luck is a bit better than theirs, Leifr."

"Whether it is or not will soon be proven," Leifr said exasperatedly, tightening the laces of his boots. "If I had my sword, I wouldn't have to worry about my luck." He darted Vidskipti a hopeful glance.

"You don't need a sword," Vidskipti said, giving Leifr a wink, or perhaps it was a nervous twitch. "You're protected under the laws of guest right until Brjaladur. You don't need me with you, either, to do what you must do. You wouldn't want to be seen with an old traveling trader such as I, lest idle tongues begin to wag and suspicious eyes be turned upon the wanderers' camp. We have no privilege of guest right; the Ulf-hedin can turn upon us at any time they wish. I wish it were not so, but it is the life we are accustomed to, such as it is."

Leifr automatically reached for the empty space where he gripped the hilt of his sword. He clenched his fist and knit his brows together dubiously as he considered. "I'm going to get Thurid out of there, so he'll be safe from all of them. At least I've still got one use of the ring and the Name you gave me."

"Save them, my lad," Vidskipti said, leaning forward, his voice sinking even lower. "You'll be needing them later. You have a slight degree of help you receive from Fridmarr's carbuncle. Now, if you were to implant it properly, you would be given another advantage. The knacker-women are clever at such things. They could do it very quickly right now, and you'd be ready to go into that Hall, and you'd have Fridmarr's help instead of being all alone. It can be removed any time, if you should wish it."

Leifr withdrew slightly from Vidskipti's intense gaze, considering, wavering over the choice. As usual, at the last analysis, he shied away from the Alfar carbuncle with all his inbred Scipling suspicion of unknown powers. He had the uneasy feeling that once he had experienced carbuncle powers, he might not want to relinquish them.

"No, I can do it without the carbuncle," he said with a shake of his shoulders. "I must go alone."

"Well then, I must be away," Vidskipti said briskly, rubbing his hands together in his usual trader manner and sidling away. "At least the arrival of the Inquisitors was good for business. I had my cart in a very good position. Everyone turned out for a look at them. Visitors from the Fire Wizards' Guild—that's something you don't expect to see every day in Hringurhol."

As he talked, Vidskipti sidled nearer to the door, and the moment he was finished he saluted Leifr with a jaunty gesture and vanished among the surrounding ruins.

Svanlaug and the others returned from their expedition into the cooking and market stalls of Hringurhol, carrying a large basket. Svanlaug went on berating Starkad over some imagined offense, and Halmur skulked wolfishly behind them, his expression alert as he scanned the surrounding ruins for signs of trouble.

"Something important has happened," he said to Leifr uneasily, passing one hand through the air to test for influences. "The Inquisitors of the Fire Wizards' Guild have arrived. They're with the Council at this moment, and the doors are locked and under guard. Rumor has it that Thurid's answered the Council's third summons."

"I've heard," Leifr said. "I'm expecting to be summoned myself at any moment. At any rate, I'm going to speak out for Thurid."

Svanlaug did not hear their low conversation, but her eyes fastened at once upon Leifr, reading his taut expression and the determined motions of his readying ritual, consisting of adjusting his boot laces, tightening his belt, and tossing his cloak over his shoulder out of the way of his sword arm. Nor could he restrain himself from reaching for the sword in its accustomed place at his shoulder, although he knew it was not there. Her sharp eyes missed none of this, including his grim, white-lipped expression.

"Where do you think you're going?" she demanded, coming around the table to look directly into his face. "We just got back with the food."

"Thurid's been summoned and I'm going to speak for him," Leifr said tightly. "Now don't get in my way. I've got only a short while until sundown to ready myself. I wish to be left alone for a while to think about it, if you don't mind."

"Well, I do mind," Svanlaug said. "How did you find out

about Thurid? Who told you? How do you know you were told
the truth? You should know there's no one in Hringurhol you
can trust!"

"It was Vidskipti," Leifr said, "and nothing you can say or
do is going to change my mind. Thurid's defending himself
against their accusations in the Council Hall at this moment,
and the Inquisitors and the Council are ready to do battle over
who gets their hands on him first. I've got to go help him."

"Vidskipti! That old vagabond! You've lost your senses!"
Svanlaug said, seizing a handful of her own hair.

"Vidskipti, the Rhbu?" Starkad gasped, his eyes growing
wide and fascinated. "Leifr, I want to come with you."

"He's not a Rhbu," Svanlaug snapped. "He's a drunken hoax,
taking advantage of gullible Sciplings!"

"And I'll come with you, too," Halmur said. "You have
friends. You don't have to face the Council and the Inquisitors
alone, Leifr."

"You can't possibly face the Council uninvited and unan-
nounced," Svanlaug declared. "That little scrounger is probably leading you into a trap. Someone probably paid him. Why
should you believe anything he says? What if those knacker-
women have put him up to some ridiculous scheme for their own
benefit? People have a way of trying to hitch rides upon our
purpose that threatens to bury our original intentions for coming
to Hringurhol."

"You must be speaking of yourself and Ulfrin, who doesn't
want to be rescued," Leifr said.

Svanlaug folded her arms and regarded him haughtily down
the length of her nose. "A way will be found to rescue Ulfrin
from her delusions," she said. "I'm no more ready to give up
on her than you're ready to give up on Thurid, Leifr. Not until
you've found your sword and freed Ljosa from her spell and
leveled Hringurhol and the Dokkur Lavardur to the ground. I
don't think that is too much to expect, as long as I'm able to
save my sister somehow. Now if everyone is ready, I suggest we
repair to the Council Hall at once. It is very nearly sundown."
She elevated her chin belligerently and met his eye with discon-
certing determination. A faint breeze stirred her raven hair, and
Starkad and Halmur added their own growls of affirmation.

Leifr could see there was no dissuading them, and he was

pierced by a sudden surge of hope and gratitude for such devoted friends.

"I wish I could take you with me where I'm going," he said. "Your friendship would lend me great courage. But I fear I cannot."

He had scarcely spoken the words when the shaky door thundered under an imperious knocking.

"Leifr Thorljotsson Scipling!" a voice rumbled. "The Council of Threttan has sent for you. Open this door and accompany us at once to the Council Hall."

Leifr opened the door to Hvitur-Fax and six hulking Ulf-hedin who were almost the size of Raudbjorn.

"The Council of Threttan wishes to speak to you," Fax said. "You need fear no harm from us or from them, until Brjaladur commences. Follow me and be quick about it. The Council is waiting."

"Is Thurid there?" Leifr demanded.

"He is," said Fax. "He has already heard the Council's demands, and they have heard his. They await your presence. Alone," he added warningly when Svanlaug stepped forward challengingly. She glared at him a moment in defiance, then looked away from his cold Ulf-hedin eyes.

"Remember the guest-right curse, Hvitur-Fax," she said. "Should something happen to Leifr, you will pay the penalty."

The tortured winding ways of Hringurhol were crowded with carts of merchants, wanderers, traveling wizards, and all the rest of the vile stew of skulking characters that cleaved to a place such as Hringurhol. Bands of Ulf-hedin from the tops of the ruins, searching for higher vantage points. A hundred pairs of eyes watched Leifr and his companions proceed from Afgang's house toward the Council Hall.

In a short while they were skirting the Ulf-hol and the grisly bone façade, the gibbets with their rotting carcasses, and the pile of the corpses of candidates who were judged unworthy of the Ulf-hedin curse. A cart was backed up to the heap, and a drab little figure in a brown cloak was supervising the loading of the bodies by a couple of dejected-looking thralls being overseen by a pair of indifferent Ulf-hedin.

Leifr's heart gave a jolt as he recognized Beitski and her sisters. He looked away and pretended to be uninterested, but the sharp senses of Hvitur-Fax had been alerted. He might have even heard his heartbeat knocking a little faster.

"The knacker-women's cart has frightened better men than you," he said, gazing intently at Leifr with his cold wolf's eyes. "And it has hauled them away, too, like refuse, to their rendering fires. This is not even your own people's quarrel. Wouldn't you rather be out of it?"

"I don't think that's possible now," Leifr said.

The Council Hall was one of the better halls still standing in Hringurhol, hung with dozens of rusting shields, prow pieces of ships, and other war trophies half swallowed by the moss chinking the stones and turves. Inside the massive front gates was a lofty courtyard faced on all sides by towering walls and windows. On the sides were the stables and servants' quarters, and rooms for guests, retainers, and resident fighting men. At one time it had been a grand and efficient arrangement, but now it had fallen into sad ruin, only partially habitable, and what parts were habitable were occupied by the roughest sort of villains and wanderers who could be found and pressed into Alfrekar's service. Only one-quarter of the grand hall retained a portion of its former dignity. Massive doors stood locked and barred, with six Ulf-hedin standing guard before them.

The gloomy yard of the Council Hall was crowded with restless Ulf-hedin, lesser wizards, charlatans, and skulking wanderers. Many stopped at a safe distance to observe Leifr being escorted under guard into the Council Hall. One of the wizards of the Council stood upon the steps, flanked by a row of apprentices, as he solemnly read aloud in a rolling monotone from a vellum.

"The first summons of the Council of Threttan calls the Scipling Leifr Thorljotsson into the Council Hall to answer certain accusations of the Council and to redress certain wrongs deemed necessary by the Council for the protection of Hringurhol and its surrounding settlements. Anyone hearing these words who produces or induces the one summoned to appear will receive a suitable reward for his services."

Hvitur-Fax called out, "The one summoned has arrived of his own free will. The first summons of the Council has been answered."

"Then you may bring him into the hall." The wizard scrutinized Leifr a moment, then rolled up his vellum and turned, entering the dark doorway of the great hall. The wagering booths were jammed with a sudden spate of business as the sporting fellows took bets on the likelihood of Leifr's coming out again. The Ulf-hedin crowded around for a closer look at Leifr, growling and brandishing weapons and prancing around in a fearsome display as if to intimidate him if they could with their half-beast appearance. The six big Ulf-hedin ignored them with supreme contempt, and the moment Hvitur-Fax turned his head, the bravado of the Ulf-hedin instantly diminished into slinking and snarling from a safe distance.

Hvitur-Fax motioned the guards at the doors aside with a slight gesture and the doors were opened before him. Leifr walked behind him, trying not to look like a captive slinking at the heels of his captor.

The interior of the hall was almost completely dark, but he was able to tell it was a massive place, with the bulk of it sunken below the present surface of the earth, as if it had been there long enough to see the remains of lesser buildings falling down around it for many centuries. A mighty domed turf roof was supported by a lacework of arches, buttresses, and fragile-looking pillars, its surface pierced at intervals by enough windows and breakage to admit a dim perpetual twilight to the floor far below. The entire hall was almost completely taken up with burial vaults and sepulchers, except for a raised dais in the center, where a couple of fires burned and Alfrekar and his Council of Threttan awaited Leifr. The ten surviving wizards of the Council were there, seated in chairs variously carved with symbols of power, enchantment, and death. Across from them were seated the Inquisitors, with Thurid in the center of them. The Inquisitors gazed upon him with scowls of disapprobation, and Thurid's expression was as tight as a clam's, his eyes narrowed to let in the least possible light.

Ulfrin, too, was there, sitting primly in a high seat of her own on the left side of Alfrekar. She avoided looking at Leifr and kept her head well elevated, gazing beyond him with an expression of lofty contempt.

Alfrekar wore his ritual headdress with its snake symbols twining among bits of bone, amulets, and tassels of fur. He raised aloft his staff, spewing tendrils of mist, and slowly passed one hand through the air.

"The Council of Threttan has summoned you, Leifr Thorljotsson Scipling,'' he intoned. ''You have been summoned here to speak to the Council concerning certain crimes committed against the Dokkalfar clans. You are involved with the wizard Thurid in a sordid crime that took place at Fangelsi in Hraedsladalur—the murder of a black dwarf smith and the theft of the valuable blue jewel he was forging magical spells upon. What concerns you is the possession of a certain sword that was wrongfully taken from the Dokkalfar holding called Bjartur.''

''Wrongfully taken according only to those who didn't want it taken,'' Leifr said. ''As to Heldur, he was keeping the helpless descendants of Slagfid in thrall to a terrible spell of no purpose except his own wicked revenge. He died as a consequence of his own evil deeds. He would have destroyed us if we had not defended ourselves. Our intention was to destroy the spell he was binding Slagfid's heirs with, and he was destroyed when he plunged into the fire of the forge to seize the orb.''

''You cannot deny that you possess the cursed sword *Endalaus Daudi*,'' Alfrekar pursued.

''No, I don't deny it,'' Leifr said. ''I have committed no crime by possessing it, although I can see that you might not have wanted it brought here.''

''On the contrary,'' Alfrekar said. ''A greater fate than all of us here has brought the sword *Endalaus Daudi* into Hringurhol at this propitious season. I am pleased to have it so nearly in my possession.''

He leaned back slightly in his chair, his eyes elevated toward the distant roof timbers, wreathed in trailing streamers of smoke. At once the temperature of the hall dropped, and Leifr was conscious of something vast and dark heaving across the high domed ceiling far above their heads. Alfrekar's aspect stiffened and changed as if a shadow had settled over him, much as Thurid changed when Gedvondur was speaking through him. His eyes rolled back unseeing, and his teeth chattered slightly in the grip of a powerful rictus.

''Who is this man?'' Alfrekar demanded in a hissing voice that carried easily over the interval of tombs in between. His sunken eyes were nothing but shadow to Leifr at that distance, but he could feel them probing at him. ''He has the form and aspect of that insinuating, treacherous Fridmarr, but there is something wrong about him. A rift between fact and appearance makes us think he's not what he seems. He is a stranger in our realm.''

"I'm Leifr Thorljotsson, the Scipling," Leifr answered, speaking into the brittle hush that filled the great hall. He scanned the rigid features of Alfrekar, drawn back in a grimace, unseeing eyes rolled upward. "Alfar call us the New People."

"Yes, the Scipling," the entity said. "I have watched his approach and brooded upon it. A lone man has come to Hringurhol, carrying the carbuncle of the luckless Fridmarr and the cursed sword of the Rhbus. And where he is, the orb of Galdur is not far behind. Beware, you wizards of the dark. The time of the wolf and raven is approaching, and ordinary means will not stop it. Free me and I will put an end to it. I will put an end to them all, and nothing will remain except darkness and ice."

Alfrekar flicked one hand faintly, his lips barely moving as he spoke. "I command you to depart," he whispered. "The Council rules the Lord of Chaos."

"Only for now," the being snarled. "What else have you to offer me?"

As suddenly as it had come, the entity departed. Alfrekar collapsed into his chair, mopping his brow with his sleeve, ashen-faced.

"Our doom has been foretold," he said grimly, casting his eye down the table at each member of the Council. "You have heard it. More must be given to keep the Dokkur Lavardur under our control."

"The Scipling must be killed," Sorkvir rasped, stepping forward in avaricious haste, his eyes burning like two embers. "I myself have brought him here like a sheep for slaughter. Hroaldsdottir has drawn him here of his own will and more surely than any binding that I could devise. Success is very near, my lord."

"I think not," Leifr said. "Kill me if you wish, but another will fill my place. As long as *Endalaus Daudi* exists, a hand will be found for its hilt."

"True words, Leifr Thorljotsson," Alfrekar said. "As long as a single Rhbu clansman exists, we will be plagued by that sword. We are most eager to welcome you into our fortress, to speak with you about the affairs that concern us mutually."

"What is there to discuss?" Leifr inquired. "We are enemies, and I am destined to destroy you."

Alfrekar pursed his dry lips tightly, like an old miser's money sack. "That is a matter for serious argument," he said. "You haven't got your sword now, but I have no doubt you'll manage to get your hands upon it somehow, and soon. You have certain friends in this place, I regret to say. Before your guest right runs out and Brjaladur begins, I wish to make you a bargain.''

''A bargain?'' Leifr repeated warily. ''Only the losers ask to make bargains.''

''Ulfrin, you may show him,'' Alfrekar said.

''Come this way,'' Ulfrin said with a resentful glance at Alfrekar as she stepped off the dais and approached a nearby tomb. ''I believe there's something in this sarcophagus that you'll like to see. She was brought here by Sorkvir in the form of a small gray cat. He wanted a safe place to store her, so Alfrekar said to put her here, knowing that you would soon follow.''

As she talked, she pushed off the cover and glanced up at Leifr, who stood as if frozen to the ground. Then he took a tentative step closer, and two long swift strides to peer into the tomb with wild hopes only half strangled.

It was Ljosa, dressed in her wedding red trimmed with white ermine fur, her pale, fine hair curling softly around her pale countenance in airy tendrils.

''She's a Ljosalfar,'' Ulfrin said with a certain air of pride, as if she had originally discovered Ljosa. ''If this is the way their women look, they're all certainly a pale and sickly lot, aren't they? Her hair is almost white.''

Gently he brushed Ljosa's cheek with his hand. She was alive; her skin was cool and soft and her breath was warm as she uttered a little sigh.

''Ljosa!'' he murmured, still half disbelieving.

''Ah! So this is the chieftain's daughter,'' Ulfrin said, nodding her head. ''I heard the tale from Svanlaug. What a lot of trouble she's caused you—and you her.''

''I thought I'd killed her at Bergmal,'' Leifr said in a whisper, more to himself than anyone else. ''She was dressed like an Ulfhedin, and it was very like the outfit you're wearing now, Ulfrin. How would you explain that?''

Ulfrin shrugged elaborately. ''It was me. Alfrekar told me I should do it. Sorkvir said that killing the girl would either break your resolve or destroy your caution to the extent that you'd come charging into Hringurhol for revenge. I was in no danger. You didn't really slice off my head; it was only an illusion, like her face. But you didn't seem to get as angry as they thought you would. They thought you cared about this girl more than anything, Leifr. But you are here, aren't you, and that's what they wanted."

"Yes, I am here," Leifr said, raising his eyes to hers with deadly calm. "And I don't like being tricked and led about by anyone."

"Don't blame me," Ulfrin said hastily. "I only did it for a lark. I didn't know what a serious business it was."

"Ulfrin, you never know how serious anything is," Leifr said.

Alfrekar pressed his hands together. "You see, you have something to lose if Hringurhol is destroyed. We must make a bargain, Scipling. We each possess that which the other wants. Strike me a bargain and you can take the maiden and turn your back upon Hringurhol forever. What I must have is *Endalaus Daudi* and the blue carbuncle taken from Heldur's forge. Bring them to me, or I fear the chieftain's daughter will die."

Leifr stood silent, his wits at a standstill. Some of the Council wizards were smirking confidently, some glowered. The Inquisitors were thoughtful and worried. Someone cleared his throat with a rasping sound. All eyes looked down the length of the table as Thurid rose to his feet.

"The matter of the missing sword," he said, after a moment of thoughtful scowling around at the wizards and Inquisitors, "raises great concern. Where is it now? Who has it? Someone stole it from the thief-takers and we have heard nothing of it since. There will be no talk of bargaining until we find out where the sword is and regain possession of it. I have my theories that its location may be known by someone in this hall, who is waiting to use it for his own best interest. Someone, perhaps a member of the Council."

"A powerful accusation," Alfrekar said. "One that you'd better be prepared to stand behind with something more than Scipling iron."

"I am prepared," Leifr said in a voice of deadly calm. "I have been given a Name and a ring of power by the all-powerful Rhbus. I also know the name of the traitor in your midst, who is most likely the one who has possession of *Endalaus Daudi* at this moment. For that name, I'm sure you'll release Hroaldsdottir."

The Council wizards muttered and nodded like a pack of dogs snarling over a bone. Alfrekar made a baleful rasping sound in his throat and his yellowish eye traveled around the ranks of the Council, flickering here and there briefly like the tail of a whip, causing consternation wherever it lingered. "That someone," Alfrekar said, "is a traitor to the Council of Threttan. When the moment comes, the traitor will pay the price. His name is also known to me, so I'm afraid you have no bargaining tool, Scipling."

In the rigid silence, Sorkvir scuffled briefly around in his capacious sleeve, pounding at something rather desperately like a dog with a biting flea. With a puff of smoke, a small curl of blue flame appeared on the back of Sorkvir's emaciated hand. Swiftly the wizard extinguished the flame, but the light of desperation remained in his sunken eye as he surged to his feet and leaned across the table.

"All of you are fools," Sorkvir snarled, "sitting here with your pious faces around this table, as if you were truly interested in striking a bargain with these enemies. We have no need of striking bargains with anyone. We have the Lord of Chaos very nearly under our control. Heldur's orb—or Galdur's orb—is within our grasp. You are wasting precious time, if all is to be complete before Brjaladur is done. We must have that orb, and we shall have it, and woe to anyone who attempts to stand in the way of the Council!"

"Time is growing short, eh, Sorkvir?" one of the Council whispered gleefully, a rat-faced individual with a bristling red beard. "Djofull can't hold you together now, but the orb will, is that it?"

"I wouldn't tell you where it is, Sorkvir, even if I knew," Leifr replied disdainfully, including the Inquisitors in his statement with a sweeping glance.

"Sit down, Sorkvir," Alfrekar commanded peremptorily, with a veiled glower in his direction. "I'll tolerate no more interruptions." He turned back to Leifr and Thurid. "Let us get on with our negotiations. The time for pride and revenge is past now. It's boiled down to a simple matter of rightful possession of Heldur's orb and *Endalaus Daudi*. You have no right to that sword. It is ours and must be returned to us before Brjaladur, or Hroaldsdottir will die."

Chapter 11

◇◇

Sorkvir leaped to his feet, facing Thurid across the table. "We must have that crystal, if we have to pry the secret out of them with hot tongs! Do you want all our labors to be for naught? Afgang and Djofull and the others to have died for absolutely nothing? Before long you'll be adding me to that list, and what do you think Hela will do to someone who has cheated her seven times?"

His wrath and fear seemed to generate the self-destructive fires lurking in his borrowed body. Small flames burst out on the backs of both hands. He quickly stifled the combustion, but his cronies on the Council drew away with expressions of horror and disgust, and the Inquisitors made subtle signs for repelling evil.

Alfrekar chuckled unpleasantly. "You and Djofull should have thought of that before you started your hideous little experiments with immortality. You're coming full circle, Sorkvir, and there's nothing anyone can do to help you. Now calm yourself, or you'll bring on your destruction much sooner than necessary."

"It wouldn't be necessary at all, if I had that orb!" Sorkvir shouted, whirling around to glare first at Leifr, then at Thurid in helpless fury.

"You won't get it as long as I can help it," Leifr replied. "Nothing would please me more than watching you burn up like a heap of rotten trash. It would have been done long ago, when I destroyed you the first time, if not for Djofull and his interference."

"Nothing would please *me* more than taking you with me to Hel!" Sorkvir snarled, starting to reach with his blackened hand for his staff lying on the floor beside his chair, but Alfrekar stopped him with a warning gesture.

"That will do none of us any good," he said with a menacing

scowl. "You forget you're not the head of this Council, Sorkvir. You won't win any concessions from the Scipling with such behavior. If you can't control your temper, we'll have to forbid your presence here."

Sorkvir glowered at Alfrekar in fury, distracted only by the sudden flicker of a flame on his cheek. He strode away from the table, slapping it out wrathfully, bestowing a blazing glare upon Leifr as he went to pace up and down in the darkness of the rows of sepulchers.

"Now then," Alfrekar said, "have you reached a decision yet? Which will it be? Hroaldsdottir and freedom, or do you prefer a continuation of warfare and death?"

The wizards of the Council and the Inquisition leaned forward slightly, all their attention trained upon Leifr in anticipation of his next words.

"I can't turn over a sword that a member of your Council already possesses," Leifr said bitterly. "Nor would I if I could, even for the life of Ljosa. But if that should happen, and she dies, the chaos of Brjaladur will look like a child's picnic compared to what will happen to Hringurhol."

Thurid snorted contemptuously. "Alfrekar, you must know that this puny Council can't control the Dokkur Lavardur forever, even with all five of those crystals you're hoarding. He'll get away from you sooner or later and smash you to shreds and continue polluting our realm with his evil."

The Council wizards glared coldly at their unwilling guests for a brittle moment.

"Well then," Fodor said, "there's nothing left we have to say to the Council, except to look well to your defenses."

"Let's not be overhasty to join in battle," Thurid said, holding up one hand warningly. "In past centuries we've seen nothing to indicate that Ljosalfar and Dokkalfar will ever change their ways on their own, and they'll no doubt continue killing and stealing from each other until one or the other is completely eliminated. But by harnessing the powers of the Dokkur Lavardur, we are giving the realm a chance for balance and peace. The evil of the Lord of Chaos will no longer be roaming free, available to any wizard or warlord for preying upon his enemies. All evil powers will be safely contained, where no one will have access to them. You have an empty seat upon your Council." Thurid gave his staff a rap on the stone floor. "Offer it to me and I shall be the peace-bride between Council and Guild, the voice of mitigation and peace."

The Council members sputtered and buzzed, shaking their heads and chewing over the idea among themselves. Even Alfrekar seemed taken aback by the idea, scowling thoughtfully, before he beckoned to Hvitur-Fax to confer with him. The Inquisitors all looked askance at Thurid, and Fodor's expression settled into lines of aggrieved disapproval.

"A seat upon the Council of Threttan," said Alfrekar, nodding his head slowly, "in exchange for the blue orb of Heldur that you hold. It shall be granted."

"And since you've already got my sword," Leifr said, "Hroaldsdottir will be delivered from her imprisonment at once, restored completely, body and spirit, with no harmful aftereffects."

Again Alfrekar nodded slowly. "Agreed, but our traitor must come forward and deliver the sword into the proper hands for administering it to the Dokkur Lavardur. Then we may release Hroaldsdottir from the spell she is under. Isn't that so, Sorkvir?"

Sorkvir uttered a resentful snort and stalked back into the pool of light cast by the lamps. He gave the stone box containing Ljosa's sleeping form a sharp rap with his staff.

"Take her if you wish," Sorkvir snarled. "While the rest of you were taking your leisure lying about in Hringurhol, I was battling everything from hostile land spirits to this maddened barbarian with the sword of Endless Death, leading him and it steadily closer to Hringurhol by dint of every manipulative method I could think of, short of killing him and dragging his carcass. I would rather have done that, but I obeyed your orders, Most High Wizard of the Council Alfrekar—" He ground his teeth over the title as if the words were venomous snakes. "I used Hroaldsdottir to control him and lead him on to this meeting. Now that we are here and I am successful in my hard-fought goal, I am turned aside and spat upon for all my endeavors. Not only that, this—this—" He waved one blackened paw in Thurid's direction, sputtering in an ashy manner and swatting at one smoking shoulder blade. "This abomination of a wizard is inviting himself to sit on our Council and mediate between us and the Wizards' Guild. You are spewing the same heresies that killed Afgang. Peace between Ljosalfar and Dokkalfar! Bah! It can't happen! Conflict maintains the balance of all nature! Never once before did you tell the Council that our harnessing of the Dokkur Lavardur was for purposes of making peace with the Ljosalfar! Always, always, it was for their destruction and enslavement!''

"Enough! You're mad!" the wizards of the Council muttered, scowling and making rebuffing motions.

Alfrekar stared at Sorkvir, with a small withered smile twisting his thin lips. "All your labors will be suitably rewarded, Sorkvir," he said. "I can imagine how hard you worked to further the purposes of the Council. You must surely have no wish except to see *Endalaus Daudi* placed in the proper hands."

Their eyes locked for a longer-than-comfortable moment, then flames burst out on Sorkvir's cheekbones, as if the fire blazing from his eye sockets were not enough. He smothered the conflagration with his sleeve and glowered furiously as Leifr took two steps to confront him.

"You still possess the black flask containing Ljosa's spirit?" he demanded. "The last I saw of it, you breathed it in and trapped her within that carcass of yours. I must be assured that you can restore her completely."

"That trick frightened you, did it not?" Sorkvir snarled with a parody of a grin, darting a vicious glare at Alfrekar. "Very well, the spell will be lifted when the sword is given to the Council. She'll awaken when she crosses the threshold of this hall, I promise you that. But it will be your task to get her there, Scipling."

"Is that all there is to it? She'll awaken and be herself the moment she's outside that door?"

"Yes, I swear it, much as I hate to," Sorkvir said. "You've been abominably lucky, Scipling, luckier than you deserve. But when we meet after Brjaladur, no ancient law of guest right is going to protect you from my wrath."

"Silence! Enough threats!" Alfrekar commanded. "We've heard all we need to hear in this matter of the Fifth Seal, known otherwise as the sword *Endalaus Daudi*. If the sword and the blue orb of Heldur are not given over to the Council by noonday of the eve of Brjaladur, our agreement is at an end. Hroaldsdottir will die, Brjaladur will begin, and your rights of guest protection are over. If there is no other business for this meeting of the Council, we will disperse until tomorrow at noonday. I extend to our guests the hospitality of this hall, and everything they require to make themselves comfortable.''

"Thank you for your gracious offer," Fodor said. "We shall stay and continue to mediate this worrisome problem of the rightful ownership of the sword and Heldur's orb." The other Inquisitors cast rather dubious glances at the tombs and statues crowding closely around, with crumbling faces and missing arms and legs.

Thurid grounded his staff with an impatient thud, bringing Leifr's attention to its charred end, where the blue carbuncle had once been fused. Nothing remained now except a few distorted smears of molten gold and silver.

"You're very kind to bestow your wisdom upon us," Thurid said, "but there's no further need. With Brjaladur so near, I'm certain you'd rather return to the Ferja side of the river."

"I'm certain we'd rather not," Fodor retorted. "This sordid affair is far from finished. Your offer of alliance with the Council of Threttan will be most interesting to the Fire Wizards' Guild."

"The Guild has done precious little about the Dokkur Lavardur," Thurid said testily. "Perhaps I can, if I'm near enough to him, instead of burying myself in the Guildhall."

"We don't bury unclean practitioners in the Guildhall," the short-tempered Varkar growled. "We purge them, then bury them outside the walls in cursed ground."

This mutual earth-pawing was suddenly cut short by an uproar from outside among the gathered wizards and Ulf-hedin; very shortly, the uproar was punctuated by the clash of metal and yells of pain. Beneath it all was a deep, furious roaring sound, like the powerful undertow on a rocky beach.

"What treachery is this?" Alfrekar snarled, and his wizards leaped up to form a bulwark on one side of the room. The Inquisitors stood against the other, with Leifr and Thurid in the middle.

"You might answer that better yourself!" Leifr retorted.

There was only a moment for three-way and highly mutual suspicion, then the door shuddered under a massive crashing attack, as if rammed with some great, door-breaking engine. Then a second charge brought the door crashing open against the wall behind it, and a huge figure of doom plowed into the room, with a trio of baying, snarling hounds holding off the attackers from behind. The apparition brandished a halberd running with blood, which whistled around suggestively as its owner contemplated the wizards backed against the wall.

"Raudbjorn!" Leifr exclaimed in delight.

"Raudbjorn here! Leifr, we get away now!" boomed a familiar voice, and Raudbjorn glared about madly for signs of objections to his plans, two-eyed once again. The troll-hounds swirled around him, gleaming teeth snapping with staccato clicks. Starkad loomed in his wake, his face pale and determined as he clutched his old sword.

Leifr opened his mouth to protest and warn Raudbjorn that this was not the time for heroics, but before he could get out a sound, Starkad lunged forward with a roar, waving his short sword.

"We've come to save you, Leifr! Charge, Raudbjorn!" he bellowed. "We've got to get them out of here!"

Both groups of wizards surged forward, some drawing weapons, some urging a peaceful resolution to the situation, but to Raudbjorn and Starkad and the troll-hounds it all looked like one massive attack. They met it with yells and with ferocious abandon. There was a brief flurry of swords and a great deal of worried shouting before the clash was over and calmer heads prevailed.

"This is Guild treachery if ever I smelled it!" Sorkvir snarled, one of those who had drawn steel, and he was sheathing it now with every sign of reluctance.

"It's no treachery of ours," Fodor retorted angrily.

"Nor of mine," Thurid said, glaring at Raudbjorn and Starkad. "I told you to stay in the wanderers' camp, you insane Villimadur, where you wouldn't get into trouble. Where did you find this young jotun-spawned ruffian?"

"I found him outside," Starkad answered, still breathless. "I thought you needed help. You've been in here so long."

"This had better not be another of your clever ploys," warned Alfrekar.

"Not Villimadur!" Raudbjorn growled furiously. "No ploy! Nothing but Raudbjorn! Leifr and Thurid safe now!"

"We're not in any particular danger, Raudbjorn," Leifr said impatiently. "We've got to talk with the Council first before we destroy it."

"Talk!" Raudbjorn snorted rudely. "Talk worth nothing! Time to go back across river, Leifr! Big storm coming outside!"

"We can't cross the river just yet," Leifr replied. "Not until our business with the Council is finished."

Raudbjorn shook his head adamantly and rolled his eyes, nostrils flaring, like a warhorse scenting battle. "No, got to get out, Leifr! Nasty storm, full of black things and eyes and bad signs in the air! This is bad place!"

"We've given our word we'll stay," Leifr said. "So we'll stay, Raudbjorn."

Raudbjorn glared around slowly at the wizards, still poised warily for attack or defense, with powerful gusts of errant influences tugging at their beards and cloaks. A few of the Council wizards worriedly rubbed amulets between their fingers, listening to the howling of the wrathful wind outside, suddenly audible in the strained silence.

Raudbjorn's shoulders sagged as he reluctantly lowered his halberd to the ground with a despondent clank. His brow knotted into an anxious scowl as he surveyed the situation and found the odds greatly lacking on Leifr's side.

Thurid eased forward a pace, causing all eyes to shift nervously to him. He raised one hand in a peaceable gesture and said, "It's all right, Raudbjorn, I've got this under control. Go now, all of you, and let us hold to the terms of our agreement. Nothing has changed."

Sorkvir was standing arrogantly aloof and watching the confrontation, with the air of a man keeping his own thoughts to himself.

"The Dokkur Lavardur is disturbed by the happenings here," he said in his dry-throated voice. "We've got enough on our hands to placate him without wasting more time with these charlatans, murderers, and thieves."

Thurid folded his arms across his chest and looked on with interest. His attitude struck Leifr as being rather smug and not unpleased with himself, as if he might be enjoying his position as the center of everyone's hopes for good or ill. Suddenly he raised his head and sniffed.

"Does anyone else smell something burning?" he demanded. "Smells like old bones and rags, as if someone were burning an old carcass!"

Sorkvir whirled around with an oath, looking hastily over each shoulder and down his sleeves at the backs of his forearms, before shifting his smouldering glare to Thurid.

"I must have been mistaken," Thurid said with a small, taunting smile on his lips.

"You won't live long enough to be mistaken many more times," Sorkvir replied in a low and furious snarl. "It will be over soon, and there's nothing you can do to prevent it. Neither you nor those Rhbus can stand against the Dokkur Lavardur in one of his rages, and he's in one now. Do you like the sound of your enemy, you bold heroes?"

He gestured with one hand to indicate the storm gathering outside. The lurking crowd of Ulf-hedin and wizards had thinned away to only the most ambitious and fanatical few, who clung to Alfrekar and the Council's presence with evident apprehension as they stood in the dooryard of the hall beneath a sky that had gone black and purple. The clouds seethed with scaly, half-perceived images that shifted the moment one looked at them directly. Instead of lightnings, a menacing green glow periodically suffused the clouds, accompanied by a grumbling of thunder. A shifty wind buffeted at the courtyard, as if testing the warriors and wizards for their weak points. The Inquisitors stood warily with their staffs in hand, eyeing the various celestial manifestations while the wind ripped at their cloaks. Fodor raised one hand in a gesture, and the wind rebounded from him with an angry shriek.

Alfrekar glared at Leifr suspiciously. "Very well, until tomorrow then," he said. He turned on his heel and stalked out the door, sparing Raudbjorn a few suspicious glances as he brushed past.

One by one the other council wizards followed suit, striving for the same defiance as they fell under the dire scrutiny of Raudbjorn's eye, which still smouldered beneath an outraged scowl. Raudbjorn did not budge a pace to make their passage any easier, and the threatening, rumbling growl deep in his chest was echoed by the troll-hounds crouching around his knees with their lips wrinkled back in hideous snarls.

Sorkvir was the last to go, bestowing his cadaverous simpering leer upon each of the Inquisitors in turn as he edged past Raudbjorn. Fodor stood glaring at Sorkvir, who stood his ground in a silent and hostile battle of wills to see which party would be the one to quit the field first. With a sudden frantic pounding at some secretive combustion, Sorkvir turned and hurried out of the Hall.

"I hope you'll be comfortable here," Thurid said, nodding slightly at a decaying figure of a warrior crumbling away atop the tomb it guarded. "Leifr and I have other friends we must visit tonight."

"Indeed!" Fodor said. "Do you mind if I accompany you and take advantage of my guest right for a view of Hringurhol?"

"You're ever welcome to take advantage of anything you like," Thurid said. "But I don't think the place we're going will be to your taste, after what I've seen of the life you live at the Guildhall. No one has any of those comforts here."

"Lead on," Fodor said. "I'm not afraid of a bit of squalor."

In spite of the manifestations of the Dokkur Lavardur overhead, the wanderers' camp bustled with a festive, gypsy atmosphere. Fires and lamps were burning brightly within the protective circle of wagons and carts. Thurid made his way to one wagon covered over with a flapping top made of hides sewn together. Inside, huddled cozily around a makeshift table with a lamp, the four knacker-women looked up from some wagering game, their eyes bright and speculative. A fifth member of their little circle also looked up from his game pieces in friendly recognition, warm and bleary with intoxication.

"Thurid, look whom we found," Ketilridir said. "He claims to be a friend of yours."

"Vidskipti!" Thurid exclaimed. "He's no friend of mine."

"How pleasant to see you again, Thurid!" Vidskipti said, as drunk as ever. "And you, too, of course, Leifr, once again. How do you like this weather we're having?"

"Less and less," Thurid retorted. "What are you doing here, you old badger? If you had any sense, you'd get yourself and all these wanderers down to the ferry before it's too late to get away from Brjaladur."

"There's plenty of time for that," Vidskipti said.

"Come in, come in," the knacker-women said, making space. "There's room for everyone in this wagon, sooner or later." They snickered at their own awful joke and shook their heads deprecatingly at their own levity.

Raudbjorn took his position outside the wagon, and no one was willing to argue with him as he selected a place out of the wind and squatted down with his halberd across his knees. He gave Leifr a wink as if to say all was well now, and the hounds also sat down watchfully beside him.

"I've come to help you out of this," Vidskipti said, lacing his fingers in a businesslike way, with a sly wink at Fodor and a conspiratorial nudge in the ribs. "Between the two of us, we'll outsmart the Council and send them packing, won't we?"

"He's got all the help he needs from me and the rest of the Inquisitors," Fodor said loftily, offended by such familiarity from one such as Vidskipti.

Thurid was about to reply, but he was distracted by a sudden flurry and struggling inside his satchel. Swiftly he removed a leather pouch and opened it, flinging it down upon the table.

"I've got more help than I want or need!" Thurid sputtered wrathfully as Gedvondur extricated himself from the bag with as much dignity as a hand could muster. He bestowed a rude fillip upon Thurid and scuttled up his sleeve.

"Greetings to all," Gedvondur's voice intoned. "I hope I shan't be prevented again from offering my advice upon this situation. After all, I've been in your shoes once before."

"Great Hodur!" Fodor exclaimed, seizing his staff. "Carbuncle possession! Don't move, Thurid! I'll get it!"

"You'll get more than you bargained for if you attempt to mess with Gedvondur," Thurid said acidly.

"Indeed you will," Gedvondur added haughtily.

"When I want your help," Thurid retorted, "I shall ask for it, and if you don't behave, it's back in the pouch for you."

Fodor blinked at him in astonishment, then turned away with a mutter and a covert sign to ward off evil.

"I could have helped you at the meeting of the Council," Gedvondur snapped, still hot from his imprisonment in the pouch.

"I most especially didn't want you help," Thurid retorted. "If any of you truly want to be of assistance, cross the river and stay out of my way. I know what must be done and I don't need anyone's help except Leifr's."

Starkad lifted his head from an uncharacteristic droop. In a faint, strained voice he said, "I think I've got myself into a bit of a fix, Thurid."

Thurid whirled around with a vexed exclamation, but the words died on his lips. With an apologetic smile, Starkad held out his hand, and Leifr was transfixed with horror to see it covered with blood, the bright, thick sort that comes from a deep and determinedly bleeding wound.

Chapter 12

◇◇

Starkad's will to stay upright slowly dissolved, and Leifr eased him to the ground, while Thurid shouted for a lantern. The knacker-women flustered and chirped in dismay.

"Bring him inside the wagon," Beitski directed, and Leifr lifted him and placed him on the clean floorboards. Thurid pulled aside Starkad's shirt to examine the injury, incurred in the brief scuffle when Raudbjorn had come barging into the hall. With Fodor gazing on with intense interest, Thurid commenced a frantic inquisition of his own into the healing properties of every stick and spell and object in his satchel. In a few moments the floor was littered with an unreasonable quantity of sorcerous things, with Gedvondur scuttling about among them, while Leifr held a thick folded pad of cloth over Starkad's wound.

"You might have said something!" Thurid admonished Starkad without looking up from his searching and reading.

"I didn't want to appear the coward," Starkad said, his voice faint and his face very white. "It wasn't such a large sword, just a slender rapier. I didn't expect its wound would bleed like a pig's gullet."

"It's what you might expect from a wound dealt by a wizard," Thurid answered grimly, his eyes meeting Leifr's with a desperate glare. Pulling Leifr outside, he continued in a low, rapid voice, "Leifr, I don't know how to stop that sort of bleeding. The wound came from a cursed sword. Treacherous fiends, they were waiting for just such an opportunity as this. Possibly we could find out which wizard did it, but I don't think we've got that much time and I doubt if the wizard would come forth with a confession anyway. Not with the Inquisitors looking for a scapegoat as they always are. By the time they finished wrangling and accusing each other, Starkad would be dead. What I want you to do is find Svanlaug."

"What about the knacker-women, Thurid?" Leifr demanded. "They brought you back to life."

Thurid glanced hastily around to see where Fodor was. "I can't, not with him here," he said. "I'm trying to get rid of him, but he's convinced he's going to see something treasonous, and he just might, if I decide to kill him."

"Ask Vidskipti then," Leifr demanded.

"That trash merchant?" Thurid snorted in fine disdain. "What could he know about healing? He's as crazy as a cow with heel flies!"

"You never know what he might have on his cart," Leifr said. "He's covered this island from end to end and seen nearly everything there is to see about it. Ask him for help, Thurid, and you may be astonished."

"I know you think he's a Rhbu," Thurid retorted, "but at this point I'll grasp whatever slender thread I can to save Starkad's life. Vidskipti as a thread is as slender as a cobweb, though," he added, bending an incredulous scowl upon Vidskipti over his shoulder. "But you've got to find Svanlaug anyway. Take Raudbjorn with you for protection. There might be a few Ulf-hedin that have never heard of guest-right protection."

"I'm away then," Leifr said, starting off with a shout to Raudbjorn and the hounds.

Turning away with a swirl of his cloak, Thurid called out brusquely, "Hulloa, Vidskipti! What have you got on that cart of yours by way of healing instruments?"

Vidskipti took on his shrewd look. "Things that will astonish you," he said. "I'll be back in scarcely a moment and you can take your pick." He wrapped his cloak around himself and plunged into the roaring darkness.

"More illicit spells," Fodor murmured, shaking his head. "If I had a healer from the Guild now, we could cure him. I shudder to think what practices could be floating around in a benighted place like this!"

"You'd be safer from them back in the Council Hall," Thurid said. "I'll have Raudbjorn direct you back there, the moment he returns, and frighten away any lurking Ulf-hedin."

"No, I'll stay here," Fodor said. "And watch."

The wagon trembled under the force of the wind. The earth itself seemed to quiver in protest under a steady assault of unseen forces.

The merchant returned swiftly from his cart and stood beside the fire with an enormous tattered old satchel at his feet, rubbing his cold hands briskly.

"You wanted to see some spells for cures," he began. "I've got dragon's marrow for curing digestive disorders and rheumatics, henbane for irregularities of the heart, witch's thimble, dogbane, alder bark, hawthorn—" He suited his actions to his words and began heaving bundles of things out of the satchel, packets of powders, heavy black bottles of infusions and unguents, and curiously carved little boxes of unknown contents.

"I don't want any of that pottering herbal drivel, you conniving trash peddler!" Thurid flared, seizing the trader's old satchel and dumping out its contents on the floor. "Let's see what else you've got here, and I'll tell you if it's worth having. I want spells carved into rune wands! I want a vellum written in runic! A stone imbued with a spell that will counteract the spell of the sword that dealt this wound! Don't you possess one item with real power in all that heap of worthless rot?"

"Well, I don't know," Vidskipti said huffily. "You can take it or leave it. I only sell the stuff, I don't use it. I'm not a wizard, you know."

"Tut-tut, Thurid, what did you expect?" Fodor said.

Vidskipti rolled his eyes in a mad fashion, then looked back into the wagon at Starkad. Glancing toward Thurid and Fodor, who had walked a few steps away to quarrel, he returned swiftly and climbed into the wagon. Thurid turned sharply away from Fodor and returned to the wagon.

Vidskipti bent over Starkad and placed one hand on his brow. The knacker-women looked at him intently, and Ketilridir whispered, "He's so cold. I can see he's still breathing somewhat, but Dokkalfar powers are invading his entire body. He hasn't the strength of his own to resist."

"He needs outside help, which is actually inside help, to augment his own powers," Vidskipti whispered in return, placing both his hands upon Starkad's head. He pinched shut his withered eyelids and spoke rapidly, in a soft voice. "Starkad, I command you to remain a little while longer. Stay the rising tide of evil and death and reach for life and light."

"You said you were no healer," Thurid said suspiciously, poking his head in after Vidskipti. "Or are you something more than you appear, as Leifr insists?"

Vidskipti turned a startled stare upon him and put his hands into his pockets. "I, my friend?" he said mournfully, "I'm nothing but a disreputable traveling trader. A bibulous, bumbling traveling trash merchant."

"About Starkad," Thurid said, his brows drawn together in a frown. His eyes darted alertly from Vidskipti to the impassive nutlike faces of the knacker-women. "You said he needed something from outside and inside. At the same time?"

Vidskipti glanced toward Fodor outside, poking at the remedies in the old satchel. He leaned forward and explained in a low rapid voice, "Inside, as from inside himself, under his own skin, and outside in the sense that it is something he wasn't born with, something that all Alfar possess to give them help when they need it. Inside and outside, don't you see what I mean?"

"Not at all," Thurid grunted.

"Try again," Vidskipti said. "But hurry. I've got important things to do before Brjaladur. I'm just a trader, not a sorcerer," he added, rolling his eyes toward Fodor, who was stalking toward him again with a handful of the cures from the ragged old satchel, holding them away from him as if they were poisonous to the touch.

"Just a hoax, you mean," Fodor retorted, finishing his perusal of the healing objects. "Much of this stuff is pure superstition, like this snakeskin. Tying that around your head won't cure headache. I'd rather tie it around your throat and see if it won't cure any more speech out of you."

"Tut-tut, keep your temper," Vidskipti advised him. "Thurid said he wanted to see cures, so that's what I brought. Now if you'd said you wanted spells—" He flapped one hand in a preoccupied manner. "Dear me, it's time to go. It seems I've done nothing but waste your time."

"I won't quarrel with that." Thurid snorted. "Remember that bit of glass you gave me for finding directions? Well, that led us right into the soup—niss and nix soup. I doubt if I could trust Starkad's life to anything that you'd give me."

"Nothing is what it seems," Vidskipti said, stopping at the door to wind a long scarf around his throat. "If you want me, I shall be at my cart, fifth one down from Smahestur's pony caravan."

When he was gone, Thurid saw that Vidskipti had left the old satchel and all his cures behind.

"Scant comfort indeed," Thurid grunted, prodding at the mess of objects heaved from the satchel. "If he'd truly been a Rhbu, as Leifr so ridiculously insists, he would have helped us. I've seen precious little help from the Rhbus, ever since I first clapped eyes upon Fridmarr and this satchel." He gave his own satchel a dusty thump and sighed deeply. "Maybe there are no Rhbus after all. Maybe this entire journey has been nothing but an absurd dream quest, which will only end in the inevitable deaths of all of us."

"The Rhbus are extinct," Fodor said. "Wanderers and madmen may claim to be Rhbus, but they all break down under inquisition and show their true colors. Renegades, all of them, posing behind a hodge-podge of powers borrowed from the Dokkalfar and other unclean sources. Now you're beginning to sound a bit more sensible, Thurid. Can't you see you're surrounded by nothing but fanciful dreamers and outright rogues? There's nothing so romantic as a lost cause, and that is just what the Rhbus are. A lost cause, a lost people. There is nothing you can do to bring them back to their former glory. The people who made all this—" He flung out his hand to encompass all of Hringurhol. "They're gone forever, Thurid. Nothing remains but these pitiful wanderers, beggars, vagabonds, and scavengers, all possessed by an undying dream of revenge and restitution. I tell you, it will never happen. Even with a sword of power and a dragon's carbuncle."

"Bah," Thurid said. "If that's how easily the Guild gives up on a cause, then I'm glad it considers me an outlaw."

With Raudbjorn lumbering at his heels, Leifr felt ridiculously conspicuous as he made his way through the wanderers' camp. On all sides, in spite of the menacing of the Dokkur Lavardur, merchants were hawking their wares from shabby carts, minstrels were tuning up their instruments, and women were cooking for the food tents, filling the encampment with smoke and savory smells, despite the blustering and blowing of the storm. The worst of its influence seemed to skim by overhead, rattling the tops of the wagons and carts and sucking up the smoke without causing too much disturbance below.

Leifr politely turned aside all the merchants who tried to persuade him to look inside their carts, while Raudbjorn dropped behind, his attention seduced by a heap of rusty weapons and armor. The troll-hounds clung to Leifr as if they never intended to let him out of their sight again, prodding his legs with their sharp noses whenever his pace slowed. They growled at the merchants and hawkers, sensing their master's impatience at the delays.

Yet another avaricious salesman lounging against his wagon suddenly unfurled himself from his cloak as Leifr approached. "Come! I've got something you must see!" he insinuated, eyes gleaming in a narrow dark face with a fanatic light. "You're just the one I've been waiting for!"

"I'll come back later," Leifr said. "I'm in a terrible hurry right now."

"It will only take a moment," the trader said, grinning with a set of longish narrow teeth. "I might not be here when you get back. It's getting awfully close to Brjaladur."

Leifr found himself standing beside a ramshackle cart while the trader flung out assorted items of no interest to anyone whatsoever, particularly not Leifr in his present mood. Just as he was about to go, thinking of Starkad's strength slowly bleeding away, the trader uttered a triumphant crow of discovery and beckoned Leifr closer.

"See here," he said, unwrapping a ragged bundle. "I knew this would be of interest to you."

It was a sword, judging by the shape of it. With a furtive glance around, the merchant unfolded the last bit of rag. Leifr's heart stopped a moment when he saw the hilt and part of an engraved blade. Reaching out, he gripped the hilt, but no answering vibration greeted his touch. It was an identical copy, but it was not *Endalaus Daudi*. Fridmarr's carbuncle burned warningly against his chest and he jerked back his hand, recognizing it as the sword Sorkvir had caused to be made in Djofullhol.

"Where did you find that?" he demanded warily of the trader, lounging against his cart yet still watchful.

"A place called Steinveggur-dahl," the trader said. "Hidden rather carelessly under a rock, as if someone had put it there in a hurry, perhaps, to get it out of sight. Have you ever been to Steinveggur, a place of ruins?"

"How much do you want for this sword?" Leifr asked, hurriedly collecting his wits. "It's not a very good one. In fact, I'm quite certain there's something evil about it, but I'm still willing to give you a few marks for it. Ten marks I'll offer.''

''Well, make it fifteen and we've got a bargain,'' the trader said, holding out his palm to be slapped, which Leifr did at once.

''I haven't got fifteen marks,'' Leifr said, wrapping up the sword quickly, glancing around to see if any Ulf-hedin were looking about. ''You'll have to trust me for it until I can get it. Do you know Vidskipti?''

''Of course,'' the trader said. ''Don't worry about it. I know where to find you. Take the sword.''

''Say nothing to anyone about this sword,'' Leifr said. ''I'm glad you came to me. I'm the only one who knows what to do with this abomination.''

Leifr whistled to Raudbjorn and hurried away with the sword concealed inside his cloak. He wasn't certain what he intended to do with it, but his head was reeling with possibilities.

Svanlaug and Halmur had a small fire burning in Afgang's ruined house, showing a ruddy glow through one window. Halmur's wolfish ears twitched, up on the rooftop against the lurid sky, and he came bounding down from his position to meet Leifr, peeling off his wolf cape.

''Starkad slipped away to follow you,'' he said anxiously to Leifr. ''Did you find him?''

''I know, and I'll tell you everything that happened later,'' said Leifr. ''First I've got to see Svanlaug.''

He greeted Svanlaug shortly. ''You must come to the wanderers' camp. Starkad's been wounded by a Dokkalfar sword and Thurid can't get the bleeding to stop.''

Svanlaug rose at once and reached for her physician's satchel. ''The fool,'' she said. ''Always trying to impress me. This time I think he may have succeeded.''

When they returned to the place where the knacker-women's wagon had stood, they found an empty space and a dozen ragged scavengers waiting to tell them that Starkad had been moved to more comfortable quarters in a nearby barn. At least twenty wanderers had gathered around, murmuring in quiet, stricken voices.

After a brief inspection of Starkad's wound, Svanlaug looked at Thurid in silent appeal. Fodor scowled over his shoulder at her in grave disapproval.

"This is wizard's work," she said. "Both wound and cure, if there is one. I'm only a simple healer of natural wounds and illnesses."

"And a Dokkalfar one at that," Fodor said sourly, turning away with a shudder of distaste as Gedvondur strutted and preened on Thurid's shoulder, making vulgar gestures when Thurid wasn't looking.

Thurid stalked back and forth, giving his cloak a lash each time to get it out of his way. "It's a Dokkalfar wound, made by a Dokkalfar weapon and hand that wielded it, and you are a Dokkalfar. It seems to me that you should be able to do something to help it if you're any kind of healer at all, Svanlaug."

"The only thing I can do is give Starkad some restoratives that will prolong his life somewhat, but unless some strong countermagic is used, I fear there's no hope of a complete recovery. There's nothing in those Rhbu rune sticks of yours that can help, Thurid?"

Thurid scowled and turned away to contemplate the clutter of wands and bundles he had heaved out of his satchel in frantic haste. "I'll look again," he muttered.

With everyone so distracted, Leifr guiltily slid the copy of *Endalaus Daudi* under some straw. Standing by helplessly, he rubbed the carbuncle with his thumb, trying to coax some communication out of it. Suddenly a strong image came into his mind, and Fridmarr's essence felt as near to him as if he had been alive.

"Wait awhile, Thurid, I've got an idea," he said in a voice almost smothered by excitement and the strong, positive feeling that Fridmarr had indeed given him the answer. He unthreaded the little pouch containing Fridmarr's carbuncle from his neck and rolled the brilliant stone into the hollow of his hand. "I know how we can save Starkad now."

Thurid stood poised a moment, still ready to fly off at any instant, his eyes fastened upon the carbuncle with sudden blazing intensity.

"Of course, that's it," he said, half to himself. "Inside and outside help. I thought it was nonsense. Svanlaug! Have you got a sharp obsidian blade in your kit? Some sinew for stitching? Get as much light around Starkad as you possibly can without setting us all on fire. Leifr, are you certain you want to sacrifice this stone? It was intended for you, and you're going to need it before Brjaladur is over.''

Leifr made a table from a smooth piece of planking and Svanlaug began laying out her tools. He put down Fridmarr's stone beside them with a hollow sense of loss, seeing the carbuncle laying apart from him on the crude table.

"I'm certain," he replied after only an instant's hesitation. "We know it will save his life, but we don't know what it would do for me. Use it, Thurid, and be quick about it."

"I've never done anything of this kind before," Svanlaug said uneasily. "Cutting into the body is an offense against nature, unless taking off a diseased limb could save the life. How do you know this carbuncle will be able to counteract the Dokkalfar spell?"

"I know Fridmarr," Thurid said, holding up the red stone. "This is all that remains of him, and he will know what to do. His wisdom will soon be Starkad's."

"Starkad needs it," Svanlaug muttered, tying back her hair and steadying her hands.

"Wait," Fodor said, aghast. "This is the rankest of perversion of powers. The theft of carbuncles is nothing short of inviting hostile possession and the transferral of unknown and unclean ability. You mustn't attempt it, Thurid. You don't know what the result will be."

"I know what the result will be unless we attempt it," Thurid snapped. "If you can't bear it, then take yourself back to the Council Hall. I never asked you to come here, snooping and prying. The only reason you're here is because you want to see me destroyed. Well, my inquisitive friend, you're going to be disappointed."

Fodor eyed him coldly. "If you had been purged and cleansed of these vile powers, most of this quarrel with the Council of Threttan would have been eliminated."

"And so would all hope of destroying the Dokkur Lavardur," Thurid answered. "Everything would depend upon those old mossbacks at the Guildhall, until the Fimbul Winter freezes them solid. I wonder if they would notice then that the Guild is falling somewhat behind."

"This talk of striking a bargain with the Council smacks of certain heresy as far as the Guild is concerned. It can't be permitted, Thurid."

"Bah!" Thurid retorted. "If you don't like it, why don't you go back to your safe and comfortable Guildhall and close the doors against the world to keep any unsettling ideas from getting in? You'll be much happier there, with your heads securely buried in the sand, and the rest of us will continue muddling along the best we can with whatever advantages we may happen to have at the moment."

"Come now, Thurid," Fodor said in a reasonable tone, "you know you can't make any lasting bargains with such rotters as the Council of Threttan. How long do you think they would hold to their end of the bargain?"

"Long enough to get Ljosa Hroaldsdottir out of that hall is enough," Thurid said.

"The Council of Threttan must not ever come into possession of that Rhbu sword and the carbuncle from Heldur's forge," Fodor said. "We cannot permit them to control the Dokkur Lavardur or our destruction is certain, no matter what they may pretend to agree to."

"It matters not," Thurid said loftily. "They no doubt think the same about us. As long as we get Ljosa safely out, the Council can do whatever they please. Then we shall deal with them in an appropriate manner."

"The Inquisitors have had generations of experience in evaluating powers good and bad. The Council are all rogues, and the Dokkur Lavardur they seek to propitiate is nothing but pure malevolence. It must be destroyed."

"The destruction of an elemental of that magnitude is no easy matter," Svanlaug said with an arrogant toss of her head. "I doubt if you Inquisitors could manage it. Once the propitiation and offerings are stopped, I believe he will depart on his own."

"No, this thing must be destroyed," Fodor said, "or it will never cease to be a bother to all Ljosalfar of the realm. I can send for a couple of Protectors to blast the creature."

"We haven't time," Thurid said. "The Council is preparing to do something during Brjaladur, which is the season when Chaos rules. If we are to do anything at all, it must be done now, without any interference."

Fodor hitched his cloak around his shoulders. "If I'm no longer of any service here, I shall return to my companions in Alfrekar's hall. Perhaps, since it is getting to be a rather wild night, I could beg the protection of your friend Raudbjorn."

"To be sure," Thurid said with a mocking half bow. "It has been a pleasant visit, Fodor. I regret that we came to no perceptible agreement on this situation."

"You still intend to bargain with them, don't you?" Fodor gazed steadily at Thurid. "You still intend to hand over the Rhbu sword and the carbuncle tomorrow at noonday? Are you truly so charmed at the notion of joining this vile Council of Threttan? Even I never expected such vanity of you, Thurid."

In the taut silence after his departure, a noisy squeaking and rumbling sound approached the door and halted outside.

"The knacker-women!" a voice of warning called out at the door, and those who were watching glided away into the shadows, suddenly remembering other places to be. Not even Raudbjorn could prevent the sister death merchants from entering the barn. Beitski approached Starkad on his pallet and touched his brow.

"No, you're not taking Starkad!" Svanlaug exclaimed suddenly, swarming forward protectively. "He's not dead! We can save him!"

"Sisters!" Thurid said in warm welcome. "Come in and help us if you can! You restored the life to me; there must be something you can do for Starkad."

"Yes, now that the Inquisitor is gone, we can get to work," said Beitski.

Ketilridir's eyes did not miss the obsidian knife on the table and the carbuncle sparkling like a drop of blood beside it.

"Leave this sort of thing to those who know somewhat of it," she said gently. "Your clumsy attempts are likely to kill the lad. Sisters, come and assist me with the placing of a guide stone. The rest of you," she added, her deepset eyes darting from Leifr to Thurid, "away with you all."

Banished to the far end of the barn, they stood a moment in silence in the white glare of Thurid's alf-light. Leifr paced up and down, Svanlaug scowled, Thurid glowered, and Raudbjorn groaned softly under his breath and mopped his glistening pate with a rag.

In a very short while Beitski called out, "It's done, and a neat job of it, too. Come and see."

Starkad no longer gleamed white like sweating marble. He lay peacefully asleep, and there was no sign that anyone had cut into him except a faint blue line at the base of his throat that looked like a healing scar already. Thurid placed his hand on Starkad's brow and nodded approvingly when Starkad moved his head and moaned. "He's coming around and he feels warmer now already. Thank you, sisters, for saving him."

Ketilridir inclined her head in recognition of his praise. "It was clever of you to think of this, Leifr, something I wouldn't have expected from a Scipling. Nothing could have helped him more quickly and more surely."

"It wasn't my idea; it was Fridmarr's," Leifr said. "And Vidskipti helped, too, did he not?"

Thurid slapped his brow and groaned. "That old trash collector? He wouldn't know a carbuncle from a peapod!"

"Nevertheless," Beitski said, "you've saved the life of your young friend. Now you should all get out of Hringurhol before Brjaladur. You are of course welcome to ride with us tomorrow in the wagon to Ferja, where we can cross the river. Running water between you and the Ulf-hedin is the only way to be safe after sundown tomorrow."

"Thank you," Thurid said, commencing to arrange his cloak and tighten his boot laces in a businesslike manner. "We shall avail ourselves of your kind offer once our business is concluded at noonday. Hroaldsdottir must be removed from the Council Hall before we leave, whether or not the traitor to the Council has surrendered the sword. We haven't got much time if we have any hope at all of retrieving it for ourselves." With Gedvondur clinging to his shoulder, he bent low over Starkad and Gedvondur's voice whispered, "Fridmarr! Can you hear me?"

Starkad stirred slightly and moaned, his pale lips half forming words as he attempted to speak.

"Patience, patience," Beitski urged. "Let him rest. You cannot speak to Fridmarr until Starkad is fully recovered. That carbuncle will tax him beyond his strength until he grows accustomed to it."

"Thurid, I must speak to you privately," Leifr said in a low voice. He led the way into the shadows surrounding the grain bins, uncovered the bundle containing the false sword, and revealed the sword hilt in a faint swath of light leaking in through a hole in the roof. "What do you make of this, Thurid? How could someone have found it and brought it all this way? I feel as if I'm being haunted by it."

Thurid wheezed slightly, his eyes glaring in the faint light as he frantically harrowed up his thinning hair with one hand, as if important knowledge lurked somewhere upon the surface of his scalp.

"Keep this thing hidden!" he whispered finally. "Don't touch it until I tell you to and don't tell anyone about it. I must think what we can do with this, Leifr."

"We can't let them have *Endalaus Daudi*," Leifr said, and Thurid nodded his head immediately. "And we can't let them harm Ljosa. Perhaps the false sword will be helpful in causing the thief of the true sword to come forward. At least it might give us time to save Ljosa before they discover their mistake."

Thurid's teeth gleamed in the faint light. "Good lad. Let the Council decide which one they want. I like this plan, Leifr."

Thurid officiously commanded Leifr to lie down and rest for the coming occasion on the morrow. The knacker-women returned to their cart. Svanlaug composed herself beside Starkad and watched his every breath intently, while the fury of the Dokkur Lavardur raged outside the snug turf walls and rattled at the ramshackle doors of the old barn.

It was near dawn when the door shook under a different sort of assault. Leifr awakened from a light doze instantly and leaped to his feet. Thurid motioned him back from the door as he cautiously approached.

"Who's there?" he demanded menacingly.

"It's Ulfrin," a low voice replied. "Please let me come in."

Chapter 13

◇◇◇

Svanlaug leaped to Thurid's side and helped unbar the door, bracing her shoulder against the furious gusting of the wind. It carried the upraised voices of the Ulf-hedin into the barn, eerie cries that made Starkad moan and toss in his restless sleep.

Thurid and Leifr shouldered the door shut again and stood gazing at a disheveled Ulfrin, panting and shivering, with her fist clutching her hood tight under her chin. Her eyes traveled around the interior of the barn fleetingly, like a hunted animal searching for refuge. The hue of her lustrous dark skin was ashen, her lips gray and dry.

"Sister!" she gasped, turning to Svanlaug, with a sudden weariness forcing her downward to sit on a low stool. She put her face in her hands a moment. "I've been searching for you. Will you take me out of here, back to the safety of our mother's tent at Bergmal?"

"Of course," Svanlaug said, concealing her astonishment at once and glaring at Thurid's openly skeptical expression. "What has happened to change your mind, Ulfrin? I didn't think you'd come with us willingly."

"I was a fool," Ulfrin said wearily. "An arrogant, blind fool." She lifted her head to listen to the door that was shuddering under the attack of the elemental forces loosed outdoors. She twitched her shoulders and shivered. "There's something rotten afoot here, sister," she whispered. "I must escape before it's too late."

"Isn't that what I've been trying to tell you?" Svanlaug demanded, pulling off Ulfrin's rain-soaked cloak and giving her own dry one to her sister.

"Yes, I know," Ulfrin said contritely. "I'm sorry, Svanlaug. Something had hold of me—my own stupid pride at the idea of taking Afgang's place on the Council of Threttan, I suppose. I should have known—I should have suspected—"

"Yes, you should have," Svanlaug snapped, shoving a pot onto the low coals. "They only wanted to use your skills, to pollute and twist your powers for their own evil purposes. Their own powers are not enough to satisfy them, so they take others and wring them dry—"

"It's worse than that," Ulfrin whispered, her eyes widening with hidden terrors. "Far worse than just that, sister. I've got to get out of Hringurhol before the drumming, before Brjaladur begins, or I'm doomed."

"Hush, you're not doomed," Svanlaug said. "You are safe now. No one is going to harm you. A Sverting birthright is the most precious of all Dokkalfar gifts."

Ulfrin nodded her head and a tear slid down her cheek. "That's it exactly, Svanlaug. I am a Sverting. But right now I'd give anything to be an ordinary Dokkalfar like you. Why didn't anyone scold me when I acted like a spoiled brat? Why didn't anyone warn me of what might happen? Everything has gone wrong here, Svanlaug. Tomorrow night I shall become the peace-bride of the Lord of Chaos."

Svanlaug clenched a double handful of hair—Ulfrin's hair—and gave her a furious shaking.

"I tried to warn you! How could you be so stupid, so thick in the head?" Svanlaug demanded, letting go her shaking when Ulfrin began to whimper piteously. "How are you going to become the bride of an insubstantial elemental, unless you're insubstantial, also? How do you think the Council plans to do that? Do you think you'll survive whatever they do to you?"

"I don't know, I don't know!" Ulfrin wailed. "I always thought I knew more than anyone else, because I'm a Sverting. Why did the rest of you allow me to behave as I did? You weren't doing me any favors or being kind to me by sparing me the work. I want to go home, and I don't want ever to leave again. I'd rather wash clothes all day or be a dyer with red and blue hands, than be peace-bride to the Dokkur Lavardur!"

"Hush, there's nothing to be afraid of, now you've come to us," Svanlaug said, smoothing Ulfrin's hair, which she had just been pulling. "Leifr and Thurid are going to get us out safely and back across the river. And Thurid knows where the carbuncle is hidden, with all its knowledge and power. Surely he can help.''

"To be sure," Thurid murmured, frowning deeply and pinching at his lower lip as he gazed at Ulfrin and Svanlaug. "And we must do it before Brjaladur, when every creature with eitur running in his veins goes mad for three days.''

Leifr scowled, coldly eyeing Ulfrin's tears and listening to her repentant sobbing. When Thurid looked at him, he shook his head very slightly.

"It's a trap, of course," he said, drawing Thurid aside and speaking softly. "Deceit seems to run in the Bergmal clan. I wouldn't believe a word of it. She's come to trick you out of the blue carbuncle, and I wouldn't be at all surprised if Svanlaug was helping her.''

"Svanlaug's not so bad as you seem to think," Thurid said. "It won't do us any harm to help them.''

Gedvondur peeped over Thurid's shoulder and added in a throaty murmur, "I wouldn't trust either of those females. I should think you've learned your lesson about women's tears, Thurid. I'd rather have a bath of eitur or dragon venom than be wept upon and begged at.''

"Silence or I'll stuff you back in your sack," Thurid growled.

Ulfrin had scarcely dried her clothing when Raudbjorn and the troll-hounds raised the alarm outside the door. The troll-hounds filled the restless night with their eager howling and cajoling for a hunt.

"Who's out there, Raudbjorn?" Thurid demanded, peering with one eye through a crack in the door.

"Ulf-hedin," Raudbjorn growled. "Name is Hvitur-Fax. Raudbjorn and hounds can have?" He ended on a hopeful note, adding a twanging sound as he tested the edge of his halberd for sharpness with his thumb.

"No, Raudbjorn," Leifr said. "We'll talk to him first, at least.''

"I like Raudbjorn's idea better," Thurid muttered.

Hvitur-Fax stepped into the barn and Leifr shoved shut the door, while Thurid posed on the edge of the firelight with his cloak billowing, his face in shadow.

"What brings you to our haven?" Thurid demanded. "We are safe from the intrusions of our enemies by the ancient privilege of guest right.''

"Guest right does not give you the right of harboring those that the Council wishes to examine," Hvitur-Fax said with a stiff nod toward Ulfrin. "I have come to fetch back the Sverting to her chambers."

Ulfrin rose to her feet, elevating her chin in the old arrogant manner and stiffening her shoulders from their uncharacteristic droop.

"There is no need, Fax," she said in a steady voice. "Why are you always following me about and compelling me to return to my rooms? Am I not trusted by the Council? Am I nothing but a prisoner here, after all?"

Hvitur-Fax replied, "Your place is with the rulers of the realm, child, not here with these poor fools. Very soon they will all be dead if they persist in challenging the Dokkur Lavardur and the Council. People such as these have no place in the return to order that the Dokkur Lavardur will bring. The Lord of Chaos himself will be bound to help us bring peace and the old Dokkalfar ways back to this realm."

"No one wants the old Dokkalfar ways," Svanlaug said. "No one wants to live underground anymore, except a few mad, old, dangerous fools such as the Council."

"Then let them all perish, if they won't live underground," Hvitur-Fax said. "There's getting to be a population problem anyway. We'll have ten underground settlements for each of the remaining tribes, instead of hundreds of small scattered clans. It will be far easier to govern, under one benevolent leader— Alfrekar. With the support of the Ulf-hedin, of course."

"Of course," Svanlaug snapped. "Until you manage to do away with him, as you did my father. If your plan comes to pass, the fortunate ones will be the dead ones."

Hvitur-Fax flicked his cloak impatiently over one shoulder. "Then you'll be one of the most lucky, woman. You, Sverting, have you made up your mind yet? Do you wish to linger with the doomed ones any longer, or do you wish to take your rightful place among the lords of the realm?"

Ulfrin's eyes darted from Svanlaug to Hvitur-Fax and back again. She replied in a voice lacking in conviction, "But she's my sister-kin. I can't turn my back on her and allow her to be destroyed with the rest."

"You've played about Hringurhol like a child long enough," Hvitur-Fax said harshly. "No doubt it's all been very amusing for you, but one day soon you'll have to put your skills to work. You weren't born a Sverting for nothing, and we haven't tolerated you for nothing. We will need a black sorceress to assist us tomorrow night in the final binding of the Dokkur Lavardur. You must be there, as the most honored guest—peace-bride of the Lord of Chaos.''

In a voice struggling not to sound frightened, Ulfrin said, "I want to go home to my mother's tent and learn my skills from her. I know the secret of the laekning, Fax, which is the cure for the Council's eitur. I'll give it to you, if you'll let me go away.''

"You're a spoiled brat," Fax snarled. "You can't tempt me so easily. Do you think your wishes come first and foremost? It's time you were taught the meaning of work and suffering. The Lord of Chaos will not be bound by any other means, and you must play your part in the grand plan of the Council of Threttan.''

"I don't want to," Ulfrin said. "I think your grand plan is not so grand after all, Fax. I want nothing to do with it.''

"It's too late for second thoughts," Fax said. "In spite of being so silly and spoiled, you're valuable to us.''

"You can't force me to go back to Alfrekar," Ulfrin retorted. "I won't stay, even if you take me there. I have my sister and her friends to help me escape.''

"You'll stay, child," Fax growled. "You'll have no choice but to stay. No one escapes from the Lord of Chaos. Come now, this isn't like the Ulfrin of old to become cowardly at the last moment, just when all the doors to the powers you've wanted are about to open to you. Unlimited realms of power will be yours—you and no other are the chosen one, the Sverting. Have you forgotten how rare and precious you truly are? Don't waste your future, even though you might be a little frightened now. After tomorrow night, you will have no need to fear anything. It is you who will be the peace-bride of the Lord of Chaos. You alone will bring about the subjection of the Dokkur Lavardur to our plans. Think of the fame, the honor, the reverence that will attach to your name forever onward from this day. He shall be the Lord of Chaos, and you the Queen.''

Ulfrin looked at Svanlaug and gathered her cloak around her with slow, deliberate motions, as if she were already studying the dignity that befit a queen. "I see this is to be my fate," she said in a wooden voice. "There is nothing I can do to avoid it. We shall go, Fax. Good-bye, sister. I doubt if we shall ever meet again."

When she and Fax were gone, Svanlaug strode around the room in a blind fury, scarcely seeing where she was walking.

"I don't understand it!" she burst out. "One moment she wants to be taken home, the next she's decided she wants to be the peace-bride of that—that creature!"

"Certainly it won't be a conventional marriage," Leifr said, "if I understand what elementals are. The Lord of Chaos is not even a flesh-and-blood person, so how could he take a wife, if he's nothing but an entity?"

"It would be only a symbolic marriage," Thurid said. "A token of the good faith of the Council of Threttan. It's a common enough tradition, even among Sciplings, although it seems more like the taking of hostages sometimes."

"She's my sister, and I don't think it's right." Svanlaug continued to pace, pulling and twisting at her hair and listening to the wind shrieking outside. "I may hate her sometimes, but I should know what's good and bad for her. I don't like this, Thurid. I want to take her out of here. It might put a halt to their entire scheme if we did. But no, you're going to strike a bargain with them tomorrow, aren't you? You're just going to let them have what they want so you can rescue Ljosa, while my sister is sacrificed to a demon!"

Gedvondur clambered out of Thurid's sleeve and gripped his forearm. Gedvondur's sly expression came over Thurid's face, and he was grinning. "I've seen plenty of demons who were subdued by women. Maybe this is just the Council's method of getting rid of the Dokkur Lavardur."

Thurid sighed impatiently and plucked Gedvondur off his arm with no great gentleness. "Get out of here and give me time to think," he said, striding across the room and back. "I sense something, a complication in our plans."

"What plans?" Leifr demanded indignantly. "Which complication? All I see is complication all around us!"

"Hush!" Thurid said with a slashing movement of one hand, and Leifr found himself silenced and calmed despite himself. With a rebuffed growl, he lay down and thought about going back to sleep.

Pausing to stand beside Starkad a moment to count his slow

and steady breaths, Thurid clasped his hands behind his back and turned to gaze into the fire with an intense, rapt expression.

Leifr awakened with a start several hours later when a rooster crowed in a rusty, screeching voice from the rafters overhead. He found Thurid still bolt upright, staring into the ashy coals of their fire, but not too entranced to notice that Leifr was awake.

"It's about time you stopped lazing about," he greeted Leifr tersely, bundling his cloak around him. "Come along, we've got things to do."

"How's Starkad?" Leifr demanded, sitting up at once.

"See for yourself." Thurid twitched one shoulder toward Starkad, who was pacing up and down peering out every crack he could find like a captive bear putting his nose between the bars of a cage.

"Leifr!" Starkad exclaimed, his eyes burning with suppressed excitement. It was the only word he spoke, but Leifr twitched as if jerked on a string, because the voice was Fridmarr's. Then Starkad continued in his own voice, "You saved my life. I shall be in your debt forever. Whatever you command me to do, I'll do it, because I'm never going to leave your back undefended until I'm either dead or too old to lift a sword for you. Tell me what I can do for you, right now. Are you hungry? Thirsty? I am your untiring servant, and you only have to tell me what to do."

Leifr clapped him on the shoulder and grinned. "You can shut up all that blather, Starkad."

"Thank you, I shall," Starkad said righteously.

"Where's Svanlaug?" Leifr asked, glancing around as he pulled on his boots and commenced lacing.

Thurid shook his head. "Shifted into that flying lizard shape of hers and gone," he said. "Still concerned about Ulfrin. Her sister is one of those people everyone worries about. A nice arrangement, if you can manage it, having everyone in the world stepping on themselves trying to take care of you."

Outdoors, the day was gray as inside the lid of a murky caldron. Noting the scaly appearance of the clouds, Leifr glanced upward frequently as he strode along in Thurid's wake, with Starkad clinging closely to his heels. The wind puffed and snarled around in an irregular manner, carrying dust and the unhealthy smell of disturbed barrows. Leifr shivered as he contemplated the thought of an enemy that covered the entire sky, hovering over him and watching him as if he were nothing but an ant scuttling erratically around the anthill known as Hringurhol.

Thurid plowed an unfailing course straight for Heidur's hill, ignoring the Ulf-hedin and wizards already going to and fro from that place. In a winding procession up the hill, they carried the great chairs out of Alfrekar's hall, along with sheep fleeces and other assorted paraphernalia needful for the coming festivities of Brjaladur.

"It's going to be quite a celebration," Thurid said, standing aside as the entire dressed carcass of an ox was carried past. "A pity we won't be here to watch."

"A pity!" Leifr retorted. "I'm afraid I just don't fancy the idea of two hundred Ulf-hedin going mad before my eyes. Thurid, we shouldn't be going up here. It's not a good place."

"Yes, this entire hill is saturated with evil forces," Thurid said, passing his hand through the air to sample it. A faint greenish glow remained where his hand had disturbed the air. "The essence of the Dokkur Lavardur dwells here like the serpent in the mound."

"Is he aware of us?" Starkad asked nervously.

"We are breathing his breath," Thurid said. "We are walking through him at this very instant. Do you think he is unaware?"

Starkad clapped his hand over his mouth and nose, his eyes wide with revulsion as they climbed. Leifr jostled him off the path as a group of straining Ulf-hedin came plodding up the trail, carrying the dragon ship on their shoulders. It swayed and surged as if it were plowing through heavy seas. Leifr flinched as a wave of unseen influence thrust at him, swelling and buffeting as the ship resisted its slow progress up the hill to Heidur's ruins. Exhausted Ulf-hedin collapsed, and others sprang into their places.

Thurid stood back and watched, his face expressionless, his eyes veiled with his own inward thoughts.

"That was our only means of escape," Leifr whispered. "Now we'll have to go two days down the river to Ferja."

"It matters not," Thurid said, falling into a position behind the dragon ship.

Within the gates of the ruin was a seething mass of Ulf-hedin, so Thurid climbed up the grassy wall and looked down inside. Leifr crouched behind a rock, appalled at Thurid's temerity as he posed himself arrogantly on the parapet, cloak flapping against the leaden sky, gripping his staff as if he were about to call down gouts of fire on the scene below.

A freshly constructed altar of rocks and bones stood in the center of the courtyard, doused with fresh blood. A recalcitrant bull was tied to a pair of posts beside the dragon ship. Individual Ulf-hedin brought their own offerings ranging from smaller creatures, such as cats, dogs, chickens, geese, and sheep, until the courtyard looked more like a livestock fair.

"Gifts to propitiate the Lord of Chaos on his wedding night," Thurid said grimly. "This is going to be a night that will shake the Alfar realm to its very roots. The Dokkur Lavardur will be bound to the wishes of the Council of Threttan."

Leifr watched, recognizing women's clothes and household possessions being brought to the ship, a rich dowry indeed. Furniture, saddles, bridles, tools, cooking implements, and food were placed inside the ship.

"These preparations remind me more of a funeral than a wedding," he said to Thurid as several horses were also added to the growing herd of gifts.

Starkad watched with a frown. "What use has an elemental for all these solid, heavy things? What good is a wife to him, for that matter?"

"All things possess a spirit," Thurid said, tapping the earth with his staff. "Everything from a fiery warhorse to a humble stone—although the spirit of a stone is very slow and dull. Objects made by human hands are endowed with a share of the maker's spirit. With the release of that spirit, the Dokkur Lavardur will be fed and strengthened, just as you are when you devour a tasty roasted fowl."

"I don't think I would enjoy a feast of spirits," Starkad said with a shudder.

A tent was erected beside the altar. The dragon ship was hauled into the inner sanctum and down between the rows of tombs to a central court. The dowry was loaded into it, and heaps of firewood stacked around it suggested more of the unpleasant process of elemental propitiation and summoning.

Shortly afterward, a deep booming sound commenced down below in the narrow dark streets of Hringurhol, and the Ulf-hedin skulking around the altar site stopped and pricked up their ears to listen. Hastily they concluded their business and departed from the hilltop. By slow degrees the booming sound approached. Looking back, Leifr saw a group of Ulf-hedin proceeding slowly up the hillside in a solemn procession.

"Seider drums!" Starkad muttered in the hoarse, unfamiliar voice of Fridmarr. His eyes blazed and he fidgeted like a nervous horse trying to make up its mind to bolt. "Leifr, we must get out of here! Come along, quickly! We'll lose our minds if we stay! They're summoning the Dokkur Lavardur!"

He started to slither away down the hillside, but Leifr gripped him by the collar.

"Not just yet, we're not going," he said tautly, his eyes upon the approaching procession.

"Don't be a fool, Leifr!" Fridmarr's voice snapped, drawing up Starkad's body in furious indignation and jerking away from his handhold. "Don't you think I've been here before? Don't you think I know what's about to happen? They're going to slaughter all this livestock until the ground is a sea of blood, and burn them all as an offering to that monstrosity of the skies."

Thurid's mouth dropped open and resolved into a rather pleased smile. "Fridmarr! You scoundrel! Mind your own business and stay out of this. I'm the wizard in charge of this expedition now, not you."

"And the result will be the death of us all, judging by the way you've managed so far," Fridmarr's voice retorted. "Now come away from here before you can't."

"We've managed at least as well as you did," Leifr said. "We're not dead yet and no one's forced us to take eitur."

Starkad swung around stiffly to look at him a long moment, and Leifr eyed him narrowly. For a moment he thought he saw Fridmarr's sardonic smile flicker across Starkad's face and Leifr felt himself heating up for a challenge. He turned his back insultingly, and when he turned around again, Fridmarr's influence had departed from Starkad's expression, leaving him looking young and rather frightened and excited. It was only Starkad's trusting eye returning his gaze.

When the drummers reached the hilltop, they silenced their drumming. Down below in Hringurhol, the drumming had signaled the beginning of the evacuation of everyone who was not Ulf-hedin. Carts piled high with household possessions lumbered southward toward Ferja; those with no carts walked, carrying their goods upon their shoulders. Straggling bands of sheep, reluctant goats, cattle, and horses joined in the untidy procession, urged along by the anxious shouts of their owners, all wincing in the brunt of the harsh, buffeting wind.

At noonday another burst of drumming from the Council Hall announced the convocation of the Council of Threttan. By this time the evacuation of Hringurhol was in full spate, a tide of carts and livestock sweeping down the hillside away from the settlement. The last to become concerned were the wanderers, who lived their lives out of carts and wagons and were ready to depart at a moment's notice at any time, so they lingered.

Thurid gripped his staff and nodded to Leifr. "It's time to go. Starkad, you can hitch a ride to Ferja with Beitski and the knacker-women. At least you'll be safe, if something should happen to us, and it's not at all inconceivable that something will. You're not coming with us, so there's no sense in pleading and begging and trying to change our minds."

"I wasn't about to," Starkad said, his voice calm. "But what about Svanlaug and Ulfrin?"

"Svanlaug is on her own," Thurid said tersely. "As always. She knows the rules here, perhaps better than we do ourselves. Don't start to fret about her now. Just get yourself out of this place if you have to."

"Of course, Thurid," Starkad said.

Thurid darted him a suspicious glance, but Leifr gave him no time to form a reply. He unearthed the false *Endalaus Daudi* from its hiding place, keeping it wrapped in its concealing bundle. Thurid poured a little oil on the cloths and set them smoldering convincingly before wrapping it all in a sheepskin.

"Gedvondur!" he snapped, peering into his satchel. "Are you ready?"

Gedvondur crept out, carrying something concealed in his palm, and leaped onto Thurid's sleeve. Thurid placed him on the charred end of his staff, gripping the end of it like a large spider. A blue light glowed between his long, bony fingers.

"You are mad, you know," Starkad said in Fridmarr's voice. "You might deceive the Council for a while, but you won't fool them for long. Have you thought about what you're going to do once they discover your clever scheme?"

Thurid turned to glower at Starkad. Poking one finger at his face, he said, "You'd better not overtax this body you've gotten yourself into, or you'll be worse off than Gedvondur."

"Very true, Thurid," Fridmarr said. "I shall let him rest. Tell Gedvondur it does no good to be angry at me."

Gedvondur ran up the staff and gripped Thurid's hand. Thurid made a spitting, sputtering sound, briefly convulsing his face into a twisted mask of hatred.

"That's enough!" Thurid snapped, evicting Gedvondur rudely and jamming him back onto the end of his staff. "All that is nothing but water under the bridge. You were friends once, you know, very close friends. I suggest you attempt to regain some of your old friendship, or at least tolerance, or I don't know how we shall all manage to abide one another's presence."

"We won't," Fridmarr muttered resentfully.

Leifr looked into Starkad's eyes. "Fridmarr, you see to it that Starkad is kept safe."

"Leifr, I can take care of myself," Starkad said in an offended tone. "I know you want me out of Hringurhol. Don't you trust me to do what you've asked?"

"Not particularly," Leifr said with a last uneasy sidelong look at him. "Especially now, when I'm not really certain whom I'm talking to."

As Leifr and Thurid made their way up the hillside, the sky darkened, although it was nearly noonday. The wind had died to an absolute dead calm and the bellies of the clouds seemed to press down on the green fells and black scarps. A sharp coldness settled in the bones and numbed exposed flesh.

The gates leading into the crumbling courtyard were closed, and Hvitur-Fax stood beside the entrance. The tops of the walls were clotted with Ulf-hedin, clinging to their lofty perches to watch as the darkness deepened and the light died.

Thurid and Leifr approached the gate where Hvitur-Fax stood guard, his breath frosting the long hairs of his wolf pelt. With a malevolent glower he stood aside, silently motioning them to enter.

Chapter 14

◇◇◇

From the outside gate to the dais in the Council Hall, the distance was about a hundred steps. On either side, the frozen carved faces on the tombs gazed into nothingness with pious disregard for their own decay and the events of mortal life happening around them. Leifr automatically counted off the steps as he and Thurid approached the Council. Flanked by two large braziers burning with a fierce bluish light, the Council of Threttan sat in their carved chairs in a half circle, with Alfrekar in the center and Sorkvir sitting at his left with a smoky pall hanging over him.

Outside, from the direction of Heidur's ruins, the seidur drums commenced a triumphant thundering roll that throbbed painfully in Leifr's ears and set his teeth on edge. Fortunately it halted just when he thought he could stand the reverberations no longer as they rolled around the ruined hall, pounding at his ears.

"The Council bids you greetings," Alfrekar said, his dry voice carrying around the hushed hall. "Will you take some refreshment, as a token of our mutual respect for the agreement we are sealing this day?" He gestured with one hand toward a small table laden with a leather bottle and two small cups. Leifr's scalp rippled with alarm, recalling the cups and flask used at the Ulf-hedin initiation he had seen.

Thurid nodded his head once in solemn majesty. "We accept your hospitality," he said gravely, "and we, too, have brought a guest-right drink to share with the Council in celebration of the new alliance that will grow between Ljosalfar and Dokkalfar." He removed a flask from his satchel and placed it upon the table with Alfrekar's bottle and cups.

"Time enough for that later," Alfrekar said, lacing his fingers together and making no move to pour the drink. "I see you have brought the sword. I assume you also have the blue orb of Galdur?''

Thurid opened his satchel and took out Gedvondur, still tightly curled around the stone in a fist, with blue light leaking through his emaciated fingers. The Council leaned forward slightly in their chairs, eyes narrowing intently as Thurid displayed his creation and stepped forward toward the dais. With obvious care he laid Gedvondur on the black cushion at Alfrekar's feet.

Then all their hooded, narrowed, malevolent eyes came to rest expectantly upon Leifr, standing with his feet planted wide in stubborn defiance.

"And the sword?" Alfrekar prompted gently, when the silence became overlong and too intense.

"I wish to see Ljosa first," Leifr said. "I want to be certain that she is alive and well, and her spirit is restored to her before I turn over my sword."

Sorkvir rose to his feet with a muttered curse and commenced slapping at a small outburst of flames. "Wretched Scipling! Have I not told you the spell will be lifted the moment she is carried over the threshold of this hall? Do you think that I have the time to carry around the burden of her curse continually?''

"I think you are a liar and a murderer," Leifr replied. "How could I ever believe anything you say, after all you have done to deceive and imprison me?''

"Sorkvir's word is the truth, for once," Alfrekar said with a deadly glance leveled at Sorkvir. "I give you my word that the spell will dissolve the moment Hroaldsdottir is carried over this threshold. See for yourself that she is alive and only sleeping." He gestured with one hand toward an open sarcophagus illuminated by a pair of whale-oil lamps. "I, too, am weary of Sorkvir's treachery. All has been long known to me about his attempt to elevate his own carcass to the high seat of the Council. As you have seen—" He gazed at Sorkvir until a thread of flame burst out of Sorkvir's chest. "—he has been chastened and soon his seat will also be vacant, after the inevitable consequences of his attempted treachery to me have reached their gradual conclusion.''

Sorkvir bared his teeth in a furious grimace. "The treachery is all yours!" he snarled, smothering a small combustion with a handful of his gown. "You planned this torture long before I planned to betray you. You would have destroyed me along with

Afgang. You've been plotting to use the Scipling against me long before he brought about the destruction of your rival Djofull. Djofull was wise in his repudiation of this Council.''

"Was he wise to have sent you to take the seat I offered him?'' Alfrekar queried sharply. "I was not deceived. I knew he had sent a viper to worm his way into the heart of the Council. But it matters not now. Djofull is dead, and you will soon be eaten alive from within by unquenchable fires. No one will ever forget your penalty for your treachery to me.''

"Gloat while you can,'' Sorkvir snarled in an undertone as he stalked away to stand in the darkness beyond the circle of the Council, surreptitiously beating at a small fire that sprang out somewhere beneath his cloak.

Ignoring their wrangling, Leifr approached the sarcophagus and gazed down at Ljosa. She looked as if she were sleeping deeply, her face faintly flushed and warm when he ventured to touch her cheek. Even the tips of her fingers were rosy, and she sighed in her sleep when he whispered her name.

"You must surrender that sword,'' Sorkvir's voice cawed harshly, cutting viciously into his reverie. "If you wish to see her awaken again.''

"You shall have it,'' Leifr said. "As soon as I reach the safety of the far side of your threshold with Ljosa.''

The rest of the Council frowned and shook their heads.

"The Council,'' Alfrekar said, "fears a trick of some sort. They insist that the sword be surrendered now, not after you have got what you want outside this hall.''

"You already have the blue orb,'' Thurid said testily. "Isn't that a strong enough testimony of our good faith? Or perhaps we should drink to one another's health to show our pure intent? Perhaps you should drink from your bottle and I should drink from mine to prove we're not trying to poison each other.''

"I accept your challenge,'' Alfrekar said. "Let us drink from the same cup to show there's no harm.''

The dark fluid was accordingly poured into Alfrekar's silver cup and he drank it off. Wiping his mouth on the back of his hand, he gazed around the silent hall a moment and handed the cup to Thurid. Thurid raised it to his lips and drank, returning the cup to the table.

"You see,'' Alfrekar said, "there is nothing to fear. We can trust each other to do the right thing.''

No sooner had he spoken when the seidur drums outside sounded a furious salvo and the distant doors burst open with a gust of cold wind, admitting Hvitur-Fax and the sound of a distant uproar of fighting. His voice boomed over the drums and the howling of the Ulf-hedin.

"Lord Counselors! The Inquisitors have broken their guest right and have attacked the shrine on Hringur-knip! I urge you to take shelter at once, Exalted Ones, while the Ulf-hedin battle with the Guild.

"And where were the Ulf-hedin that guard the jewels of the Pentacle of Chaos?" Alfrekar demanded, gripping the arms of his chair, his face livid."

"It's almost Brjaladur," Fax said. "The guards deserted their posts, leaving the shrine and the jewels unprotected. When they are found, they will be put to death."

"Unprotected!" Alfrekar screamed. "The greatest treasure of the realm! Fax, if the Pentacle is destroyed, you shall have to pay for this dereliction with your own hide and perhaps your life."

Hvitur-Fax shrugged. "You may not get the chance. The Inquisitors threatened to destroy the Pentacle of Chaos, the altar, and the dragon ship if we do not relinquish all our holds upon the Dokkur Lavardur. They also demand the return of their prisoner Thurid, as well as the outlaw Scipling Leifr Thorljottsson."

"That will never be," Alfrekar's dry voice said. "The Inquisitors are too late. We have the fifth jewel of the Pentacle of Chaos now. The Inquisitors have failed." He reached out and plucked up Gedvondur from the cushion and held up the hand, letting the rays of blue light filter down in the ruddy gloom of the ancient hall's atmosphere. "Let the Council of Threttan and the Lord of Chaos be one in purpose and power. My friends of the Council, let us not take shelter like cowards while the Ulf-hedin begin a useless battle that will only result in the destruction of our altar to the Lord of Chaos. We must go and reason with these mad Inquisitors. They won't dare oppose the completed Pentacle of Chaos."

"The sword! Take the sword!" Sorkvir rasped, lunging into the light like a smoking, tattering scarecrow falling off its pole.

"Not until Ljosa is safely outside!" Leifr answered in a furious shout over the distracted babbling of the Council as they leaped to their feet, clutching their staffs and preparing to do battle with the Inquisitors.

"Those fools!" Thurid growled in mighty affront. "Breaking the guest right! We had no part of their decision! Drat those Inquisitors! Why can't they mind their own business? Come along, I'll attempt to reason with them, which is smarter than trying to fight them. Leifr, come with me. We'll be back for Ljosa the moment we reach an agreement with the Inquisitors."

Leifr shook his head doggedly. "I've gotten this close to her now, and I'm not leaving until I can carry her outside to safety. You don't need me to tip the scales in your favor against the Inquisitors. There are only six of them and eleven of you, plus hordes of Ulf-hedin. Whatever happens, I'm going to get Ljosa out of here."

"Fair enough," Alfrekar said, "so long as you hand over that sword now."

"That I won't do," said Leifr. "I'll stay here on vigil until you return and we can make the exchange as I proposed, outside, with Ljosa safe."

"I haven't time to quarrel about it now," Alfrekar snapped. "Stay here until we return then, but I advise you not to spend your time thinking up treacheries. Ask Sorkvir how well treachery is rewarded in Hringurhol."

"The seidur drums will begin again very shortly," Thurid said to Leifr in a low voice as he passed by. "If I'm not back by then, you'd better get yourself and Ljosa out of here."

The sounds of fighting intensified, punctuated by the shriek and sizzle of ice-bolts and fire-bolts colliding. Leifr crouched beside Ljosa's tomb in the failing light of the braziers, wincing at the echoes and the bursts of stray influences ricocheting around the Council Hall. Outside, he sensed a heavy black nothingness pressing down upon Hringurhol, as if the Dokkur Lavardur were greedily absorbing each blast of energy and sponging up each trace of life force freed from the dying Ulf-hedin. With the sky so dark, Leifr had no idea of the passage of time, except that it seemed terribly long, surrounded by the tombs of the forgotten rulers of ancient Hringurhol.

Suddenly the seidur drums commenced with a rumbling crash that reverbrated in the echoes of the old Hall. He tried plugging his ears, but it did nothing to stop the terrible pounding inside his head. All his bones and body to its very center were gripped in the inexorable rhythm of the drums. He waited, hoping it was only another warning, urging those not Ulf-hedin of Hringurhol to hasten their departure, but the drumming did not stop. It would continue until every living thing in Hringurhol was captured in the meshes of its power. He had to act now, or he would have no volition of his own to act with.

The Inquisitors took possession of the ruins of Heider, with one Inquisitor positioned at the ruined gateway, gazing stolidly at the Ulf-hedin menacing and capering at a safe distance. Above, in the empty windows and arches, the Inquisitors lit fires to prevent a stealthy attack under cover of the Dokkur Lavardur's gloomy cloud. Fodor placed himself in an archway, taking a commanding viewpoint of the hilltop, the altar and dragon ship behind him in the ruins, and the pathway leading up from Hringurhol below.

The Council proceeded through the waves of frantic Ulf-hedin like a dark and stately ship cleaving troubled waters, trailing clouds of mist and war banners.

"Silence the drums!" Alfrekar commanded, and Hvitur-Fax relayed the order, silencing the drums immediately.

Alfrekar approached, stepping into the cleared circle surrounding the redoubtable Varkar, who stood with his arms folded impassively before him, gazing straight ahead with the implacable calm of a man who fears no death.

"Fodor!" Alfrekar called. "Is this the way Ljosalfar settle their disputes? Sieges and warfare? You've always claimed to know the better way, but surely this is not it!"

Fodor's voice came down from the arch. "This is an unclean place and we are going to destroy what you have done here. This is the end of your scheme to harness the Dokkur Lavardur to your wishes, Alfrekar."

"The mad fool!" Thurid muttered with a snort. "Fodor, you madman! Listen to me!"

Thurid strode after Alfrekar, passing the spot where he had stopped and not halting until he was almost face to face with Varkar, who suddenly unbarred his arms and extended his staff warningly.

"Varkar! Let him pass!" Fodor called down.

"Bah!" Thurid said into Varkar's grim face. "Killing me is not your lot in life, as long as Fodor is alive. He's reserved that special privilege for himself.'' He circumnavigated Varkar and halted below Fodor's arch, glaring upward.

"I know what it is you truly want," Thurid said. "All you've ever wanted since the moment you heard my name was the privilege of destroying me. Well, now you've got your opportunity. Why don't you come down here and we'll match our powers, Fodor. You're afraid I might have strengths the Fire Wizards' Guild doesn't have. You're afraid I might know something you don't. What the Fire Wizards fear, you destroy. Perhaps it's time for some new Inquisitors, Fodor. Perhaps you've outlived your usefulness. Perhaps your narrow opinion of good and evil powers has crippled the Guild instead of strengthening it. Something is rotten in the Fire Wizards' Guild, Fodor, and I believe it is you!''

"Is this a challenge to the Guild?" Fodor demanded.

Thurid hurled his satchel on the ground. "No, it's not a challenge to the Guild!" Thurid roared. "It's a challenge to you and your carking vulture Inquisitors! I've had enough of your following and hounding and threatening and purging! Either the Inquisitors will leave Hringurhol alive or I shall, but tonight is going to decide it for once and for all! Let Brjaladur begin with our challenge!''

"Brjaladur has gotten to your senses!" Fodor said. "You must be insane, Thurid! We have no desire to destroy you, only to improve your powers and skills.''

Thurid thrust his staff in the direction of the Council, backed by ranks of lesser wizards and hordes of snarling Ulf-hedin. "This is no time for improvements. If bloodshed and mayhem are not what you intend, come out of that shrine and speak to me like a man, not a siege holder!''

Fodor disappeared from his arch, and in a few moments the Inquisitors appeared in the doorway of the ruin, hesitating warily on the broken threshold. Thurid strode forward, his staff spewing blue vapor.

In a low growl he demanded, "What do you think you're doing, you fool? I've got the situation well in hand.''

"Yes, you've turned over the blue orb to them!" Fodor said. "And you intend to give them the sword of Endless Death! Don't you realize you can't negotiate with these brigands? They want nothing but our destruction, and you're giving them the tools to do it with!''

Alfrekar edged his way around the scowling Varkar and his spewing staff, his eyes darting back and forth between Thurid and Fodor.

"We desire no one's destruction," he said with a final glance over his shoulder at Varkar. "The annihilation of the Ljosalfar tribe would accomplish nothing. Are we not all children of the same father, who sired the thirteen tribes and scattered us over the face of the land? We may quarrel from time to time, but with the protection of the Dokkur Lavardur, we who love the darkness will have the shelter we need from the heat of the sun. The Council does not want destruction; we want only peace with our kinfolk, the Ljosalfar."

"Not that we've noticed lately," Fodor grunted. "The tide of Dokkalfar possession is threatening to push the Ljosalfar off Skarpsey entirely and into the sea."

"Changes will be made, of course," Alfrekar said.

"Perhaps we should talk about it," Fodor said. "A genuine truce must be hammered out before I'll consent to return this hilltop to you."

"Very well," Alfrekar said. "We have until midnight to reach an agreement. At that time, we must make our offerings to propitiate the Lord of Chaos, or I fear his wrath will be turned against us."

"Midnight?" Fodor repeated, rubbing his chin dubiously. "That's not much time. This should prove to you the inadvisability of feeding something that has more strength than you do. How do you know he's going to be satisfied with what you have to offer?"

"We are offering a peace-bride," Alfrekar said. "He will be bound to keep the peace."

Fodor shook his head. "I've seen it fail many times before. His kind is not to be reasoned with or propitiated. Our only deliverance is the destruction of this altar."

"Give us just until midnight to prove our reasonable intent," Alfrekar said. "At that time, if the Dokkur Lavardur is not given what has been promised, he will destroy us all and it won't matter if you have blown the altar to powder. If the Fire Wizards' Guild truly wants peace, I doubt if you'd wish for such a thing to happen. It's better to have the Dokkur Lavardur contained by someone than to let him run rampant at the beck and call of any vengeful practitioner who desires to work a mischief."

Fodor retorted, "The Dokkur Lavardur is more likely to run rampant at your beck and call than at any other's. This useless talking is at an end. We shall not allow you to gain the control of this airborn monster."

Signaling to the others, Fodor turned on his heel and strode back into the shrine.

"A most unreasonable man," Thurid mused. "Blind in both eyes to the possibilities and deaf in both ears to the voice of reason. I truly apologize for my fellow Ljosalfar. I thought he would see the need for striking a bargain, as Leifr and I have done."

"I don't believe anyone is completely deaf," Alfrekar said, "especially to the seidur drums. We shall drum them out of our shrine and perhaps then they will be more eager to come to terms. A simple protection spell—haeli, haetta, haela—repeated in sets of threes will divert the influence if you become too uncomfortable. Over the years we've learned to resist it."

"Haeli, haetta, haela," Thurid muttered as Alfrekar gave the signal for the drumming to begin.

With rising dread, Leifr realized he was twirling Vidskipti's ring over and over in his pocket. Thurid was not coming back to advise or help him, and the drumming sounded as if it would go on all night this time. Finally he slipped the ring on and waited hopefully to see if he felt any different, or if he could hear or see any better, but there was no change that he could detect. He could hear the Ulf-hedin outside the Hall, tramping up and down in anticipation of the Brjaladur rituals, keeping time with shouts and screams to the pounding of the drums. The weighty influence of the Dokkur Lavardur pressed down upon Hringurhol until Leifr felt the breath was nearly crushed out of him.

The great broken dome of the Hall creaked and groaned threateningly, with occasional bursts of lurid blue flame skating along the arches and shadows. Suddenly the roof-darkness above exploded with ominous grinding, creaking, and breaking sounds, and larger samples of the roof came crashing down among the tombs in showers of dust. In the silence that followed the breaking of the dome, Leifr could hear the Ulf-hedin raising a savage, triumphant yell outside from the direction of Heidur's ruins, followed by a mighty rolling of the drums that soon settled again into the mesmerizing rhythm he was already too familiar with. Now, however, the reverberations seemed to shake toward the great domed roof itself and its supports. More dust, mortar, and stones dropped down, veiling the hall in choking clouds. Intermittently larger pieces came down, and one was larger than the largest of the tombs, crashing down like an avalanche.

Leifr climbed into the sarcophagus and knelt, lifting Ljosa up into his arms with her head resting against his shoulder. As he paused a moment, judging the best course to take through the tombs and up the steps to the door, he thought he glimpsed human shapes moving through the gliding veils of dust and shadow, and they looked like the shades of warriors, all trooping out of that doomed hall, moving purposefully and in silent haste.

Even the wraiths of those buried here were abandoning the place.

He began to hurry through the tombs. Ljosa shifted restlessly in his arms, and suddenly something that felt like a wing brushed across his face. His arms tingled strangely and Ljosa felt suddenly lighter. Looking at her, his heart lurched with horror. He ought to have known beyond a shadow of a doubt that the word of neither Sorkvir nor Alfrekar was worth a pinch of salt in a high wind. She was changing shapes, glowing with a sinister green light. Her face shrank rapidly into the black countenance of a swan, and her restless thrashing turned into the determined beating of huge wings that hammered at him with bruising blows from the hard edge of the first joint. The black swan hissed at him furiously, its long neck curling like a sinuous black snake as it bit at him with its bill. Its heavy webbed feet clawed frantically, straining to escape.

Leifr winced and ducked as the creature struck at his face, probably hoping to blind him. He gripped its neck and bent its head down under his arm and restrained its beating wings with all his might and staggered onward.

The form of the swan vanished like a dwindling candle flame, and Ljosa's true shape was restored. Leifr struggled over a heap of fallen masonry, scarcely able to keep his feet under him, blinking at the irritating trickle of blood leaking into one eye from a gash the swan's bill had made in his eyebrow. His battle with the swan must have tired him; Ljosa's weight in his arms slowed him down and made him stumble. He looked at her, relieved to see she was herself again.

Leifr stopped and took a good grip on her as she began to writhe and twist in his arms. Scales crept up her neck and covered her face and her arms. Her hands were converted to claws and her face was that of a lingorm, its jaws parting in a deadly hiss. A cloud of venom seared Leifr's face, almost blinding him with pain, and sharp claws dug relentlessly into his shoulders. The creature's barbed tail lashed at him, slashing his cloak to ribbons and ripping holes in his tunic beneath. His flesh was likewise scored, exacerbated by the venom of the lingorm's barb. Wherever he gripped the beast, its scales cut his hands like knife edges, and it managed to sink its fangs into his upper arm before he was able to grab its snaky neck. Its coils wrapped around his legs, trying to halt his advance toward the doorway.

Leifr's answer to the lingorm's deadly antics was to squeeze it harder, until it uncurled its tail and began thrashing around violently. Its baleful yellow eyes gradually turned purple and its forked tongue lolled out of its mouth. Gradually the dragon spell dispersed, and again Leifr was holding Ljosa. He rose shakily to his feet, gazing up at the stairs ahead of him and the doorway above. He had only a dozen more tombs and heaps of rubble to negotiate, those stairs to climb, then Ljosa would be free.

He didn't pause to assess his injuries, knowing that they were considerable, and if he was aware of how damaged he was, he might not be able to reach the door. During his Viking days he had seen warriors who were already dead men fighting long beyond the boundaries of mortal pain, kept alive by will alone, dying only when the battle was over and the enemy destroyed. Once beyond that threshold above, he had no thought for himself, only the hope that Ljosa would be free at last and someone would take her back to Gliru-hals where she had been born.

The pain in his lacerated hands subsided to a dull burning. He was scarcely aware of anything except the necessity for reaching the stairs, hardly hearing the drumming and the tumult of fighting outside the hall. Ljosa was shifting shapes again, just as he reached the foot of the stairs. He stopped, waiting to see what creature he would be battling next. Whatever it was, he would be steadier on level ground.

Ljosa's form glowed with red light, shrinking steadily and glowing more brightly until he was clasping nothing but a solid heavy bar of red-hot metal. His hands blazed with searing pain, but he summoned the will not to let go and started up the stairs, forcing his agonized legs to leap up two stairs at a stride while the heat of the bar traveled up his arms and into his chest. He could scarcely breathe with the terrible heat wracking his lungs, making each breath agony. The last five strides up the stairs were in virtual darkness as the fire threatened to burst his skull. The door stood open, a pale rectangle in the fiery darkness crashing down around him. He plunged through the doorway, oblivious of all else, clasping the fatal iron to his breast, knowing that there would be no more transformations, desiring nothing but the end of this torment. The fiery glow of a bonfire showed him a wall of leering, snarling Ulf-hedin awaited him, their teeth bared in welcoming snarls, their black claws reaching out at him. With his last ounce of resistance, he threw back his head and summoned the shout from unknown depths of determination. One voice against all that uproar of pounding and yelling made no sense, and he was certain the only one who heard the words was himself.

"Komast Undan!" he yelled as loudly as he could into the deafening cacophony.

A windy roaring sound commenced in the clouds above, gaining in volume and angry howling pitch as if some massive angry creature were gathering strength for an attack. The earth underfoot trembled slightly with ominous promise and the echoing roof chambers boomed and grumbled as more dust and pebbles sifted down from above. Then a mighty wave of force swooped down from the darkness, swallowing up the bonfire flame and magnifying it a dozenfold. It leaped onto the skulking Ulf-hedin with a roaring crackle, igniting their fur in halos of blue flame. Yelling, they threw their wolf capes on the ground and charged away in terror, beating at cloaks and sleeves that also flamed with a fire that would not be smothered. A few lingered a moment in a vain attempt to trample out the flames, but when their boots and leggings also acquired the eerie blue flames of the capes, they speedily abandoned their efforts and departed, howling.

Leifr's fiery consciousness sank slowly into darkness, like a funeral ship giving way to the dark sea. He dropped to his knees, still clutching the burning bar, letting it fall with a sizzle onto the earth. A few drops of rain hissed upon it virulently, dissolving in puffs of steam. The drums were silent, not an Ulf-hedin stirred. Looking up toward Heidur's ruins, he saw a ring of bonfires around a tent.

"Thurid!" His lips were too seared and his throat too dry to form the name. The silent call drained the last of his strength, and he sprawled forward on the faint green stubble of grass.

As Alfrekar had predicted, the Inquisitors were more amenable to bargaining once their ears had been subjected to the pounding of seidur drums for an hour or more. The only pity was the waste of the time necessary to drum them into a state of reluctant submission. Upon one point, however, they refused to budge.

"We must have Thurid," Fodor said repeatedly. "We shall send another representative from the Fire Wizards' Guild to sit in the Council of Threttan."

Thurid listened impassively to the arguing, pressing the tips of his fingers together in a narrow tent. His attention kept straying back to Leifr, waiting in Alfrekar's Hall. He became more uneasy the longer the arguing went on. Suddenly something went through him like an arrow and he leaped to his feet, startling the Council and Inquisitors.

"Enough of this pointless arguing," he said roughly. "If I am the bone of contention here, then let me decide what must be done. I shall go with the Inquisitors, if only to settle this quarrel before midnight. But the person who will take my place will be Gradagur, my old teacher and friend, not a regular Guild Fire Wizard. I think that will be agreeable to both sides, once the Guild gets accustomed to a such a new and startling idea."

"Gradagur!" the Inquisitors muttered. "It's doubtful he'd be acceptable to the Guild."

"Then he must be a good sort," Alfrekar said. "If you insist upon taking Thurid, then by all means let us have Gradagur. I think I've heard of him. He has marvelous visions of future events that no one can understand. We can accept Gradagur, if Thurid recommends him."

The hoary old wizards of the Council scowled and pulled their lips and ears in thought and reluctantly nodded.

"I must get back to Leifr," Thurid said, nervously tossing his cloak over his shoulder. "I feel quite certain that something has gone wrong, leaving him there alone in that Hall with nothing but draugar and tombs and Ulf-hedin. Being a Scipling, he's not good at resisting temptation.''

"This will be the last delay we grant you," Fodor warned, "so don't try to stretch it into another attempt to cheat us out of our confrontation. You wanted a challenge, Thurid, and I don't intend to miss it, either. To ensure your cooperation, I've prepared a rune stick. A drop of your blood is all I require to bind you to your agreement.''

"Just make it quick," Thurid snapped, pulling out his own knife and jabbing a hole in his thumb.

The Council followed at the heels of the Inquisitors, grumbling suspiciously and keeping a wary interval between themselves. Alfrekar beckoned to Hvitur-Fax.

"Is the Pentacle now securely guarded?" he demanded.

"As well as can be expected during Bjaladur," Fax said gloomily. "You know well that all the packmasters are being challenged for their positions. The fighting won't end for three days. I myself shall stand guard at the shrine. No one will have the temerity to challenge Wolfmaster Fax.''

"No one can say what might happen during Bjaladur," Alfrekar retorted. "But so far, things are working out in our favor.''

Chapter 15

◇◇◇◇◇◇◇◇◇◇◇◇◇◇◇◇◇◇◇◇◇◇◇◇◇◇◇◇◇◇◇◇◇◇◇◇◇◇◇

Outside the Council Hall, the lingering Ulf-hedin gathered in a wary circle around something on the ground, sniffing from a cautious distance. They melted back at the approach of the cloaked wizards. Sorkvir's presence was betrayed by the pall of acrid smoke that continually followed him, like a malingering trash fire. Thurid plunged forward with a choked exclamation and halted beside Leifr's motionless form, a darker shadow in the gloom cast by the Dokkur Lavardur rumbling and roiling overhead. He knelt down, touching Leifr lightly and finding no response.

"It was a trick!" he gasped. "You've killed him!"

"Success at last," Alfrekar said with a harsh chuckle, reaching out to prod at the sword hanging sheathed at Leifr's back. A warning puff of smoke oozed from the rags wrapping it. "We're rid of you, Thurid. We've got the blue orb of Galdur. The sword remains, and the Scipling is dead. Take him away, Fodor, and if you've got any sense at all you'll see to it he's left with no more powers than a newborn kitten. We swore an oath in blood and runes, and it must be upheld."

"I don't like your manner of upholding your oaths and bargains," Fodor said to Alfrekar. "But as long as I've got what I came here for, I'm content to leave you to the mercies of the Dokkur Lavardur. I don't think you'll last long, Alfrekar. Come along, Thurid. There's nothing more we can do here. I'm truly sorry about the Scipling. You did agree to surrender."

Thurid heaved himself onto his feet, reeling a little before he steadied himself with his staff. "Very well," he said. "This is the end of it then. I've failed."

Fodor patted his shoulder in a comradely manner. "Not so much as you think, Thurid. Let's get out of this place before they start that horrid drumming again."

"We shall give you long enough to get as far as the barrow field to the south," Alfrekar said. "And then we shall start the drums for the summons to the wedding feast."

The Ulf-hedin pressing near enough to hear responded with a throaty muttering of approval.

When the Inquisitors were gone, Alfrekar bent to the sword and began tearing the wrappings off. The oiled rags inside the outer layer were finally supplied with air and burst into flame. Alfrekar leaped back with a curse, then began kicking the outer rags back until the fire was extinguished and only a wisp of smoke curled up from the sword.

"Cursed Rhbu metal!" Alfrekar snarled, belatedly making a sign in the air. "Don't anyone touch it. I'll put a neutralizing spell on it later so it can be handled. Is the Scipling truly dead?"

"Almost certainly, or he soon will be," Sorkvir replied resentfully. "No mere mortal Scipling can survive a retrieval spell. Now you've got the Rhbu sword—not that you'd feel any gratitude for all the work I've done to get it into your hands. Without me, you'd be as far from it as ever. It would still be buried in Bjartur. And who was it that gathered the five stones for you?"

Alfrekar turned his back and spoke to the rest of the Council, leaning dubiously on their staffs and making signs behind their backs.

"I knew he'd try to save Hroaldsdottir, like the fool he is," Alfrekar said, almost chortling with satisfaction. "Sciplings do have a morbid tendency to martyr themselves."

"Everyone who deals with you becomes a martyr," Sorkvir growled hoarsely, swatting at a burning coal simmering inside his cloak. "After all I've done, this is my reward."

Alfrekar returned sharply, "You needn't expect any mercy from me, Sorkvir, not after all you've done against me. The sweetest portion of all is knowing I'll soon be rid of you—but not too soon. It's so pleasurable watching you struggle and burn, trapped in that wretched carcass. Unlike a mortal, you don't even have the option of suicide to deliver yourself from intolerable circumstances. There is no quick and merciful death for a draug, only disruption, dismemberment, and endless struggling to regain a body to carry you around again. Only the sword of Endless Death can deliver you to the peace of the goddess Hela."

Sorkvir lifted his head and listened. The slinking Ulf-hedin stopped their bickering, pricking their ears. The rhythmical squeaking of a wheel and the rattle of a wagon penetrated even the thunder of the seidur drums.

"Stand back, please," a thin voice called, piercing the din and causing the Ulf-hedin to shrink back abashed, hushing the drums and halting their dancing and prancing. "We've come to claim what is ours, unless you want to quarrel over a bit of useless offal."

The knacker wagon rolled to a halt, and the drums were silenced as the four bent figures of the knacker-women dismounted and stood in a row, expectant and tattered as old ravens waiting to be fed. Their bright eyes darted hungrily over Alfrekar and Sorkvir and the other wizards standing nearby, making covert signs to ward off bad luck.

Alfrekar stepped forward cautiously and cut the thongs that bound the sheath and gingerly laid the sword in its smoldering wrappings upon the ground at his feet.

"Go ahead, take him," Alfrekar said to the knacker-women with a shudder of distaste. "He's done for and we've got all we want from him. You're welcome to him, as well as whatever else you find. It will save us the trouble of a burning with Brjaladur so near."

The knacker-women lifted Leifr's inert form among them, loading him into the back of the wagon along with quite a load of seared and blackened Ulf-hedin. Then Beitski swiftly commandeered the bar of metal that was now cold and dropped it into her wagon, also, as her legitimate salvageable goods. With a ponderous rattling and squeaking the cart moved away, a bleak blot upon the festivities of Brjaladur. After it was well away, making another stop for another burned carcass, the seidur drums resumed their jubilant pounding.

From the interior of the old barn, Starkad listened to the drums, striding up and down while Raudbjorn sat with his back to the wall, watching him. The dark eyes of the troll-hounds also watched his useless pacing, their chins on their paws, frequently groaning and sighing with impatience.

"There's the drums again!" Starkad exclaimed. "What does it mean, these stoppings and startings? Where's Beitski and the knacker-wagon? What if she doesn't come back for us? We've got to get out before we lose our senses to those cursed drums.

But where is Leifr? How can we get out of Hringurhol without Leifr?''

"Leifr said to go," Raudbjorn said, rumbling uneasily. "Warriors must follow orders. Go we must. Leifr ordered."

"We can't go and leave him here," Starkad retorted, flailing his arms around a moment, then clasping them together again as if he were battling with himself. "A warrior also must think for himself and make decisions, if something has happened to his chieftain. A warrior doesn't merely carry a weapon and use it when commanded. A warrior has to use his brains, too."

Raudbjorn furrowed up his forehead anxiously at the mention of thinking. After a moment of great effort, he said, "Maybe Leifr needs our help."

"Exactly!" Starkad replied, his face drawn and pinched-looking, falling into the harsh lines of Fridmarr's countenance. "We can't just go off and leave him here if he's in trouble. Not after all he's been through."

"We'll go then," said Raudbjorn, his features beaming with the pleasurable thoughts of the coming battle.

The troll-hounds leaped up with a sudden salvo of barking and growling, clawing at the door in furious haste.

"Halloa!" a muffled call came. "Hold back the dogs! I've got news for you!"

Raudbjorn commanded the dogs to lie down and Starkad opened the door. Halmur tumbled inside, his wolf cape bristling. Tearing off the wolf scalp, he scanned the inside of the barn quickly.

"You've got to get out of Hringurhol," he said. "The drums have begun in earnest. Everything's finished. We've failed completely. Thurid's been handed over to the Inquisitors by the Council of Threttan, and I heard that Leifr is dead."

"Dead!" Fridmarr's voice repeated, and Starkad turned pale, stricken by a sudden tremor from within.

"Yes, it was the trickery of Sorkvir again," Halmur said bitterly. "Ljosa was in the depths of a spell when Leifr tried to carry her out of Alfrekar's hall. He's only a Scipling; he couldn't have retrieved her unaided, unsuspecting. Now they've got the sword and the blue carbuncle stone. All is lost. You've only got moments to escape with your lives. You must follow me quickly and I'll take you out through the drains. I know where the bars are off so we can get through."

"No," Fridmarr's voice said, and Starkad shook his head. "We're not going until we know Leifr truly doesn't need our help."

Then Starkad's own voice added fiercely, "We'll go after him. Where should we start searching? And what about Svanlaug and Ulfrin? We can't leave them, either. We've got a great deal of unfinished business to attend to. I'd like to get my hands on Sorkvir, just once, and I'd tear his head off his shoulders, if he's truly done something to Leifr."

As they made their way toward Alfrekar's hall, they encountered the knacker wagon rattling along with a load of badly scorched Ulf-hedin. Starkad shoved Raudbjorn into a dark alleyway between two walls and they hid there until Beitski was safely past.

The Council Hall was dark, and the Ulf-hedin were hurrying away from it as if anxious to be someplace else. The acrid smell of powerful spells still lingered in the air, and the stench of burning hide and hair.

"Something happened here," Starkad said.

"Plenty of dead Ulf-hedin," Halmur whispered grimly, looking after the wagon. "Something has happened, but it seems to be over now."

"There will be plenty more happening before this night is finished," Fridmarr's voice said dryly. "Maybe your carcass will be among the dead in the knacker wagon, pup. The moon is in full phase. Even if it's hidden behind the Dokkur Lavardur, you'll still feel its effects. With eitur in your veins, you'll be as mad as the rest. When it begins, take care you're nowhere near us or we'll be forced to kill you."

"Kill Halmur?" Starkad interrupted. "We couldn't!"

"We could to save ourselves," Fridmarr said grimly.

"We won't," Starkad said. "I'd rather carve you out again and throw you where a pig could swallow you!"

"And you'd suffer the consequences," Fridmarr retorted. "Far worse than the pig, I assure you. Halmur will have no choice in the matter and neither will we. Now that's enough of this sentimental babbling. Get up to Heidur's hill and see if Leifr's there."

Starkad chose a rocky ravine as an alternate route to the ruins at the top and urged Raudbjorn along, still grousing and rumbling anxiously at the worrisome notion of disobeying Leifr's last orders.

Fridmarr remained silent until they reached the ruins of Hei-dur. In the forecourt, a huge heap of half-burned offerings to the Dokkur Lavardur lay smoldering and stinking, with several Ulf-hedin poking more wood into it in a halfhearted attempt to reignite it. A tent had been erected, and more Ulf-hedin were tearing it down and carrying away the chairs and table from inside in a disorderly and distracted manner.

The seidur drums roared from every pinnacle, and the Ulf-hedin were beginning to fall under their power. They leaped and danced in ecstasy, and some stood turning around and around in one spot, their snouts pointed skyward. Starkad was re-minded of the year his brothers' cattle got the circling disease and circled mindlessly until they dropped from exhaustion and starvation.

"Get inside the hall," Fridmarr whispered. "Leave Raud-bjorn outside in case something goes wrong. Never put all your warriors into jeopardy."

Bolstered by Fridmarr's advice and encouragement, Starkad boldly plunged from shadow to shadow, skirting knots of Ulf-hedin in the throes of ecstasy. Hvitur-Fax himself stood guard-ing the doors of the hall, and Halmur laid a warning hand upon Starkad's arm.

"I'll distract him," he whispered before slipping away.

In a few moments a wrangling brawl broke out, and the Ulf-hedin took up the chant of "Ogra! Ogra!"

An arena cleared out before Hvitur-Fax, with Halmur strut-ting around in the empty space shouting challenges into the din of the chanting. Hvitur-Fax shook his grizzled head in disgust and folded his arms in refusal, but the chanting grew louder and more frenzied.

"Coward!" Halmur shouted, dancing around the cleared space in time to the chanting and the drumming. "Ragur! Hug-laus! Do you want to be known as the one who refused the challenge, Fax? I dare you to fight me for Wolfmaster! This is Brjaladur! This is the time for measuring up and fighting and madness!"

Starkad watched, open-mouthed, until Fridmarr gave him a sharp nudge. "Are you going to sit here gawking or are you going to get inside while Fax is diverted?"

"Leifr said you were a crotchety old thing," Starkad growled, slipping warily along the wall. With a final glance over his shoulder, he darted through the doorway and into the sacred precincts of the shrine. In awe he looked around at the carven tombs and tall pillars and arches that had once held up great domed roof, like the trunks of a forest of dead trees, now faintly lit by the fire from the braziers. Starkad shuddered and made a sign to ward off evil that covered all unfamiliar situations, including architecture he didn't comprehend.

At the far end of the ruins reposed the dragon ship, with its grimacing dragon face pointed slightly skyward, as if it, too, yearned to be out of this place. Starkad's skin prickled with intimations of evil as his eyes came to rest upon a set of doors leading into a sort of inner sanctuary with a roof still intact. Two braziers burned on either side of it, illuminating the images of the five Great Seals embossed in the blackened wood.

"What about Halmur?" Starkad whispered. "Is he going to be killed?"

"I doubt it," Fridmarr replied testily. "Although he would be better off. Usually they don't allow young pups to waste their lives challenging such as Fax. On the night of Brjaladur, such things are expected. Come on, keep moving, don't stop to gawk now. I still can hardly believe Leifr would have wasted my carbuncle on a calf like you. Can't you hurry a bit before we're caught?"

"What should I do?" Starkad asked nervously, still glancing from side to side.

"Well, look around. What else can you do? See if Leifr is here, alive or dead. They might put him with that ship as an offering to the Dokkur Lavardur. Can't you stop that shaking?"

"I can't help it if I'm nervous," Starkad muttered.

"Frightened, you mean. I know exactly what you're feeling, so don't try to fool me."

With a sudden thundering of drums and a shrilling of pipes, the Ulf-hedin came trooping into the ancient hall, herding several new recruits ahead of them, stumbling and confused from the effects of the eitur.

"Quick!" Fridmarr said. "Hide yourself!"

Nimbly Starkad scuttled through the tombs, darting apprehensive glances over his shoulders. The Ulf-hedin came trooping onward, straight toward the dragon ship. Starkad hurried ahead of them and vaulted over the gunwale of the ship and flattened himself among the trunks and heaps of offerings.

"Very good!" Fridmarr said, his voice scarcely a murmur inside Starkad's head. "Now we'll be among the first to be taken when they offer up this stuff! I couldn't have picked a better spot!"

"I can't move now; it's too late! The drums!" He rolled back and forth in agony, clutching his head with his fists.

"Put your fingers in your ears or you'll be entranced along with the Ulf-hedin!"

"Don't be ridiculous," Starkad said, wincing at the recurring echoes answering from the walls that yet stood. "Warriors don't put their fingers in their ears. What good would it do anyway? It's too loud!"

The Ulf-hedin procession wound through the tombs and formed a ring around the dais. The sound of the drums throbbed and vibrated until the air was filled with dust sifting down from above. Starkad struggled to resist its force, swaying as he crouched in the ship, feeling dizzy and short of breath. Even the earth underfoot trembled. It was irresistible, and he knew that he was doomed unless the drumming stopped.

The mighty reverberations of the drums provoked some of the Ulf-hedin to acrobatic leaps, twists, and turns, with the snapping jaws and glazed glaring eyes of mindless frenzy. Others danced in place, unable to keep their feet still, and a few rolled on the ground in the agonizing grip of visions and trances. Some howled in a dreadful chorus, almost lost in the noise of the drums.

The newest Ulf-hedin writhed in pain, holding their hands over their ears, trying to resist the madness, but they were helpless against the eitur-induced frenzy, and all were soon howling or jittering or dancing with the rest.

Starkad gazed at the open door above, still blowing blasts of cold air into the hall. Surrounded as they were by these mad, hairy creatures, he knew he didn't dare risk a wild dash for freedom.

Holding to the side of the ship for support, he braced himself against it, struggling as if the pounding of the drums were a heavy surf crashing around him. Fridmarr nudged Starkad sharply, a rather painful twinge under his scalp. "Now's your chance to do something. Pay attention."

"I am paying attention," Starkad retorted with as much force as he could muster mentally. "Do you think I'm asleep?"

"I wasn't certain," Fridmarr returned.

"What do you expect me to do?"

"What can you do? What have you been trained at?"

"Nothing besides tending sheep and milking cows. What did you expect, with me coming from a place like Fangelsi?"

"You're little better than a Scipling. I'm afraid to channel much of my power through you for fear of destroying you with something you're unaccustomed to tolerating. This entire situation is intolerable. Gedvondur and I had a better chance than this."

"Not that I've noticed," Starkad muttered.

With a final agonizing roar of the drums, the pounding suddenly was silenced, leaving Starkad almost gasping with the sudden relief. The only sound was the measured tread of an approaching solemn procession, carrying banners and clan symbols on standards. In the midst of the approaching procession walked Ulfrin, decked in a bride's red finery and holding her head at a haughty pose. Hvitur-Fax, evidently no worse for his battle with Halmur, paced in somber dignity behind her. Starkad sat up a little more for a better look at her, working himself into the space below the prow of the ship, where the neck of the dragon arched upward.

Ulfrin stopped beside the dragon ship, where Fax lifted her up and placed her within on a carved chair that looked like a throne. "It's hours until midnight, Fax," she said in a rather petulant voice. "Why do I have to sit here this whole time and listen to nothing but the beating of those wretched drums? I can think of many other things I would rather do with the last few hours of my life on this earth. It doesn't seem fair that I should be bored to death first, and then killed."

"You should think about your great good fortune," Fax said. "You aren't going to be merely killed. Think of yourself as being freed and lifted to the wondrous power and freedom of the elemental life-form. No one can say nay to the wind or the storm, and that power will be yours. You should not be afraid, for you are a Sverting, and one of the most chosen ones of all the Alfar."

Ulfrin gazed steadily before her, not betraying the slightest glimmer of dread. "I keep thinking of my sister," she said. "I never treated Svanlaug very well. I envied the freedom she had. No one trotting at her heels attending to her, listening to her every word, or telling her how hard she must work to reach her potential. I often wished she were the Sverting and I were the common one. I shall miss her, Fax. I wish I could talk to her during these last hours. I have many things to say to her that can't be said later, when I have nobody to speak with.''

"I shall have her found and sent here," Fax said. "I know she's still about, trying to find you. If it will ease your mind to spend these hours with her, she will be brought. I see no reason why she couldn't go with you as your handmaiden if you wish it. She has a bold spirit that would be a suitable attendant for yours.''

''Thank you, Fax, you're most kind,'' Ulfrin said.

As Fax departed, he stopped and conferred a moment with eight or ten Ulf-hedin, who subsequently stationed themselves in a row beside the dragon ship, keeping the rest of the Ulf-hedin at a respectful distance. Starkad ventured to peek out at them, watching their enraptured antics, despairing of making a clean escape.

When Fax returned, Svanlaug was brought along behind him by two burly Ulf-hedin. Struggling, protesting, and sputtering like a mad cat, she was hoisted into the dragon ship with Ulfrin and placed upon a chair.

''Ulfrin!'' she spat. ''Is this your idea of revenge? You must be gloating that I'm going to die along with you!''

''We shall not die, sister,'' Ulfrin said, turning her placid face in Svanlaug's direction. ''We shall live forever as part of the great Lord of Chaos. I shall be his Queen, and you shall be my sister forever.''

Svanlaug looked at Fax and the Ulf-hedin guarding the dragon ship and the sanctuary.

''This time, sister, you have sprung the ultimate trap,'' she said grimly, ''and I see no deliverance or escape. Tell me, Fax, is the Scipling truly dead now?''

''Yes, beyond a doubt,'' Fax said. ''At last we shall have some peace in Hringurhol. Brjaladur and the wedding of the Lord of Chaos can proceed now without interference.''

''Then I have no hope for deliverance?''

''None at all,'' Hvitur-Fax replied with a ghost of a wolfish smile. ''Tonight shall see the riddance of quite a number of troublesome responsibilities we've had to endure since the arrival of Afgang and his talented daughters.''

"If I could escape," Svanlaug snarled, "I'd have your pelt to make slippers of!"

"There is no escape from this hall," Fax said. "The Ulfhedin are guarding the doors, and the walls are too steep and high to climb."

"I have no desire to escape," Ulfrin said in lofty serenity. "This day is the most glorious day of my life, and so it shall be with yours, sister, whether you know it or not. You shall thank me, when we are part of the great elemental spirit of the Dokkur Lavardur."

"But I don't want to die!" Svanlaug exclaimed, her voice awakening the echoes.

"Fax," Ulfrin said, "I wish to speak to my sister and calm her fears. Please take the Ulf-hedin and retire from the hall for a short while. It's not fitting that she should follow me when she is not in a peaceful and accepting state, as I am, welcoming the freedom from the burdens of the mortal flesh."

Fax made a short half bow and summoned up the nearby Ulfhedin with a gruff shout. They trooped away down the corridor through the tombs.

The door opened briefly as the Ulf-hedin departed, letting in the sounds of the uproar outside. Before they were halfway up the corridor, Svanlaug scuttled over the gunwale and started across the pavement toward the sanctuary. Starkad glanced at Ulfrin, sitting upright and staring before her as if she had not seen Svanlaug making her escape.

"Ulfrin!" Starkad whispered, but she made no sign that she had heard him and went on staring into nothingness.

"Svanlaug!" Starkad said. "What are you doing? Are you going to leave your sister?"

"What are you doing here?" If a whisper could be a scream, Svanlaug uttered it. She swooped back and fairly dragged Starkad out of the ship by his neck.

"I came to look for Leifr," he choked as she shoved him down behind a heap of broken masonry and glared over it like an eagle with prey.

"Leifr's dead," she snapped. "You idiot! You fool! You're going to ruin everything! Now follow me closely and do exactly as I tell you!"

"But Ulfrin!"

"Silence! I know exactly what I'm doing!"

She scurried across the floor to the set of doors that led to the inner sanctuary, ducking between the tombs.

"Starkad, come!" she added in a commanding tone, beckoning. She crouched beside the doors, working an opening spell upon the wards that guarded them. Starkad sputtered protests and warnings, but she ignored him entirely. Exuding a cloud of cold mist, the doors opened and Svanlaug dragged Starkad inside, quickly closing the doors after them. With his hair lifting off his scalp like a sheaf of wheat, Starkad gazed around at a deserted room lit by a pair of braziers at the far end. The walls of the room were plastered with bones and skulls, intertwining in patterns that drew the eye in sinister directions and spirals. The Pentacle of Chaos winked from the encrustation of bones. Five skulls formed the points of a large pentacle, surrounded by smaller bones, and in each skull reposed a glowing stone. Below, standing between the braziers on a cairn of bone and rocks, reposed the black flask of eitur and the gold flask containing the antidote. Beside the flasks lay a familiar sword, gleaming in the dull red light of the braziers. Starkad inhaled a quick breath and took a step forward, but Svanlaug silently thrust out a restraining arm and shook her head. The cairn of bones and stones was also the reposing place of a few chosen skeletons, some of which were comparatively recently perished. Chains held the old carcasses in place against the cairn, with the wrists held in shackles and the feet likewise bound. This altar was nothing like the one outside in the courtyard; it radiated a sense of grim purpose, and the flat surface of the main altar stone had a well-used sheen through a blackened substance that seemed to be dried blood.

Starkad gripped Svanlaug by the tail of her hood, arresting her approach to the grisly shrine. His every nerve and cell cried out in objection to approaching the hideous object. To his eyes, the cairn suddenly took on a significance that was beyond his power to grasp, and the sense of standing in near proximity to such an object of powerful mystery overwhelmed him with terror and the conviction of his own inadequacy.

"Svanlaug!" he sputtered in a choking voice, trembling in the primitive fear that gripped him. "It's the Council's Pentacle of Chaos! Don't go near that thing! It's death!"

"Yes, there's a guardian spell here that would make you think that,'' Svanlaug said grimly, swatting the air with her hand. ''Not knowing it was only a spell concocted by Alfrekar to protect the jewels, a lesser man might easily believe that to approach is to die. He might even oblige the enchantment by doing so. But the jewels are on that cairn, Starkad, and I must have them if we are to stop the Dokkur Lavardur. Stay back here where you won't feel the influence so strongly, and try to retain a slight hold upon your common sense. Look at the jewels and be strengthened.''

Prying off Starkad's restraining grip, Svanlaug pointed out the subtle sparkles of green, blue, yellow, amber, and red glinting from the eye sockets of skulls. Starkad tried to convince himself that the dark terror emanating from that heap of rock was nothing but a clever spell directed toward the primitive region within him that dictated his sense of self-preservation. He found that his knowledge of the spell helped only somewhat; its force still assaulted his fears, leaving him trembling and sweating.

Svanlaug advanced one slow step at a time, her hand outstretched before her as if bearing an invisible shield. When she was almost within reach of the nearest stone, which was the blue one, it dropped out of its socket obligingly and a dark shadow scuttled up her arm like a rodent with the jewel in its mouth.

''Gedvondur!'' Svanlaug gasped, reeling from the startlement of it. The hand gripped her forearm, Gedvondur's voice sputtering furiously through Svanlaug's lips, ''That poor body on the cairn! Look at it!''

''I am looking at it,'' Svanlaug said grimly. ''It looks as if the poor devil died a terrible death.''

''I know! I know!'' Gedvondur's voice exclaimed. ''That's my body! I thought it was burned to ashes, but it's not! If Thurid's got the proper spells in that satchel, he could restore me to my own body! I could be a man again, instead of a scuttling spider! We must get to Thurid and go through the wands in that satchel! I know he can do something for me! There must be some spells!''

''Gedvondur, Thurid's no necromancer, and besides, the Inquisitors have taken him away,'' Svanlaug said. ''Leifr is dead, there's no one left to finish what we've begun except me and Starkad and you and Fridmarr. That body is nothing but worthless dust to you now. You're lucky you're as alive as you are. Do you want them all to have died for nothing? You, Fridmarr, Leifr, my brother, my father?''

"You call this being alive?'' Gedvondur demanded bitterly, and he flung himself off Svanlaug's arm to claw his way up the side of the cairn of skulls.

"Gedvondur! Come along!'' Svanlaug said. "We're not leaving you here. What do you think will happen the moment they discover you're not Galdur's carbuncle? They'll be delighted to finish you off completely this time. You'll probably end up as a belt buckle or something.''

Starkad reached out to grab him, but Gedvondur responded with a hostile burst of sparks and Starkad jerked his hand back, shaking it frantically. He grabbed again, with the same result.

"Gedvondur, you fool!'' Fridmarr's voice flared. "If you ever regarded me as your friend and companion, you must come away instantly!''

"He wants to stay,'' Starkad said, shaking his head to clear it from the ringing headache Fridmarr was giving him. "He'd rather perish here with the rest of himself than go on as he is.''

"Then we'll leave him!'' Svanlaug exploded. "We've got so little time! If we're caught here, it will mean instant death! Grab those jewels and the sword, Starkad! Make yourself useful!''

Drawing some deep breaths, Starkad reached out cautiously and plucked the green gem from its eye socket. Instantly a terrible screaming sound pierced the heavy stillness of the hall. Starkad seized the skull and dashed it on the floor and crushed the shattered remnants, but the screaming continued. Waves of evil powers emanated from the cairn, driving Starkad back pace by pace.

"Svanlaug!'' he cried between clenched teeth. "We've got to get out of here!''

"Not without the stones!'' Svanlaug scrambled over the shrine to seize the other jewels, leaving the robbed skulls screaming their terrible summons.

A hand reached up and gripped Starkad's forearm suddenly, as if the corpse chained to the cairn had suddenly come to life. Starkad responded with a great yell and a leap into the air. A chain rattled and a dark form rose up, still clinging to him in grim determination. Starkad surged backward, his ears ringing with the shrill uproar of the screaming skulls. The clinging creature seemed fastened to him with claws of iron, and its desperate eyes blazed almost in his face.

"Save me!" a voice croaked.

Chapter 16

◇◇◇

"Svanlaug!" Starkad shrilled, his throat almost too paralyzed to emit anything but a shriek.

It was no corpse, but a very different Ulfrin from the placid creature in wedding finery sitting in the ship. Her hair hung in ragged strands, her face was smeared with dirt and grimy tears, and she wore only a torn, stained white gown meant to be an undergarment to a gown. Chained by her ankle to the cairn, she clung to Starkad pleading and weeping. For an instant Starkad thought she must be another spell calculated to detain them, but the sight of her terror-stricken eyes and raw fingers and the bloody weal around her ankle convinced him she was no fraud.

"I'm here, I'm here, sister!" Svanlaug exclaimed, jerking frantically at the chain. "How am I ever going to get you out of this? I never thought they'd chain you! Starkad, help me!"

"You'll never break it that way," Fridmarr's voice said. "Stand aside and let me try it."

"What do you want me to do?" Starkad demanded, seizing the chain for a mighty and possibly self-destructive effort.

"No, no, you fool," said Fridmarr. "Listen to what I'm telling you and do what I say."

Starkad dropped the chain and his heroic pose and looked around blankly for a moment. Then he gripped the chain with one hand and quietly rubbed the metal with his thumb. Svanlaug and Ulfrin watched as if frozen, and presently the metal began to change shape. The heavy link gradually relaxed and straightened out enough for Starkad to slip it through the next link, and Ulfrin was free.

They turned to make their escape, and found the doorway blocked by Hvitur-Fax. Slowly he lifted one hand and made a banishing gesture toward the wreckage of the screaming skulls, and they vanished in a swirl of dust, silencing their screaming instantly. He looked at Ulfrin in her white shift, standing frozen in a crouch. His gaze did not miss the shackle still fastened to her leg and the red weal around her ankle.

"You aren't where I thought you were," he said, his gaze falling next upon Svanlaug. "I was deceived."

Svanlaug lifted her chin and answered, "Yes, a leikfang. One of the better ones I've done. When I couldn't find Ulfrin in her rooms, I had a vision of her chained here by the Council. So I created the leikfang and sent for you to bring her here."

"The Council would not do this," Fax said.

"They chained me here in this terrible place, Fax," Ulfrin said, her voice trembling. "They want to sacrifice me to the Dokkur Lavardur! It's not a wedding, as they say! I'm nothing but fodder to appease that monster!"

"Hush!" Fax said. "Not in this place!"

"Please let me escape!" Ulfrin continued. "I don't want to die, Fax! You don't want me to die, do you? You've been my friend for many years. Since my father was killed, I've had no one here in Hringurhol except you that I counted as a friend."

"I cannot," Fax said. "Much as I would like to let you go, I'm bound by the eitur in my blood to serve as Wolfmaster to the Council and the Lord of Chaos."

"Then come away with me, Fax," Ulfrin said. "What if you don't survive another Bjraladur? Can you really endure it once again, and a hundred times more, until eventually you are destroyed by the fighting of Brjaladur? I can save you, Fax. I want you to come with me, and we'll be free, together, away from the Council and all this evil. I shall cure you of your Ulf-hedin curse."

For a long moment, Hvitur-Fax hesitated and his eyes came to rest upon the altar and the two flasks.

"I could not," he said. "I could not free myself and leave all those others to suffer."

"We can free them, too," Ulfrin said. "I know how the antidote is made. There's the eitur and the antidote, free for our taking. I can cure the Ulf-hedin completely of this curse and you will all be free."

"But it's only a small flask," Hvitur-Fax said. "How can you cure all the Ulf-hedin with such a small amount?"

"I am a Sverting," Ulfrin said with a shadow of her former hauteur. "I know where this small amount came from, and I

assure you, there's more than enough to cure twice as many Ulf-
hedin of their curse. I'm not the daughter of a healing physician
for nothing. Take the flask and drink it, Fax. Drink it all; I can
refill it.'' She held out the golden flask to him, and after a moment he took it, uncorked its neck, and swiftly drained it.

''I don't see any difference,'' Starkad said nervously as they
all stood gazing rigidly at Fax, who still clutched the flask in
one hand.

Then his features convulsed in a grimace, bathed in a fine
sheen of sudden sweat. Doubling over, he reached out to steady
himself against the wall.

''Fax! Have I killed you?'' Ulfrin exclaimed.

''We must make haste,'' he said, shaking his head. ''Brjaladur begins in earnest at midnight, while the Council is in here
conducting their rituals. Everything must be as they left it. The
stones must be put back into the skulls. The sword must not be
touched. The bride of Chaos must be ready. This flask—'' He
held it up, fumbled it, and let it drop to the stone floor. ''It must
be refilled.''

Ulfrin picked it up and turned back to face the dreaded altar.
Steeling herself, she approached it and knelt down before it as
if she were offering adulation, but in a moment Starkad realized
she was searching for something on the ground, prying with her
fingertips between the stones. Soon she had raised one of the
stones. Starkad persuaded himself to step forward and help her
turn the stone back and shove it out of the way. Beneath, dark
water rippled and purled. The light of the braziers showed narrow steps descending into the water, which was icy cold to the
touch when Starkad tested it with one finger. It gave him a shiver
from the end of that finger clear down his spine. Ulfrin filled
the flask, and Starkad shoved the stone back into place.

''Everything is as it should be,'' Svanlaug said. ''Now let's
get out of here.''

With a choking sound, Fax slithered down the doorframe,
sinking to his knees, then slowly sagged into a helpless heap
while Ulfrin struggled to help him. The Ulf-hedin pelt fell away
like an old worn hide, the fur matted and lifeless, the eyes of
the mask nothing but gaping holes. His face was as colorless as
the belly skin of a dead fish.

''What have I done!'' Ulfrin cried. ''He's dying! Fax, can you
hear me? What's happening to you?''

"Ulfrin, we've got to leave," Svanlaug insisted.

"Not without Fax," Ulfrin said. "He's been my only friend in this horrible place. I want to save him, Svanlaug. I can't imagine living without him."

"What rubbish!" Svanlaug fumed. "What would you do with a man at Bergmal? How ridiculous!"

"I like him, Svanlaug, he's been very kind to me."

Still arguing, they dragged Fax out of the way of the doors, depositing him safely out of sight behind a sarcophagus, and closed the doors once again.

Outside, the seidur drums commenced their thunderous pounding, and the earth underfoot trembled in sympathy. The voices of the Ulf-hedin rose in a yammering, howling shout of terrible victory.

"We're not going to get out!" Svanlaug exclaimed, grabbing a handful of Ulfrin's hair and giving her head a furious shaking. "All my working and planning and suffering from one end of the realm to the other, because of you and this useless hulk, will all come to naught! The Inquisitors have got Thurid and Leifr is dead! You had to try to cure Fax; you thought you could save him! Well now, we can't even save ourselves!"

"I'm sorry, sister, sorry for everything!" Ulfrin whimpered. "I'm truly not worth all your trouble. I don't know why I'm so confused. A Sverting should have all the answers."

Svanlaug gave her hair another yank. "Now we'll all be fed to the Dokkur Lavardur! We'll be nothing but chaos!"

Ulfrin lifted her head and gazed around. "We could do as the Council do to avoid Brjaladur," she said, and pointed to a half-open sarcophagus. "They lie in these and sleep away Brjaladur once the Dokkur Lavardur has been fed. Into there, and we shall be safe. But what about poor Fax?"

"Poor Fax is beyond caring," Svanlaug said. "Leave him where he lies. Maybe he'll come out of it, but I think you gave him too much of that antidote. If it comes out of that well, it's no doubt a Rhbu well, filled with who knows what powers and influences. You probably poisoned him, sister, purged him of everything as neatly as the Wizards' Guild will do to Thurid."

Ignoring Ulfrin's protesting, Svanlaug shoved and pushed him into the sarcophagus and climbed in after her, with Starkad close behind. It was a roomy vault, intended to hold the carcass of the decedent as well as plenty of his personal wealth and possessions deemed necessary for the next life. The three of them were able to hoist the heavy stone lid almost shut, leaving only a crack for air. It was also possible to press one eye at a time to the crack for a narrow view of the doors with the Seals and the dragon ship reposing nearby. The still form of Ulfrin's leikfang was waiting for the arrival of the Council.

The Council came treading solemnly in, with a great fanfare of drumming and a dismal screeling of pipes. Banners and standards trailed sluggishly on their poles on the thickening air as the dank clouds pressed down into the hollow bowl of the ruined hall. An atmosphere of dread and anticipation smothered the festive antics of the enraptured Ulf-hedin, muting the leaping and dancing into uneasy muttering and twitching.

Alfrekar strode boldly at the head of the procession, marking each step with a rap of his staff, spuming a cloud of mist. He positioned himself before the doors into the sanctuary, glancing left and right at the assemblage of lesser wizards, Ulf-hedin, and the image of Ulfrin in the dragon ship. His lips were moving, but the sound was obscured in the throbbing beat of the seidur drums. The wizards of the Council muttered in unison as they solemnly positioned themselves around him, beards and cloaks gusting in the bursts of cold wind skidding around the interior of the ruined hall.

"Haeli, haetta, haela," Ulfrin muttered, repeating the formula over and over, scowling and pressing her fingertips into her temples.

Starkad moaned, first trying to plug his ears with his fingers, then repeating the words along with Ulfrin and Svanlaug. With each repetition, the dreadful attraction of the drums lessened.

Above, the weighty pressure of the Dokkur Lavardur crushed down upon the ruin, which offered some protection against the hurricane of winds tearing at it ferociously. The clouds glimmered with half-smothered lightning, and a continuous rumble of thunder added a menacing background for the seidur drums.

Several Ulf-hedin opened the inner sanctuary doors at Alfrekar's command, falling back in awe too great even to risk looking within. Alfrekar strode through the doorway with the Council still mumbling and spewing mist behind him, quickly sketching protective circles around themselves when they came to a halt at various positions around the walls of chamber. Alfrekar traced a five-pointed star on the paving stones and positioned himself before the altar as twenty of the newest inductees were led forward. They were in such an ecstatic delirium from the pounding of the drums that they were scarcely aware of their surroundings or the awful fate that awaited them.

Ulfrin turned away from the crack, but Starkad watched, bound by a terrible fascination, as Alfrekar spread out his arms skyward, invoking a mighty and unheard curse, and suddenly the twenty acolytes dissolved in a cloud of dusty particles and a thunderous explosion of wind.

Starkad flattened himself then in the bottom of the sarcophagus, scarcely daring to breath. Surely an entity with such power would know exactly where he was and would extract him from his hiding place like a cloud of dust, siphoning him out bit by bit.

Svanlaug also winced away, but in a moment she had her eye to the crack again, kneeling upon Starkad for padding until he freed himself and returned to watching.

With a sudden mighty crash, the drums were silent. The silence filled the ruined hall, freezing the packs of Ulf-hedin in the midst of their cavorting and dancing, reducing them to a sea of silent watchers as the still, red-clad form of Ulfrin's leikfang was led forward without resistance.

Svanlaug scowled in mighty concentration, orchestrating every move of her creation. The leikfang was lifted and bound to the altar by two wizards, who stepped quickly back into the safety of their guardian circles. Alfrekar placed the false sword also upon the altar before him.

Then he commenced a long peroration of invocations and words of power unintelligible to uneducated ears, his arms uplifted, his eyes scanning the vast darkness pressing down on the hilltop. It was no earthly language he spoke, and his face gleamed with unholy rapture. Starkad's hair bristled as the sense of evil powers summoned and rampant oppressed even the three occupants of the sarcophagus.

When Starkad thought he could not stand another moment and the air seemed too thick to draw a breath of it, Alfrekar took up the sword in both hands, holding it aloft with the point downward. Svanlaug watched intently, rigid with concentration, as the tip of the sword hovered over Ulfrin's breast.

Then Alfrekar drove the blade into her chest with all his might, and the seidur drums rolled like thunder. With a swelling cre-

scendo, the thunder from above drowned out the puny reverberations of the drums, and Alfrekar stood gripping the sword
as if transfixed by some overpowering revelation from the entity
lurking above. The Council darted questioning glances around
at each other. Ulfrin's rigid body seemed to darken and shim-
mer, while the sword suddenly gleamed with a lurid greenish
light that spread upward to Alfrekar's hands and arms to his
grimacing face, frozen in an expression of horror.

In the uneasy silence, Sorkvir cackled in his harsh voice.
"Triumph, my friend?" he gloated. "It is not so sweet, is it?"

Before the eyes of the Council and the watching Ulf-hedin,
the blue stone in the Pentacle of Chaos suddenly dropped from
its moorings in the eye socket of a skull and tumbled away at a
cartwheeling gait across the altar, adding a few rude gestures
before vanishing into the folds of Alfrekar's cloak.

"Fools!" the voice of Gedvondur boomed out from Alfrekar's stiff lips. "It is I, Gedvondur! You thought you defeated
me, but I have returned! You are doomed to destruction, you
fools of the Council! Your offerings are all incomplete or false!"

"Gedvondur! Stop him! He's got the jewel!" one of the wizards roared, and three of them surged forward, converging on
Alfrekar's frozen form.

"I haven't got it!" Gedvondur shouted. "And neither do you!
Beware the wrath of the Lord of Chaos!"

The words rang around the chamber, followed by a dull explosion and a gust of stinging dust particles. The false sword
whirled in midair, shattered into several large pieces, and the
forms of Ulfrin and Alfrekar and two nearby Ulf-hedin vanished
entirely, except for drifting shreds of cloth and hair. A roaring
sound filled the hall, rising to a shattering scream of sheer disembodied wrath. In confusion, the Ulf-hedin surged forward at
the dissolution of Alfrekar, then backward in disarray. The
screaming of the wind intensified, plucking Ulf-hedin off the
walls as they climbed toward windows to escape and whirling
them away into oblivion. Portions of the walls themselves crumbled and dissolved, pelting everyone with flying debris in the
ensuing mad crush as the hall emptied.

The Dokkur Lavardur continued to rage and scream in fury
long after the hall was deserted. Even the earth underfoot seemed
to recoil in shuddering waves.

When all was still, Starkad opened his eyes and took his hands off his ears, lifting his head slightly from his curled-up position. Nothing showed except a faint crack of lesser gloom around the end of the sarcophagus and a dark lump that was Svanlaug curled up in a protective ball. She looked at him silently, her eyes gleaming faintly. He straightened and peered out through the crack.

Outside, the hall and the sanctuary were empty, with the doors shattered from pounding against the walls, the imposing Seals torn from their fastenings and gone. The winds had died to perfect deadly calm, and the eastern sky was glowing with the faint light of approaching dawn. Nothing remained of the grand scheme of the Council except the four jewels glowing faintly in their pentacle of skulls.

"We must have them," Svanlaug whispered. "We can't leave them for the Council to use again."

Remembering how Alfrekar had exploded into dust particles, Starkad replied fervently, "I don't care. I won't touch them. All I want is out of Hringurhol. I'm going back to Fangelsi and I'm never going anywhere again."

They pushed back the lid of the sarcophagus and crept out stiffly, straightening tenatively from their long, cramped vigil. With dread, Starkad watched Svanlaug reach out and pluck the first stone from its skull, expecting the dreadful screaming to start again. Instead there was only silence. Quickly Svanlaug removed the other three jewels, placing them in a row on the altar.

Totally rapt, Starkad scarcely noticed a dark shadowy figure when it suddenly detached itself from a gloomy corner and lurched forward. Ulfrin fell back with a muffled cry, and the familiar rubbishy burning smell of Sorkvir suddenly filled the air with its stinging stench. He swayed on his feet, looking at them with reddened eyes, dull in their sunken hollows. Starkad and Svanlaug also cowered away from the smoking apparition.

"It was good of you to save me the trouble of taking those stones," he rasped, reaching out with one seared claw of a hand to scoop the stones into his other hand. "The time was drawing awfully short. Thanks to your help, I shall preserve myself once again. I have triumphed over Alfrekar at last, and the Council is mine. In time, the Dokkur Lavardur will be my servant, also. Now then, I need a volunteer. You'll be the one." His hand shot out and seized a handful of Starkad's collar, twisting and winding him closer with irresistible draug strength until Starkad could scarcely breathe, face to face with Sorkvir, seared and smoldering only inches away.

Sorkvir's hand suddenly convulsed and his claw opened, releasing Starkad as he staggered back with a strangled cry. Something had a grip on his wizened throat, shaking his head to and fro like a dried weed stalk. A steady growling burbled from his lips, sounding much like the voice of Gedvondur. Starkad trembled, resisting, then he pitched into the battle also, unable to refuse the prompting of Fridmarr's fiery impulse burning within him.

He wrestled Sorkvir to the ground and held him there while Gedvondur fastened himself to Sorkvir's wrist. Svanlaug and Ulfrin pried at his brittle fingers in an attempt to wrest the four jewels out of his grasp.

"Once-dead is not a match for me!" Sorkvir snarled, hurling Starkad and the two women backward with a potent rebuffing spell. Gedvondur tumbled away like a dead leaf.

Ulfrin gathered herself up and sprang to her feet, her eyes flashing. She spread out her hands in a banishing gesture and cried out, "Release those jewels, you dried piece of carrion! Dare you challenge the power of the Sverting?"

"Bah! You're nothing but a child playing at grownup games!" Sorkvir snarled, making a stabbing gesture toward her and spitting out the words of a spell.

Ulfrin rebuffed the spell, turning it back upon its maker, sending Sorkvir hurtling backward against the wall with a dusty concussion.

"You forget who I am," Ulfrin said.

"It was nothing but a lucky coincidence," Sorkvir snarled, fumbling around in his sleeve to smother a fire. "A mere girl could never defeat a wizard of the Council!"

"Olagi! Leysa upp!" Ulfrin replied, pointing to the ground at Sorkvir's feet. The paving stones shimmered and vanished with a sizzling sound, the dust from them scattering on the wind. "You see, Sorkvir, I know the powers of chaos. I was intended as the bride of the Dokkur Lavardur from birth, so I learned all I could about him. Surrender the jewels to us or I shall start dispersing you bit by bit."

"Do it and be done! I dare you!" Sorkvir spat.

"And have you floating around bodiless to torment us?" Ulfrin retorted. "I think not. Now at least we have the smell of you for a warning of your foul presence. Give us the jewels. I command you."

"You will die!" Sorkvir raised his hand to direct a spell against them all.

Starkad trembled in the grip of invisible influences grinding and clashing. He could see Sorkvir's lips moving, uttering words, but all he could hear was a shrill ringing in his ears, muffling the words Fridmarr was chanting.

The ringing shifted to a sharp squeaking, accompanied by the rumbling of heavy wheels jolting over stones. Sorkvir's concentration faltered as the knacker wagon came trundling into the hall down the corridor of tombs.

"There you are," Beitski said, her wizened little face wreathed in a cadaverous smile. "We've been looking forward to this for a long time, Sorkvir."

Sorkvir gripped his staff, the waves of his spell falling around him in diminishing gusts and spurts.

"There is no escape, Sorkvir," Beitski said. "Get into the wagon and we shall attend to what's needful. You are an abomination that must be eradicated from the earth. One journey through death is all that is allotted to mankind."

"I have the jewels," Sorkvir said in a snarl, holding them aloft and shaking his fist. "I can live forever!"

"You are a mistake," Beitski said. "You won't be permitted to live forever. Come along now, you know what is fitting and proper."

"I won't! Not yet!" Sorkvir retorted, and he hurled the jewels toward the unclean altar where they clattered and bounced among the stones and skulls and bones. With a harsh laugh, he turned and dived into the protection of the jumble of tombs, flitting from one to the next.

"Let him go for now," Beitski said, raising a restraining hand when Starkad started after Sorkvir. "There is no escape for him, after all. We shall have him for the plucking one day soon. Our first concern is the jewels. Find them, sisters."

Ulfrin stepped back as the three knacker-women dismounted from their wagon and commenced searching for the scattered jewels.

"They aren't yours," Ulfrin said. "What do you want with them? You're nothing but bone-pickers!"

"Everyone's bones are picked by someone sooner or later," Beitski replied with a shake of her head. "Get into the cart, all of you, and I shall carry you away from this place. I think there's also another one we should have, over there behind that tomb."

"Fax? You can't have him, even if he is dead," Ulfrin said with a sob catching in her throat. "And we're not going with you, you old death-ravens. Why is everyone so afraid of you? You're nothing but a pack of old scavengers!"

"There's nothing to fear," Starkad said, speaking in Fridmarr's voice. "While we're at it, we'll take Gedvondur's old carcass, too. No sense in wasting a scrap of anything useful if we can help it."

"What a wise young man," said Beitski. "Our philosophy exactly. Life is a wasteful process sometimes. Someone has to put things back in order. Sisters, let us unload our burden from the cart to make room for living passengers."

The four jewels were soon found, and the knacker-women commenced unloading their sad cargo in a busy, cheerful fashion that did not suit their occupation. All the bones and skulls in the wagon were heaped up on the paving stones of the well, along with the limp body of Hvitur-Fax and three huge fireblackened cauldrons. Starkad watched uneasily for a body that might be recognizable as Leifr's, but most of them were too burned to identify.

Three of the knacker-women remained at the shrine, while Beitski climbed onto the seat of the wagon.

"You must leave Hringurhol now," Beitski said as the cart rumbled slowly over the rough paving stones of the settlement. "There is nothing more for you to do, except to go to a place of safety and wait. Return to our little house outside Ferja, and we shall join you when Brjaladur is done with and our business is finished."

"You're not staying on another night in Hringurhol, are you?" Svanlaug demanded. "There's two more nights of Brjaladur! You were lucky enough to survive one!"

"We've got business to attend to," Beitski said in surprise. "Did you not see the corpses littering the byways? There are two more nights of Brjaladur, and more Ulf-hedin will die. Someone must take care of the results of their madness, or Skarpsey would soon be neck-deep in wandering draugar. Go on yourselves, though. There's no need for you to stay any longer.''

By the time they reached the wanderers' camp at the far south end of the settlement, dawn had arrived and the sounds of Brjaladur were diminishing to intermittent howls and screams coming from inside the ruined halls. The knacker-woman stopped at the old barn.

''I can take you no further,'' Beitski said. ''My sisters and I have a great deal of work to do. Remember, you must leave Hringurhol now, while the Ulf-hedin are asleep.''

The troll-hounds crept out of the barn to give then a faint-hearted welcome and returned to nose at Raudbjorn and whine anxiously. Clutching his halberd, Raudbjorn sat morosely with his back to the wall, ignoring the icy brunt of the wind as he bleakly guarded the last stronghold he knew to guard, scarcely rousing himself from his gloom to grunt at them in greeting.

''We'll just have to walk, then,'' Svanlaug said to Ulfrin, watching the ramshackle wagon rumble away, back toward Hringur-knip. ''In two days we'll make it to Ferja, if we travel by day as well as night.''

Ulfrin stood rooted to the ground, her hands hanging down at her sides. ''I can't leave now,'' she said. ''The least I can do is see to it that Fax's death is properly avenged upon Council. I killed him—my only friend in this horrible place. I thought I was helping him.''

''Help him, indeed you did,'' Fridmarr's voice said briskly. ''The life of an Ulf-hedin is far more miserable than death. Death is often a very practical arrangement for people who can't get out of what they've gotten into.''

''Ulfrin, we can't stay!'' Svanlaug protested. ''We won't live through another night! Not after what I've done to Alfrekar! That leikfang of you blew him to Niflheim! What do you think the Council is going to do now?''

''They'll certainly think twice about extending us the privileges of guest right again,'' Starkad said judiciously.

''The Council is one of my smaller worries,'' Ulfrin said. ''The Dokkur Lavardur was not pleased with their offerings. The sword was false, the fifth jewel was false, and his intended bride was nothing but a trick. So Alfrekar was taken in my place. If anyone should remain and face the wrath of the Dokkur Lavardur, let it be me. You go ahead and escape, with Starkad and Raudbjorn.''

Starkad turned his head at the mention of his name. ''I agree with Ulfrin. We're not finished here,'' he said in the voice of Fridmarr. ''I'm not leaving until there's been an accounting for my friends who are lost. The Council will pay dearly for what happened last night. Go ahead if you wish, but I shall remain until I'm satisfied.''

Svanlaug glowered at Starkad. ''That's easy for you to say, Fridmarr, when Starkad is the one who will suffer for it,'' she said. ''The knacker-woman was right. We must leave Hringurhol while the Council is in disarray and the Ulf-hedin are sleeping off Brjaladur. There's nothing else we can do here.''

''Nonsense,'' Fridmarr said. ''We can find *Endalaus Daudi*, perhaps. All I need is to lay hands upon Vidskipti and wring a few secrets out of him.''

''And what would you do with Leifr's sword?''

''It was once my sword, you recall.''

''When I was a child,'' Ulfrin whispered, ignoring their quarreling, ''I used to think there was nothing so fine or mysterious as the secret rituals and sacrifices of the Council to the Dokkur Lavardur. Now I wish they were all a thousand miles underground, buried and dead. If I could, I'd pluck the Dokkur Lavardur out of the sky and squeeze him into nothingness. I'd make chaos out of the Lord of Chaos.''

''It's all right now,'' Svanlaug said. ''Soon we'll be safely away from Hringurhol forever.''

''No, no, they'll come after me,'' Ulfrin said. ''I know they will. I'm the only one they think is a suitable bride for the Dokkur Lavardur. They'll search and they'll find me wherever I go, wherever I try to hide. Leifr would have saved me, but I was blind, I was stupid, and now he's dead.''

Svanlaug answered with rare patience. ''There's no hope, sister. If we stay we're all doomed.''

''That's not true,'' Starkad murmured, his own voice coming faintly, completely exhausted from his efforts with the chain and Fridmarr's power coursing through him. ''We've got Fridmarr. As long as I'm alive, we've got hope. If Leifr were here, he wouldn't leave until he had destroyed that wretched Council and put an end to their ambitions.''

Svanlaug shook her head. ''It's all very bold to talk of destroying the Council, but what can the three of us do without Leifr and his sword? While we talk, we waste time. They'll be hunting us down like rats. Whatever the Council does against us will take place at midnight. By then we could be safely on our way to Ferja. We could be across the water before they can catch us.''

Ulfrin shook her head slowly. ''Sister, I shall not leave Hringurhol until I have destroyed the Council and the Second Seal forever, for what the Ulf-hedin curse has done to Fax.''

Svanlaug seized a handful of her own hair. ''Am I going to escape to safety alone? No one is coming with me? What sort of friends are you?''

''Go if you wish,'' Ulfrin said. ''I'm not surprised at you, sister. When we were children, you always left your work before it was finished.''

''That's not true!'' Svanlaug retorted. ''You're the one who never finished anything! You were never compelled to do anything you didn't want to do! If you stay here and get killed and sacrificed by the Council, I won't be at all sorry! It serves you right!''

''Yes, I know,'' Ulfrin said, elevating her chin and clenching her jaws. ''But I shall stay, and I shall not fail. I have set my mind to it, and once a Sverting makes up her mind, nothing can stop her. The Council of Threttan must perish.''

Svanlaug moaned and flung herself down on a straw pallet and draped her forearm across her eyes. ''Then I suppose I am doomed along with the rest of you.''

Hringurhol remained as silent as an abandoned ruin, silently counting off the hours until the muzzled light of the sun began to diminish. Then the silence was disturbed by covert stirrings, muffled voices, and occasional glimpses of slinking Ulf-hedin. Overhead, the great mass of the hovering elemental entity gleamed with secretive glimmers of lightning, rumbling with suppressed thunder. The clouds roiled like the scales of a great monster slowly wallowing through troughs of mist. The reluctant smoke from bonfires crept across the ground as if chastened by the spectacular display in the sky.

Starkad awoke from a restless sleep and prowled around the barn, eyeing the sky nervously and wondering what Fridmarr was going to require of him next. Tentatively he attempted to summon forth the voice of the carbuncle, but it remained stubbornly silent. Ulfrin and Svanlaug gazed at him expectantly, and Raudbjorn had sharpened his halberd in expectation.

Outdoors, the voices of Brjaladur became more insistent; screams, howls, and the sounds of fighting rose from the streets of Hringurhol. Suddenly something collided with the door, clawing at it, a voice gasping out, "Starkad! Let me in! Only for a moment!"

Starkad pressed his eye to the crack in the door, then hastily pulled back the bolts and bars securing it.

"Halmur!" he exclaimed in shock as a ragged, bloodstained figure reeled through the doorway and collapsed at his feet. Halmur twitched and trembled and his eyes glared with a feral light.

"It's the Brjaladur curse!" Ulfrin said. "Don't trust him for an instant!"

"There's not much time," Halmur whispered. "I came as soon as possible. Tonight all of Hringurhol is allied against you. They know where you are and they're coming for you. There's only one safe place: Heidur's ruins. They won't dare touch you there."

"That much is true," Ulfrin said. "For the Ulf-hedin, it's a place of destruction."

"Go, and hurry," Halmur said, shutting his eyes in shuddering misery. "Leave me here. I shall hold them off as long as I am able to fight."

"We can't just leave you here," Starkad said.

"We can't take him," Ulfrin said. "When the madness comes upon him, he'll see us only as his enemies."

Starkad demanded, "Isn't there any more of the antidote?"

"There's a limitless supply of antidote," Ulfrin said, "but time is getting very short. We must get to Heidur's hill now, or there's no hope."

"I'm not leaving Halmur to die," Starkad said. "Look at him. He's not going to make it through another night of Brjaladur."

"Then bring him along," Ulfrin snapped. "I'll attend to him when we get to Heidur's hill. Sentiment has no place when it comes to survival, Starkad."

"If not for sentiment," Svanlaug said, "none of us would be here now, so you can shut your mouth, sister. Take hold of his arm and help Starkad carry him. When you're tired, I'll take your place.''

In the gathering darkness, they left the barn and sought the sheltering gloom of a ravine. A lurid flare suddenly lit up the night with a rush of warm wind, followed by a rumbling explosion. Starkad seized Halmur and they tumbled into the safety of some dense, thorny bushes, followed by Svanlaug, Ulfrin, and, with some heavy crashing, Raudbjorn and the troll-hounds. Scarcely able to draw a breath in the thinning atmosphere, Starkad looked on in disbelief as the old stable disintegrated, bit by bit, sucked away into the dark maw of the Dokkur Lavardur hovering above. It melted away as if it were a tallow candle, finally vanishing with a scream into the funnel of darkness in the sky.

Chapter 17

◇◇◇◇◇◇◇◇◇◇◇◇◇◇◇◇◇◇◇◇◇◇◇◇◇◇◇◇◇◇◇◇◇◇◇◇

When Leifr opened his eyes, he was first astonished that he had done so, having looked death in its red and burning eyes and given himself up for its taking. The smell of moist earth and young green grass was in his nostrils, cooling his spirit with its sweetness, and he realized he was lying facedown with his cheek pressed to the earth. Rain pattered around him softly, running down his neck. He licked his lips and tasted rain. As he blinked at the drops running heedlessly down his face, he looked at his hands, which had been nothing but blackened bone clenched around red-hot iron, and found them whole and healthy, quite capable of opening and closing in the most miraculous manner.

Slowly he gathered himself and sat up with his knees bent under him. He felt no pain at all, which made him reconsider his original surmise that he was still alive. Next he got to his feet, noting that the flaying tail of the lingorm had done no damage to either his flesh or his cloak, nor had its teeth left any mark where it had savaged his arm.

The soft, steady rain had settled the dust, and all of Hringur-hol was softened with fog. Judging by the gloomy light, it could be either dawn or just before twilight. He heard not a sound. As nearly as Leifr could tell, no living thing remained here except himself. He wiped some of the mud off his face and turned back to look at the doorway of the Council Hall. It was shut now, and the earth of the dooryard was trampled with many foot-prints. Cutting across them all were the wheel marks of a wagon and a single horse. Thoughtfully Leifr touched the small foot-prints that surrounded the place where he had lain. The prints were only moments old.

Behind him he heard a light footstep on a stone and a startled gasp. He whirled to confront whoever had chanced upon him, reaching by reflex for his empty sword sheath.

Ljosa in her red finery stood staring at him, her fine hair curling in mist-tendrils where it lay damp on her neck and forehead. She raised one hand vaguely to start a warding-off motion, but her hand dropped to her side as she stared at him, her face pale and empty of any expression except numb wonder.

"Ljosa! Are you back among the living?" he asked anxiously. "Completely? Nothing has been held back? Nothing has been lost?"

"You're alive," she said. "I thought you were a draug. I'm alive, and free of Sorkvir at last. I feel I've come back from a long journey but I don't know where I am." Drawing a shivering breath, she shut her eyes and sank down on part of a wall.

In two quick strides Leifr was beside her, steadying her gently and letting her head rest on his shoulder, feeling the living warmth of her and her soft breath with a sense of amazement and relief. An owl glided to a silent landing on the broken rooftree of a nearby ruined house, greeting the approaching night with a series of rusty hoots.

"I'm more surprised than you are that we're both still alive," he said. "You don't remember what happened? Being carried out of the Council Hall? The transformations?"

Ljosa shook her head, with a nervous shiver running through her slight frame. "I don't know. I woke up here, next to you, with your arm shoving my face into the mud. I thought it was all a nightmare—the swan and the lingorm, and then I thought I was burning up, on fire like a torch. But the rain put an end to it. I sat up, and I saw no one except four old women and a wretched-looking wagon, all of them just standing and watching with their hands folded as if they were pleased about something. When I called out to them for help, one of them came over and took a gold ring off your finger. I was angry, but she gave it back to me, and here it is."

She untied a handkerchief, revealing three crescent-shaped parts of a broken ring. With a gasp she exclaimed, "It was whole when it came off, I swear it!"

"Vidskipti's ring," Leifr said. "It's all right, Ljosa. I think this was intended to happen. Never mind, maybe someone can melt it down and remake it one day. Luckily it was taken off when it was, or I might have gone on sleeping until it was too late."

"A magic ring." Ljosa hastily pushed the ring as well as the handkerchief into his hand. "I'd get rid of it. It may give you amazing powers, but it takes something else away from you."

"It was a gift," Leifr said. "From a wise old friend. I don't believe he intended me any harm. Well, I fear there's no strength left in this now." He tied up the broken ring again and thrust it into an inner pocket, secretly pleased that he had also managed to get away with Ljosa's handkerchief. Glancing around suspiciously, his natural caution alerted him to possible threats in the brooding calm of Hringurhol. Not a soul stirred among the huts and hovels and deserted ruins. "It's so quiet now. Too quiet. Brjaladur will be starting up again soon."

"Brjaldur? What is Brjaladur? I know nothing about what has happened here," Ljosa said with a shudder. "The last thing I remember clearly was Djofullhol, in my fylgja-form, when Sorkvir was restored to life. Everything after that is like a bad dream."

"We've got to get out of sight," Leifr said, still scanning the alleyways of the settlement warily. "I shall tell you all about it later."

A sudden movement caught his attention and he crouched down behind the wall, pulling Ljosa down beside him. A dark, furtive figure scuttled out of the rubble, glancing about on all sides, then paused suddenly to flog at himself in a rising cloud of murky smoke. Sorkvir gazed around a moment, cocking his head to listen to the first tortured howls of Brjaladur. One of the seidur drums sounded a warning through the twilight like the soft thrumming of the owl's wings. Leifr crouched lower, and Sorkvir glided out of sight, disappearing into the Council Hall. For a moment Leifr pressed his forehead against the cold mossy stones of the wall.

"It's not over then," he muttered, half to himself. Then he raised his head and listened, hearing faint voices coming from inside the hall, raised to quarrelsome shouts.

"What is it, Leifr?" Ljosa whispered. "Where is your sword? I don't like the feel of the atmospheres here."

"Nor do I," Leifr said grimly. "It's the Council of Threttan, quarreling. My sword was stolen from me; but, from the sound of this arguing, I might have some hope of doing what I came to do, even without *Endalaus Daudi*."

With Ljosa shadowing his heels, he crept forward to the door. This time no Ulf-hedin were standing guard. He eased it open a slight crack by pressing on it gently. Through the crack he could see fires lit within, and the irritable voices carried to his ears far better. Cloaked wizards were pacing around in a fury, while some sat stoically in their traditional chairs, with their beaky hoods turning back and forth as they watched the others, whispering among themselves like conspirators.

Leifr pushed the door open farther and darted inside, followed by Ljosa, after losing a brief argument about leaving her behind. She closed the door quickly, but even so, the fires on the braziers dipped and climbed in the sudden gust of wind. They crouched behind a crumbling sarcophagus near the door, with the carven image of a man clutching a sword to his chest with an expression of raddled dissatisfaction on his pitted visage.

The wizards paused in their arguing and glanced around suspiciously. Sorkvir was seated in Alfrekar's chair, exuding a subtle cloud of murky smoke. He continued speaking in his grating voice, by now almost inaudible for its dry hoarseness.

"Cowards, all of you," he rasped. "Listen to me. I have the wisdom of seven lifetimes. Who is better qualified to take Alfrekar's seat on this Council? Alfrekar, the fool, the unworthy! If not for his bungling, the propitiation would now be complete, the Dokkur Lavardur would be bound to do our will forever, and the destruction of the Ljosalfar would be complete. Who among you still wants to go whining away like a whipped cur?"

The wizards stood still, their secretive eyes sliding around to avoid looking at one another.

"The Lord of Chaos has turned his back upon us," a burly wizard with a white-streaked red beard intoned. "I for one don't intend to wait around and see what happens. We've lost whatever meager hold we may have had upon him. He's going to do with us whatever he wishes, and I don't think it's going to be pleasant, after seeing what he did to Alfrekar."

"The Dokkur Lavardur won't be cheated," a hunched little stick of a wizard in a russet hood said. "He's quiet now, but he's probably plotting something."

"I don't like this calm, either," another said, shaking his head. "It's not natural for him."

"Old women!" Sorkvir spat, peering around at them with his eyes glowing a baleful red, like a cat's. "I forbid you to leave Hringurhol. I have taken Alfrekar's place, and I shall tell you when you can abandon what we have begun here so long ago and at what great cost. The Sverting woman is still within our reach. The Ulf-hedin are yet bound by the curse of eitur, are they not? Did the Lord of Chaos not take the twenty Ulf-hedin we offered? The Rhbu sword is somewhere in Hringurhol, I feel it in my bones, and it will surface again. When it does, we shall have it.''

''But the jewels!'' the red-bearded wizard said. ''We've surely lost them now, after last night. The Ulf-hedin are scattered and uncontrollable without Hvitur-Fax, and those infernal knacker-women have set up their stinking rendering pots in the sanctuary of our Shrine of Chaos.''

''Perhaps,'' another voice said, ''the Dokkur Lavardur will never be bound.''

''Silence!'' Sorkvir commanded, freezing them all instantly to listen. ''I know where the jewels are. Getting them back into our possession will be as easy as gathering eggs. Those four knacker-women have got them. Neither would I be astonished if they also possessed the fifth stone, the carbuncle of Galdur.''

''The Inquisitors have got that,'' the red-bearded wizard said. ''It's well upon its way to the Fire Wizards' Guildhall by now. When they took Thurid, they took Galdur's stone. I knew we should have killed Thurid.''

''Raudkell, if you don't be silent I shall be forced to make an example of you,'' Sorkvir snarled, pointing a dried and bony finger at him.

''And that would leave only nine of the original Council of thirteen wizards,'' Raudkell said, clasping his hands behind his back and rocking on his heels. ''Nine cannot hold the Dokkur Lavardur, and that nine includes a draug in a very unstable condition of incipient combustion. What will happen to us when you finally burst into flames? What do you think that great beast out there will really do, if he decides to do it?'' He brandished his arm skyward, including all of Hringurhol in his gesture. ''I say we take refuge while we can. A feeling of doom hangs over this place now, and I think the doom is ours.''

''Absurd,'' a few of the other wizards muttered, loudly enough to make themselves noticeable by Sorkvir. Their spokesman edged forward a step, a younger wizard simmering in the stifled ambitions of one who has been kept at the bottom of the heap for too long. ''We've all worked at this too long to abandon it now,'' he said, with eyes flashing. ''Gaining control of the

Dokkur Lavardur will make us the masters of all the realms. We've come so near, too near to give up at the first failure to appease him. Alfrekar was hasty and foolish. He should have recognized a false sword, and almost anyone can detect a leik-fang. We can find the true sword, we shall have the jewels if they are yet within Hringurhol, and we can still capture the Sverting. We have lost nothing of value, except possibly Alfre-kar, who has since proven himself an unfit leader of this Council. We have two more nights of Brjaladur. If we move quickly, all will not be lost.'' He turned to Sorkvir, a lean and wolfish pale face peering out from under a ragged hood. ''You say the jewels are yet within the ruins of Heidur's well? Then we shall retrieve them for the use of the Council.''

''Syndugur, you are wise beyond your years,'' Sorkvir said. ''One day you shall be rewarded for your loyalty. The knacker-women have got the jewels. Their very presence is a desecration to our Altar of Chaos.''

''Those old crones have reached the end of their arrogance,'' Syndugur said, straightening his wizened frame and his murky eye taking on the sheen of self-importance. His four cohorts nodded in silent agreement. ''Why should anyone fear a pack of old carcass-pickers? What hold do they have upon all these simpleminded fools who fear them so? Are we of the Council as ignorant as common people? The jewels shall be returned, and the knacker-women will no longer be a trouble to us.''

They strode away, leaving the three recalcitrant ones eyeing Sorkvir dubiously. Raudkell shrugged his shoulders and gath-ered up his staff, giving its serpent carvings a ritual rub for good luck. ''Then I suppose it falls to us to find the Sverting,'' he said. ''I don't think it will be so easy to convince her this time that it is an honor to become the bride of the Lord of Chaos. She's getting a nasty cunning streak from that sister of hers.''

''I've heard enough of your whining,'' Sorkvir said. ''I won't forget your reluctance, Raudkell. Unless you redeem yourself somehow, I fear you may suffer for it later.''

''Well, then, I shall go find the Sverting. She can't be far.'' Raudkell gathered his thick shoulders in a shrug.

''The knacker-woman took her to the old barn near the wan-derers' camp,'' Sorkvir said impatiently. ''I've saved you the necessity of a search. Go and get her, and I don't care how you do it. Also bring me the one called Starkad. He's got something

I would like to possess. You remember Fridmarr, don't you, Raudkell?''

''Fridmarr!'' Raudkell thrust out one foot, which was a gnarled stump of blackened wood. ''I owe this to him. On every cold and rainy day when that stub throbs like coals of fire, I wish I could get my hands upon his throat.''

''Well, he's not got a throat any longer for you to get your hands on,'' Sorkvir said. ''Just the person who carries him around. Fridmarr's carbuncle is mine, so spare me that greedy gleam in your eye. I also want the body of the youth Starkad brought to me. It should serve me well for many years to come.''

Raudkell's lip curled with disdain. ''I shall do what I can, but I'm not yet convinced a draug can be a Grand Wizard. Who's going to help you make the switch to a new body? Djofull was skilled at necromancy and disembodied things, but no one else has his filthy talent.''

''I shall do it myself,'' Sorkvir snarled.

Raudkell was about to reply when a tearing shriek pierced the unnatural calm of Hringurhol. The wizards clapped their hands over their ears in agony, except for Sorkvir, whose singed and blackened ears were far beyond feeling any pain. Clutching his staff, he leaned forward to hear it better, his eyes glaring as he bared his teeth in a calculating grin.

''The sword!'' he exclaimed in triumph, when the metallic screech had ceased. The wizards cautiously unplugged their ears, cringing in expectation of another shrill blast. ''It's the sword of Endless Death being sharpened! Find it now, you fools, and the Lord of Chaos is ours!''

By unspoken consent, Leifr and Ljosa silently crept out of the hall during the diversion of another grinding shriek from the sword. The sound pierced the air of Hringurhol, awakening a chorus of dolorous howling from the Ulf-hedin. It seemed to come from everywhere, echoing and reechoing off the ruined walls of the ancient structures.

''Which way? Which way?'' Leifr clenched his fists and swung around, listening in all directions.

''From there!'' Ljosa whispered, pointing toward Heidur's well. Eerie lights flickered through its hollow arches and windows, and the sky entity lowered over the ruins with flickerings and dour rumblings of its own.

With the sounds of Brjaladur increasing on all sides, Leifr hastened toward the hilltop shrine as fast as he dared; Ljosa clung to the hem of his cloak like a burr. Suddenly a brilliant flash lit up the sky. In the sudden oppressive darkness, Leifr and Ljosa crouched in the lee of a wall. Looking back, they watched in horror as the black sucking maw of the elemental devoured the roof of a stable, transforming turf and timbers to nothing but dust. How such a thing could happen was beyond Leifr's understanding. A solid structure could not simply dissolve, like salt in water! A few moments of such incomprehension was all he could tolerate. It was the same old stable that had sheltered them after Starkad was wounded. He shuddered at the sudden nothingness and the thought that his companions might still have been inside, and were now nothing but dust being absorbed into the incomprehensible sky monster known as Chaos.

He seized Ljosa's hand and dived into a ditch running along a wall. When he was out of breath and well away from the phenomena of the Dokkur Lavardur, he stopped and looked back warily, gasping for breath.

At that moment, another thin scream cut through the sounds of Brjaladur.

Leifr swung around like a lodestone, facing the black outline of Heidur's ruins. "It's there," he said. "Whatever else may have happened tonight, I know where to find *Endalaus Daudi.*"

"No, it must be a trick," Ljosa answered. "The evil I feel coming from that hill is almost as thick as the Dokkur Lavardur. I feel as if we'll dissolve, as the stable did, if we go up there."

Leifr's skin prickled and his neck hairs bristled in agreement, but he shook his head.

"I'm going up there," he said. "You can come with me, or I'll find a safe place to hide you."

"There are no safe places," Ljosa said. "I'm coming with you."

Halfway up the hill, Ljosa suddenly reached out and stopped him with one hand on his sleeve. When their feet were stilled, they heard voices coming faintly from the towering ruin cresting the hill. Singing or chanting echoed from the shattered walls, rising up in an almost visible cloud of influence that caused the Dokkur Lavardur to roil and flicker above it menacingly. In mounting fury, gusts of icy wind slashed at the hilltop, loaded with spatters of cold rain, but the chanting continued. The elemental struck at the towers repeatedly with lightning, but the bolts shattered before they reached it, showering the settlement below with flashes of light.

The chanting continued, its sweetness urging Leifr and Ljosa to hurry onward, breathlessly eager to see the singers of such a melodic chant. No one stood guard, either swept away by the fury of the Dokkur Lavardur or sensibly taking shelter somewhere. As they crossed the threshold of the vast circular hall, the wind ceased abruptly. The piercing, sweet chanting continued, but they could see no one. Leifr blundered against several tombs in his haste, his eyes fixed upon a circle of firelight glowing in the center of the ruin, illuminating rows of tombs with their intricate carvings of men, women, monsters, and beasts. A lone figure inhabited the circle of firelight, seated at a grindstone, treadling away steadily and holding up a long gleaming sword blade to consider its sharpness. Almost tenderly he put the blade to the stone with a rending shriek, amplified by the echoing walls of the ruin. After more consideration, the sword was thrust into the fire, then tempered with a vicious hissing and steaming. All the while, the sweet chanting continued, surrounding the hall and its forgotten tombs and forgotten dead.

Leifr felt no desire to move or approach Malasteinn during his work. He crouched down behind a tomb and watched, with Ljosa kneeling beside him, also watching and hardly breathing, her eyes almost translucent in the soft glow of fire and forge. The wizened smith sharpened a few lesser blades next, whose voices were a mere musical singing as they met the whirling grindstone.

With reluctance Leifr's ears became aware of an intruding sound: the rapid and furtive trampling of several pairs of boots scuffling up the rough path toward the front doors. Then a single cloaked figure appeared in the paler rectangle of the doorway, pausing to speak to the others behind him. Even without hearing the voice, Leifr recognized Thurid instantly from the profile of his nose and brow and scrubbily bearded chin.

"Come along!" Thurid commanded sharply. "Enough precious time has already been lost. Not to mention lives," he added in an embittered tone. "Something at least will be salvaged from this hideous debacle."

The moment Thurid turned to look within the hall, the circle of illumination surrounding Malasteinn vanished. Leifr leaped to his feet with a resounding shout that echoed around the ruined walls.

"No! Wait! Don't go!" He plunged a short way toward the place where he had seen the smith, but a shout from Thurid brought him up short.

"Leifr! Is that you? I thought you were dead! You're not really dead at all, are you?" Thurid pounced upon Leifr and shook him by the shoulders and wrung his hand and patted him on the back, thus reassuring himself it was not a draug he was dealing with.

"Thurid! Did you hear anything? Did you see?" Leifr sputtered in a choked voice, twisting around to look again for Malasteinn, but no sign of him remained except for a long needle of light standing vertical in the place where he had been.

Thurid's eyes bulged, glistening in the sickly light cast from the inner burgeonings of the Dokkur Lavardur.

"The sword!" he cried, raising his hand to point, but Leifr was already bounding through the tombs and defaced statues in a torturous course toward it.

Leifr found *Endalaus Daudi* with its point securely buried in a solid paving stone, with a small puddle of melted stone girdling the metal of the blade. Pausing, Leifr gazed around at the walls of the ancient place, for an instant seeing not the derelict ruin but a gracious hall crowned by a vaulted dome supported by slender pillars and arches nearly lost in the silky gloom of the intricate ceiling. He heard a ghostly thread of the same sweet chanting that had called him here, and just as suddenly it was gone again. He shook his head, not hearing the chanting any longer. Instead, he heard the clumping of Thurid's boots making their purposeful way toward him, followed by the six Inquisitors, muttering querulously and gripping their smoking staffs as they advanced.

Leifr glared at them severely, and they halted at a respectful distance, gaping at the sword standing trembling on its point. He put a hand upon its hilt, feeling the welcome humming of its power. With a quick, sure pull, he removed the sword from its moorings and held it aloft, gleaming and casting off little slivers of sparks.

"This is most irregular," Fodor said, shaking his head and passing a hand over his brow. "I think when I return to the Guild, I shall resign my post as Chief Inquisitor. I never dreamed there was so much knowledge that the Wizards' Guild simply ignores. I feel all atremble in this place, like a child at his first examination.''

"Didn't I tell you what an ignorant pack of fools you were?'' Thurid demanded.

"Almost continuously,'' Fodor agreed, seconded by murmurs of agreement from the other Inquisitors.

"Although,'' Varkar added in his sardonic voice, "it would surely take an ignorant pack of fools such as we are to return to Hringurhol during Brjaladur, even for the carbuncle of Galdur. Listen to that din!''

The Ulf-hedin sounded their dismal cries from all quarters of Hringurhol.

"Well, then,'' Thurid said, "let us attend to our business and be on our way again. You see the dragon ship yonder. That's our prize. It must be returned to the river.''

"What!'' the dismayed Inquisitors sputtered. "Why on earth? There's no way to steal a dragon ship without being seen!''

"Isn't it a bit heavy for just the eight of us?'' Einkenni added, still out of breath from his climb up the hill.

"Nine,'' Ljosa said, gliding out of a shadow and taking a cautious position on the far side of Leifr.

"Excellent! Nine, then!'' Berjast exclaimed harshly, flinging his hands aloft. "At least we won't be getting in one another's way! Why didn't anyone listen to me when I suggested using the Protectors to flatten this place and be done with it?''

"Because it was a poor idea,'' Fodor said. "If Thurid says we must remove the dragon ship, then we shall remove it, if that's what it takes to obtain Galdur's carbuncle.''

They advanced upon the dragon ship cautiously. Thurid ran his hands over it anxiously, examining it for signs of damage, while the Inquisitors watched him as attentively as if he were a sleight-of-hand artist. Leifr walked around and gazed at the ship, shaking his head slightly. From nose to tail it was at least eighty feet, one of the larger warships he had seen in his brief career as a Viking in the Scipling realm.

Ljosa shadowed him, darting dubious glances between Leifr and the Inquisitors. Outside the walls, the Ulf-hedin howled and fought in the fury of Brjaladur, and the raging Dokkur Lavardur engulfed more of the settlement with a bellowing roar.

"Whatever happens here tonight,'' she said in a low voice,

"know that I don't intend to end up as Sorkvir's captive again and I don't want to be swallowed by that thing." She glanced upward with a warding-off gesture. "I have enough power left for one last escape spell—for the two of us. I don't know where we will come out, but anywhere is better than here with Sorkvir."

Leifr nodded in agreement, his throat tight and dry.

"We must have a chain of power to move this ship," Fodor was saying, and commenced directing them to stand with one hand on the shoulder of the next person and one hand on the ship. "United in purpose and effort, we will move this ship to the river. Close your eyes and picture it moving over the land and toward the water."

Leifr did exactly as he was told, without questioning the wisdom of imagining a ship moving, when he knew that the only way to do it was on rollers or skids. To his amazement, the ship shuddered and jolted forward perhaps a foot.

"We should have it there by the end of the year, at this rate," he grunted.

The Inquisitors backed up and gazed at the ship a moment in silence, then at Thurid.

"You're certain we must do this?" Fodor asked.

Thurid nodded vigorously. "This ship is a priceless creation, crossing and recrossing the way it does without human hand upon the oar and tiller. Why do you think the Council was intent upon offering it up to the Lord of Chaos, as they call him?"

Thurid glared at the ship, an imposing figure in a billowing cloak dimly lit by the crackling and fulminating of the Dokkur Lavardur overhead.

"There must be a better way!" Fodor said.

"Then you tell me what it is!" Thurid growled, distractedly plowing through his hair with one hand, the practice that, over a lifetime, had rendered Thurid's hair very fine and thin. "I wish we had Raudbjorn here!"

Leifr leaned against a tomb, clasping his arms over his chest in discouragement. "I'm afraid Raudbjorn went up with the stable," he said gruffly, "so there's no sense wishing for something that is gone."

Nevertheless, he thought wistfully of Raudbjorn and his enormous strength, wondering if that great strength and loyalty were now being used to fuel the unwholesome energies of the Dokkur

Lavardur, to be used against them in their last desperate struggle to thwart the elemental's dominion.

"I'm beginning to regret this decision," Fodor said, after a much nearer outburst of Ulf-hedin howling and fighting. "We shouldn't have come back. They'll be upon us at any moment, surrounding us. We can't hope to hold off several hundred crazed Ulf-hedin. With or without saving this ship, Thurid, we must leave while we can. We do have one of the five stones, at least, do we not?"

"What a lot of carking and crying," Thurid snorted. "I thought you Inquisitors were the most bold of all the Fire Wizards' Guild, and here you're ready to show the white feather already. Well, I assure you, there's plenty of spells in this satchel to protect us for a great long while." He opened his satchel with a flourish and began examining rune sticks.

"Leave our defense to me," Leifr said, putting his hand upon the welcome warmth of the sword's hilt. "*Endalaus Daudi* and I will keep the Ulf-hedin out, and you figure out how to move that ship."

Leifr strode to the archway and planted himself there with *Endalaus Daudi* glimmering in his hand. Below, scattered fires dotted Hringurhol, showing glimpses of Ulf-hedin running and fighting or staggering around in death throes. It was indeed a night of misrule and chaos, with the Dokkur Lavardur exulting over it all, capriciously tossing men and animals about in mid-air, pausing to dissolve the tops of the jagged ruins, and ripping the roofs off houses and barns like a hungry bull grazing in a field of hummocks.

In the light of a particularly fulsome display by the Dokkur Lavardur, an apparition suddenly rose up from behind a heap of rock, lurching toward the ruined hall. It was a huge, deformed creature that instantly put Leifr in mind of the Flayer of Fangelsi.

"Stop there!" he commanded with an aggressive brandish of the sword. "Come forward only if you wish to die for once and for all! It's Endless Death I'm wielding, and it's waiting for your blood!"

"Leifr? Leifr Scipling Thorljottsson?" a deep and throaty voice rumbled. The slouching figure straightened suddenly, dumping a burden off its shoulders precipitately and taking two swinging strides forward. A splintering crack of lightning revealed a great round face, split by a broad grin, small almond-shaped eyes beaming down at him half obliterated in joyous creases.

"Raudbjorn!" Leifr exclaimed, jolted breathless by a great friendly clout on the back and a mighty squeeze that threatened to lift him off his feet. The troll-hounds leaped up around him all the while, snapping at his ears and nose in an ecstasy of welcome.

Starkad shoved his way through the hounds and whacked his palm, grinning malevolently as he pranced around in a warlike fashion, saying "Now we're going to see a massacre! Ulf-hedin will be stacked up like firewood from here to Ferja!"

"Enough, enough!" Svanlaug interrupted, striding past them with an impatient kick at the hounds. "The guards have deserted their posts. Heidur's well is ours. Raudbjorn, you've dropped poor Halmur like a sack of grain! Let's get inside and prepare our defenses. It won't take the Council long to figure out where we're hiding. Now that we've got the sword again, I'm beginning to feel almost hopeful. Starkad, you help Raudbjorn. Take Halmur to the well under the altar. Ulfrin, you're not going to knuckle under again, are you? You're going to cure Halmur, aren't you?"

"No one is going to knuckle under unless it's you, dear sister," Ulfrin spat as she strode past, her head carried arrogantly high.

Svanlaugh paused and greeted Leifr with a twitch of one shoulder and a grim little smile. "It's about time you showed up to help," she said. "I haven't had an easy time of it, managing all this by myself. I've got Ulfrin back, at least, and you've got *Endalaus Daudi*. I see you've also managed to rescue the chieftain's daughter."

Ljosa stepped out of the shadowy archway and she and Svanlaug exchanged a level stare.

"Yes, and Thurid and the Inquisitors are inside, trying to get the dragon ship out," Leifr said. "We're glad of any help we can get."

"I should think so, if those Inquisitors are involved," Svanlaug retorted, tossing her mane of black hair in exasperation. "Everything is a perfect muddle now, thanks to them. They'd better not attempt to interfere again; I fear my patience is wearing terribly thin. All I want is to get out of here alive, with Ulfrin—and to do as much damage to the Council as I can on my way out. You'd better come along and see what can be done with Halmur. He's in the mad stage of Brjaladur. If he wasn't already nearly dead, you'd have to kill him. I'd leave him to his friends to tear apart, except that he came to the stable to warn us away. We at least owe him the effort of trying to cure him. Have you seen the knacker-women?''

"Where, here?''

"Of course here,'' Svanlaug snapped. "We left them here. They wanted us to leave Hringurhol, but we came back to make certain the Council was done for, since everyone else seemed to be either dead or gone. Have you looked yet in the altar room? I'm beginning to have a feeling about those knacker-women, Leifr. They're not what they seem.''

Chapter 18

Halmur growled and snarled as Raudbjorn hoisted him to his shoulders, despite his struggles to free himself. As Leifr followed Raudbjorn into the hall and toward the altar room, he felt as if he were once again at Fangelsi, contending with the Flayer and Uncle Ketil.

"What is this interruption?" Fodor demanded, drawing back in alarm as Halmur was carried by him, kicking and snarling, with eyes gleaming in mad fury. As Ulfrin brushed past him, he summoned a flare of light to his staff's end and stared after her in amazement.

"Hide that light!" Svanlaug commanded. "If the Council sees lights up here, they'll be down on our necks before you can draw your next breath. It was good of you to return Thurid to us, though. I guess you're not such a bad sort after all."

Fodor glared after her haughty shoulders and sputtered, "We are the Inquisitors! Not such a bad sort indeed! If anyone is considered bad, it is certainly not Inquisitors of the Wizards' Guild!"

Several of the other Inquisitors shook their heads, and Berjast remarked gloomily, "If we were not Inquisitors, we should have to turn ourselves in for examination, after all that has passed here tonight. No one better find out we've been guilty of an unorthodox alliance with Dokkalfar, Sciplings, renegade Rhbu wizards, Svertings, and now Ulf-hedin!"

"We won't tell a soul," Varkar growled. "Especially if we're all dead."

The tall doors to the altar room were closed, the remnants of the great Seals glowing with a dull light. In the shadows nearby, the knacker wagon lurked like a shabby skeleton. Ulfrin positioned herself before the doors and stood still a moment, breathing deeply.

"Something is wrong here," she said. Fanning the air with her fingertips, she turned slowly toward Leifr. "All the influences of the Dokkur Lavardur have vanished. The ancient abomination of Heidur's well is returning. The return of that sword has a great deal to do with it."

"What ancient abomination?" Leifr demanded, his hand on the hilt of the sword.

"Open the doors," Ulfrin said.

Starkad sprang forward and fearlessly pressed his shoulder to the door, trundling it open with a complaining of old hinges and a mossy grumbling.

Within, the chamber was lit by two braziers leaping up toward the distant ceiling, and candles and oil lamps stood on every available surface, dotting the blackened old tombs and seats and perched on niches in the walls. A slight figure knelt upon the paving stones of the buried well and straightened when the doors opened, stepping around a watery pinkish pool staining the floor near the well. Ulfrin took a backward step, raising one hand in a shielding gesture. Leifr half drew the sword, then thrust it back into its sheath and hurried forward to intercept the small slinking figure.

"Vidskipti!" he exclaimed. "What are you doing here? Are you the ancient abomination?"

"You could say that of a man who always seems to be in the wrong place at the right time," Thurid said caustically, his eyes darting left and right as he strode into the altar room with a businesslike toss of his cloak over one shoulder. Swiftly he tested the influences of the place, one eyebrow hiking upward in suspicious amazement.

Vidskipti spread his hands apart apologetically and shrugged his ragged shoulders. "Leifr, my friend of friends! I see you have your sword back. I hope you won't be angry at me for stealing it from those thief-takers. I kept it in safekeeping for you until it could be sharpened. From what happened to Alfrekar, *Endalaus Daudi* itself could not have done a much better job on him. The sky beast thought they were trying to trick him with the leikfang and the false sword." He added a nervous cackle and wrung his bony hands, glancing at the Inquisitors with an appeasing grimace.

"What are you doing here?" Leifr demanded. "You should

have got yourself out of Hringurhol for Brjaladur, unless you enjoy more trouble than you can handle.''

Vidskipti rubbed his nose and shook his head. ''Trouble is the wrong word for it, Leifr. Come in, come in quick, all of you, and you shall see what I mean. What's that you've got, an Ulf-hedin in full Brjaladur? I suppose you want the antidote for the curse, don't you?''

''Yes, he's a good friend and ally and we must cure him if we can,'' Leifr said, his eyes darting around the brilliant room. ''What have you been doing in here, Vidskipti?''

''Never you mind,'' Vidskipti said. ''I need a bit of help in a chore I've started, and the lot of you are going to help me in a small bit of housecleaning. This unclean altar is the abomination of Hringurhol, if anything is, covering the well of Heidur, and it must be scattered. The lot of you should manage it nicely. Carry the stones out to the main hall and scatter them around. It will greatly hinder the furtherance of the Council's vile plans with the ruling entity.'' He motioned significantly upward, loath to speak the name lest it become a summons, and knelt down beside Halmur, churning and trembling in a weakening frenzy.

''Halt!'' Fodor said. ''No one shall enter this place until we've thoroughly examined it.''

The Inquisitors glided around the room, sampling the air, the designs on the walls, and the water of the well for influences.

''Where are the knacker-women?'' Svanlaug demanded. ''I wish to speak to them.''

Vidskipti rolled his eyes around furtively and bunched up his skinny shoulders in an elaborate shrug. ''Who can say about the knacker-women?'' he replied.

''Oh, this place is loaded with strange things!'' Fodor said in poorly concealed excitement. He knelt on the curbing of the well and sampled a drop of the water on the end of his tongue. ''Wonderful things! Nothing like this has been on the face of the earth for a great many years! It's a wonderful curiosity. I pronounce this place clean and safe to enter.''

Vidskipti's eyes burned in a fever of impatience. ''Well, I could have told you that,'' he sputtered. ''Time's running out for this young lad. Get some water from the well and force it down his throat, no matter how he struggles. He won't want it, because of the Ulf-hedin curse, but it will cure him, and cure his wounds, as well.''

"What do you know about healing?" Svanlaug snorted.

"Only a few things," Vidskipti said. "Fetch me a draft of water from the well and I shall show you."

"But it killed Fax!" Ulfrin exclaimed. "If you give that to Halmur, he's going to die, and horribly! It's vile and dangerous! The Council has tried for years to keep it covered with this altar!"

"This well is the most pure of all water," Vidskipti said, trailing a handful through his fingers. "It will harm no one except those given over to the Dokkur Lavardur or creatures like him. This is one of the most ancient beneficial wells that used to encompass Skarpsey like a chain of safety and healing. Places like this have sprung up to attempt to destroy them." He made a contemptuous gesture at the unclean altar. "Bring forward your Ulf-hedin. I know this water is going to cure him."

Ulfrin herself took the horn cup from Svanlaug and turned toward the well. Vidskipti alone had removed some of the paving stones, revealing more of the curbing and the narrow stair winding downward, disappearing into the black water. Carefully Ulfrin filled the cup and returned it to Vidskipti, where the Inquisitors stood in a judicious ring with their eyes upon the proceedings, keenly searching for signs of aberration.

Vidskipti forced a draft of the water between Halmur's teeth while Leifr, Starkad, and Raudbjorn maintained a good grip on him to restrain his struggles. Svanlaug kept herself out of the reach of the water as it was slopped and sputtered around, but her eyes were avid as she watched. As the water trickled down Halmur's throat, it also soaked the outside of him and bathed his wounds during his struggles to escape, making another pinkish bloody pool on the paving stones of the ancient well.

The wolf skin peeled away from Halmur in a lifeless heap. Leifr seized it and gave it a contemptuous toss, not intending for it to land in the well. It settled on the water with a simmering hiss, with tendrils of steam rising around it as it blackened and curled, smaller and smaller until it was entirely consumed in a cloud of mist.

Fodor and other Inquisitors exchanged a long glance, shaking their heads slightly, and the wise and gentle Skyldur raised his eyes skyward with a long-suffering sigh.

"I wish I had not seen that," he said. "This is not conventional sorcery. I shall have to consider all this later."

Vidskipti held out the cup again. "If we bathe his injuries in this water, he will quickly heal," he said. "This well was blessed by the Rhbus in ancient times. I doubt if it has lost its efficacy."

Kneeling down to scoop up another cupful, Ulfrin gasped and backed away, pointing into the water, where some indistinct white shapes floated just beneath the surface. "Something's in the well!" she said, her voice hoarse. "I think it's—people!"

Hastily she poured out the cup of water, and it flashed red in the light, stained by blood. Everyone surged forward with a collective gasp, peering and pointing into the water, where indistinct pale shapes floated just beneath the surface, unnoticed until now.

Without much trouble, Leifr and Thurid dragged one of the corpses out of the water. It was small, like a dead wet bird, clad only in a plain white shift. Thurid peeled back some of the wet strands of hair to look at the face. He stiffened and covered the body with his own cloak.

"It's the knacker-women," he said in a low voice, turning his face away. In the strained silence, everyone heard every word. "All four of them."

"Killed and put into the well!" Leifr looked first at Thurid, then at the Inquisitors, then at Ulfrin for an explanation. They all stared back at him and at the four miserable little corpses staining the water with their blood.

"Who could have done it?" Svanlaug murmured. "What harm did they ever do to anyone?"

"Raudkell," Leifr said, glancing toward Ljosa, who turned her stricken face away from him.

"The water is polluted now," Ulfrin said. "Whoever did it knew exactly what they were doing. This well water was the closely guarded secret of the Council. This is the cure for the Ulf-hedin curse—or was. Only the most loyal, like Fax, were given the antidote. It prevented the effects of Brjaladur. I don't know if it will ever be the same now. What has it done to Halmur? I know it killed Hvitur-Fax, and that was before this pollution."

In the silence, as everyone hesitated, watching Halmur writhe and choke, a voice from the doorway said in a soft growl, "Hvitur-Fax is not so easy to kill."

A white-haired figure stood framed in the doorway, then strode forward to kneel beside Halmur, silencing his wolfish snarling and snapping with a quelling gesture. "Be silent, young fool, you're not a wolf, and you won't be acting like one much longer. The water will cure him. He will suffer, but not as much as he suffers now."

"But the blood!" Ulfrin protested. "The well is desecrated! Something terrible has happened here! The poor old knacker-women were slaughtered and thrown into the water. That's something the Council would do, just when we are so near overthrowing them!"

"The water is yet pure," Fodor said, kneeling beside the well, testing the water with his hand. "As the Chief of Inquisitors, I give you my solemn promise that no one with a grain of truth and light in them will perish if they drink the water of this well. It's a Rhbu well and they were good and honorable people. I'm not afraid to drink it myself." To demonstrate, he pulled his horn cup from his belt pouch and downed a good measure of the water. Promptly he began to choke and wheeze, staggering around the curbing waving off the concern of his companions. "It's nothing," he said, red-faced and chagrined, "just too many years of following the narrow line of the Guild. I insist that the rest of you try it, so you'll see your faults. It will open your eyes amazingly." Done with choking, he stood still and gazed around, blinking his eyes as if dazzled by what his inner vision was showing him.

Thurid rose to his feet and rubbed his hands briskly. Halmur's struggles abated somewhat, settling to a weary moaning and twitching. "There, I think that should be enough for him. Let him soak it in for a while and perhaps he'll be on his legs in a bit. I know full well the restorative powers of these waters, and so do you, Leifr. If not for the knacker-women and this well, we'd both be nothing but charred rubbish and Fax would be out there as mad and foaming as the rest of the Ulf-hedin. You're nicely mended, wouldn't you say, Leifr?"

"Then all those transformations and tortures were not illusions?" Leifr asked, glancing at Ljosa.

"Certainly not," Thurid said. "It was a complicated retrieval spell, filled with nasty wards and counterspells and you attempted just to walk through it. Luckily Beitski came along when she did." Thurid stopped abruptly, as if something were stuck in his throat. He hemmed and coughed a moment, dabbing at some moisture in his eye before resuming gruffly, "We'll fill up what vessels we have and take some with us. There's nothing more we can do here, and the time is growing very short. If the Ulf-hedin don't discover us here, the Council surely will. Where's that pesky Vidskipti? He seems to know so much about things, he might tell us how to get that ship down to the river.''

Vidskipti, however, had vanished. A quick search of the outer vault revealed no trace of him.

''Drat him!'' Leifr muttered, eyeing the dragon ship towering over him. ''Just when we could use his help! It's like a Rhbu to leave you dangling on your own hook.''

''Fridmarr!'' Thurid swung around and glared at Starkad. ''You've had an easy time of it, riding along and letting everyone else do all the work. If you're worth a grain of salt, you'd better tell us how we're going to get this ship out of here.''

Starkad and Fridmarr both ignored him, turning away to examine the dragon ship. Starkad raised one hand to run it along the gunwale. ''Again we meet,'' Fridmarr's voice whispered. ''This time you'll be saved, my friend.''

Alertly Fodor shadowed Starkad, scouring him with a searing glance from head to toe. ''This fails to surprise me, considering the rest of your associates. What fylgja-draug are you possessed by?'' he demanded. ''Wizard, Dokkalfar, troll, or Ulf-hedin, perhaps? Oh, the work to be done here! The purgings I could do!''

Starkad turned and faced him, with Fridmarr's keen and sardonic expression hardening his youthful features.

''You'd better think of something useful to do,'' Fridmarr's voice rasped. ''You've done precious little to help this enterprise. Fetch that bucket and begin wetting down the hull of this ship. It's getting too dried out, like the brains of most Guild wizards.''

''There's no water, except that in the well,'' said Fodor. ''Should it be used for such a mundane purpose?''

''Yes,'' Fridmarr snapped, ''and be quick about it unless you want to be fodder at a Brjaladur feast. They don't bother to cook anything for these three days, you know. Thurid!'' He swung around and arrested Thurid in midstride, interrupting a furious bout of ransacking his satchel for rune sticks. ''This ship must be returned to the river before it is destroyed, either by the Ulf-hedin or drying out. Leave off that pottering around with sticks! You know that's not the solution!''

"There's nothing here about moving a ship!" Thurid fumed. "Fridmarr, these rune wands have been dreadfully inadequate. Why weren't the Rhbus better prepared for emergencies such as this?"

"Thurid, it's time you ended your subterfuge," Fridmarr said. "Where's the blue orb? You'll never move this ship without it, or else a dozen more men and some rollers."

At the mention of the blue orb, the Inquisitors watched Thurid attentively. In the interval of silence, the hypnotic thrumming of the seidur drums commenced.

Thurid cocked his head a moment to listen, then slapped his belt pouch as if suddenly remembering an inconsequential thing he had forgotten some time ago. With a theatrical gesture like a sleight-of-hand trickster at the autumn sheep fair, he palmed the blue orb and held it aloft, shining softly on his hand and bathing his narrow, intense face in blue light.

"If it's time, it's time," he said in a solemn pronouncement.

Varkar elbowed Berjast and muttered, "I knew he had it all along. You owe me fifty marks in silver."

Thurid climbed upon a tomb, putting him on the same level as the carven dragon's head. Looking down on the rest of them with a solemn, benign expression, he held up the blue carbuncle, shedding sparkling rays all around in restless swaths of light.

"This is a solemn moment," he said. "I feel it calls for a speech. We are very near the end of our journey together, and our goals very nearly realized. A great many others who are dead would be pleased to see what we have accomplished thus far, and perhaps they are able to see us from whatever place they've gone to, and I'm certain they would approve of all that has passed so far."

"They wouldn't approve of any more wasted time," Fridmarr's voice interjected. "And neither do we. Listen to those drums, Thurid. Let's get out of here."

"Well, it's rude to be so hasty and unceremonious about it," Thurid grumbled.

"Plagues on ceremony!" Fridmarr snapped. "Get done with it, Thurid! We can be on the other side of the river and have a ceremony, if you wish it, or even two or three of them. But now we must move this ship."

With no further ado, Thurid inserted the carbuncle stone into the forehead socket of the dragon ship and tamped in a bit of rag to hold it in place.

"Now then," he said with dignity as he climbed down from the tomb, "we shall try it again."

The wizards commenced a lengthy chant in unison, putting on strained and pious expressions. In the midst of it, the ship suddenly gave a lurch forward. The chant faltered a bit as they opened their eyes in astonishment, then it resumed with more hopeful energy than before. The ship gave another lurch, followed by a good long slide toward the archway. The wizards moved after it, still chanting their words of power. After a short halt, it commenced a steady, purposeful, rumbling glide down the pathway between the tombs, setting a course for the arch leading to the outside.

Thurid skipped out of the way, swooping down on Leifr and Raudbjorn, who were standing in awe, awash with mysterious pricklings and goosebumps of ignorant unease. Svanlaug and Ulfrin crouched beside the well, with Hvitur-Fax looming protectively behind them.

"Move along," Thurid snapped at the Inquisitors, all brisk bluster now that things were going well. "The ship is moving of its own will now. Your escape is all but guaranteed, once we get the ship to the river, across it and to Ferja. Ljosa, into the ship with you now. Svanlaug, Ulfrin, you certainly can't stay here. The ship will ferry you to the other side of the river, and you can go happily your own way, preferably back to Bergmal and contented obscurity for the rest of your days."

"Yes!" Svanlaug said. "The Council is finished, wouldn't you say, Ulfrin?"

"Hvitur-Fax," Thurid continued, "you, too, are welcome to ride to safety on the skirts of the all-powerful magic of the magnificent Rhbus. But you must be quick or you'll be left behind."

Hvitur-Fax gazed after the ship then at Ulfrin and Svanlaug. "You must go," he said. "But I shall stay. I've got my poor Ulf-hedin to attend to. Now that these doors are open and the back of the Council is broken, this well and its cure are available to any Ulf-hedin who chooses to free himself of his curse. Those who don't are going to be at the mercy of the rest of us who have been delivered. What do you say, Halmur? The two of us against all the Ulf-hedin?"

He extended his hand to Halmur, who was nearly awake now,

crouching on the paving stones as weak as a new-hatched bird, shaking his head as if he were still dazed. His wounds were healed now, as whole as if no teeth or claws had ever touched him. Even his clothing was restored to what it had been. Halmur felt of his arms and legs as if he needed constant reassurance that he was indeed healed and whole. He nodded his head slowly and his face broke into a grin as he clasped the hand of Hvitur-Fax. "We shall get the cure to as many of them as will take it," he said. "There won't be many who will refuse."

"And I shall stay, too," Ulfrin said. "Not one Ulf-hedin will remain."

"And we shall stay, also," Fridmarr's voice said. "The Dokkur Lavardur is not destroyed yet, even if we have broken the back of the Council."

"Well, then!" Thurid exclaimed. "Who else wants to stay on and fight with the elemental?"

"We do," Fodor said, scanning the other Inquisitors with a quick scowl.

"Then no one intends to escape while the escaping is good?" Thurid demanded, and no one replied. "Well, Leifr, it will be our duty to see the ship into the water. This site is indeed safer than Ferja now."

"But Thurid," Ljosa said, still kneeling on the cold stones beside the wretched little carcass of Beitski. Tears trailed down her cheeks, shining in the firelight. "We can't just leave the poor knacker-women like this, with no burial or burning or barrow, can we? Not after all they have done to help us. Can't we do something for them?"

Thurid paused and his snappy manner sagged a little. He looked from the bodies to the dragon ship, which was struggling mightily to rise over a series of crumbling steps. In a subdued voice he answered, resting one hand soothingly on her shoulder, "Ljosa, your heart is soft and gentle, even after all the miserable misadventures that have befallen you, through no fault of your own. Never should a fine-spirited woman have to endure the heroic travails of us menkind. I'm afraid we must leave them as they are for now, my girl. We shall take care of them later. And if we're not successful in the coming battles, at least the Ulf-hedin can't savage their poor bodies, if they are safe in the waters of this holy well. There is nothing in any of those goodly women that will fail to enrich those beneficial waters. After all they have done for me, for all of us, this is the last poor favor I can do for them. It's a pitiful world sometimes, is it not?''

By the time the ship had trundled itself through the arch to the outside, it was gaining speed. Leifr and Thurid hurried to catch up with it, catching hold and tumbling themselves over the gunwales to land inside. The going was smooth, mostly over the soft green sward and rocks thickly coated with moss. An occasional boulder scraped along the bottom, but no damage seemed evident.

The Ulf-hedin spied the ship sailing and raised a clamorous shout of alarm, but the majority seemed to be of two minds about the dragon ship conveying itself purposefully toward the river. They started to pursue, but stopped short and turned aside, repelled perhaps by the sight of Thurid standing amidships with his feet planted wide, holding his staff aloft and spewing a trail of threatening smoke and sparks. Most of those who did opt for pursuit halted suddenly when Thurid summoned forth a menacing burst of alf-light, which cut through the gathering twilight like a bright sword blade.

Then the wolf-horn of Hvitur-Fax sounded from Hringur-knip, and even the most determined of the Ulf-hedin abandoned their pursuit and obeyed the summons.

''Good old Fax!'' Thurid exclaimed. ''Exactly at the right moment!''

The ship turned toward the river, drawn as if by a lodestone. As it swung about, the wizards of the Council came into view, forming a line directly across the path of the ship, holding their staffs aloft in a manner determined to put a halt to their escape. The smoky form of Sorkvir stood to the fore of them.

''I command you to stop!'' he demanded, his voice harsh but piercing, even above the grinding rumble of the ship's hull. ''You have stolen the property of the Council of Threttan! Surrender yourselves, you thieves and murderers!''

''Stand aside or be destroyed!'' Thurid roared, still planted amidships with his staff held at ready. Leifr leaped onto the seat behind him and unsheathed his sword. Baring it to the charged atmosphere of the oppressive elemental caused a crackling shower of sparks to spatter from its gleaming metal.

Leveling his staff, Sorkvir directed a bolt of mist and ice toward the ship. Thurid countered it swiftly, throwing back a crackling wave of fire and smoke that drove the wizards into the cover of walls and corners of fallen buildings. The inevitable progress of the ship did not abate; it plunged willy-nilly onward, leaving a black scar behind it as it passed over the green earth. The Council followed at a safe interval, blasting bolts of ice and clouds of freezing cold, which Thurid turned back upon them with waves of fire, so the occupants of the ship were alternately bathed with numbing cold and searing heat until, with a final burst of speed, it plunged down the bank and into the river with a triumphant splash. For a moment it drifted sidewise, turning slightly around. In a matter of moments it was too late to think about jumping back to land.

"Thurid! We've got to get out of this!" Leifr shouted over the roaring of the river.

Thurid crouched in the bow and cursed, eyeing the spraying rocks rapidly approaching. "Come on, ferryman, do your duty! Bring us to land!" he shouted in helpless fury as the ship was dragged across a shoal of rocks. Leifr looked back at the rock where the ferryman was chained and saw him stand up, arms outstretched like a bird about to take flight.

At that moment, an ice-bolt from Sorkvir caught the ragged figure in a burst of green light. The hapless form of the ferryman flew into the air, knocked from his perch by the force, then dangled by one foot from the chain. Not sparing him even a glance, the Council darted along the bank of the river from one obstruction to the next, sending blasts of ice and power toward the ship. Leifr could hear their voices calling upon the Dokkur Lavardur for assistance. He spared the heavens many an anxious glance while the ship lurched from one protruding rock to the next in a doomed fashion. Thurid dashed from one end to the other, muttering frantically. Suddenly the ship righted itself in the water, swerved around a tremendous boulder, and began churning steadily across the current.

The deck of the ship heaved and tossed, slippery with melting ice-bolts running over the planks in tendrils of mist and green slime. Leifr winced as a blast shattered directly overhead, but Thurid's alf-light swept the dark sky, dissolving the deadly shards of ice into drops of vapor that stung the skin.

The ship veered around and streamed straight back toward Hringurhol, bearing slightly upstream and bucking furiously against the current with an ominous creaking of timbers. The Council welcomed their return with showers of icy brume and gusts of repelling powers. The sky roiled, shuddering with livid light that illuminated the river and its banks and the ruined halls of Hringurhol with a pale and sickly gleam, like rotting wood in a bog. Leifr was certain he saw scales, claws, tail, and glaring eyes, swirling around in no conventional arrangement for any beast he knew. The Council had grouped themselves on a hillock and stood chanting, invoking the sky beast for their assistance and protection.

As Leifr was clinging to a precarious perch in the bow, the ship suddenly heaved and tossed, standing nearly on its tail and shaking him from his perch. He slid backward, gripping the nearest seat, thinking they must have struck a rock just beneath the surface, although he had heard no sound of it.

"Thurid! We've sundered!" he shouted.

"Hold fast to something!" Thurid shouted back. "Stay with the ship!"

The deck was cracking and bowing upward in the center and the gunwales were breaking away. Tar and planks were coming loose with sharp reports as the entire ship shuddered. The ship stood still, lodged upon an outcropping of rock. It was most certainly breaking up and sinking. Thurid came scrambling forward, fumbling with his satchel and a handful of rune wands, slipping and groping his way over the bending planks.

"Thurid, we're sinking!" Leifr shouted. "We're going to die if we hang onto it any longer!"

"No, we're not!" Thurid bellowed over the snapping and creaking and groaning sounds. His hair and beard stood out in crackling streamers and his eyes glared with a madman's fearful glee. "We're going to fly!"

A high windy scream almost deafened them. The sides of the boat, which Leifr had once thought so cunningly carved to look like folded wings, suddenly unfurled themselves with a mighty flapping and thundering, shaking off layers of pitch and tar and creating a hurricane that lashed the water to white foam. The spine of the ship arched with a tremendous creaking and clattering as planking and benches tumbled off into the water, thrust aside as great rocky knobs rose through the wood. Leifr was dumbfounded, but a part of him was still convinced they had run up on the rocks, so he flung his arms around the nearest boulder, thinking it was better to hold on to the rock than be swept away into the water. More huge rocks jutted up through the planking of the ship in a regular row. Thurid seated himself astride the rocks, with one before and one behind, and hauled Leifr into a similar position ahead of him. The deafening screaming and hissing had not ceased, nor had the hurricane of wind and the mighty cracking like a dozen enormous sails of warships. Still convinced the ship was breaking up, Leifr saw the prow bend around so the carved dragon head was looking straight at him for a moment, and he saw the blue orb set blazing in the third eye socket of the beast, with two luminous golden orbs gleaming below and to each side, flickering with the clear membranes that functioned as eyelids for lizardlike creatures. A cool breath fanned Leifr's face as the creature snorted softly at him, and its mouth opened to emit another of the piercing screams, showing rows of razorlike teeth and a long, curling black tongue.

Thurid roared some words at the creature and the beast answered with a deafening scream, lashing its head from side to side in a shower of flying tar, revealing gleaming scales underneath.

Leifr swayed on his perch, light-headed. The dragon ship, which was a ship no longer, rose out of the water with a powerful beating of wings that buffeted at the Ulf-hedin and wizards below, sending them scuttling for cover.

"Now we're going to have some fun, Leifr!" Thurid called with a nervous cackle.

"Thurid! This isn't going to work!" Leifr moaned. "You can't do this with a ship!"

"Ship, my hind foot! This is a real dragon, Galdur the Sorcerer, and I've freed him from the Council's spell! He owes me a few favors, don't you think? Now then, we'll see how he responds!"

Thurid's voice commanded in the language of the Rhbus, and the dragon obligingly drew in a vast creaking breath and blasted it out again, directed at the boat stand not far below. Orange flames scoured the stones, igniting the fur of several Ulf-hedin unlucky enough to be caught by the exploding fireball. One foolishly brave wizard paused to send an ice-bolt upward at the dragon, but it shattered harmlessly against the creature's plated breast. Angered, the dragon stooped like a hawk, making a snatch at the offending wizard with its front talons. Leifr glimpsed the stark terror on the fellow's face for an instant before he dodged into a crack in the rocks, and the dragon's claws clasped only the empty air where he had stood an instant before.

"Come now, Galdur, time for eating later!" Thurid called. "You've got larger fish to fry than that!"

The dragon rumbled like a landslide between Leifr's knees and turned his head in the direction of Hringurhol, circling until he gained sufficient altitude. Leifr clutched the bony hump before him, wanting to shut his eyes against the unnatural sight of the settlement below, but the old exhilaration of flying with the mad wizard Gradagur had returned. Then Galdur went into a long glide, gathering speed.

"Now!" shouted Thurid, and the dragon spewed a tongue of flame all along the battlements of the Ulf-hol. The Ulf-hedin had already gone into shameless retreat at the greatest speed they could manage. As the fiery breath of the dragon touched the walls, their forms changed from crumbling ruins to the crisp outlines of newly hewn stone.

As Galdur swept over the settlement, Leifr gazed down and beheld a group of people with torches simply standing and staring upward. Leifr realized they were singing some sort of chant, and Galdur also heard it and banked steeply, his neck stretched out as he peered down at them. Then he gave another piercing scream, a cry of rapturous joy. Leifr clung to his perch as the dragon swooped above them, making a burbling, rumbling sound like a geyser about to erupt.

"It's that crazy vagabond Vidskipti!" Leifr shouted. "And the rest of those wanderers! Don't they know they could get burned to cinders?"

Thurid turned slightly to shout back, "They're in no danger! He's their own kind! Galdur! Leave them! We'll be back!"

Galdur obligingly turned and swooped over the hall, where Hvitur-Fax and the others were besieged inside by a ravening swarm of Ulf-hedin outside, still in the grip of Brjaladur.

"Galdur!" Thurid called, pointing below with his staff. "Friends of ours are in there! We must save them before the Ulf-hedin get in!"

Galdur burbled a reply, a fiery sound like a violently boiling cauldron. Not a wing tip stirred as the dragon turned and banked, with no sound except the whistle of wind over his wings and the deadly singing of his whipping tail. The wings, Leifr realized, were not the dragon's sole means of flight. He settled gracefully on the crumbling battlement of Hringur-knip, using his wings and tail to balance there. For additional effect, he swelled up his chest and uttered a shrieking hiss, shaking his armored head menacingly.

The Ulf-hedin forgot their battering at the doors and took to their heels, except for a few who were too witless to do anything but stagger around in circles, bellowing for a fight.

Galdur puffed up again and blasted at them with an angry hiss of stinging vapor that brought them to their senses instantly and sent them scuttling away, shedding their wolf skins, with panicky glances backward at the apparition whetting his horns on the wall until they gleamed with the same eerie gleam as *Endalaus Daudi*.

Galdur whistled piercingly, adding a few coughs and grunts for emphasis as he writhed his head around in a fearsome display of horns and teeth and gleaming eyes. To Leifr's surprise, another whistle answered him. Leifr glanced all around, able to see quite well in the thick predawn gloom. The short night was nearly spent, and even the Dokkur Lavardur could not smother all the light of the sun struggling to penetrate the swirling black elemental clouds.

The last remaining domed roof of Heidur's ruins suddenly uttered a grinding creak, and a fragment of stone the size of a large table was thrust upward from beneath.

"Thurid! What is this?" Leifr exclaimed.

Thurid clung to one of Galdur's spinal protrusions, gaping like a small boy attending his first autumn fairing, delighted to behold all the unaccustomed sights.

"Silence, Leifr!" he commanded. "Just watch and you'll see miracles!"

Chapter 19

◇◇

The remaining portion of the roof cracked like an egg pipped by a hatching gosling. The hole became much larger, then a small head and long snaky neck thrust through the hole for a quick survey of the outside. A huge body lunged through the hole, glistening with a deep amber light radiating from its glossy skin. Another dragon climbed to the top of a parapet, flung back its head and uttered a piercing shriek toward the roiling sky entity, which responded with a roar of thunder and a powerful swat of wind.

Craning his neck from side to side and gazing upward, Galdur answered with a challenging screech that set human teeth on edge, flapping his wings in a mighty hurricane that sent the reformed Ulf-hedin below scuttling for cover among the tombs.

"Galdur, you may set us down below, in the cleared space," Thurid said, pointing to the center of the hall.

Obligingly, Galdur leaped down from the parapet. Leifr shut his eyes, bracing himself for a thunderous landing with certain injury, but Galdur glided down the short distance and lit as lightly as a dry leaf drifting down from a tree. With legs that still trembled somewhat, Leifr climbed down the corrugated sides of the massive creature and leaped the last few feet to the welcome earth.

Meanwhile, a second dragon had joined the first, with scales as red as rust. Frills like a massive heavy mane ornamented this dragon from head to tail, diminishing into spiky bumps at head and tail tip. This creature joined the first in an ear-splitting challenge to the Dokkur Lavardur swirling above them. Their trumpeting and head tossing reminded Leifr of rival stallions working themselves into the proper fury for a fight.

"Are they hungry, do you suppose?" Leifr asked nervously, interrupting Thurid's open-mouthed admiration of the red dragon.

"I daresay they might be," he said agreeably.

Two more dragons appeared, golden and green, climbing through the hole in the roof as if it were an eggshell. They preened and aired their wings, flapping mightily, and tried their voices as if they had been silent a long time. Instead of harsh hissing and screeching, their voices were a melodious caroling of mighty, powerful sounds that defied description. It put Leifr in mind of the roar of a huge, musical waterfall or the powerful spring wind sweeping over moors and fells. It shook him to his core, and he knew he would never again see or hear anything so fine and splendid.

Then all five dragons launched themselves into the air for a flight around Hringurhol, screeching and blasting gouts of flame and black smoke as if for the sheer joy of seeing Ulf-hedin and ice-wizards scuttling for shelter.

"Leifr! Thurid!" someone shouted, and a familiar figure vaulted over a tomb and loped toward them. It was Starkad, a welcome sight in his flapping, ragged attire, grinning with the satisfaction of knowing he had annoyed someone. Behind him, the Inquisitors rose up from their hiding places, testing the atmosphere for hostile influences, waving an assortment of devices and amulets, and all nattering at once as they made their way toward Thurid in considerable excitement. Behind them Ljosa, Svanlaug, and Ulfrin were quick to follow.

"Fridmarr!" Thurid's greeting was stern, and he made a conspicuous effort to draw his features into a scowl. "Didn't I leave strict orders that no one was to come out of the sanctuary until I returned? What has happened here? I shouldn't have let any of you out of my sight!" His gaze settled indignantly upon the Inquisitors, still arguing and sputtering among themselves in high excitement and peering upward anxiously at the dragons.

Starkad beamed, a curious mixture of Fridmarr and his own mischief running through his expression. "What a worrier you are," he said. "You should know I'd be all right. I know this place from long experience."

"Starkad doesn't," Thurid said sharply.

"Yes, I do," Starkad said. "I know a great many new things now, with Fridmarr to tell me."

"More's the pity!" Thurid added.

Fodor greeted Thurid with a disheveled flourish of his arms. "Magnificent! Extraordinary! The dragons are splendid, aren't they? The Guild declared dragon fylgjur obsolete long ago, but I think that was a mistake. We've had nothing but trouble with air elementals such as the Dokkur Lavardur ever since. I didn't know whether to believe Fridmarr when he told me who they are.''

''Who who are?'' Thurid demanded.

''And look who's back,'' Fridmarr went on, but it was Star-kad's exuberant enthusiasm as he pranced around and beckoned impatiently to someone lurking behind the front row of tombs.

A blocky, dark-haired Alfar stepped from behind a sarcoph-agus, holding his shoulders in a stiff, defensive manner as he glanced suspiciously from Leifr to Thurid. With a rolling gait he advanced, planting his feet firmly with each step and not taking his eyes off Thurid. His face was not handsome, being rather coarse and set into lines of strength and determination. Piercing dark eyes sparkled beneath jutting black brows. His beard and hair were a mass of wiry curls, slightly silvered.

''So,'' he said, halting abruptly. ''Here I am. Do you know me? You ought to; I've carried you this whole way to finish the job I began.''

''Gedvondur!'' Leifr blurted, drawing back a pace.

''Of course,'' Gedvondur retorted. ''And now no one is go-ing to take advantage of me any longer since my old form has been restored. No more rude tossing into a satchel or a sack or an old boot. No more hot coals, either.''

Leifr felt his heart stop beating for a moment. Gedvondur— the name meant Bad-tempered, and Gedvondur had the peevish look of a chronically ill-tempered person who was unafraid to use his vile humors to good effect.

''I hope you'll let past mistakes be forgiven and forgotten,'' Leifr said. ''It's not as if we don't have a few things of yours to forgive. In spite of everything, at least you got restored to your own body now. It was lucky you got to the knacker-women before they were killed.''

''Knacker-women!'' Gedvondur tossed back his head with a short bray of mirth. His eyes followed the five dragons as they curveted and spiraled through the murky air. ''A clever dis-guise, was it not? Even I was deceived.'' He said something more, but the roaring scream of the Dokkur Lavardur buried it as wind and stinging pellets of ice suddenly dashed at Heidur's ruins. The half-broken dome of the altar room offered partial protection, so they raced into its shelter and stood there in aston-ishment, watching the dragons darting through the sky. Unlike birds, their flight was erratic and nimble, more like the flight of bats. They were able to stop and hover before plummeting away, often tumbling head over tail, as if they were playing with the mighty elemental that blasted at them. Curtains of fog and darkness brushed the earth, hurled aloft like nets at the dragons, and lightning stabbed at them to the accompaniment of roaring thunder. The humans watching stood transfixed by awe, and even Gedvondur let a respectful expression smooth his swarthy and cynical features.

Quite suddenly, the five dragons turned as one and came tilting earthward at a perilous speed, drawing up just short of destruction among the jagged ruins of Heidur's well. For a moment they hovered, not a wing stirring, then settled gracefully into the midst of the tombs. For a moment they preened themselves, holding their wings aloft and shivering the translucent membranes like a thousand panes of colored glass before folding them away. Their images continued to shiver, however, dissolving into a mist that obscured them completely. When it vanished, five people stood there, talking and embracing with the fervor of old friends reunited, four women in gray gowns and cloaks and one man attired in black.

"It's the knacker-women!" Thurid suddenly declared in a shout of recognition, breaking the respectful silence of all who watched. Gripping his staff, he strode forward to meet them, his shoulders stiff and his head jutting forward. By his posture, Leifr knew he was acutely aggrieved at being excluded earlier from this bit of knowledge. Leifr hurried after him, making a few unnoticed tweaks at his billowing cloak to restrain him.

"I thought you promised to tell me all," Thurid greeted the knacker-women and the wizard Galdur, who all smiled at him with an air of anticipation. They no longer appeared shrunken and pinched with poverty and lean living. Their age was great, Leifr realized, but it set upon them in a mantle of knowledge and experience and vitality unrivaled by youthful beauty. Galdur's age was incalculable, irrelevant in the warmth of the waves of approval and encouragement eddying around him and touching anyone who came near. In his presence, Leifr felt strengthened in every fiber, as if he could do anything Galdur suggested.

"I thought," Thurid continued, "you supplied me with much more knowledge when you brought me back from Hela's gates. You told me I should recognize all things needful. You did tell me that the dragon ship was Galdur the Sorcerer, trapped by the Council in a spell. But you somehow neglected to tell me that you were the remaining four dragons of the Rhbus. Had I known, I might have got those four stones earlier and avoided a great deal of trouble. And grief, I might add, after we found your bodies in the well and supposed you were killed."

The four women were laughing silently at him, still smiling at Thurid in gentle calm.

"Thurid, Thurid!" Beitski said. "All things come in their own good time, and even grief and pain are good teachers. It wasn't for you to restore our carbuncles to us. It was a thing we had to do for ourselves, while no one was nearby to interrupt. I doubt if you would have understood, so it was well that the Inquisitors took you away for a short while."

"Just to get me out of the way!" Thurid snorted, rather faintly, his tone diminishing in its indignation. "Well, who am I to criticize the actions of my betters? I am, after all, your servant, if I am to be considered an adept wizard of the Rhbu tribe."

"Domari is the Judge," Beitski said, with a deferential nod to her sister. "She is the most wise of us and she must give you the answer to that."

Domari, the most white-haired of the sisters, returned the nod graciously. "Thank you, Bryti, but you are the Steward who has nurtured us through these lean times. Nor could we have survived without the guidance of Fylgyd to reassure us that we would one day be restored to our powers, and the faith of Verdugur the Worthy to flog us along when we were discouraged."

"Hear, hear!" Galdur murmured in a comfortable rumbling voice.

"As the last Judge of the Rhbu tribe," Domari continued, "I deem it fitting to award Thurid the status of Wizard of the First Rank for his service and progression toward full knowledge."

"I did no more than any of the others who were with me," Thurid said. "Perhaps less, even. I was selfishly pursuing a path for my own benefit, while they were earnestly devoted to helping someone else: Leifr to rescue Ljosa; Svanlaug to save her sister; Fridmarr and Gedvondur to help me. No, I'm not at all sure I deserve the First Rank or even to be an apprentice."

"Nonsense," Galdur said. "Rhbu wizards are as scarce as hen's teeth these days and we aren't going to let you off easily, I'm afraid."

"Rhbu wizards!" Fodor murmured, rolling his eyes skyward and making some hasty signs to ward off bad luck. "The scourge of the Fire Wizards' Guild for many a year, until the practice of dragon hunting so drastically reduced their numbers. With such powers, why are dragons unable to defend themselves against the weapons of the dragon hunters?"

"Those great shooting weapons have been brought through the gates from the Scipling realm," Galdur said. "Powerful though dragons are, Scipling weapons and Scipling knowledge destroy us. Traffic between the two realms must be stopped, if any dragons and our ancient knowledge is to survive. We have all gained immeasurably from the New People; but, even though their intentions are not hostile, they are more capable of destroying both Ljosalfar and Dokkalfar than any spells and elemental furies we wizards can concoct."

"Tell me," Leifr said, "have I done your realm any harm? It was the least of my intentions to do damage here with my presence."

Wise Domari shook her head. "You have done no harm, Leifr Thorljotsson, only good because you are a good man, honest and true in all you do. No one else could have been trusted with the sword of Endless Death. You have used it with only just cause, not for your own evil gain. Many a lesser man has used it and died. Yet we feared for you, this close to rescuing your loved one from the clutches of these evil Councilmen. Had you touched one of them in vengeance with that sword, you would have perished, and only moments from realizing the deliverance of the realm from the Lord of Chaos. For that reason the sword was taken away from you until your selfish desires no longer stood in the way of your judgment. Should you choose to stay, there is yet work for you and that sword. There is much happiness and much good, but I fear there is also sorrow for you on the opposite side of the balance beam. What is weighed on one side must be balanced on the other in this realm. In your realm inequity seems to abound, but here we must balance good and evil as we go. You have already endured much for our cause, and it grieves me to tell you that you must suffer more. If you do not wish to continue, we must send you back to your own realm before the third night of Brjaladur. During these seasonal changes, the gates between our realms are most easily negotiated. But if we are to defend ourselves from the dragon hunters, as Galdur has said, the gates must be changed, and they must be changed on the third night of Brjaladur. Go now and you will be safely returned to your family and kinfolk and all will be as if you never left them. But if you stay another night in Hringurhol, it will be as if you had been gone three hundred years by the next time we can send you back. All that is familiar to you will be gone. Everyone you knew will be dead. No one will remember your name. This is the price you must pay if you decide to stay in our realm. You will be a hero here, *Endalaus Daudi* will be yours to keep for as long as you are faithful and just. I shouldn't wonder if you became wealthy and influential, and you shall certainly have friends in high places. If you don't choose to pay the high price of this life in the Alfar realm, you must be returned to your own realm before midnight tonight."

Three hundred years. Leifr trembled at the thought of it, picturing his parents and brothers as he had seen them in happier days, and as he had seen them last, grieving over his outlawry as if he were already dead and his head handed over to the chieftain he had offended. He glanced at Ljosa, and she immediately lowered her glance to her feet. It occurred to him then that she would have seen Fridmarr in Starkad, living again and no doubt loving her still.

"I shall have to think," Leifr said. "I can't answer you right now."

"Very good," Bryti said, with her same old birdlike Beitski mannerisms. "You go ahead and weigh your options. At any time before midnight we can send you back and all will be as if you had not left. What were you doing just before the moment you entered the gate to the Alfar realm?"

"I was fighting off a pack of thief-takers," Leifr said. "They were in a fair position, too, to get what they had come for. Is that what I'd be sent back to?"

"Just that," said Beitski.

"And would I remember any of what has happened to me here?"

"For as long as you live, you'll remember," Bryti said. "But we couldn't send you back to die at the hands of thief-takers. We'll see to it that you survive that day, at least. I shouldn't wonder if you saw someone you knew, from time to time, come on a visit to the Scipling realm, although such things are going to be far more difficult than they once were, I'm afraid."

Leifr felt the sword hilt beneath his hand. Without asking, he knew it could never leave the Alfar realm, so he had better put it to good use while he could. Gruffly he said, ''Time is wasting. What's to be done now with the Council of Threttan and the Dokkur Lavardur?''

''The Council has been summoned,'' Galdur said. ''So far they are choosing to ignore their summons, however. It may be necessary to ferret them out and bring them to an accounting for their crimes.''

''I can fetch them,'' Leifr said, ''with the aid of *Endalaus Daudi*. I don't think they'll refuse, unless they've gotten into that warren of tunnels under the Ulf-hol. Getting them out of there could be difficult, but Hvitur-Fax knows every inch of it, I should think.''

''We shall give them every opportunity to be reasonable,'' Galdur said, and the four sisters nodded their heads in agreement. ''But this time they shall not get the better of us.''

Leifr spent the day resting and considering his situation. The five Rhbus and Thurid spent their time in some much-needed housecleaning; by sundown the holy well of Heidur had been cleared of the unclean altar stones and all traces of the Council removed from the chamber that surrounded it. A few shaky Ulf-hedin presented themselves to be cured of their curse, under the watchful eyes of Hvitur-Fax, the newly appointed guardian of the well. Ljosa stayed completely out of sight, and Svanlaug and Ulfrin could not get enough of surreptitiously spying upon the five Rhbus and quarreling in low voices. Clearly, Svanlaug had had enough of Hringurhol and everything in it, but Ulfrin wanted to linger.

Gedvondur and Fridmarr, along with Starkad as a natural consequence, sat and argued ferociously over what had gone wrong when they had attempted to disrupt the Council's Pentacle of Chaos years before.

Throughout the day, the Dokkur Lavardur buffeted at the ruins of Heidur's well, and the sky thickened once more to empurpled, swollen masses of lowering cloud. As Leifr skulked about, brooding over his situation, he watched the menace of the sky touch down like the funnel of a waterspout, siphoning away a turf house and barn and some livestock in a shrill roar of dissolution. Nothing was left behind except the flinty heart of Skarpsey that lurked not far beneath its velvety green coat of moss and grass. Leifr clutched the small ball of fine linen that contained the three broken pieces of the ring of strength. It was used up, as was the spell Vidskipti had taught long ago. All he had left was the sword, and he could not imagine how he would use it to challenge an entity that filled the sky from horizon to horizon, capable of engulfing a house and barn and five cattle in a single breath. The dragons might possibly drive it from the sky, but it didn't seem to be a thing anyone could battle with a sword.

Gazing southward through the rising mists that heralded the approach of night, he saw the deserted wanderers' camp, barren of carts and cookfires and blattering sheep. Its desolation filled his heart with a similar desolation, echoed by the resounding, exhausted silence of Hringurhol. Only a small solitary fire winked in the jumble of a fallen building, a lone red twinkle in the feathery gloom.

Suddenly it seemed to Leifr that he smelled sausages cooking. He could almost see them, skewered on sticks, oozing grease that dripped into the coals with wisps of bright flame and sizzled away in wisps of black smoke. In an instant his lassitude and indecision vanished, and he found himself slithering down from his high perch and out the main doors of the ruin before he took time to think about it. With his hand upon the hilt of *Endalaus Daudi*, he traversed the wreckage of Brjaladur, seeing ruin and havoc and mayhem on all sides. The mindless wrath of Brjaladur turned against anything made by human hand, and when there was none of that to destroy, the Ulf-hedin turned upon each other in a frenzy of hatred and self-destruction.

He approached the small fire, discerning a ragged form crouching beside it. Sausages indeed sizzled invitingly on skewers, dripping grease onto the coals.

"Vidskipti! You knew all along about the knacker-women!" Leifr greeted him. "You were there and you helped them with their restoration, didn't you? I've known a long time you were a Rhbu, and now there's no denying it."

The figure by the fire lifted his head, letting the drooping hood fall away, revealing the singed and blackened face of a skull, with eyes that blazed like coals.

"No, there's not, is there?" the dry voice of Sorkvir rasped. The sorcerer reached out with one claw to seize his staff as Leifr gripped the pommel of his sword.

An icy blast numbed Leifr's hand and rooted him to the ground, scarcely able to breathe.

"We're not quite finished with Hringurhol yet," Sorkvir continued with a harsh sputtering that might have been a cackle, or a sign of some grave malfunction in his borrowed body. "You may think we've lost all cause to continue our fight, with all our offerings to the Dokkur Lavardur destroyed, but now, thanks to our meeting, it is not quite all lost yet. At least I shall have the satisfaction of seeing you and that cursed sword finally destroyed, beyond anyone's redemption. Those confounded, interfering Rhbus may have their well again, but the Dokkur Lavardur will have you to feast upon and the Ulf-hedin will have all the dragon meat they can hold. The glory of the Council of Threttan will be known and feared throughout all the realms!"

Leifr folded his arms to show his disdain. "You're mad," Sorkvir," he said. "The fire eating you has got to your brain. Nothing can save the Council of Threttan now. Compared to the Rhbus, you're nothing but paltry, conniving tricksters."

Another shadow stirred in the darkness of the shadow, and Raudkell's face appeared in the smoldering glow of the fire, scowling and wary.

"The Council conquered the five dragons of the Rhbus once," he said. "This time they'll be destroyed utterly, carbuncles and all, with no hope for any clever retrieval."

"You're fools to try it again," Leifr said.

Sorkvir rose to his feet, exuding a cloud of smoke and trickling ashes. "But we are desperate, and the desperate always make one more attempt," he croaked. Flinging out one hand, he riveted Leifr to the spot. "There's the bait in our trap," he said to Raudkell. "Now where are your men?"

Raudkell beckoned, and three slinking figures crept out of the shadows.

"Where is your instrument?" Sorkvir demanded. "Bring it forward and put it into position. We have little time before our powers wane at midnight."

A horse was led forward, blindfolded with a rag tied around its head. Behind it rolled a small cart with no sides, and Leifr recognized the deadly, dragon-destroying weapon he had first seen in Ormur-rike.

"No!" he growled, feeling Sorkvir's spell fading away from him. His rigid fingers closed around the pommel of *Endalaus*

Daudi. "You won't kill them! You'll be dead yourselves, forever in the cold grip of Hela."

"Silence!" Sorkvir sputtered, swatting at a few sullen curls of flame that wisped from his chest, burning within the hoops of his ribs like an incongruent human lantern. All his vitals were turned to ash, charred and rattling within a stretched and withered cage of bone and skin.

Holding his arms in a summoning gesture, his raddled sleeves fell back, revealing arms that were scarcely more than blackened sticks held together by the knobs of joints and stringy tendons. Unclean words spewed from his lips and the wind began to shriek around the ruins in gathering fury. Leifr was too cold and stiff even to feel its buffeting, but he knew when it suddenly snatched him off his feet, tossing him aloft like a calfskin over the jagged ruins of Hringurhol. One drop, one swoop, and he knew his life would be ended. Scarcely able to breathe, his chest burned as he struggled for a ragged breath, and his vision was whirling, blurring, even without being tossed and twirled around on the blasts of elemental wind. Below he glimpsed Heidurhol, the well of hope, and the diminished figures of his friends standing and looking skyward. It would be the last he saw of them and of the life he had once known as an earth-walking creature. All around him, surrounding and filling him, he felt the presence of the Lord of Chaos, greedily plucking at his living essence.

A circle of fire blossomed on the darkening earth, and a vast dark shape ballooned against the phosphorescent sky. A piercing call quavered over the ruins of Hringurhol, echoed by others rising in a carol of melodious chanting and singing. Numbly Leifr thought it was the last and best thing mortal ears could hear, the singing of the Rhbu wisewomen whose knowledge made them dragons.

With a shriek of tearing wind, the light was blotted out of Leifr's vision, but only momentarily, and the heat of a large passing obstruction thawed the spell that bound him. It was Galdur hovering beside him, wings outstretched, his mighty voice rumbling and fulminating deep within his great bulk. A roar came out of him that shook the air, driving back the intruding elemental with a reedy scream of retreating wind.

Leifr's clawing hands found a purchase on a rough, scaly neck, and he flung one leg over as if he were mounting a horse. Sliding downward over protrusions of increasing size, he landed in a fairly comfortable niche between two rocky humps on Galdur's shoulders. When he was well settled, Galdur swooped like a falcon upon the knot of wizards and dragon hunters crouching below.

"Galdur!" he shouted into the wind, directing his voice toward the great head that floated somewhere on the end of a vast long neck stretched out before him. "Don't go after the wizards! Let them go! They've got dragon hunters and one of their terrible engines that kill dragons!"

Galdur banked and veered aside with a derisive snort as the engine exploded with a puny gout of flame and a small, flat report. Something whizzed past, more slowly than an ice-bolt, but Leifr knew Scipling iron was far more deadly to a dragon.

"Galdur, go back!" shouted Leifr. "It will kill you!"

Reluctantly the dragons all returned to Heidurhol and settled to the earth, shifting forms almost the moment they touched down, casting up great shimmering clouds of dust and power.

"The Anathema is back!" Briti exclaimed. "No spell can block its course once it is launched!"

"The Sciplings have truly created a monstrosity of destruction," Verdugur agreed, shaking her head. "I foresee nothing but grief and warfare for the Sciplings if they persist in making and using such things."

"If only it weren't solid iron," Galdur said, "our powers might have a chance against it, but iron is the most cold and unfeeling of all the metals of the earth, the outcast, the renegade metal, with a character intractable and rebellious. Opposition is essential in all things, but why did the Sciplings feel drawn to manufacture with iron?"

Leifr realized they were all looking at him for the answer, but all he could do was shrug his shoulders and feel ashamed of his fellow Sciplings for possessing such a taste for battle and adventure and domination.

"We haven't your powers to create metals such as this," he said, putting his hand upon *Endalaus Daudi*. "Iron is the hardest and the strongest thing we can find. All we can do is heat up a forge and batter away at red-hot iron until it bends to our will."

"Indeed, Sciplings are willful people," Galdur said.

"What can we do with the Anathema?" Fylgyd asked. "I can see no course of action except to retreat. I don't wish to perish again, pierced by one of those iron balls they hurl. Death of a fylgja-form and being robbed of one's carbuncle are dreadful trials.''

"I don't think we could pose as humble knacker-women again," Domari said.

Galdur chuckled dryly. "It was indeed a comedown for you, wasn't it, sisters? The experience should have cleansed you of any lingering residues of harmful pride, I should think, to have been brought so low by a crude Scipling instrument."

"It was a good experience," Verdugur said. "All things that happen to us, whether pleasant or not, are intended to make us stronger and wiser. As knacker-women, we learned a great deal about living by our wits and calling upon the knowledge we had stored in our memories, instead of relying so greatly upon the power of our carbuncles. We healed a great many people of their ills and safely directed a great many harmful spirits to Niflheim, so they can never return. If we should lose our carbuncles again, we can accept and benefit from whatever lot befalls us."

Thurid came striding across the hall, winding among the tombs with a flaring of his alf-light that indicated a similar fiery elevation of his temperament. To Leifr, with admirable restraint, he said, "Your absence was noted by several of us, and it excited considerable apprehension. Losing you now would be a dreadful pity, as near as we are to eliminating the Council and the Dokkur Lavardur from our realm." He looked at the five wise ones with a hopeful flicker in his eye. "At least, I hope we are near to it."

Galdur took two quick steps away, then returned with an impatient swirl of his cloak. "The Anathema that destroyed our dragon forms has returned, Thurid. The Council has brought dragon hunters into Hringurhol, armed with the Anathema. In spite of all our powers and wisdom, we are defenseless against it."

"Not entirely," Thurid said. "It is a Scipling weapon, and we have a Scipling here among us. Leifr, how can we destroy the Anathema? If you don't think of something, we might lose Heidur's well to the Council."

Chapter 20

◇◇◇◇◇◇◇◇◇◇◇◇◇◇◇◇◇◇◇◇◇◇◇◇◇◇◇◇◇◇◇◇◇◇

"I've never seen anything like it, even in the Scipling realm," Leifr protested. "How do you expect me to know how to destroy it? You're the wizard, you think of something. Haven't you got something in your satchel for conveniently destroying anathemas? Or Galdur—maybe he can tell you how to destroy a solid hunk of iron so heavy that it takes a horse to pull it around."

Thurid glared at him and strode away with a snapping of his cloak toward the circle of light where the five Rhbus were conferring.

"You could always ask Vidskipti for his advice again," Gedvondur's voice said behind Leifr. "Provided he's anywhere within miles of Hringurhol. He was here the last time, when Fridmarr and I made our attempt. I suspect he's somewhere a healthy distance from here, laughing up his sleeve even now at the antics of these foolish Ljosalfar."

"No, he's not," Leifr snarled. "I know he's not. He's a Rhbu, and not just an ordinary one. He gave me a ring and a Name to use on this journey."

"And where are Vidskipti's ring and Name now?"

"I used them up. Look, here's the pieces of the ring, if you don't believe me."

Gedvondur examined the three pieces of the ring, scowling and breathing rather heavily over them through his large hooked nose.

"Rather fine gold for a scruffy old wanderer," he said. "And did this ring work for you?"

"Yes. It was a ring of strength. I used it up carrying Ljosa out of the Council Hall. If I hadn't had it, I suppose Sorkvir's retrieval spell would have killed me. I used the last of the Name then, too."

"Well. It's lucky you did, I suppose, or you'd be dead now. This Hroaldsdottir has caused you a bundle more trouble than she's worth, I'd say."

"It was my fault she got caught up in all this," Leifr said, "so I had to get her out of it."

"Even if there's scant chance of any reward," Gedvondur added unnecessarily. His eyes traveled to the high wall of the surrounding ruins, where Leifr recognized two figures, standing alone in a high place to talk where no one would disturb them. One was Ljosa in her red gown, and the other was easy to identify as Starkad by his rough thatch of pale hair blowing in the wind.

"I suspected as much," he said with a negligent shrug. It was as he had feared all along, then. Fridmarr had always been the one she cared for, and now he was alive again in another form. "It doesn't really matter to me, as long as she is safe and alive. What could I do about it anyway, even if I chose to? I'm only a stranger in this realm, after all."

"Bah on women, in other words," Gedvondur said with an astonishingly appealing grin, something like the toothy expression of a dead badger lying faceup in a ditch. His teeth were small and pointy, and his eyes screwed up until they were nearly shut. "Now that we've got this Anathema to think about, there's no time for any distractions, anyway. I've been talking to Hvitur-Fax, and we've come up with a scheme that just might work. Thurid would never approve of it, but we know what an old woman he is."

"Will it work before midnight?" Leifr asked. "That's my last chance to get back into my own realm."

"It will work in no time at all, if you'll just give me the chance to tell you about it," Gedvondur retorted testily. When he scowled, his black brows made his face look even more like the barred mask of a stodgy old badger. "Come along, we'll get Fridmarr and go talk to Fax."

"Fridmarr seems a bit preoccupied," Leifr said.

"Nonsense," Gedvondur snorted. "Come along."

Ljosa watched their approach with no great favor, Leifr thought.

Her greeting was delivered with an icy, clipped tone. Her eyes flickered from Gedvondur to Leifr. "I suppose you've come with some great scheme to save us all and destroy the Council and their Anathema.''

''Perhaps,'' Leifr said. ''We can't leave things as they are now.''

''Why not?'' she demanded. ''You've done the Council plenty of damage. You've dealt it a death blow, I should think. Why not leave now while we're all still alive? You don't have to make an entirely clean sweep here to destroy what they were working on.''

''It will be better if we don't leave them anything to build a new attempt upon,'' Leifr said.

''War and death are all you think about,'' she accused, including them all in her searing gaze. ''Or is it revenge? Sorkvir will burn himself out soon enough without your help. The Ulf-hedin will never have another leader like Fax. The Rhbus will stay and defend the well, and most of the Ulf-hedin will eventually come to be cured. The Council will scatter and the Dok-kur Lavardur will leave. There's no sense in continuing the fight, except for the sheer love of a battle.''

''I've never walked away from an unfinished battle yet,'' Leifr said.

''Neither did Bodmarr or Fridmarr,'' Ljosa returned. ''And look how they turned out. Bodmarr dead and Fridmarr—'' She waved a hand at Starkad and the look she cast at him could have withered young corn. ''I don't know how you could have given such a carbuncle to a mere child such as Starkad. At least he can fight now, and I suppose that's what matters the most to such as you.''

Gedvondur and Leifr exchanged a guilty glance.

''It is rather important sometimes,'' Leifr said.

''Sciplings!'' Ljosa exclaimed. ''That's the only way you know to settle your quarrels! If someone steals your horse or rides through your crops or looks at you strangely, you simply go and kill him and pay a blood price for it and everyone is pleased that justice has been served.''

''Justice is not what's important here,'' Gedvondur said, shaking his head. ''It's like killing a nest of snakes. You've got to kill them all before they multiply again.''

''Exactly what I would have expected from you!'' Ljosa snapped at him. Then she rounded upon Starkad, who winced under the attack. ''And you, Fridmarr! You think you can hide behind Starkad, but I know you're listening! I've had more than enough of heroics! If you persist in this insane battle, don't trouble yourself ever to speak to me again. And you, Leifr, you shouldn't even be here at all. I blame Fridmarr for bringing you into this, but I blame you for not getting out of it while you can. Leave now while you still can, Leifr. A few more hours, and you'll be trapped in our realm forever. Is that what you want? Don't you want to go home where you belong?''

Leifr stood staring at her, letting his hesitation grow too long. Gedvondur abruptly seized Starkad by the arm and towed him out of hearing range. "Come along, you great calf," he muttered. "And Fridmarr, I want to talk to you."

"Perhaps I should go back," Leifr said to Ljosa. "It's not as if I've got much of a life to go back for, outlawed and hunted as I am. I once thought that I could stay in your realm with you. In the Scipling realm, marriages are arranged by the families, and a man never has to speak for himself this way to a woman, as if he were begging a boon or buying a farm. I don't know what words to use. I do know you've been in my thoughts so long and with such concern that I can't imagine going away from you. It's a great, hollow feeling when I think about going back to the Scipling realm and leaving you here and never seeing you again. We should stay together, as man and wife, after all we've gone through. For me, at least, there will never be another woman half so brave and quick and strong."

Her eyes studied the ground, then turned away toward the distant horizon. She shoved back the pale clinging mist-curls from her face in exasperation. "Leifr, you must go back to your own realm," she said. "Leave the Ljosalfar realm to its own battles. I'm not ungrateful for all you've done for me, but you can't expect me to be your reward for being such a great and noble hero. You expect more of me than I am. My father and all my brothers are dead, there's no gold or name or even honor I can give you. I'm no longer a chieftain's daughter. Enough blood has been shed. I'm sick to death of fighting and honor and pride. If you truly want my favor, you'll turn your back on all this and try the peaceful route for once."

"I can't abandon you here like this," Leifr protested. "With Sorkvir still alive, the Dokkur Lavardur as thick as ever, and the Council still holed up in Hringurhol. I'd be a coward to go back to my own realm now."

"If you stay," she said, "I shall never speak to you, either. Go to the Rhbus and tell them you want to go back before the gates change time between the realms. It will be midnight soon. If you listen to Gedvondur and Fridmarr and do what they want you to do, your only chance will be gone forever."

"It is Fridmarr, isn't it?" Leifr said. "You've never forgotten him, and now he's back. Well, I shall leave you to him then and I won't trouble you again."

"Fridmarr is dead to me," Ljosa retorted. "As dead as Bodmarr, my father, and all the rest of my close family. I have nothing and nobody, and I am nothing and nobody. Stay away from me, Leifr, or my bad luck might rub off on you. Go back to your own realm. Even as an outlaw, you'll have a better chance there than I do here."

She strode away, leaving Leifr gaping after her in dismay. Gedvondur and Starkad returned, with Fridmarr quarreling in an undertone with Gedvondur.

"Angry, isn't she?" Fridmarr greeted him. "She was after me, too, trying to get me to give it up now we've got their backs to the wall. She's not got our instincts for warfare, I fear. We can't give it up now, Leifr, but you ought to go back to your own realm while you can."

"Are you going back, Leifr?" Starkad added anxiously.

"No, not before this is finished. I've never been one to turn my back on a fight," Leifr said grimly. "Especially one I've come to care about a great deal, such as this one."

"Then come along," Gedvondur said. "Time is wasting."

In the final night of Brjaladur frenzy, it was a simple thing for the three of them to don three cast-off wolf skins and walk boldly up to the Council Hall where the Anathema stood, with its attendants lounging carelessly nearby, secure in their superior knowledge of how to operate the vile creation. Other Ulf-hedin lurked near it, brawling among themselves and gazing at the Anathema with undisguised reverence and curiosity. Occasionally one of them went near enough to sniff at it warily and peer down its long dark throat. Once an Ulf-hedin ventured to lay a hand upon it, jerked it away with a howl of pain and dismay, and went careening away at a staggering gallop, his offending hand smoking.

Gedvondur chuckled dourly under his wolf skin and elbowed

Leifr. "Scipling iron," he grunted. "It's an anathema to them, as well. You're the only one who will be able to touch it."

Leifr looked at the thing, thinking it was like nothing Scipling he had ever seen before. The smell lurking around it was sharp and exciting with destructive promise.

At sundown, barely distinguishable by any discernible action of the smothered sun, the Council emerged from the hall and took up a cautious position behind the Anathema. Sorkvir moved to the fore, facing the dragon hunters and smoldering like a burning rubbish heap. The dragon hunters, capable of finding and slaying the largest and most dangerous of living beasts, shrank back from him, making warding-off signs behind their backs.

"It is time to do as you promised," Sorkvir said in a fiery, croaking voice. "If your device is as powerful as you say it is and Heidur's well is destroyed, along with the people defending it, you'll be rewarded as we agreed upon."

"We won't fail," one of the dragon hunters answered. "This machine will knock down those walls and your Ulf-hedin can have whoever's inside that's not a dragon. If any dragons come out, they're doomed."

Taking care not to touch the exposed metal of the Anathema, the dragon hunters turned the device and positioned its maw so it pointed toward the hilltop of Heidur's well. The surrounding Ulf-hedin grew silent and still with fascination as they watched the dragon hunters preparing the engine by pouring a black grainy substance from a small keg into a horn cup, measuring it out carefully before pouring it into the machine. Then a large metal ball was wrapped in a bit of rag and tamped down the long throat of the Anathema. Motioning the curious Ulf-hedin back, the dragon hunter ignited a grass wick and pushed it into a hole on the closed end of the device and put his fingers into his ears. The Ulf-hedin likewise plugged their ears and winced away.

The Anathema exploded with a deafening roar and a belch of flame, leaping backward against the chain that anchored it to a ring in the wall. The Ulf-hedin fell back, yelling and howling and leaping into the air in wild exultation.

Ears ringing, Leifr opened his eyes and looked toward Heidur's ruins. To his amazement, a section of the wall was collapsing.

For a moment he was dumbfounded. Then a sense of awe and admiration spread over him as he immediately recognized the Anathema for the most wonderful device a besieging warrior could ever desire. Enormous pride flooded over him that the humble Sciplings could ever have invented such a useful weapon.

"It shoots things!" he exclaimed in a delighted sputter. "From a distance! You can knock down an entire wall and be completely safe!"

"Very clever," Fridmarr grunted. "Think of the hole it could make in a person, or even a dragon. Yes, you Sciplings are masters of invention and destruction."

"For all my knowledge of magical powers and properties," Gedvondur said, "I've never yet seen anything like it that didn't have some kind of sorcery behind it. I can scarcely believe my eyes. Are we quite certain it isn't possessed of magical qualities?"

"Only the fact that it's made of iron gives it any powers at all," Fridmarr said.

"What about that black powder they poured into it?" Starkad interrupted. "Wasn't that a magical substance? They were certainly cautious with it."

Gedvondur rubbed his chin dubiously. "We shall have to examine it more closely to determine its exact properties."

The small keg of powder had been taken into the hall before firing the instrument; now it was brought out again and the device was prepared for another firing. Gedvondur nudged Leifr sharply and glided forward through the crowd of Ulf-hedin, other Dokkalfar, and wanderers who had stayed to brave Brjaladur. This time, while everyone was plugging his ears and gazing at Heidur's ruins in fearful anticipation, Gedvondur crept up behind the dragon hunters, awaiting his opportunity. They brushed by him imperiously, swabbing out the throat of the Anathema and readying another shot.

Leifr and Starkad waited in the shadow of a broken corner of wall. Leifr found he could not bring himself to speak to Starkad or Fridmarr, keeping his face expressionless and turned well away from them.

"You're angry," Fridmarr's voice said, and Starkad added, "Yes, I thought so, too. What's the matter with him, Fridmarr?"

Leifr cast him a brief glower. "This is no time for idle chatter," he retorted.

"It's as good a time as any," Fridmarr said. "I know you better than you know yourself, Leifr Thorljotsson. I think the problem is still Ljosa, as it has been since you saw her first at Dallir."

"I saw her first by no means," Leifr said. "She is free now to do as she chooses and I have nothing to do with her choices."

"You should talk to her," Fridmarr said.

"I did," Leifr said. "I only make her more angry whenever I try to say anything. She's had enough of men who fight for honorable purposes, and I can't say that I blame her. Men such as we are tend to die rather frequently. It's no wonder women lose faith in us."

Fridmarr sighed. "It's a sad truth, Leifr. But I assure you, she's got no use for me now that Starkad's carrying my essence around. She thinks I ought to have stayed dead. But I couldn't, not knowing what I knew about the Council and the Dokkur Lavardur."

"I'm glad you stayed," Leifr said. "I couldn't have come so far without you."

"And I would have died," Starkad said. "You're not a bad influence at all, Fridmarr. Not like Gedvondur. I feel I've finally got some wisdom. Leifr, are you going back to your own realm, once the Dokkur Lavardur is finished? Would you take me with you, if you are?"

"I can't, Starkad," Leifr said. "And I wouldn't if I could. You belong here."

Gedvondur crept through the shadows, keeping his wolf cape pulled low over his face. With so many curious Ulf-hedin sniffing about, he managed unnoticed to tip out a small sample of the powder from the keg into the palm of one hand. He sniffed at it, and ventured to taste a bit of it on the end of his tongue.

"Here, you, get away from that! Do you want to get blown to Niflheim?" one of the dragon hunters exclaimed suddenly, brandishing a club at Gedvondur, who drew back his teeth in a vicious snarl that sent the fellow stepping hastily backward. Gedvondur scuttled away into the shadows to rejoin Leifr and Starkad.

"It's a simple concoction," Gedvondur said. "I've seen a few sleight-of-hand experts use it for casual entertainments, but never for anything as spectacular as this. It's the force behind the Anathema.''

"Then we'll steal it," Starkad said. "And destroy it. Then the Anathema will be helpless."

Gedvondur shook his head. "Not for long. Any pothering alchemist can make this powder. It wouldn't take them long to have another batch made. It's the thing itself that has to be destroyed."

"What about Galdur and the knacker-women?" Starkad asked. "If they've got no real powers, why did we bother saving them?"

"They have knowledge, you idiot," Fridmarr snapped. "They aren't destroyers, they're creators. They are the opposite of Chaos. Without such people to balance Chaos, we'd all very soon slide right down into anarchy and ruin. As you can see, the Dokkalfar are already near to it. Unless some of the Rhbu are saved, somewhere, this entire realm will be swallowed up by Chaos. Not a pebble will remain resting upon another. Such is the nature of Chaos."

As they watched, a dragon hunter emerged from the mouth of a nearby alleyway connecting the hall to the stables, and he was carrying another cask of the powder. The Council wizards guarding the Anathema shoved at the curious Ulf-hedin, cursing and thrusting them away with their staffs.

"Follow me," Gedvondur whispered. "Stay close."

The alleyway reeked of garbage and the smell of Ulf-hedin. Gedvondur summoned a small glow to the end of his staff to light the way. He led them around a heap of dead Ulf-hedin, frozen in various stages of transformation from wolf to man.

Gedvondur stepped over the carcasses. Then he stopped and raised one hand warningly. Leifr crouched with the sword ready in his hand, with Starkad also armed with his old pitted sword from some barrow near Fangelsi. Ahead, in the musty darkness of the stable, stood the dragon hunters' cart, still hitched to a horse, which was sighing wearily and shifting its weight from one leg to another.

Gedvondur brightened his flame for a closer look. A dark figure leaped down from the tailboard, sputtering and cursing.

"Get rid of that flame!" the fellow snarled, his ragged and stained clothing identifying him as a dragon hunter. "Don't you know what could happen if the least spark touches this powder?

You wizards think you've got power from your magic, but there's more power in this cart than five hundred of you mumbling fools have got. Get away from here, nobody's allowed."

"Not allowed?" Gedvondur said in a wondering tone. He took a step forward. "Me, not allowed? You're the stranger here, with your lumbering cold iron Anathema and exploding powders and iron missiles that tear great holes in dragons. No, you're the one that does not belong, my friend. You're the one who should leave this place and never come back."

The dragon hunter closed his mouth and backed away, like a bristling dog whose hackles have suddenly fallen, becoming a frightened cur. His teeth chattered in the waves of terror Gedvondur wafted toward him. Trembling, he staggered backward as if his legs would scarcely hold him up, making jerky motions to ward off evil.

"Away with you!" Gedvondur snorted in contempt. "And stay away from dragons!"

The dragon hunter whirled around and dashed out through the alley in unreasoning panic. Leifr shivered in the tendrils of Gedvondur's fear spell, remembering it well. Gedvondur's voice chuckled softly in the dark as he climbed onto the cart.

"Starkad, there's a back door to this place. Get it open and stand back."

Another fiery explosion from the Anathema covered their escape from the stable, concealing the sound of the wheels rolling over the paving stones. The few Ulf-hedin who stopped to look at the cart suspiciously were sent on their way by Gedvondur with frightened yelps. The horse slowed its pace as the road steepened, leaning into the harness and straining with the load.

"Throw out those iron balls," Gedvondur directed, and since no one else wanted to touch them, the duty fell to Leifr. He tossed them into the ravine, lightening the load as they went, until nothing remained except kegs of the exploding powder.

The Council Hall stood deserted and dark, its glories of the Council and its schemes neglected now in the excitement of the Anathema. Gedvondur drove the cart right inside through the front doors into the darkness and silence of the tombs. Only the faintest glowing knob on the end of his staff softly illuminated the dark, showing the thirteen imposing seats of the Council sitting empty, except for a startled rat that was tearing the stuffing from one of the cushions for a nest. It glared at them a moment over a mouthful of horsehair, then scuttled away with a flirt of its ropy tail.

"Take the horse outside and set it loose," Gedvondur said, climbing down off the cart and starting to unhitch the harness. "No sense in blowing up a perfectly good cart horse."

"What are you going to do?" Starkad whispered, his eyes as wide and suspicious as the rat's.

Gedvondur approached the rear of the cart and pried open the tops of several of the kegs.

"Now—" he chuckled wickedly, feeling around in his pockets. "We need a bit of a wick."

Disappointed of that search, he pulled a handful of dried grass out of the stuffing of his boots and twisted it into a crude wick. Pinching it between his fingers, he induced it into a smoky little flame.

"There's a great deal of wood and timber in this old hall," Gedvondur said. "As long as we're ridding ourselves of the powder, we might as well make a spectacle of it. First we destroy the Council Hall, then the Council itself."

"Wait!" Leifr said, sniffing the air. "I don't think we're alone in here!"

A distinct rubbishy burning smell came to Leifr's nostrils. He whirled around, studying the gloomy ranks of tombs standing silently like a petrified audience. With a rasping cough, the raddled figure of Sorkvir stepped out from behind a nearby tomb. A slight blue nimbus of flame surrounded him.

"If a wick is what you want," he greeted them with a rattling sound in his chest like an old gourd, "I would be happy to supply you with a flame. Gedvondur, you're back again."

"Yes, it's Gedvondur," Gedvondur answered. "With the Bjartur sword and the five dragons of the Pentacle."

"It's the day of Reikna, Sorkvir," Fridmarr's voice said. "The day of reckoning for all your wrongs."

"And Fridmarr, too," Sorkvir rasped, attempting to shake his head, but the motion was slight with such a dried and stiffened neck. "What a pleasant reunion. Gedvondur, you're looking well for a corpse. Draugar usually don't look so healthy and strong."

"Not usually; but, then, I'm not a draug," Gedvondur said, showing his teeth in a nasty smile. "I've been restored—and perfectly. Down to the last hair, tooth, and toenail, Sorkvir old friend. I've certainly done better than you. Don't you wish you had access to such power, such perfection? I don't see how you and Djofull could content yourselves with such lumbering, crude, inept attempts. And not only inept, Djofull's experiments are obviously short-lived, necessitating the continual switching from one body to the next. Poor old Djofull, meandering around in his benighted way, would be distressed to see his work being slowly consumed by spontaneous combustion. Knowing what I know now, I can say with perfect candor that Djofull was miles off the track. If he'd lived another thousand years, he would never have discovered the correct principles of revivification. Look at yourself for an example. It's quite pathetic, really. No Dokkalfar will ever discover the secrets of the ancient Rhbus. And to think, those knacker-women were here under the Council's noses all these years, and the Council members, in their supreme ignorance, bricked over the well, doling out mere pittances of it to cure chosen ones. When you think of what they might have been doing with it, instead of conjuring elementals they couldn't hope to control—''

Sorkvir shook his head stiffly from side to side, making rattling, gagging sounds of mounting fury.

"Silence your idle chatter!" he snapped. "Help me out of this and I shall repay you. Put me into another form before Hela gets her claws on me, and I'll make you wealthy. I know where the Council's treasure lies. I know all the secrets of its powers, and they are yours, Gedvondur, if you'll see to it that I migrate into another living body before it's too late."

"Don't be absurd," Gedvondur said. "Why should I want to do that? I've lived solely for the chance of destroying you and the Council one day. Reikna is here, Sorkvir. You've got no chance of killing those dragons. You've lost Heidur's well, you've lost the Council, and you've lost the Dokkur Lavardur."

"Be that as it may, we've still got the Anathema, and the Anathema will destroy those dragons," Sorkvir rasped, shuffling forward toward the cart. He faced Gedvondur and Leifr over the tailboard. Stretching out one hand, glowing with its halo of flame, he went on, "I could blow us all to Niflheim with just a single touch. It would afford me some satisfaction to destroy that sword."

"Stop," Leifr said, raising the sword threateningly.

"Do you think I'm afraid?" Sorkvir sneered. "Oblivion would be a welcome release, in my condition."

His hand hovered over the open keg of powder. Leifr took a step forward. Sorkvir beckoned him forward, his seared and blackened face withered into a permanent grimace of hatred.

"Come, come," he whispered. "This is your final chance, Scipling. You want your revenge, don't you? Perhaps you can stop me before I touch this powder. It's a reasonable gamble, isn't it? Or are you a coward?"

"Come away from that cart and I'll fight you," Leifr said. "Whatever spells you care to throw at me, go ahead. I challenge you, and I'll let you take the first blow."

He moved away to a safe distance and fanned the air with the sword, making a deadly humming sound. Sorkvir turned his raddled grin upon Leifr and shook his head.

"No, it's not going to be like that," he said. "Come closer. See if you can stop me. Whether you're there or here, it makes no difference when I light this powder. You especially I would like to see die, Scipling, with your abominable good luck and your self-sacrificing piety and your supposed Scipling courage. Bah! I spit on you and your courage and everything you hold dear!"

"Come away from that!" Leifr commanded as Sorkvir hovered near the cart and the open kegs.

Sorkvir beckoned, grinning like a skull on a pike. "See if you can stop me, Scipling."

Leifr sheathed the sword, suspecting that Sorkvir might explode like a pitchy log if he hacked him through with it. Flaming parts would fly everywhere, igniting the powder. He strode forward, quelling a rising tide of revulsion, and, ignoring the blue glow of flame, he seized hold of Sorkvir's arm, as a wrestler would. The arm was disgustingly light and brittle, and he didn't feel the flame at all. His object was to toss the draug away from the cart, but with his cunning draug strength, Sorkvir instantly seized hold of him, swarming across his back and wrapping his spindly arms around Leifr's throat in a smothering choke hold. Shoving his face near one of the kegs, Sorkvir thrust out his hand to touch the powder. With a roar of fury and terror, Starkad plunged into the battle, seized the arm, and wrenched it around with a snapping, crackling sound like a dry stick breaking. With a careless toss, Sorkvir flung Starkad aside, bowling him into Gedvondur.

"Let me fight him, Leifr!" Gedvondur snarled. "Stand aside! Let a revenant fight a revenant!"

Leifr would have gladly obliged him, but Sorkvir had a grip on him he couldn't break. Gasping for air, he plunged around among the tombs trying to dislodge the burning draug, with Starkad and Gedvondur tearing at him in a frenzy. Starkad twisted on one leg until the charred foot came away in his hands. He flung it away with a shout of disgust, rubbing his hands frantically.

Sorkvir repelled them with ease, his unnatural draug strength unabated. Scraps of half-burned cloth and leathery skin were torn away in the struggle, but still Sorkvir maintained his hold, forcing Leifr, half dragging him, inexorably toward the cart and the powder.

With one hand Sorkvir reached out, almost touching the edge of the nearest keg, slightly releasing his grip upon Leifr's windpipe. The attempt afforded Leifr an opportunity to draw a deep breath, and he flung Sorkvir's crushing grip off him. The draug spun away like a useless heap of blackened sticks and rags. Heedless now of possible consequences, Leifr whipped the sword from its sheath. Sorkvir sprang to his feet at once, his object the cart and the powder. With a roar, Starkad leaped at the draug in an attempt to slow his dive at the powder. It was enough; Leifr gripped *Endalaus Daudi* and took a level swing at Sorkvir, scything the air in a motion he had mentally rehearsed thousands of times, now seeing it enacted in minute and perfect detail. The sword cut in a gleaming half circle, connecting perfectly with Sorkvir's neck. The draug's head spun around, clipped off neatly like a seed pod on a dry stalk, still grimacing with mad draug fury. The body still stood where it was, unaffected by the removal of its head, spouting bright orange flame where a mortal body would have spouted blood. The head flew in a continuing arc, following the sword, and landed on the floor of the cart between the kegs.

Gedvondur and Starkad's mouths were opened in a silent shout of horror. They dived forward as the flaming head ignited a greasy rag tied to the sides of the cart. A tongue of flame shot upward as the rag blazed into fiery life.

Chapter 21

◇◇◇

Thurid winced as yet another explosion shook the tottering walls surrounding Heidur's well. The Rhbu sisters exclaimed and clucked over the damage in dismay, looking to Galdur for an answer.

"You'd better get out while you can," Thurid said to Galdur and the four sister Rhbus. "A little while longer and those walls will no longer hold the Ulf-hedin out."

"We aren't leaving you and we aren't leaving the well," Bryti said with her old Beitski certitude. "Let them do their worst, we can mend it."

"This is a different sort of chaos," Galdur said, shaking his head uneasily. "It doesn't come from our realm, sister. We can't repair it."

"Where's Leifr?" Thurid growled, lashing his cloak aside as he paced up and down the length of the altar room. "I ordered everyone to take shelter in here when those explosions started shaking the walls down. Drat that Scipling! He's always got to be independent!"

Ljosa lifted her head, and Svanlaug's sharp gaze did not miss it.

"You know something about it," she said sharply.

"Has no one missed Gedvondur and Starkad also?" Ljosa asked. "And where Starkad goes, Fridmarr goes."

"Fridmarr!" Thurid muttered, grinding his teeth in an agony of self-accusation. "I might have known! Fridmarr and Gedvondur are out to salvage their pride from their last defeat! Where did they go? What are they going to do?"

"They asked about wolf skins," Hvitur-Fax said, glancing toward the heap of wolf skins cast off by the Ulf-hedin who had crept in during daylight to be cured.

"Gedvondur mentioned some scheme of his," Ljosa said. "I

tried to persuade them not to attempt anything. Why couldn't we have escaped, while all of us are still alive? Now Brjaladur has started again and it's too late to escape. Was that such a terrible thing to ask? Why not leave the Council to destroy itself? Does this senseless fighting always have to take away everyone that I care about?''

The question hung in the air a moment. Then suddenly a brilliant orange light blossomed over the settlement below, bursting in through the remaining windows of Heidur's ruins as bright as noonday. A muzzled explosion sounded, followed by a chorus of shouting and screaming from several hundred throats at once. Thurid clambered up a wall for a look and saw the Council Hall engulfed in flames, its roof entirely gone; the pieces of it were settling down over the houses, stables, and hayricks of Hringurhol in a storm of fire and flaming timbers. The Dokkur Lavardur recoiled with a scream of wind, which instantly fanned the flames to twice their size with a greedy roar and sucked the flaming materials skyward until it seemed that the clouds themselves had burst into fire. Ash and soot and black powder filled the air, exploding in firestorms when flame and drifting powder came together.

''More Brjaladur mischief!'' Thurid exclaimed, snorting in the sooty air. Suddenly he clutched his temples as a searing vision filled his skull with blinding orange flames and the roar of fire exploding like a sea of destruction. As plainly as if Leifr were standing within three feet of him, he heard Leifr's voice calling his name.

Staggering, he nearly fell down off the wall in his haste to descend.

''Leifr's down there!'' he gasped. ''Galdur! We've got to rescue him! He's in a high place, I'm sure of it!''

''It's terrible weather for flying,'' Bryti warned, unfurling her cloak like wings and shaking off the soot and black powder. ''We shall have to be cautious, sisters. This is like no ordinary fire we've ever seen. Thurid, you mustn't use your alf-light, or we may all be fried in midflight. The air is full of the essence of the Anathema.''

As the five Rhbus shifted forms, Thurid turned to face Ljosa, who was staring stonily down the hill toward Hringurhol, already grieving in her silent, angry way.

''Svanlaug,'' Thurid said. ''Raudbjorn. If we should not come back from this, see to it Ljosa is taken back to her relations near Dallir.''

Raudbjorn shook his head, looking from the dragons to the inferno below. He flung his halberd on the ground, lamenting, ''Worthless dung-heap! What good to Leifr now? Send Raud-bjorn into flames!''

''No, Raudbjorn,'' Thurid said, climbing up the shoulder of the fylgja-dragon. ''This is no longer a battle for ordinary warriors and weapons. Heidur's hill is only island in a sea of fire. Two hundred crazed Ulf-hedin will be heading this way. Someone courageous must remain behind to hold them back.''

Raudbjorn's face lit up with a combative gleam. He snatched up his halberd instantly. ''Ulf-hedin! Hah! Raudbjorn's kind of enemy!''

The dragons launched themselves into the air, with Thurid clinging to the perch between Galdur's shoulders where a gap in his spines would have made a good space for a saddle. The light of the fires shone through the gossamer veins of their wings with the sparkling colors of their jewels. Viewed from above, Hringurhol was like a bed of hot coals dancing with columns of flame, fanned into a furious inferno by the raging of the Dokkur Lavardur above. The wind screamed, lapping flames and embers high into the sky, while the survivors ran aimlessly to and fro like ants, perceiving themselves trapped between the flames of Hringurhol and the dragons sailing overhead in the sky.

''Go to Heidur's hill!'' Thurid bellowed, amplifying his voice by means of power to carry over the roar of the fire. ''Go to the well and you'll be safe!''

Some of the hapless creatures heard and understood, Ulf-hedin with their pelts blazing, ordinary Dokkalfar, wanderers, and wizards who had thought to lie low in Hringurhol and avoid the nuisance of moving house for the uproar of Brjaladur.

''There! There! I see them!'' Thurid screeched suddenly, leaning precariously over Galdur's side and pointing to a parapet standing above a sea of blazing rooftops and haystacks. Three singed figures racing along desperately, trying to find a safe course through the fires, halted suddenly and waved their arms, trying to shout over the roar of the flames.

The dragons hovered over the fire, tilting and bobbing in the overheated updrafts. Warily they swooped lower and came to rest lightly on the wall, their scales gleaming and brilliant. Galdur furled his wings in a cloud of flying particles of light. Before their eyes he altered his shape again to that of a long ship.

"In you get!" Thurid commanded, looking rather tumbled about after righting himself on the bottom of the ship.

Leifr, Gedvondur, and Starkad clambered over the gunwale and fell gratefully inside the ship. As Leifr lay there a moment, gasping in the cooler air and limp with the gratitude of deliverance, it seemed to him that he could almost see through the sides of Galdur's dragon-ship form. He watched the ruin of Hringurhol sailing past below, with everything combustible burning with a vengeance. Then the dragons rose to the relative safety of the sky, where the Dokkur Lavardur buffeted them with screaming blasts of wind and hail that melted into stinging sooty spatters in the heat of the fire. Galdur surged through the storm's powerful billows, pitching and tossing like a ship on the sea.

Suddenly the fierce elemental winds withdrew so abruptly that the air was dead calm, and there was no sound except the muted crackle of the fires below.

Leifr shoved Starkad's limp form off him and sat up to look around them, watching the sky elemental. The clouds glowed with a dull and menacing light, coiling about themselves like the writhing of monstrous snakes, with a background accompaniment of muted thunder. With the air whistling softly over their wings, the dragons sailed back over the walls of Heidur's well, where the Ulf-hedin had arrived in a pressing crowd around the walls of the ruins. As the dragons passed overhead some of them broke and ran for the protection of the shadows, others stood still and gazed skyward with the calm dejection of doomed creatures awaiting their slaughter. Raudbjorn stood braced in the doorway, swinging his halberd, alongside Hvitur-Fax and Halmur, the guardians of the well and the cure of the Ulf-hedin curse.

"A pathetic ending to a most exciting Brjaladur," Thurid said. "You were lucky to have survived it. I can't wait to get my hands on Gedvondur." He turned to the third sooty figure, still huffing and wheezing on the floor of the ship, down between the rowing benches.

"The Anathema," Gedvondur gasped, waving one blackened hand in a weak triumphant gesture, "is no more. We have conquered it. The thing is even now melting in the fires of Hringurhol. The day of Reikna arrived and is nearly passed. The Council is destroyed and Sorkvir is dead.''

"Dead at last," Leifr added with a grim and sooty grin, touching the hilt of *Endalaus Daudi*. "There's no one to rescue him from Hela now. Not a scrap of him remains, Thurid. I hacked the head off him, and while he was looking for it, the cart with the powder caught fire. We ran for our lives, but Sorkvir was still inside the Council Hall when the powder exploded. It was astonishing, Thurid. You wizards have got powers beyond a doubt, but it's nothing like the explosion that we saw.''

"Leave it to the ignorant and barbaric Sciplings to discover the more potent methods of destruction," Thurid said sourly. "Whose idea was this escapade? You might all have been killed.''

"It was my idea to go after the Anathema," Gedvondur said, his face rakishly smeared with soot. "It was well worth it to restore our honor, eh, Fridmarr?'' He gave Starkad a nudge with his foot.

Starkad groaned at the disturbance. Fridmarr's sharp voice retorted, "We'd all be dead again if not for Thurid and the Rhbus, you ass. This was exactly how we got into trouble the last time. You, plunging ahead with some insane idea, overfilled with undeserved confidence. This is the last time, Gedvondur. I'll never take your word for anything ever again.''

The dragons' forms billowed like images seen through the distorting curtain of fire. Watchfully they craned their long necks, scanning the sky, the jewels in their heads casting beams of light ahead of them.

Suddenly a torrent of darkness descended like a net, pouring from the roiling cloud cover above. Verdugur dodged it, calling out a warning in a windy whistle. Galdur altered his course abruptly, causing his passengers to roll around a bit in confusion before they steadied themselves again. Another spurt of blackness erupted from the clouds, missing the dragons and settling to the earth, swallowing a flaming hayrick and a stable as water would extinguish an ember. No walls or ruins remained, just a crater of darkness plunging into the earth itself. It had the cold blackness of the midnight sky in midwinter.

"Chaos!" Thurid gasped.

Hovering over the site, the four sister Rhbus began to sing, a mighty sound that set the air and probably the very stones to vibrating underfoot. A pale cloud settled over the darkness, softly taking form under the protective wings of the dragons, until the house and hayrick and all that had been destroyed was renewed again, new and whole and clean, as it had once been long before the decay of Hringurhol had set in. Flowers, grass, and trees grew again inside the enchanted circle of the dragons' restoring powers, while the fires and soot still ruled outside.

The elemental retaliated with a furious blast, a cyclone of destruction that sucked away a swath of houses and barns and byres and a host of screaming inhabitants. In an instant nothing remained but silence and emptiness, and a cavern gaped in the face of the earth where the houses had stood, as if it had swallowed them up. The dragons sailed away in retreat when more curtains of oblivion were cast at them, blacker than the surrounding night. Then the Chaos moved toward Heidur's hill, swallowing up the flaming ruins of Hringurhol without a sound. The sounds of fire and voices diminished gradually until it was well-nigh silent in the ravaged plain where the settlement had stood.

Transfixed by horror, Leifr stood in the prow of the ship, helplessly watching the darkness spreading inexorably toward Heidur's hill. All was swallowed up before it, hills, ravines, jutting scarps of rock, and nothing but emptiness was left behind. Even the ruins crowning Heidur's hill dissolved like sand on the beach under the merciless advance of the brutal waves. Just as he was about to despair and fling himself overboard into the nothingness, Bryti's great singing voice filled the silence with a strong, vibrant note like the roar of a high sea during a storm. The other dragons joined in, with Galdur adding a mighty bass rumble.

The cloud of pale light hovered over the gaping void, grew larger and larger, swelling until the black pit was obliterated. As the mist cleared, towers and pinnacles took form on Heidur's hill, standing like needles against the muddy sky. It was more splendid even than the half-ruined Fire Wizards' Guildhall, enough to take the breath away from one who had never seen anything much grander than the towering turf hall of the chieftain of the Four Quarters. The restoration of Hringurhol swept down from the hill like a flood, replacing houses, halls, and hovels alike in perfect condition, without so much as a doorstep or kitchen garden missing.

The Dokkur Lavardur retreated with tempestuous screams and howls of wind. Around the horizons, the clouds were thinning away to smeared streaks and streamers, as if frayed by the conflict with the dragons. Early dawn light crept beneath the inky skirts of darkness. The elemental lashed around in a fury of destruction, smiting down the tops of hills and crags and stretches of verdant hillsides, but the restorative powers of the five Rhbu sorcerers negated the effects of Chaos, returning what was gone with new splendor. Twice the Dokkur Lavardur engulfed nearly all of Hringurhol, and twice the dragons restored it. The dragons passed over and over, combining forces like great shuttles weaving a web of healing and life. The cloud cover diminished with each attack, until nothing remained but scattered black puffs of cloud rapidly fraying away in the light of the rising sun. Long and unaccustomed shadows were cast over the new settlement of Hringurhol, falling away from new-built walls of houses, barns, and paddocks and roads paved with cobblestones. White walls gleamed in the rosy dawn glow, inviting the return of the people who had once built them, so long ago.

The dragons settled to the earth outside the entrance of the edifice that guarded Heidur's well. Its roofs and spires were now intact and shining with the crisp sparkle of new-cut stone. The Inquisitors stood waiting, awe stamped upon their upturned faces. Skulking Ulf-hedin scuttled away at once, goggling in extreme discomfiture as the dragons shifted forms in a misty cloud that felt cool and cleansing on the skin. Looking down at his singed and charred clothing, Leifr saw it restored, the threads busily reweaving themselves, the soot and dirt falling away, until his attire was as clean and new as the day his mother had made it for him. The burns and blisters he had acquired from his battle with Sorkvir vanished in the bathing mist rising from the Rhbus as they shook off their fylgja-forms.

The night had passed. Voices were lifted up in celebration. Brjaladur was over, and the exhausted Ljosalfar Ulf-hedin were lying in heaps in the welcome sun, their wolf pelts cast away. Very humble now, the Dokkalfar took uneasy refuge within the walls of Heidur's tower under the stern eye of Hvitur-Fax. Already the cure was being given to them, with the accompanying unpleasant sound effects, and none were allowed to escape.

Midnight and Leifr's last chance to escape back to the Scipling realm had passed unnoticed. Nor did anyone seem to remember his plight in the excitement of the defeat of the Lord of Chaos. The first of the newly cured Ulf-hedin tottered around in glad astonishment, greeting their friends and rejoicing in their new-found freedom. The five Rhbus and Thurid were holding a court of homage in the central courtyard outside the tower, which Leifr deftly managed to avoid, although he heard Thurid calling for him to join them. As he hurried out of the courtyard, he was recognized, thanked, congratulated, pawed, and blubbered over until he wished he could fly to escape so much gratitude. People of all sorts were coming out of their hiding places, astonished at the changes wrought upon Hringurhol and upon themselves.

Everywhere he looked, Leifr saw nothing but strangers. Ged-vondur and Starkad had gone in search of something to eat. Rejoicing in an opportunity for self-importance, Ulfrin and Svanlaug chivvied the reluctant Ulf-hedin toward the well and their deliverance. Even Raudbjorn stood beside the door with his halberd, puffed up and scowling with pride, enjoying his status as an object of terror to be looked upon and feared.

Of Ljosa he saw not a sign. Perhaps she had already found passage westward, back to her own people. Walking blindly, he made his way down the hill, which was crowded with troops of ragged wanderers hurrying to Heidur's well to see the five Rhbu sorcerers. The settlement below was filling up with the returning residents who had crossed the river for Brjaladur. Their amaze-ment knew no bounds as they contemplated rotting turf houses now neat and square, collapsing barns and byres rendered hab-itable, and miry roadways dry and paved with stone. The Coun-cil Hall and other important structures stood in pristine splendor; as he passed, Leifr glimpsed the tombs and carvings inside also whole.

On a sudden whim, Leifr turned aside from his blind wan-dering and entered the Council Hall, suspiciously keeping his hand upon his sword. Once inside, he saw his precautions were needless. Lamps and candles illuminated the dark interior cor-ners, and morning sunlight poured in from high windows. Sev-eral cloaked figures stood high above on a balcony, measuring with some instruments. At a long table along one wall several people were seated, going over the contents of scrolls and vel-lums. More scrolls were stored on shelves and in boxes, along with precious volumes made from binding many of the vellums together. One aged Rhbu seemed to be in charge of all the manuscripts, finding and returning them to their appropriate places.

It was a busy place, and the longer he looked around the wider his eyes were opened. Groups of students and apprentices vanished among the pillared walkways at the heels of their instructors. Stairways gave access to rooms and chambers above, which had been missing in the days of the Council of Threttan. At some point, the hall had lost its upper level, and a turf and timber roof had replaced it.

Curious and unafraid, Leifr climbed one of the stairways, occasionally returning a preoccupied nod from someone coming down. As Leifr pursued his exploration of the upper hall, he saw small cubicles of rooms where a solitary person could pursue his own quest for knowledge and power, away from the busy hum of voices and the whisper of passing feet below.

As he trod softly down a narrow and rather dark hallway of the small chambers, he suddenly felt a cold presence at his back. Turning, he saw nothing to alarm him; but as he proceeded on his exploration, he kept touching the hilt of *Endalaus Daudi*. The coldness followed him through an open rooftop celestial observatory and back into another corridor of cells, some occupied and some vacant. His heart began to pound as he approached a gallery at the end of the corridor, where a door stood half open. The cold sensation pressed at him urgently, urging him forward. He stopped and looked at the door, silently drawing his sword. The sinister sensation reminded him of the aura of influence that surrounded Sorkvir, chilling and repelling anyone who came near. Warily he sniffed for a scent of burning rags and flesh.

"Come in, Scipling," a voice called out suddenly. "I've been expecting you since dawn."

Leifr pushed the door aside and stepped back a pace, avoiding the treacherous area of the threshold until he had made the appropriate sign to avoid the evil of boundary places.

A small, very old man who looked like Leifr's grandfather stood gazing back at him, steadily, with no fear in his expression, only a deep and almost friendly curiosity. He even wore the many-peaked blue tribal hat of his grandfather's clan and the long gray gown of a shepherd, as his grandfather Ord-sannur had persisted in doing long after he was too wealthy to be a shepherd. Leifr lowered his sword, unable to believe his eyes.

"Who are you?" he demanded. "You look like my grand-father, but I know he's dead."

The man clasped his hands together with a pleased nod of his head. "Ord-sannur—True-word. I knew him well; we were enemies. Yes, enemies, and you are very like your stalwart grandsire. Likewise, you and I are enemies."

"Who are you?" Leifr demanded.

"I am called the Dokkur Lavardur by some. I have many names, but you've heard of that one, I'm certain."

"You're the Dokkur Lavardur? The Lord of Chaos? Here?" Leifr demanded, raising the point of his sword again.

The little man nodded his head briskly. "So I am called by those who admire me," he answered in a rather piping, penetrating voice. "Or simply call me Chaos. And I'm always somewhere. I can see I'm different from what you expected. You'd hoped for a monster, didn't you, a powerful dragon or lingorm, spitting ice and venom, a frost giant towering in the sky, a great hairy troll like Ognun, or some dreadful creature that you could easily kill and relish the job while you were doing it. No, I'm afraid all you've got is me, and I'm not a kill you're going to boast about, am I? That must be a source of great disappointment for a warrior like you."

"But I saw how you filled the sky with monsters, and wind, and storm," Leifr said. "Now you're really nothing but this? Was it all just an illusion, nothing but a glamor spell?"

"No, indeed, it was I, spread quite thin but just as strong," he said with an airy gesture that cast a brief dark cloud around him like a wind-tossed cloak. "The form you see before you is only a condensation and an arrangement that is calculated to make you feel most comfortable. Sciplings, I am told, are savage fighters and bold leaders and even intelligent, but easily frightened by what they don't understand. You have an intelligent look about you; perhaps you will understand what I have to say to you and the boon I have to ask of you."

"Boon?" Leifr surveyed him suspiciously. "I don't need to give any boon to you. If you are indeed Chaos, there is nothing I can give to you. Chaos is death and disorganization."

"Now you mustn't be so suspicious and reluctant to try new ideas," Chaos said. "That must be another Scipling characteristic. I shall remember that, when I move back into your realm one day. Yes, I was there a great deal in the earlier days of your people, but I must say they had a particular knack for defeating Chaos, with their namings and walls and fences and boundaries and possessings of everything and putting names and owners to all the land. Just the din they make going about their normal daily business is repelling. I shouldn't be at all astonished to find them one day dividing up the air above among themselves. You might as well lay claim to the seas while you're at it, and the sun and stars above. What a strange lot you New People are. For all that claiming and naming and inventing, you've still got a great deal of ancient Chaos within you, so I'm content to let your realm tumble on as it is. Inevitably you'll be mine one day, and I shan't have to do a thing to claim you. You really don't comprehend how all this is possible, do you?"

"No," Leifr said. "All I do know is that I was sent or brought to this realm, to Hringurhol, to get rid of you and the Council. The Council is gone now, and you are here, and I am here. Only one of us will remain."

Chaos sighed. "That's the talk of brawling fighting men. This is not that sort of trial. I'll ask you a second time, will you grant me a boon?"

Leifr swayed between the desire to refuse and his own curiosity about what such a powerful entity would want from him, a lowly utlender from the Scipling realm.

"Will you leave, if I grant you this boon?" Leifr asked warily.

"I shall leave, utlender," Chaos said. "The Rhbus and you have won this particular battle. The Council of Threttan is defeated. There is nothing to bind me to this place any longer. As the victor in this battle, you must award the defeated one boon."

"A boon? What can I give you? You're an elemental thing. I could no doubt put my hand right through you."

"No, no, I'm as solid as you are, right now." Chaos pounded himself on the chest and held out his arm. "Here, touch, feel that I'm as real as you are and quite capable of demanding a boon."

With utmost reluctance, Leifr accepted the challenge and touched the arm proffered him. "It's not like a living thing," he said. "It's as hard as iron."

"It's a simple boon," the Dokkur Lavardur went on. "Nothing but the answer to a question to satisfy my own curiosity about the New People."

"Well, if that's all, go ahead and ask your question."

"It has two parts," Chaos said, taking up a glass flask from the table. The glass was green and thick, but still translucent. He shook it idly, corking the neck with one thumb, and a faint cloud of mist materialized inside. "Here is the first part—a simple question. Are you truly stronger than the elder races? Are you truly the ones most fit to inhabit the earth and be its masters?"

"I don't know about that," Leifr said, sheathing the sword, which he knew to be useless against something like Chaos. "From what I have seen of the powers of the Rhbus and the Ljosalfar and Dokkalfar, mere Sciplings with no powers seem well-nigh helpless, unless given some token of power such as this sword, which was given to me. I don't believe that Sciplings are ever going to displace the elder races."

"The elder races are in decline even now," Chaos said, holding up the flask and looking into it. "They have been declining for a great long while, and the advent of the New People has hastened the downward slide. Things such as the Anathema are brought into the Alfar realm to fight Alfar battles. Warriors such as yourself are brought through the gates. The cost of these things is invisible, but great and painful. The gates must be forever closed, if the Alfar realm is going to survive, but Alfar and Sciplings alike have seen what the other's realm has to offer. No one will ever be able entirely to stop the draining of the one into the other. It seems that everything is coming out of the Alfar realm and flowing into the Scipling realm."

The mist in the flask took on form. Chaos held it close to Leifr's face, forcing him to gaze within the mottled glass. With a shock, Leifr recognized tiny images of Thurid, Ljosa, Starkad, and everyone else he had met in the Alfar realm, including Sorkvir and the Council and some Ulf-hedin and Dokkalfar. The tiny forms of the dragons flitted around like trapped moths, flickering with puffs of smoke and flame, and Vjdskipti's form gave him a cheery wave through the bubbles and swirls of the glass.

Leifr took an involuntary step backward, his hand upon *Endalaus Daudi*. "What have you done?" he gasped. "You've got all my friends trapped in that bottle!"

"No, no, your friends are quite safe where you left them," Chaos said. "This is only for the purposes of demonstration. Sciplings must be shown everything in great detail so their simpler minds will understand. What I have contained in this bottle is the essence of all the peoples of this realm, all the Thirteen Tribes of the Alfar, both Ljosalfar and Dokkalfar. Now watch carefully, this is the second part of my boon that I have asked and you have granted."

"I don't want to grant anything else," Leifr said, shivering and drawing back another pace. "You said you were defeated, so take yourself away now."

"Your friends will come to no harm," Chaos said. "This is nothing but an illusion to show you what is in this fluid."

He held the flask over the flame of the whale-oil lamp burning on the table, and the tiny figures inside began to steam and melt like tallow. In a moment nothing remained but a dark-red fluid swirling around inside the glass. A familiar sweet smell issued from the bottle, tickling Leifr's nostrils invitingly.

"Eitur!" he exclaimed.

"Only one of them," Chaos said. "There are many eiturs in existence. You have seen that this is nothing to be afraid of, it's only the essences of your friends."

"And also of my enemies," Leifr added. "I saw plenty of Dokkalfar and Ulf-hedin in there."

"True, you did. But that shouldn't frighten you. You've overcome all your enemies, with no personal advantage you stand to gain from it. At almost any moment you could have been killed. Did you know that only mortals can be martyrs for a cause? You have but one short little life, yet you risked it for your friends and their cause. What strange and noble creatures you Sciplings are. You have seen that there are ways for Alfar to live on and on, nearly forever, and ways to retrieve them from Hela's realm once they have actually made it there. Had you actually given up the ghost during your retrieval of Ljosa Hroaldsdottir, not even the four worshipful lady Rhbus could have fetched you back again. Perhaps there are those in your Scipling realm who possess such powers of retrieval and repair, but I don't believe they are many. Sciplings have but one journey through death and there is no return. Yet you were willing to perish for the sake of freeing Hroadlsdottir and driving me out of this part of the realm. I doubt you even realize the power of martyrdom, do you?"

"Do you expect me to drink that?" Leifr demanded, his eyes still upon the flask.

"It is the boon you agreed to," Chaos said, gently swirling the fluid inside the glass. "If you swallow this and lose your life, the Ljosalfar hold upon Hringurhol will be immeasurably strengthened. Your name will never be forgotten by the Rhbus. It will be as if you never died and were yet with them, a leader and warrior more powerful than any draug dredged from his barrow. Each one who knew you will then carry a portion of your bravery and self-sacrifice with him forever, a blazing carbuncle of memory that will pass from generation to generation in the way of the endless legacy of power given by carbuncle stones."

"It would be better if I did die, it seems," Leifr said wryly.

"And if you survive—" Chaos drew up his shoulders in a shrug. "It will be a sign to me that you mortals are not going to be easily defeated. Worse yet, it would mean that your new race is capable of absorbing all of the elder races and prospering for it. I would prefer to think that you will die of all the ancient poisons and villainous deeds of the elder races. I would prefer to have you as a martyr in the Alfar realm than to think of Ljosalfar powers spread around among the Sciplings, and Dokkalfar evil lurking below the surface, all mixed in with Scipling attributes in a soup of strengths and ills that invites Chaos on one hand and drives it out on the other. Are the New People that strong? Can you assimilate so much old evil and not fall completely into chaos of your own making? I must know the nature of my mortal enemies. If your people are indeed that strong, then perhaps I am defeated forever."

He held out the flask to Leifr.

"If I die of this poison," Leifr said, "then your next target is going to be the Scipling realm. You think you'll have an easy time of it, spreading Chaos through my realm. We might be mortal and you might think us weak because of it, but we are the New People, and you'll see that we are strong enough not only to survive, but to conquer Chaos."

Leifr took the flask and raised it to his lips. The drink was more bitter than he had expected from its smell, but he drained it all, feeling no immediate ill effects except a rather pleasant warming sensation in his belly.

Chaos watched him expectantly as he strode up and down the length of the room, taking glimpses out the windows at what he hoped was not his last look at the emerald hills of Skarpsey, now radiant under unaccustomed blue skies. The wanderers were setting up their camp again, and the day-faring inhabitants of Hringurhol were moving back in. He strove to picture his own realm, which he would never see again, nor the faces of his father, mother, and family. His unnoted death in an invisible realm might well be the cause of Chaos descending upon the Scipling realm, triumphant and confident of eventual destruction of the busy Scipling race, now scuttling to and fro, buying, selling, stealing, fighting, exploring, conquering, marrying, birthing, and dying, all unsuspecting of the threat that hovered over them.

Gazing out at the busy Ljosalfar and descendants of the Rhbus, he could not believe that their entire race was foredoomed to extinction. With the sun shining down like new-minted gold, the threat of the Lord of Chaos seemed a remote, half-forgotten nightmare, dimly remembered after a long and restless night had finally given way to day.

Leifr turned around after a long moment of futile waiting for the eitur to take effect.

"It seems that I have passed your test," he said. "The New People have defeated you once again, Chaos."

Chaos raised on hand in a resigned gesture. "Do not grow careless with overconfidence," he said. "I shall always be with you, waiting for you to weaken. Though you may overwhelm the earth one day with Sciplings and Scipling ignorance, your people's disbelief in the unseen realms changes nothing. I have always been here, and I shall be the last thing the last inhabitant of this world sees in his last moment before his eyes turn to particles smaller than dust."

"No," Leifr said. "If someone doesn't summon you and work to keep you present, as the Council did, then you'll have no foothold."

"Farewell, then, until we meet again." Chaos darkened, diminishing rapidly, still holding up one hand in admonition, until the image of the entity had dwindled to nothing but a pillar of shadow. Then with a shriek of wind, the shadow dispersed. An unseen force ricocheted around the walls, catching up dust and bits of gravel like a whirlwind; then it vanished into the clear sky with a final desolate howl.

Chapter 22

◇◇◇◇◇◇◇◇◇◇◇◇◇◇◇◇◇◇◇◇◇◇◇◇◇◇◇◇◇◇◇◇◇◇◇◇◇◇

During the next days at Hringurhol, Leifr was often reminded of the terrible gap that now separated him from his ancestral home. More straggling bands of impoverished Rhbus returned to Hringurhol amid the tearful, rejoicing celebrations of families reunited after long and unhappy separations. Leifr watched them with envy, picturing himself returning to the arms of his own family. Even if he had managed to get back through the gate in time, he would have seen them only a few days, and then he would have been off again, since the term of his outlawry had several more years to run. When it was finished, if he had been lucky enough to survive it, he would have returned home and never left again. But all that was idle daydreaming. They were all gone, and he would never again have that opportunity.

Svanlaug and Ulfrin were the first to leave the company, departing at sundown several days later as soon as the sun was beneath the horizon.

"It's been an unlikely partnership, Leifr," Svanlaug said, shaking hands with him briskly, "but one that has worked well for us both, I like to think. My father Afgang is avenged, the Council is smashed, and my sister Ulfrin is delivered. My only complaint is this garishly bright hot sun, but I suppose it will be good for the dragons. When I get to the Prestur clan, I'm going to start a move to put a stop to dragon hunting."

Thurid also shook her hand. "It will go badly for any dragon hunters I encounter," he said darkly. "Farewell, Svanlaug. I expect you to make something of yourself now, instead of pottering around with herbs and cures. But I hope we never cross paths in opposition."

"We won't cross paths after we've built bridges," Ulfrin said. "You may take the word of a Sverting for that. I've learned to think more kindly of day-farers now, and I always will. Good-bye, and may we meet again in happy times."

Mustering all their dignity, the Inquisitors ventured forth rather warily and took their departure on the following day, bidding Thurid farewell as gloomily as if they were laying him out on his funeral pyre.

"Should you ever decide to return, Thurid, we'll be waiting for you," Fodor said with a sorrowing sigh. "I regret that we couldn't convince you to join the Fire Wizards' Guild. The longer you remain here, the more difficult it will be for you to root out the insidious Rhbu influences."

"You'll wait in vain," Thurid said. "I've discovered my place, and it is among the Rhbus. If you should ever tire of upholding the time-raddled and sometimes useless traditions of the Guild, you know where to come looking for the greater truth, Fodor."

Shaking their heads, the Inquisitors departed Hringurhol in haste, obviously anxious to leave it and their shattered convictions behind.

Leifr felt more lonely than before. Thurid was almost completely preoccupied with his new mentors, the five Rhbu sorcerers. Ljosa avoided him, allowing him only distant glimpses of her. Starkad was preoccupied with his new and astonishing friendship with the restored Gedvondur, and the two of them endlessly discussed plans for Dallir from sunup to sundown, making themselves wealthy landholders a hundred times over. It was no surprise to anyone when they began preparations for the long trek back to Dallir, pressing Leifr and Thurid to accompany them.

"But I'm not ready to leave yet," Thurid protested when they told him of their plans. "Look at the wonders unfolding before my eyes, the hopes, the possibilities! Even our sour old friend Gedvondur is a shining example of what can be learned from the Rhbus. Imagine, his dried carcass was restored to perfect life and health. If that's what I am going to learn, then I must stay a while longer."

Galdur shrugged and nodded, turning a sly eye upon Thurid. "Such healing is commonplace magic for Rhbus. Our knowledge goes back beyond the first people, Thurid, back beyond as far as the black void from which came the earth and its peoples. But I fear it will cost you, Thurid," he added, just as Thurid's mouth was almost watering with yearning after such knowledge.

"I don't know if you'll want to pay the price. You've had a comfortable and safe life in Dallir. You might not want to forsake it and the friends you now hold so dearly."

"And if I choose to return to Dallir, what would I lose?" Thurid inquired, instinctively clutching his satchel and tightening his grip on his staff.

Galdur nodded and sighed gently. "The satchel and its spells and history belongs with the Rhbus. You'd have to leave it. You'd be just as you were before, a teacher of young children and the scourge of the farm help. In this realm, as you know, nothing is given without something being taken away. It's the first law of gaining magical power."

Thurid turned his hunted gaze upon Leifr. "What should I do, Leifr?" he asked in a low voice.

"Stay," Leifr said. "There's nothing for you to go back for."

Thurid scowled, drawn backward by old memories. "But Dallir is standing vacant. It needs someone to tend its fields and keep the trolls off the housetops. You must go, Leifr. It belongs to you as much as to anyone, since there's no one else to claim it."

Starkad turned his peculiar Fridmarr stare upon Leifr. "Come with us, Leifr," he said. "I've changed my mind about being a wizard. I don't think there's a place for me here with the Rhbus, as there is for Thurid. Besides, Fridmarr wants to be taken home. Leifr, let's you and I and Gedvondur take Dallir and make it into a prosperous farm."

"A veritable seat of knowledge and power," Gedvondur added. "The pair of you need a wiser head to govern your impetuous energies. With Thurid out of the way, Solvorfirth needs the wisdom of a wizard to protect it. I can heal the peasants of their ills and teach those little brats of the settlements their runes as well as Thurid could—probably better."

"You, a teacher?" Thurid snorted. "With your bad temper? The little demons need patience and kindness. Don't think you're going to take my place, you bandit. I have a very strong interest in what goes on at Dallir!"

"There's only room for one wizard at Dallir," Gedvondur said haughtily. "See to it you don't stay long when you come to visit."

Leifr shook his head, tempted but not quite enough. "I belong in the Scipling realm. I feel as if there's a hole there where

I should be, and I'm somewhat unnecessary here, now that I've done all I can. Maybe I should go back to the Scipling realm, even if everyone I know is dead.''

His glance in Ljosa's direction was bleak, but she did not try to dissuade him. She only looked uncomfortable, frowning slightly and keeping her eyes averted.

Thurid continued, ''Ljosa, you'll go to your relations in the north, I suppose.''

Ljosa's aloof eye flickered as she slowly shook her head. ''My home is Gliru-hals,'' she said, ''and I'm going back there to clean up the mess Sorkvir left behind.''

''Raudbjorn go with Leifr,'' Raudbjorn rumbled. ''Dallir, Scipling realm, all same to Raudbjorn.''

''Fridmarr left a rune wand,'' Leifr said. ''Raudbjorn's got it in his trophy bag. I think he'll fit in rather well, where I'm going.''

Thurid nodded as if his head were almost too heavy to lift. ''I'll be sorry to see you go, Leifr, but if that's what you think you want, I'll see what can be done.''

Thurid and Leifr walked apart from the others, sunk in a silence too painful to trivialize with mere words.

''The packet,'' Leifr said, stopping suddenly. ''Elbegast gave us a packet to summon him with. Let's use it. He said it was for direst need, and I need to get back home.''

Thurid darted into the gatekeeper's hut, already rummaging through his satchel, eyes gleaming and intent as he flung out handfuls of stuff. Some of it he examined incredulously, shaking his head.

''Hah! Here it is!'' he exclaimed at last, holding up a small, wax-covered bundle, somewhat worse for wear. ''Ready, Leifr? I'll burn it, but I'm not certain what's going to happen. Be prepared for anything.''

Leifr nodded, and Thurid cast it upon the small fire smoldering on the hearth under a pot of rhubarb soup. At once the wax melted and the contents ignited with a sputtering whoosh. Colored smoke spewed into the air. With watering eyes, Thurid coughed and fanned at the cloying clouds.

''I fear something's gone wrong,'' he said with a sneeze. ''It might have gotten wet or contaminated by something else in that bag.''

"Maybe this is Elbegast's idea of a prank," Leifr said darkly, his eyes streaming.

"Come, let's get out of here until the smoke clears," Thurid said. "It might not be healthy."

Leifr stood up to follow him outside, his sodden spirits sinking down to his toes. A shoal of Thurid's admirers were waiting outside, who all wanted to touch his staff and satchel for good luck, invite him to dinner, and offer him a place to stay for the night. Even the smoky atmosphere of the gate-tender's hut was preferable to all that adulation, so Leifr ducked back inside and sat down, waiting for the smoke to clear.

When it did clear, he saw Vidskipti seated at the table, spreading out a small and tasty feast from his battered old pouch.

"Leifr!" he greeted him in delight. "Sit down and help me eat this. You look as if you're in need of nourishment."

Leifr sat down on the edge of a chair, warily going over what he might say to this curious individual without offending him or sounding ridiculous.

"Elbegast," he said. "You've been with me all along and I didn't even suspect it."

Vidskipti was nothing like the Elbegast he had met long before at Hjaldurshol. The ragged little wanderer gazed at him with an amused quirking of his lips.

"There are many things you don't suspect," he said in a tone of merry reproof. "Won't you have one of these filled pastries? They've got some kind of fruit in them, I think."

"I want to go back to the Scipling realm," Leifr said.

"Well, now," Vidskipti said thoughtfully. "You know it won't be the same. The gates have shifted, like circles within circles."

"It doesn't matter," Leifr said. "There's nothing for me here."

"I've looked and tried to find out what I can," Vidskipti said. "There are distant relatives of yours now living, but they have little recollection of you. Only a name in their family history, and it the name of an outlaw who vanished when young. Your mother's house burned down during a feud a hundred years ago, and a different house was built. Some of the barns and paddocks are the same, but it's still different. Very different, Leifr. Three hundred years have passed."

Leifr sank back farther in his chair, suddenly seeing nothing before his eyes except blinding visions of the home that he would never see again.

"It belongs to strangers now?" he asked.

Vidskipti nodded again, his features drawn up in painful lines. "And you would be a stranger to them, I'm afraid. You couldn't tell them who you were. The old beliefs have been sadly discarded. You could always go back to a wandering life. Or outlawry or thief-taking. I fear that's all that would be open to you now, if you returned. I could send you, but I fear you'd always be an outcast, alone and miserable."

"I wouldn't belong there," Leifr said, more to himself than to Vidskipti as the grievous truth of his situation sank into his heart more cruelly. "No more than I belong here."

"You have friends here," Vidskipti said. "Many friends. You're a hero in Solvorfirth, and you always will be. I'd like nothing better than to see you go back there and set up with Starkad and Gedvondur, and eventually you'll take a wife and there'll be a family and it will be home to you, Leifr."

Leifr slowly shook his head. "I can't go back there. Not with Gliru-hals—I'm doomed to be a wanderer, landless, lordless, luckless. And if I stay here, I shall have the privilege of growing old and dying while the rest of my friends enjoy their long Alfar lives. I may have twenty or thirty good years left, compared to your hundreds."

"Tut-tut, Leifr, nothing is impossible. There are ways of preserving life—" Elbegast began.

"Not for me," Leifr growled. "I've seen enough of Djofull and Sorkvir's attempts to extend life, and enough walking draugar to last a lifetime. Nothing like that will ever be tried on me. If I'm going to die so quickly, it doesn't much matter which realm I choose to do it in, does it? I'd better just get on with it as soon as I can."

Angrily he leaped to his feet and strode away, out of the gatekeeper's hut, shouldering his way past knots of evening strollers without seeing them. He stopped on the edge of Heidur's hill, looking west again. West always seemed the direction of home, and it always would to him. Kraftig whined and thrust his muzzle into Leifr's hand, pawing at him gently, urging his master to stroke him and be comforted.

"That's a poor reward for all you've done here," Elbegast said, catching up to him. "Take your happiness in what small pieces it can be found, Leifr. If you can't have the whole cake, get what crumbs you can. Dallir will be a good life for you for as long as you choose to stay.''

"You're meaning Ljosa, aren't you?" Leifr asked harshly. "You know she'll have nothing to do with me. How can I live at Dallir, with Gliru-hals just over the hill, reminding me how I've failed with her? To her, I'm nothing but a Scipling barbarian.''

"How do you know that's the way it will be?" Elbegast demanded testily. "Are you a foreseer now? Wounds will heal. People can get accustomed to living with horrendous losses. You've lost nearly everyone you ever cared about, I know. Nobody is asking you to live in joyous revelry for the rest of your days. But there is peace, Leifr, somewhere, and you can find it. I know it's not in the wandering, warfaring life, unless death is the peace you're looking for.''

"Maybe it is!" Leifr retorted savagely. "I've certainly courted death in one way or the other for most of my life. Death is the only bride a warrior ever takes.''

Whistling to the troll-hounds, he turned and hurried down the hillside, sliding and stumbling in his haste to get away. For the rest of the day he avoided everyone, seeing that he was the only one among them who had no future worth contemplating. The bitter bile of regret and bereavement rose in his throat like poison. The place where his heart had been, and everything that had once caused him to care about anything, was now a seared, aching void. A part of him questioned whether he could go on living with such a feeling, and another part told him that, if he did go on living, it would be with this hidden area of uncured pain buried inside him forever.

For the next fortnight or so Leifr lurked about Hringurhol, shunning his friends and the elaborate feasts that each Rhbu family felt obligated to present in celebration of the return to Hringurhol. Most of his time was spent in restless walking as he explored the region of Hringurhol, watching deserted farmsteads being taken up by the returned Rhbus, and a few new ones being built. He lent a hand at these, working in grim silence until he was exhausted at the end of the day. His idea was to make himself too exhausted to think much about the loss that had befallen him, but the same thoughts marched endlessly around and around inside his head.

Thurid tried to stay beside him and cheer him up, but he did his best to discourage all kindly endeavors with some rather churlish retorts to the well-intentioned inquiries and remarks, when he could not avoid them altogether. Raudbjorn he tolerated, because Raudbjorn seldom spoke anyway.

"What are we going to do with him?" Thurid suddenly blurted out one evening, when Leifr forsook the cheery fire and excellent company of the five Rhbus and Elbegast for the wind and gloom outdoors. "Look at all the terrors he's gone through, and now he's laid low by a simple case of heartbreak. He's homesick, can you believe it?"

Galdur looked up from the cup he was idly twirling around, gazing into the miniature maelstrom he was creating.

"Certainly I can believe it," he replied. "I've been trying to figure out some form of comfort for him, but there's no reckoning with certain very human feelings. There's no healing the pain he feels."

Domari the Judge shook her head, cowled in soft gray wool like mist. "Sciplings spend all their restless lives getting away from home and then trying to get back home once they've lost it. Not like Alfar, whose home is the realm."

"But is there no healing?" Fylgyd the Guide asked in a tone of gentle inquiry. "No help from his friends?"

Galdur sighed and drew up his shoulders in a shrug. "He yearns for a place of his own, with roots centuries deep and the dust of his ancestors mingled in every step of the soil underfoot. Without it, he's a homeless wanderer."

Thurid turned to Elbegast. "When will he stop this useless grieving? Doesn't he value our friendship enough, after all we've been through together, to take some sort of comfort from us? Isn't there something we can do to set him to rights again?"

"Sciplings are difficult creatures at best," Elbegast said, rubbing his scruffy Vidskipti chin and narrowing his eyes in thought. "Though their minds are veiled to much of our common knowledge, raw emotion is almost as powerful for good or evil as our magic. I fear he'll gnaw away at himself and pine for what's not until he's too bitter and sad to recover."

"Unless some substitute is found." Bryti the Steward raised her eyes to Thurid's.

Thurid sighed with a short burst of exasperation. "For seemingly simple and primitive characters, Sciplings are far too complicated in the head for their own good. I don't see how I can help him, when he'll scarcely talk to me. And I wouldn't dare any sort of a spell. It would be too much like holding him captive."

"The way for him is being prepared, even now," Verdugur the Worthy said, her clear eyes scanning the dimness of the rafters above, without seeing them. "The answers lie waiting to be recognized. You, Thurid, hold the key to every question."

Thurid harrowed up his hair distractedly as he strode up and down, muttering. One of his hasty and ill-attended passages past the hearth nearly overtook the cat fylgja of Ljosa, dozing on the warm flagstones. She hissed at him and betook herself to a safe perch on the table.

"And you Rhbus, of course, won't tell me what to do," Thurid said, casting a hopeful eye toward Galdur. "Not a single inconsequential favor in exchange for breaking you out of that boat spell, I should hope?"

"Thurid," Galdur said patiently. "Stop your chattering and listen within. You have the answers already."

"And you know what they are!" Thurid fumed.

"Of course," Galdur said mildly. "And that is precisely why I can't give them to you. We who know some of the secrets of the future cannot impart them to those who don't. It would be altering the entire Web of Life."

"Well, we can't have that now, can we?" Thurid growled testily, glaring around the room for clues, perhaps, when his feet ceased their restless questing. He hurled himself down in a chair and rested his elbows on the table, his fingers pressed against his temples. "So I must find the answer somehow. I must think!" Gently he pushed away the cat fylgja, who butted him affectionately in the ear and trailed her plumy tail across his face.

Astonishingly, Ljosa in her fylgja-form was Leifr's most persistent comforter. The gray cat shadowed him around Hringurhol and even followed him far afield in his rambling expeditions, appearing like a shadow when he sat down to rest or get a drink of water. She sat and stared at him with large, unblinking, amber eyes, primly staying just out of reach with her toes arranged in a neat bunch and her long tail curled around them. For several days, Leifr only glared at her in anger and wounded pride and strode away, but it began to seem to him a rather ridiculous treatment to give to a mere cat.

At last he began to talk to her, without really intending to, and he felt rather ridiculous at first.

"I suppose you think I'm an even greater fool now," he blurted out to her one day on the windy battlements as she sat staring at him. "I know you've never thought much of me at any time. But talking to a cat has to be the ultimate folly. You probably don't understand a word anyway, in that form. You wouldn't even talk to me in your true form, though. Dirt beneath your feet is more important to you than I am."

The cat yawned and began to lick one silken paw. Leifr had to smile at his own ridiculous behavior, but he was rather proud of it. Once he had started, it was easy to continue, and he talked to Ljosa on his walks and his rambles through Hringurhol, often with her walking along shoulder-high on a wall beside him.

"Can you imagine what it's like suddenly to discover that you've been dead to your own family for three hundred years?" he asked her one day during his lengthy pacing of the western battlements, stopping suddenly to face her. She sat down and began to wash the backs of her ears with one paw. "They must have grieved for me for a while. I know my mother would have, and my sisters, at least. Even my father, old Thorljot. My mother was his third wife, and he was rather old to have another another family—especially a son like me. I never brought them anything but grief. I would have made it up to them, if I could have gone back. But now I never will. They got old, my brothers and sisters married, had children, and they all lived and died in their own way, and I was never there to see it. If only I could have seen my mother's face one more time. If only I could have seen the little children coming along, keeping our family name strong. There must be plenty of descendants now, but I wouldn't know them. My life is gone. It's over, but I'm still here. And I'm alone."

The cat was washing her back now, reaching around as far as she could, with one forepaw off the ground.

"I've traded everything I valued for this sword," Leifr went on. "I didn't strike a very good bargain with the Alfar realm, did I? I wish I could see my parents' faces just once more. I wish I could tell them I was sorry to be such a wild, bad son. I'd like to make amends with my older brothers, too. What a useless clot they thought I was. I'm afraid they were right. Even now, after this thing I've done for the Rhbus. They think I was so splendid and brave, but that's not true. Most of the time I would have turned back in an instant, except that I'd gotten you mixed up in this mess. It would have been better if I'd broken my neck when Jolfr jumped off that cliff into the tarn behind your hut. Thurid would have found some other stupid oaf to carry this cursed sword.''

The cat had finished her washing, which left her fur swirled into scallops. She moved a little closer and rubbed the side of her face on the toe of Leifr's boot, purring audibly and looking sleepy. Leifr cautiously extended one hand, and she came up to rub her head on his knuckle. A tiny scrap of pink tongue bestowed a quick lick on his hand, then she sauntered casually away and disappeared behind a pillar.

''What, tired of hearing all my troubles?'' he said to her with a wry chuckle. ''It is rather boring stuff, isn't it?'' Leifr watched a moment to see if she would reappear, perching in a sunny spot or just crouching and watching him, as she often did. He didn't see her, so he turned back to his solitary contemplation of the west, which was his habit when his mood was lower than usual.

Hearing a footstep behind him, he turned to scowl in the direction of the unwelcome intrusion.

Ljosa stood there, wearing a long straight blue gown gathered from the shoulders and a soft cloak and hood of darker blue. She came forward a few more steps, gazing straight at him with the directness of a cat, with an expression of suppressed suspense and knowingness that made his heart sink with the realization that she had listened in her cat form, and she now knew almost everything about him.

''Do you know what I disliked most about you?'' she said without preamble, and went on without waiting for an answer. ''It was your complete, unselfish willingness to sacrifice yourself for someone else. I'd never seen anyone so uncalculating, so open to injury. You're a fine fighter, Leifr, with a sword and shield, but otherwise you're so unprotected. It must be the way Sciplings are. You're almost as much a child as Raudbjorn is.''

''So you did understand everything in your fylgja-form,'' Leifr said, finding it oddly easy to talk to her now, as if he and she were old friends. ''Well, any man who is fool enough to talk to a cat is a fool indeed. I'm sorry you disliked me so much for what I felt I had to do. It's the Scipling way to risk your life for your friends—even to die, sometimes. I can't believe you would have liked me better if I'd turned my back on you."

"No, I wouldn't have, it's true. But you're frightening in your loyalties, Leifr. It creates a sense of obligation that can never be repaid. For what you did for Fridmarr before he died, no one can ever pay you."

"I don't want to be paid," Leifr replied, amazed. "I don't do this sort of thing for money. I'd burn towns or sink boats for money, but nothing like pretending to be Fridmarr so Fridmundr could see him one more time."

"You see? You're peculiar for even consenting to do it. Nobody else would have done so. And that's not the only instance."

"Someone needed to do these things," Leifr retorted in prideful exasperation. "It seemed that I was the only one available in most cases, so I did what I could; after a while, Thurid's endeavor became my endeavor, so how could I escape from it? It was larger than myself."

Ljosa nodded. "So now what are you going to do, since the great endeavor is over?"

Leifr shrugged and sighed moodily. "You should know that's what I've been trying to decide. I've babbled to you like an idiot about it every day for hours. I didn't know you were really listening."

"Cats always listen, even with their backs turned. But now it's my turn to give you some advice, Leifr."

"Advise away, I'm willing to listen, at least."

"What you need to do is to return to Dallir. It's your home now, and you've got to begin remaking a life for yourself. You're not the wandering, warfaring sort. Your life means more to you than a short, brutal, day-to-day existence, like a beast's. You're made of finer stuff than that." Her forthright gaze dropped earthward and a faint rosy blush colored her cheeks. "I've come to know you as if we'd known each other for years and years. If you went away, you'd leave a great emptiness. I want you to stay."

Dumbfounded, Leifr could only stare at her for a moment. Then in a gruff voice he added, "I'm not sure that would be the easiest thing for me, living so close to you at Dallir. You know I have a feeling for you that can never be cured. It's foolish and my own fault, I know, but I'm afraid it would make me act ridiculous from time to time, and everyone would know.''

''Well, I have a solution for that.'' She sounded as awkward and uncomfortable as he felt, but he was too distressed with himself even to look at her. ''I know you can't ever replace the family and parents you have lost by becoming trapped in this realm. But what you must do is start to rebuild your family feelings, so you won't be alone anymore. I'll confess that I thought you were a vain, pleasuring sort, who wanted the worst sort of reward—a chieftain's daughter to wed, an inheritance, some honor, and then you'd go on your merry way boasting about it, with never a true thought about me. After my father was killed, any title or position I might have possessed was gone, so you would have been disappointed in your ambitions. I may be poor now, but I still have too much pride to give myself away as mere currency.''

''I never regarded you as an opportunity for my own advancement in the world,'' Leifr broke in. ''I thought of you as a fine and abused person, needing rescuing, from the first time I saw you herding sheep.''

''Yes, I know that now, after crossing half of Skarpsey together, for the most part. One thing that you will learn about me, Leifr, is that I am very tough and determined, and not at all fragile. When I make up my mind to do something, nothing can stand in my way for very long before I break it down or get around it. I hope you or your pride won't stand in my way.''

Leifr had to smile at her more tenderly than he intended. She was a small mite, for all her determination, standing there confronting him with her fists braced against her hips, looking up at him. Delicate-looking, she reminded him of a fine sword of brightest steel forged by a master smith, not to be taken in hand by anyone less than the most worthy. The wariness and suspicion were gone from her manner, and she smiled and flushed pink, radiating a barely suppressed secret glee.

''I won't interfere with anything you propose,'' he said dutifully, straightening his shoulders. ''If you still have enemies, set me to killing them. If it's lands you want, I shall conquer them for you.''

''Good, good, but it's nothing so drastic. I've thought about it a long time, what would be a suitable payment for your rescuing me,'' she said, held up one hand to his lips as he began to protest, thus startling him into silence. "You must listen carefully now. We have become very well acquainted, since our first meeting, and I am pleased to call you my friend and protector. I want to give you a new family, with your own little boys and girls to dandle on your knee, a wife standing at the loom in your house, and plenty of interfering aunts and uncles and cousins to share your feast days with and to go to visit for weddings and funerals and birthings and illnesses and birthdays. And when you grow old, there shall be sons and daughters beside you to ease your burdens. That is what you have sacrificed by coming into the Alfar realm, and, as our laws work, nothing is given without something being taken away. I am the debtor, and this is how I shall repay you."

Leifr shook his head. "Don't torment me, Ljosa, with visions of what I can't have. You forget, I'm mortal. I'm going to age and sicken and die in a very short while, compared to you Alfar. I'd never live to see my children become men and women. And what sort of curse would be such a mixed heritage for them? Powerless in a realm of power?"

"I have asked the Rhbus about it, and they said that the strongest traits from Scipling and Alfar would be combined in such offspring. Your courage and loyalty. My sense of pride and honor." She flushed more pinkly and her eye flashed when he stood as if rooted, staring at her in amazement. "I really do think it best for you, Leifr. I shall make a good wife for you. I shall temper your excesses and protect you from your own generosity and compassion, or I'm certain you'd fill up the house with all manner of homeless wretches with their sad stories of wasted fortunes and bad luck. You won't like all of my aunts and great-aunts, I'm afraid, but they only bark a great deal and never bite, like old dogs, without meaning most of it. My uncles and cousins are all rather jolly, pleasant folk, and they'll make you welcome. I thought that you could join Dallir to Gliru-hals and leave Starkad and Fridmarr to manage Dallir. We'll live at Gliru-hals in the summer and Dallir in the winter. Dallir gets less snow, and it's so much more cozy. Dallir won't have certain dark memories woven with it, either. You promised not to stand in my way, Leifr, and there's no way this will work without your approval. I have taken great gifts of freedom and deliverance from you, and now this gift of your future is what I offer you in return. Now will you come with me?"

Her smile was coy, but her manner was confident. For a moment Leifr was almost blinded by the visions of the future she was holding out to him, and to a homesick Scipling they were visions of wonderful beauty and warmth. He was stunned speechless by the magnitude of what she was giving.

"But I can't," he croaked finally, shutting his eyes and his heart once more with a painful gasp. "I'm mortal. I don't think it's worth your time, when I've got so little left, compared to you."

She sighed and stamped her foot slightly. "I must remember to be patient," she said, as if to herself. She shoved back her blue cloak from her arm, bare to the shoulder, where a gold broach held the cloth gathered. She turned over her left arm's soft underside, where he saw something like a chain of beads beneath the skin. "Do you see here, these little bumps beneath the skin, here where I can hold them close to my heart? These are the tiny young carbuncle stones of my children that I shall someday bear. Nothing old and terrible will possess them; these are new stones waiting to grow and give long life to their owners."

"But the messages," Leifr said. "Carbuncle stones are always whispering in strange voices—"

"These stones will whisper nothing but love," Ljosa said. She covered her arm again and gazed at Leifr squarely, so he had no place to hide from her eyes. "I should know, because I formed them, and my mother formed mine before me, and I was a beloved child. Now, will you allow Thurid to take one of these little stones and plant it in your flesh so you may live far beyond your mortal span, or do you choose to remain miserable and fearful, snapping at people like an old, sick dog under the porch when they try to feed you?"

"An old, sick dog?" Leifr repeated with a fiery snort. "Is that what they're all saying about me?"

"That and worse," Ljosa said, folding her arms and shaking her head. "They think you've used up all your courage, to be frightened by a mere child's carbuncle stone. You'd scarcely feel it at all."

"A child's carbuncle. I would be stronger than it?"

"Most certainly. It would take a great deal of training to teach it powers and memories and voices. No more than you wish to possess, of course."

"But it would extend my lifespan?"

"Unless you went off and got yourself killed somehow. It won't take the place of common sense."

"But it would mean one less child for you. I can't ask you to make such a sacrifice, not for a beaten-up old Scipling outlaw."

"Oh, I'm satisfied with the trade, and my family will adjust to the idea eventually. Perhaps you've changed your mind, however. I assure you, there will only be a small opening cut wherever you wish for greater strength, and only a very little blood."

"Blood and wounds and pain are nothing to me," Leifr said, with a prideful glint in his eye. "I'm no man or wizard's servant, living or dead. Nor am I an old, sick dog under the porch. But this little stone of yours sounds like something I can accept—even welcome."

"Well?" she prompted. "Are we even now?"

"Perfectly even!" Leifr said, still unable to believe his luck.

"Then it's high time we went home," she said, and reaching up and, bending his head down to her, she kissed him once. She nestled against his chest with a sigh. "For too long I've been like a weary bird, flying and flying through storms and winds, but now I've found my nest. I knew, I hoped you'd always come after me, even when I was so hateful. The very first time I saw you at Dallir, I knew I'd lost my heart completely." Lightly he pressed her slight body against him, feeling her quick-beating heart and the tiny wings of her shoulder blades. "It wasn't a comfortable feeling."

"What?" Leifr exclaimed, shocked out of his blissful contemplation of the feel and fragrance of her in his arms, with her silvery hair tickling his nose.

She laughed and skittered away, breathless.

"We'll have a Rhbu wedding here in Hringurhol, Leifr. Then a tremendous celebration for the family at Gliru-hals. It will last a month, at least. Thurid says there's a caravan coming through that will carry us home."

"Thurid!" Leifr was shocked out of his rosy visions. "You've told him already, before even me?"

"Yes, and he's rather grouchy about it. He says there'll be no end of trouble with half-Alfar children."

"It's no concern of his!" Leifr snorted, darting a fiery glare toward Heidur's well. "He's got a terrible talent for meddling where he shouldn't!"

"And look where it's taken him," Ljosa said softly, fitting her hand into his before it could make a fist. "As well as us. You'd better thank him for it."

"I will," Leifr said, reaching out to stroke away a filmy lock of hair blowing across her cheek. "Every day for the rest of my life, I'll thank him."

She kissed his fingertip, like the quick lick of a cat, and skipped away down the rough path to the settlement below, where cooking fires were rising in straight plumes into the blue sky. When she had vanished, Leifr started off in his usual course along the top of the battlement, passing the snoring, strong-smelling heap that was Raudbjorn and the three troll-hounds. Raudbjorn's sleep was full of uneasy twitches and snorts and groans.

Leifr's eyes scarcely registered on Raudbjorn. With a sudden leap and a whoop he slapped Raudbjorn on the chest, startling the troll-hounds into ferocious barking and growling. Then he broke into a run, suddenly dying to see Thurid and Starkad and Gedvondur, as if he hadn't seen them in months. All at once, he was starving for some jolly conversation as well as good food.

Raudbjorn leaped to his feet, snorting and sputtering, pawing for his halberd, on his feet and ready to fight before he was completely awake. In consternation Raudbjorn gazed after Leifr a moment, leaping and almost flying down the battlement. Then a wide, slow smile began to split his broad countenance. He rummaged in his trophy bag, dropping several blackened and disgusting objects before finding what he wanted. He tapped his great, black-seamed palm with Fridmarr's rune stick, wrinkling up his brow in a painful effort to think. Then he gave it up with a huge sigh.

"Too hard to think," he confided to the hounds, who panted up at him with slant-eyed approval. "Raudbjorn do what feels right."

Taking a firm grip on the rune wand and gritting his teeth, he snapped it in half, then ground the two halves into splinters under his heel. Chuckling mischievously and winking at Kraftig, Frimodig, and Farlig, he shouldered his halberd and followed Leifr at the slow and sedate tread of the faithful, all-knowing, self-appointed guardian.

About the Author

Elizabeth Boyer began planning her writing career during junior high school in her rural Idaho hometown. She read almost anything the Bookmobile brought, and learned a great love for Nature and wilderness. Science fiction in large quantities led her to Tolkien's writings, which developed a great curiosity about Scandinavian folklore. Ms. Boyer is Scandinavian by descent and hopes to visit the homeland of her ancestors. She has a B.A. from Brigham Young University, at Provo, Utah, in English literature.

After spending several years in the Rocky Mountain wilderness of central Utah, she and her husband now live in a log home in Utah's Oquirrh mountains. Sharing their home are two daughters and an assortment of animals. Ms. Boyer enjoys horseback riding, cross-country skiing, and classical music.

Enjoy
the Wonder
and
Wizardry
of
Elizabeth
H. Boyer